Michelle,

Please enjoy!

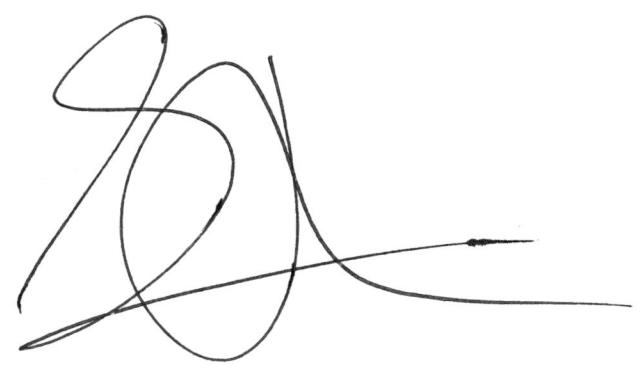

Selina Rossman

FIRST ON SCENE: A HOWLING SIRENS NOVEL

Copyright © 2024 Selina Rossman

This is a work of fiction. Certain long-standing locations, institutions, agencies, and public offices are mentioned, but the names, characters, events, and incidents are the products of the author's imagination. Any resemblance to actual persons, living or dead, or actual events is purely coincidental.

No part of this book may be reproduced, or stored in a retrieval system, or transmitted in any form or by any means, electronic, mechanical, photocopying, recording, or otherwise, without express written permission of the publisher.

Published by Carson Press, LLC
Boston, Massachusetts

ISBN: 979-8-9904684-3-6

This book is dedicated to
my fellow first responders and all those still
racing the reaper.

Prologue

Illuminated in an unflattering glow from the fluorescents above, the desolate fast-food restaurant housed abandoned tables slick with smears of old sauces and strewn in crumpled wrappers. The thick scent of greasy, fried food hung heavily in the air, a stark contrast to the allure of burgers pictured above the counter where a bored college student stared down at his phone, biding his time until close.

An incongruent pair of men occupied the only clean table. With his back to the front entrance, a clean-cut, blonde man in a gray suit sat up straight and smiled warmly, even if it didn't reach his bright blue eyes. Slouched across from him, a disheveled man with a mane of unkempt, muddy brown hair and a scraggly beard remained indifferent to his dining partner.

"Aren't you tired of living like this?" The blonde asked, peering intently across the table.

What does this pretty boy with his suit and coiffed hair think he knows about me? Sure, I let him pick me up on the corner. It doesn't mean I need him. I'm just here for the free food, he thought, sucking at an empty socket in his jaw where a tooth used to be. Straightening in his seat, he crossed his arms over the faded Van Halen T-shirt he wore and scowled. "Living like what?"

The well-dressed man shook his head, reclining and draping an arm over the backrest of the booth. "Don't you want to be respected? Empowered?"

The homeless man scoffed. "Power ain't nothing but an

illusion. The sooner you learn that, the better off you'll be. And trust me, I got plenty of people that respect me."

"Oh? Do tell." The blonde condescended, his thin lips curling into a sneer.

"I got my old lady, and I got that red-headed kid that works the ambulance. It's enough." The homeless man declared and took a big bite out of the hamburger in front of him, chewing with his mouth open.

A tinge of green coloring his cheeks, the blonde man huffed out a sigh and leaned forward, using his elbows to support himself. "You truly don't crave more? Not even a warm bed to fall into at the end of the night?"

I bet he thinks I don't see the way he looks at me. Judgemental prick, the homeless man thought, clenching a fist in his lap.

The blonde let out an exasperated sigh. "Look, I can get you whatever you want. I belong to a group that can make it happen."

I'll just indulge him long enough to finish my meal. Ain't no sense in wasting free food. Hell, maybe he'll even kick in a few bucks to "persuade" me. Taking a big bite of his burger, the homeless man chewed thoughtfully. He wasn't buying what he was being sold. He'd met men like this before. "This group of yours got a name?"

"Not officially, but you could describe us as a brotherhood of sorts." The blonde man shrugged and casually licked the grease of long-since devoured burgers from his fingers.

Yup. This guy is trying to get me to join a cult. Covering up a knowing smirk, the homeless man took another bite out of his burger. He used to be a private investigator, and he could still smell bullshit a mile away.

"So, what do you say?" The blonde asked, leaning forward.

"I'm fine with my life just the way it is." Shaking his head, he popped the last of the burger into his mouth.

Keeping his features neutral, the blonde man pulled out a business card from his pocket and slid it across the table. "I think you're making a mistake, but here, if you change your mind."

First On Scene: A Howling Sirens Novel

"I won't." He assured the other man and stood without picking up the card. *Should I ask him for a few bucks? Nah, he didn't get what he wanted; he ain't gonna give me nothin' else.*

Turning to leave, he could feel the other man's eyes boring into his back, making the hair at the nape of his neck stand on end. *He's probably not used to being told no. I better get out of here. You never know what these cult weirdos will do,* he thought, making a beeline for the Burger King's exit.

The warmth of the Indian summer day that had let him wear a T-shirt and torn jeans had faded with the setting sun. The last rays of red painted the westward sky and flickering street lamps began to replace the daylight. He needed to hurry if he was going to make it to his campsite before it was too dark to navigate the woods.

Shrugging off the odd encounter with the blonde man, he hurried towards the tree line. The other man's pitch had been weak, like even he didn't believe his words. Listening to it had barely been worth the free meal, but at least it had gotten him close to home. It's why he had insisted on that particular Burger King.

Glancing over his shoulder to make sure he was alone, he darted into the quickly darkening woods. Long shadows spilled onto the path, reaching for him like outstretched claws. He knew it was just the pine trees in the fading light, but it still creeped him out. Every small rustle of leaves made him jump. For weeks, animals had been crashing through the underbrush near his campsite, and he didn't want to run into whatever had been making the noise when he could barely see.

Stumbling up the steep incline, he braced himself against a tree. A wave of nausea assaulted him, and his body ached. Full belly or not, he'd gone too long without a drink. A bottle of vodka was waiting for him in his tent. If he was going to stave off the tremors, he'd need to hurry.

He finally reached the small clearing that held his two-person camping tent to see that the flap was open. It was never open. *Is my old lady here? Thought she wasn't coming until tomorrow. She better not be in there getting fucked up without me,* he thought, pinching his lips together.

Selina Rossman

He strode forward but froze as something moved inside the tent. Mouth going dry, he squinted, straining for a better look. *What is that? Can't be my old lady, its too big. Is it a bear?*

A tremor rippled down his left arm, and his fingers began to quiver. *Shit, I need that vodka.* Curling his hands into fists to keep the shakes at bay, he shuffled closer to the tent. *Should I just wait for it to leave? Or could I lure it out? What would I even lure it out with?*

Edging closer to the entrance, he could hear something large shuffling around inside. Swallowing down another wave of nausea, he leaned forward and peered into the tent.

With a deafening snarl, a blur of black and white shot out of the tent and headed straight for him.

He bolted. The booze would have to wait.

He stumbled back the way he'd come on trembling legs. Panting and sweating, he glanced behind him, but all he could see was darkness.

His foot snagged on a rock, sending him sprawling. "Fuck," he grunted and forced himself to his feet.

Blood pounding in his ears, he staggered forward, his legs threatening to give out. Something heavy struck his back, and he collapsed under its weight. Face down in the mud and leaves, he struggled against the beast holding him down.

Rivulets of hot drool ran down his neck. The foul-smelling liquid dripped into his eyes, and he clenched them shut. The beast rumbled out a threatening snarl, and agony clamped down on his shoulder.

Unable to lift his head, only the dirt heard him scream.

Chapter One

Painted in fading shades of pink with a slanted roof and a dingy white door, the building resembled a small house. Its unassuming exterior wasn't welcoming, but it also didn't immediately raise any alarms. It wasn't uncommon for an ambulance base to be nestled into a residential neighborhood.

Kitty approached what would be her home away from home for twenty-four hours at a time and tucked her black motorcycle helmet under an arm. The location might be new, but the gig was the same. She was a Paramedic, and not even moving across the country could change that. Hopefully, her new employers invested in their people.

Finding the ID scanner and keypad, she punched in the code that she had been given during her online orientation. The heavy door stood firm. Frowning, she punched in the code again and gave the door a shove. It didn't budge.

Hell, she thought, putting her shoulder to the door and giving it another shove. The door lurched open, and she almost dropped her helmet as she stumbled inside.

The door clicked shut behind her, leaving her alone in the poorly lit hallway. At least she was out of the hot summer sun.

Above her, the fluorescent lights flickered ominously, and the dark walls on either side of her threatened to close in. Suddenly nauseous, her stomach roiled. *Breathe! You can't start a career here known as the nervous puker*, she thought and ran her tongue over her dry lips.

Inhaling deeply, she slowly released the breath, repeating the process until the anxiety faded. Feeling better, she took in her surroundings and wrinkled her nose. The walls consisted of wood paneling that had been painted a chalky white. *Who paints over wood paneling?* she thought, scrutinizing the narrow hallway. Eager for a way out of the gloom, she searched for an exit.

Opening a door to her left, she found herself blinking rapidly as she left the dingy hallway behind. Squinting until her eyes adjusted, she glanced around the room. The first thing she noticed was a brick fireplace. She had never worked anywhere with a fireplace before and would have been excited if it weren't for its obvious disrepair. Frowning, she examined the hearth, which was littered with feathers and nesting material. *Did a bird escape from the chimney?*

Before moving, she had heard rumors of beautiful stations and top-of-the-line equipment. It sounded like a dream come true, and apparently, that's all it was, a dream. This place was nothing like the bases she'd been in down south. You could eat off those floors.

A quick scan of the room revealed windows with missing screens and broken vinyl blinds. A muddy-colored carpet ran wall to wall, and the theme of painted paneling continued. To her right stood a sturdy wooden desk. Perched on top of it was an ancient desktop PC. The computer looked like the finest equipment 1995 had to offer. Patting the smartphone she had tucked into her uniform's breast pocket through her leather jacket, she confirmed that she was indeed still in 2012.

What kind of shithole did I agree to work in? Pinching the bridge of her nose, she squeezed her eyes shut. Someone cleared their throat to her left. Her eyes flew open, and she whirled towards the sound, finding herself face to face with a scruffy-bearded man. She took a staggering step backward. *How the hell did I not notice him?!*

Forcing a smile, she willed her thundering heartbeat to slow and took in the man in front of her. He wore an ill-fitting uniform. Stained and untucked, the faded white button-down

First On Scene: A Howling Sirens Novel

had clearly seen better days. The polyester material strained against the man's large gut, buttons threatening to pop at any moment, and his navy blue pants seemed clean enough but were awkwardly tucked into a pair of unzipped boots.

"You must be Catherine." He snatched up her hand in greeting, his meaty paw engulfing her much smaller hand. She flinched, fighting the impulse to jerk away. She hated being touched by strangers and loathed the name Catherine. No one had called her that since she left home.

"I go by Kitty," she said sharply, snatching her hand back and shoving it into a pocket.

"I'm Tim, one of the per diem guys here," he continued, oblivious to her discomfort as he turned to indicate the two lumpy green couches on either side of the room, hemorrhaging stuffing.

He leaned over and retrieved a bottle of diet soda from between the cushions of the nearest couch, taking a long swig, some of the brown liquid dribbling out of his mouth and into his beard. Capping the bottle, he wiped his mouth with the back of his hand. "This is the day room, but the P1's crew sleeps here. We don't have beds here. The higher-ups don't like them."

Grimacing, Kitty shook her head and looked away.

"You're riding with P2 today, but they're out on a run," he went on, leading her back the way she'd come. "I'll give you the grand tour in the meantime."

Oh goodie, she thought facetiously, *if this is the caliber of people I'll be working with, I won't make it here a week. I thought Massachusetts was supposed to have higher standards. Even the bible thumpers down south had their shit together better than this guy!* With a frown and a soft huff, she followed him at a distance while he clawed at his face.

"Those are the bedrooms for the 9-1-1 crew. You can get to one of the bathrooms through either room." Not bothering to stop, he pointed at the two doors on their right. Taking a few more steps toward the end of the hallway, he paused. "We only piss upstairs. If you have to take a shit, use the bathroom downstairs."

7

Selina Rossman

Nope, definitely not going to last here. I know I need the cash, but I can't possibly partner with people like this, she thought, rubbing at the back of her neck.

"When they actually put up a basic life support crew, they hang out here during the day but post up near the hospital at night. We just don't have the space for them. Most of the time, though, it's just the medics here." Without looking in her direction, he led them out of the hallway and down a flight of stairs.

Grimacing, she descended the staircase. Her boots crunched on the carpeted floor with each step she took. Layers of dirt and untold amounts of bodily fluids had created a crispy film. Kitty gagged at the thought of all the filth tracked in over the years.

The flight of stairs ended in a landing that overlooked the ambulance bay. A rickety banister separated her from the open air. Exposed wires hung menacingly from the ceiling, reaching for their next victim. She was suddenly glad for her short stature. She figured an extra two inches could mean electrocution.

To her left, wooden stairs crept towards the ceiling. A circular, indoor running track ran the entirety of the bay. Looking up, light peeked out at her through rotted floorboards. Out of the corner of her eye, she caught Tim staring at her. *I don't think he means to be creepy, but ugh.* Kitty ran a hand through her short, bleach-blonde hair. Usually, the boyish crew cut deterred men. It's part of why she had gotten it, but it didn't seem to be working today.

"That's the old track. You can technically get up there, but I wouldn't recommend it. It's not stable. Even someone your size would fall through." He commented, slumping his way down the remaining stairs.

What does he mean by that? Did he just call me fat? She was only five foot three, but she was fit; she had to be to do this job. Still not sure how offended she should be, her curiosity won out, and she followed him down the remaining five stairs.

"What was this place?" she asked, catching up with him.

"It was a YMCA back in the day, but it's been an ambulance

First On Scene: A Howling Sirens Novel

bay for ages. Apparently, haunted spaces are fine for first responders but not gym rats." He shook his head.

"What do you mean, haunted?" she asked, chewing on her lower lip. She loved most things occult, but ghosts had never piqued her interest. Why would they? Being forced to roam a plane you couldn't interact with for all of eternity sounded terrible. Now shapeshifting, on the other hand, that sounded like freedom.

"Rumor has it that three teenagers died here by jumping off the track. No one knows if it's true or not, but the place was shut down for years before ambulance companies started using it."

Shrugging off her horrified expression, he walked further into the bay.

Unsure of what to say, she silently trailed him around a parked Honda and into the kitchen. The floor was made up of dingy, yellowing tiles. *Is this the shitty yellow-brick road? Does it lead to hell?* Smothering a snicker, she looked around. *Nope, no emerald city here.*

A filthy crockpot, grease-caked microwave, and some unwashed dishes lingered on the counter. The stove was covered in food debris. To her surprise, the sink was clean. *It's probably never been used before*, she thought, wrinkling her nose. The kitchen lacked a dishwasher but had two overfilled trash cans. *This place is gross, and there is no way we don't have a rat problem here.*

Just off the kitchen was the second bathroom, an oddity at best, a health hazard at worst. A grubby curtain hid the shower from view. Across from it was a ceramic sink coated in what she could only assume was soap scum. The toilet stood on a wooden platform. *Talk about a porcelain throne.* Wrinkling her nose, she tightened her grip on her helmet. She had yet to find somewhere clean enough to put it down.

Tim continued the tour, and she gladly followed him out into the bay. Concrete flooring ran the length of the enormous oval space. It was easily large enough to house three box trucks for the paramedics, a van ambulance for the basics, and a few personal vehicles. The bay door didn't look large enough

Selina Rossman

to accommodate a van, let alone a box truck. *It must just barely fit*, she thought, eyeing the savaged door frame. Hunks of plaster had been torn free on either side of the wall. *It's a good thing I can drive because parking here is going to be a bitch.*

Tim muttered something about getting his lunch and ambled away in the direction of the kitchen. Glad to be rid of him, she wordlessly watched him go.

Wandering outside, she stopped. To her surprise, a river ran behind the building. Sunlight danced languidly along the water's surface while a pair of white herons glided overhead. The corners of her mouth turned upward. She loved being near fresh water. The creak of weight on wood drew her attention. *Oh no, did the rats find me?* she thought, turning her head towards the sound.

A woman with long, golden brown braids drawn up into a simple bun eyed her from her perch on the picnic table. The woman's dark onyx skin exuded a natural radiance, and her full lips begged to be kissed. Kitty stared back, losing herself in two pools of amber-flecked hazel. Lips parted, she drank in the sight. She didn't believe in love at first sight, but lust? She believed in that.

Blinking slowly, she realized the owner of those perfect eyes had spoken to her. *Shit, how long have I been staring at her?* she thought, choking on her own saliva and flushing brightly.

"What?" she coughed out, clearing her throat and playing with her shirt collar.

"I asked if you ride?" the woman said, flashing her a smile and nodding towards the motorcycle helmet still tucked securely under her arm.

Kitty jerked her head up and down enthusiastically. "I sure do!" *Holy shit, say something better than that!* she thought frantically, feeling the heat in her cheeks intensify.

The other woman abandoned her seat and approached her. She was taller than Kitty by a few inches, but few people weren't. Still smiling brightly, the woman held out a hand once she was close enough. "I'm Zuri, it's nice to meet you."

"Kitty. Nice to meet you, too," she murmured, shaking the offered hand.

First On Scene: A Howling Sirens Novel

Zuri leaned in closer and lowered her voice. "I'm sorry that the first person you met was Tim. He's a creep. Don't worry, though; you'll like the team you are riding with today. Both Angell and Eric are good guys."

Behind her, a door slammed, making her jump. Dragging her eyes away from the goddess lingering in front of her, she glanced over her shoulder in time to see two men walking away from what she guessed would be her ambulance for the day.

Head held high and broad shoulders thrown back, a tall man strode towards them. Cocoa-brown eyes peeked out from under sable locs. The man ran his fingers through his hair, pushing it out of his eyes. The bright smile he offered was a dashing contrast to his dark umber skin, and his cookie-duster mustache gave his face character.

Unlike Tim, he exuded professionalism. His freshly pressed uniform and spit-shined boots immediately put her at ease. This was closer to what she had expected.

"Hi. You must be our third for the day. I'm Angell. The slowpoke behind me is Crash," he said loudly enough for the man behind him to hear. The other medic, a pale, gangly redhead in his mid-twenties, was equally professionally turned out. "My name is Eric," he said with a brief scowl at his partner.

This asshole," he continued and prodded Angell in the side. "is going to be one of your regular partners. I hope you're ready."

Angell laughed, his shoulders shaking good-naturedly. "Okay, so maybe Crash is just a nickname.

Eyes flitting between Angell's warm grin and Crash's scowling face, she smiled. *Maybe this place won't be so bad after all.*

"What do you go by?" Angell asked.

"You can call me Kitty," she said, her breath catching in her throat as Zuri came around to stand next to her.

"Great!" Angell rubbed his hands together excitedly. "Eric's right. I am going to be one of your regular partners. Let's go get breakfast, and I'll show you around the town." Glancing at

Zuri, he paused. "Want me to pick you up something from the crepe place?"

Zuri shook her head. "No, I'm good. Just hurry back so I have someone to talk to besides Tim. If he goes off on one more rant about how he has been wronged at his other job, I'm going to kill him," she huffed, crossing her arms.

"Come on, you know he only picks up a shift once a month or so. You can put up with him for twelve hours. I believe in you!" Angell fist-pumped the air. Zuri rolled her eyes and retreated to the picnic table.

Taking a breath for what felt like the first time in ages, Kitty stripped off her leather jacket and followed her new partners back to the ambulance.

"I can't eat anything here!" Eric whined as he led the way into the small cafe.

"Oh please," Angell rolled his eyes, "you still drink coffee, right?"

"Of course, I still drink coffee! How else do you expect me to function for twenty-four hours?" Eric held the door open for them and shot Angell an exasperated look.

"Okay then. I'll buy you a coffee. A nice boring coffee with no sugar, no milk, and no taste." Angell playfully shoulder-checked his partner before striding past him.

"Not all of us need a fru-fru drink to enjoy our caffeine!" Eric sniped at Angell's retreating back.

Suppressing a grin, Kitty wandered through the open door into the cute little bistro, brightly lit and with small tables and cushy armchairs scattered throughout the space.

She inhaled deeply and licked her lips at the tantalizing smells of cinnamon, brown sugar, and vanilla wafting through the air. She loved cinnamon. Every Christmas, she hoarded all the cinnamon & spiced vanilla body lotion she could get her hands on lest she should run out during the year.

Following in the boys' wake, she ensured that all of her gear

First On Scene: A Howling Sirens Novel

was still there. *Phone, wallet, lip balm, pen, notepad, trauma shears, stethoscope, pen light, tourniquet.* Running through her mental checklist for the third time today, she patted her pockets to confirm that nothing had magically disappeared.

She wasn't normally this particular, but it was her first day working in a new system. She had to prove herself. That meant being ready for anything. She just had to figure out what to do with the portable radio. Like most of the equipment she had encountered thus far, it wasn't new or top-of-the-line. Clipped onto her belt, the plastic body hung like a lead weight at her side. She had run the coiled cord up her back and clipped the push-to-talk microphone onto the front of her shirt. It felt awkward. She needed to get a strap like the ones Angell and Eric wore. Made out of simple black leather with a holster for the radio base, space to run the cord, and a spot to clip the PTT mic, it was exactly what she wanted.

"What can I get you?" Kitty looked up from her inventory into the annoyed face of the pretty brunette behind the counter.

Fuck! I need to be less in my head today, she thought, reaching for her wallet as she ordered a cinnamon latte and a sweet crepe.

"On the house," the woman said, waving away the money.

"Don't expect to eat for free unless she is on. She's got a soft spot for anyone in uniform because her dad was a Boston cop," Angell murmured into her ear before smiling at the woman and chirping. "Thanks, Rachel!"

The woman looked up from preparing their drinks to wink at him. Swaggering, he led them to a table on the far side of the restaurant.

"He thinks he is so smooth…" Eric grumbled softly enough that Rachel couldn't overhear.

"Don't be jealous," Angell shot back.

Grinning, Kitty curled up in one of the plush armchairs. *These two bicker like an old married couple. At least it'll be an amusing shift.*

"So, what's your story?" Angell asked, settling into the chair opposite her.

Selina Rossman

"I grew up in the South," she began, letting her natural accent come through.

Eric's eyes widened at the twangy drawl, all too common of a reaction north of the Mason-Dixon line. It's why she suppressed it most of the time. "It doesn't mean I'm a hick, you know!"

"Alright then," Grinning widely, Eric removed his hat and ran his fingers through his unruly carrot-collared hair. Shoving the cap back onto his head, he leaned forward, ready for the rest of her tale.

"I'm from Morris, Alabama. It's a bit north of Birmingham." She paused to greet Rachel, who had appeared at their table, arms laden with their food and drinks.

Rachel blew a kiss at Angell and headed back to the counter. Her curvaceous hips swayed with each step as Angell grinned widely, his eyes glued to the woman's retreating form.

They've definitely hooked up, Kitty thought knowingly and took a sip of her latte. The soothing combination of cream, cinnamon, and honey did wonders for her first-day nerves.

"I'm honestly not that exciting," she explained, suppressing her accent once more. "I'm twenty-three. I got my medic ticket back home and then moved here. So, I'm still pretty new, but I do have experience working in a busy 9-1-1 system as a basic." She took a sip of her latte. "I've only been in town for a couple of weeks."

Angell swallowed a mouthful of his peppermint mocha latte."What made you choose Massachusetts? "

She shrugged. "I just needed a change of scenery, and I heard that Massachusetts had solid EMS protocols." *And actual protections for people like me.* She took a bite of her chocolate and strawberry crepe and groaned. "This is so good!" Chewing slowly to savor each bite.

Watching Eric nurse his hot coffee and stare longingly at baked goods on the counter, she frowned. She couldn't understand why he was depriving himself. It's not like he was out of shape. *Is he vegan or something?* She wondered as she polished off her breakfast.

"What about you guys?" She asked as the silence stretched

First On Scene: A Howling Sirens Novel

out uncomfortably.

"He's a born and raised mass-hole," Angell said, thrusting his thumb in Eric's direction.

"I can speak for myself!" Eric grumbled, shaking his head and grinning ruefully at Kitty. "Have you even been here long enough to hear that term?"

She shook her head. Apparently, she had a lot more to learn than new protocols.

"A Mass-hole is someone that lives here. We're called that for the bad driving and general standoffishness you see in folks up here."

"To put it mildly," Angell interjected.

Eric rolled his eyes. "Anyways, I'm actually from Hudson. I grew up here with half the cops and firefighters in this town, which is nice most days. I like that I get to serve my hometown."

Before she could comment, Angell launched into his backstory. "I'm a transplant like you but I'm from Mexico originally. We moved to Worcester when I was six. My parents ended up getting divorced and my mother moved back to Mexico City. I spent every summer out there with her so I speak fluent Spanish when needed."

"Do you speak any other languages?" She had once read somewhere that it was easier to learn languages once you were bilingual.

"Besides English?" He joked, grinning broadly.

Blushing, she looked at her feet. *Was that rude?*

"He's also fluent in asshole," Eric offered helpfully, and the two men laughed.

Rolling his eyes, Angell continued. "There is a pretty big Brazilian population in town, so I've learned to speak a little Portuguese, as well."

"Poorly," Eric added, winking at her and grinning. "So, what do you do for fun?"

Nibbling on her lower lip, Kitty thought about it. *What do I do for fun?* She'd spent the last two years working, busting her ass to pass paramedic school and lying to her parents so she could keep going to classes and working the rig. It hadn't left her much time for fun.

"Too personal?" Angell teased.

Shit, I'm doing it again! I have to answer people quicker! Grinning up at him sheepishly, she decided to just be honest."I used to be really into hiking, and I still love reading, but I didn't have much free time while going to school. I guess I'll have time to get back into hiking now."

Angell nodded knowingly. "Yeah, medic school is pretty life-consuming. It was honestly the best time of my life, but I'm glad it's over. Working to get by and making time to study was exhausting. I'd wake up in the middle of the night, a book page glued to my face with drool."

"I can't even make fun of him for it because the same thing used to happen to me. Falling asleep face down in your paramedic book is a right of passage around here," Eric said, giving Angell a playful shove before draining the last of his coffee and looking down at the empty cup remorsefully.

"If you want to get back into hiking, I can make some suggestions for you. We even have some local waterfalls that are super easy to get to," Angell said and ran his fingers through his dark locs. "If you want, you could come with us. We usually hit a trail once a week during the summertime. Hell, we'll make a whole day out of it and take you to some of the local breweries."

"Sure, that would be great," Kitty said, making a mental note to buy the first round of beers for taking her under their wings.

"So, did you move up here with anyone?" Angell asked, fishing for more information.

"Nah, just me." With a shake of her head, she downed the last of her latte.

"Alright, he grinned. "I guess there is only one thing left to ask. Boys or girls?"

Eric blanched and smacked his partner. "What the hell, man?! Sorry, I forgot to warn you about how intrusive he is! You don't have to answer that."

"It's okay," she assured him and turned a hard stare on Angell. "The hair doesn't give me away? Are you blind?"

First On Scene: A Howling Sirens Novel

Angell roared with laughter while Eric groaned. Unable to help herself, she laughed.

When she moved to Massachusetts, she'd decided to lean into the dyke chic look and had shorn off her shoulder-length locs, dyed her mousey-brown hair bleach blonde, and called it a day. Now, even her own mother wouldn't recognize her.

"Not blind. I just don't like to assume," Angell assured her, causing Eric to have a coughing fit.

Sighing softly, she snuggled deeper into her seat. This was going better than expected. Massachusetts had been the first state in the country to recognize same-sex marriages. So she knew she'd be safe legislatively, but you never knew when you were going to run into a bigot.

"Alright, let me guess. Both of you are straight?"

Angell rolled his eyes. "As if. I'm Bi, so you can just call me an equal opportunist. Now, the prude next to me, on the other hand, is straight."

"Hey! We've had this conversation. Straight doesn't mean rigid, and just because I have standards doesn't make me a prude!" Crossing his arms over his chest, Eric glared at his partner. Softening his gaze, he turned to her. "You don't have to worry about people giving you shit for being gay. People around here don't care who you sleep with as long as you can do your job. Oh, and of course, that you don't do it in the back of an ambulance. That's gross."

"It's not gross if you wipe the truck down first!" Angell argued, giving his partner a playful shove. "You're just jealous I get more action than you do!"

"You're dirty," Eric informed him with another shake of his head.

"So, like I said, a prude."

Grinning, Kitty caught Eric's eye. "So why does he call you Crash?

Eric groaned as he raked a hand through his orange locs. "I didn't have the smoothest entry into EMS. When I first started driving an ambulance, I hit everything but the lottery."

"And?" Angell asked, poking his partner in the side.

Eric cleared his throat while rubbing the back of his neck.

Selina Rossman

"And when I got my medic, I had some rough calls. While I was still riding third, we had this guy code after he snorted enough cocaine to kill a horse. I thought I got the tube, but apparently, I was in the stomach."

"Okay?" Kitty said, not understanding what the big deal was. Everyone made mistakes sometimes.

"And then—" Angell pried.

"And then the dude puked half-digested ramen up the tube into my mouth," Eric grumbled, wrinkling his nose. "I can still taste it sometimes."

"Ew!" Kitty exclaimed.

Laughing, Angell patted Eric on the shoulder. "Okay, now tell her about that other time—"

Three high-pitched beeps interrupted their verbal sparring, and Kitty jumped.

"Medic Two, please respond to 472 Main Street for the unresponsive male. Police will meet you there."

"Saved by the bell," Angell said, winking at his partner as he clicked the radio mic. "We have it. Please show us en route." Standing, Angell strode towards the door. She and Eric followed suit.

It was time to get to work.

Chapter Two

Eric parked in front of the base, yawning widely as he got out of the car and looked around. Kitty's motorcycle was nowhere to be found. She refused to get a car despite the cold weather, and he hated to think about how she'd fare once it started snowing. He foresaw her bumming rides from her partners when the cold weather hit in earnest.

A yellow Volkswagen beetle pulled into the lot, blocking his car in. He squinted at the driver, a familiar-looking woman with dark skin and a mop of curly black hair. The passenger door popped open, and Kitty, sporting a blush and a lopsided grin, stepped out of the car. Muttering something he couldn't hear to the driver, she winked and shut the door. The beetle peeled out of the lot.

Kitty straightened her collar and smoothed out the creases in her uniform shirt as she walked up to him, grinning. "Hey."

Smirking, he rested his hands on his hips. "And who was that?"

Rubbing the back of her neck, she glanced in the direction the car had gone. "Uh, you remember that triage nurse I was flirting with last week?"

"Which one," he teased.

Flushing, she scuffed her boot against the concrete. "Anyways- I crashed at her place last night, and she offered to drop me off."

Barking out a laugh, he shook his head. "What do you think Zuri's going to say about some other woman sniffing around?"

Kitty's head snapped up to stare at him wide-eyed. "Here?" She squeaked. Turning a deeper shade of red, she cleared her throat. "She's here today?!"

Shrugging with false nonchalance, he turned and walked towards the front door. He didn't know if Zuri was actually on shift or not but he loved teasing his partner. Kitty'd had the hots for their co-worker since her first day of work four months ago, but still hadn't worked up the courage to ask her out. He didn't understand her hesitation considering how fast she went through nurses.

Walking into the day room, Vivian and Tim were already there waiting for them.

Pushing a strand of curly, red hair behind her ear, Vivian smiled brightly and tossed him her keys and radio. "Truck should be all set," she chirped and darted out of the room without another word.

He couldn't blame her. If he'd been stuck with Tim for twenty-four hours, he'd flee at the first sight of relief, too.

Frowning, Eric eyed the man before him. It had only been a few weeks since he'd had the displeasure of working with Tim but their time apart had transformed the man into someone new, someone worse. Pockmarks lined his hollow cheeks, and sunken eyes peered out at the world from beneath the baseball cap pulled over his face. The once tight uniform shirt now swam around his gaunt frame, reminding Eric of a sick kid playing dress up. *What the hell happened to him?*

Ignoring Eric and Kitty, Tim kept his eyes glued to Vivian's retreating back.

He looks like shit, but he's the same old scumbag, Eric thought and stepped into Tim's direct line of sight, blocking Vivian from view.

Tim fished the truck keys out of his pocket. Pushing himself to his feet, he slammed them down on the desk and scowled before stalking out of the room.

Kitty sidled up next to Eric. "He's lost a lot of weight. You think he's on something?"

First On Scene: A Howling Sirens Novel

Eric scoffed. "I'd bet my life on it." Folding his arms across his chest, he shook his head. "I know we need people but shit, I think we can do better than that!"

Kitty shrugged. "I don't know, man. They let you in on a truck."

"Hey, I'll have you know, I'm the world's okayest medic," he jested and shoulder-bumped his partner.

Rolling her eyes and grinning, Kitty headed for the ambulance bay. "Come on, we should check out the truck before it gets busy."

They descended the stairs and crossed the bay.

Kitty's eyes immediately darted to P1's open door.

Smirking, Eric prepared to tease her about her *girlfriend* but the tones dropped. Three loud beeps shouted down at them from the ceiling, and the words died on his lips.

"P2, Engine Two, car two, please respond to 36 Front Street for the allergic reaction."

Striding towards the ambulance, he clicked his radio mic. "P2 has the call. Show us responding, 36 Front Street."

Kitty sped towards the driver's door, and he swore. Her driving always made him queasy. He knew she wouldn't wreck, but the feeling of impending doom always crept up his neck whenever she got behind the wheel.

Kitty screeched out of the base, leaving the sirens on wail and driving at breakneck speeds around the rush hour traffic.

Swallowing hard but unable to tear his eyes from the road, Eric clawed blindly for a hold on the door, curling his fingers around the handle and squeezing hard enough to make his knuckles blanch.

The truck stopped abruptly, and his chest collided with the taut seat belt. They'd beaten fire and police to the scene.

With a soft grunt, he released the belt and jumped out of the ambulance. He was tempted to kiss the ground, but there wasn't time; he had a job to do. "I got the monitor," he called to his partner and shouldered the equipment.

Striding towards the house, he took the three steps in two long strides and banged on the front door. "EMS!" He shouted and tried the door knob. It was open. He pushed inside and stopped short. The only way to get to his patient was by climbing a long, steep staircase with narrow steps. It was a New England special. "Fuck," he grumbled and started climbing.

The stairway was narrow, the walls pressing in on him on either side. The space was too tight for him to pass with gear slung over his shoulder, so he shifted the monitor to his chest, holding it awkwardly against his body.

Behind him, he could hear Kitty cursing softly as she struggled to climb the stairs and keep the first-in bag in front of her.

Legs burning, he cleared the stairs and stepped through an open doorway. He made two quick turns and found himself in a kitchen. Directly in front of him, a white man in his thirties sat bolt upright in a chair, his chest heaving with every breath.

A thick tongue protruded out from between swollen, grayish-blue lips, and a sea of angry red hives covered the man's face and neck, his blotchy red skin stretched tautly over his grotesquely bloated features. Wide, panicked eyes locked onto Eric, and he could hear the man's stridorous breathing from the doorway. He needed to act fast. If he didn't, the man's airway would close, and he would die.

He didn't know what was taking Kitty so long, but he needed the rest of their gear.

"I'll be right back!" He shouted at the patient as his heart leaped into his throat. Dropping the monitor, he turned on his heel and sped back the way he had come.

Skirting to a stop at the top of the stairs, Eric peered down at his partner.

Having made it only halfway up, Kitty panted as she braced herself against the wall, the first-in bag balanced precariously on the step in front of her. "Sorry," she gasped, looking up at him, "asthma."

Shit. She needed a breathing treatment, but their patient needed an Epi-pen more. Kitty would have to wait. Guts twisting with guilt and throat constricting painfully, Eric swallowed hard. "Throw me the Epi pen!"

Wracked by a coughing fit, Kitty pressed a hand to her chest and hunched over the first-in bag, digging through its contents. "Here," she rasped out, raising the medication above her head and hurling it in his direction.

Don't fuck this up, Eric thought, clutching the door frame with one hand and leaning into the open air above the stairs. The Epi-Pen sailed end over end, losing altitude as it got closer. Clinging to the door jam by his fingertips, he thrust out his free hand and snatched the autoinjector out of the air. *Yes!*

Throwing himself backward, he stumbled inside. Finding his footing, he sprinted back to the patient and dropped to his knees next to the flushed, gasping man. Popping the top off the pen, he drove the enormous needle into the side of the man's leg. The man didn't even flinch.

"Don't worry, sir. The medication will kick in a couple minutes," he promised as he hooked the patient up to the monitor. By the time he had a set of vitals, the patient had begun to breathe easier.

"Thank you," the man mumbled past swollen lips.

Eric eyed the monitor. Surprisingly, the patient's oxygen levels looked good. "Sir, I have to go check on my partner real quick. I'll be right back."

The man gave him a curt nod.

Kitty wasn't going to last much longer without a breathing treatment. Jumping to his feet, Eric sped out of the kitchen and back to his partner. He reached the top of the stairs and stopped short. He was too late.

While he'd been tied up treating their patient, the fire department had arrived on scene and started Kitty's care. She looked up at him, a nebulizer mask secured to her face, and gave him a thumbs up.

Eric's shoulders sagged with relief. He'd made the right call.

The radio went off, and he jumped.

"P1, Engine One, Car Three, please respond with animal control to the Cellucci park for the reported wolf attack."

Frowning, Eric stared at the radio. *A wolf?*

Chapter Three

Doing her best to drown out her partner's constant whining with the sirens, Zuri swerved around a stopped car and huffed out an irritated sigh. It was barely seven-thirty, and she was already over it. She'd figured that since Tim had worked the night before, he wouldn't be her problem, but unfortunately for her, she'd been wrong, and his self-inflicted thirty-six-hour shift only made him bitch more.

"Who gets attacked by a dog at this hour?!" Tim complained, clawing at his face and glaring out the window. "And why are they calling it a wolf?! How are people this stupid?"

Zuri pulled to a stop behind the fire engine, throwing open the door as she killed the engine and flipped off the lights. *I'd let a dog bite me right now if it'd shut him up*, she thought resentfully.

Drawing a deep breath, she shouldered the first-in bag and frowned at the earthy musk on the wind. Wrinkling her nose as she strode around a police car, she kept her head on a swivel, looking for the scent's cause. Behind her, Tim continued grumbling under his breath as he clawed at his face, gouging his skin. She hoped that his constant scratching wasn't a case of fleas. Or worse, bedbugs.

She caught sight of a dark-skinned man with a gaunt face and long, dirty dreadlocks that she was certain she'd seen

First On Scene: A Howling Sirens Novel

before at one of the homeless shelters in town. He was dressed in a baggy T-shirt, sweatpants two sizes too large for him, and had a clean, white bandage that hugged his upper arm. Hands curled into fists at his sides, he scowled at the officers flanking him. "No!" He shouted suddenly. "I'm telling you, I was attacked by a giant wolf!"

A short, muscular officer ran a hand through his clean-cut, blonde hair. "Sir, we know you were attacked," he soothed as Zuri reached them. "But I saw the bite mark before fire patched you up, an animal didn't do that. A person did."

"Just listen," the man pleaded.

"Great," Tim muttered as he came up beside her, "a fucking psych." Stinking of stale coffee and unbrushed teeth, his hot breath tickled her cheek. Reflexively, she stepped away from him and towards the patient.

"Hi, Sir, I'm Zuri. Can you tell me your name?"

Lips parted, the man shifted his agitated gaze from the police to her, but before he could speak, his eyes rolled into the back of his head, and he crumpled to the ground. Shaking violently, he thrashed his head against the concrete as his teeth gouged his protruding tongue. Blood rushed down his face from a scalp wound.

"Shit," Zuri yelped and surged forward to roll the man onto his side and keep him from doing further damage to himself. The sharp metallic tang of fresh blood stung her nostrils and made her empty stomach growl hungrily. *Not now*, she told her stomach and took a deep breath. The sour scent of alcohol and a familiar musk clung to the man. Furrowing her brow, she struggled to place the smell. *What did this?*

"I could use some he—" The words died on her lips as she looked at the empty space where Tim had been standing. "Great," she muttered bitterly and glanced at the two officers now kneeling beside her. "Can you guys go get me the stretcher?"

Both men scrambled to their feet and sprinted for the ambulance, returning quickly with Tim in tow. One of the officers helped her partner lower the stretcher to the ground and they hoisted the still seizing man off the ground. Rushing him back to the rig, they loaded him inside and Zuri climbed in.

"I'll set up an IV while you draw up meds," she said and reached for supplies. "Do you want a driver so I can stay back here with you?"

Training narrowed eyes on their patient, Tim shook his head. "Nah, just get up front and go."

"But we have to stop the seizure," she argued and continued what she was doing.

"I'm the fucking medic," he snapped and yanked the IV catheter out of her hands. "Go drive."

Glaring up into his scowling face, she bared her teeth. "Fine," she growled and left before the impulse to bite him won out. Seething, she slammed the double doors and stomped her way to the front of the truck. His piss-poor patient care was just one more reason to hate him. Any other paramedic would have let her help. Hell, they would have expected it.

Blowing out a frustrated breath, Zuri climbed into the driver's seat and started the truck. The engine rumbled to life as she hit the emergency master button to turn on the lights. The button glowed green, but nothing happened. *Not now*, she thought, her heart racing as she glanced into the rearview mirror at her useless partner. If she couldn't respond to the hospital, Tim would definitely kill the patient.

She closed her eyes and took a deep breath. Her relationship with electronics was awful on the best of days but always got worse when she was stressed. *Be calm*, she repeated to herself, shutting her eyes and focusing on breathing.

Zuri jumped and her eyes flew open as someone rapped loudly on the window beside her. Cheeks heating with embarrassment, she rolled down the window. "Uh, yeah?"

"Everything okay?" The blonde officer asked, frowning.

"Just a little electrical issue," she muttered as she hit the emergency master again. The lights flicked on, and her shoulders sagged with relief. "All fixed," she said and threw the truck in drive.

Chapter Four

The battered steps creaked disconcertingly beneath his scuffed boots. The monitor strap bit painfully into his shoulder, but it was nothing compared to the bite of the wind. Cresting the top of the stairs, he finally reached the dilapidated structure. With faded, peeling green paint and crooked shutters, the building had seen better days. The front door groaned open, revealing a familiar robed figure, and Angell trembled. Hooded head cocked to the side, a skeletal hand beckoned him forward. Rooted to the spot, he blinked rapidly. *Is Kitty seeing this, or am I hallucinating?* he thought, worrying at his lower lip between his teeth.

Searching for his partner, he looked over his shoulder. She wasn't there. Returning his gaze to the darkened doorway, he blanched. The Reaper had been replaced by the figure of a white, nude man. A sallow face peered out at him, tears dripping down his cheeks and mouth agape in a silent moan.

"No!" He hissed through gritted teeth and stumbled back. Losing his footing, he tumbled down the jagged steps. Pain lanced up his flank, and he struggled to draw a complete breath.

Something sharp needled him in the side, jarring him awake. Swatting at whatever was prodding him, he gasped for air. Taking a couple of deep breaths and willing his pounding heart to calm itself, he looked up into Kitty's concerned face.

"Are you okay?" She asked, watching him closely through narrowed eyes.

Swallowing hard, he nodded. "Yeah, just a nightmare."

She patted him on the shoulder. "I still can't believe you slept through the sirens." She shook her head and opened her door. "Come on, nap time is over. We have a job to do."

He nodded tiredly, watching Kitty tumble gracelessly out of the huge vehicle, barely catching herself before he smoothly exited the ambulance. He couldn't help feeling sorry for her and ever grateful for his long legs. The rigs weren't designed with short people in mind.

It had already been a miserable shift and he didn't want to add night terrors into the mix. Every frequent flier in town had conveniently decided that they *needed* to go to the hospital today, and what was worse, they still had drunk drivers and drug overdoses to look forward to. He didn't know what he had expected. After all, it was Halloween *and* a Saturday night. At least the trick-or-treaters had gone home, and he wouldn't have to worry about them running in front of the truck anymore.

Opening the back doors, the stagnant scent of BO and fresh vomit accosted him. Their last patient had been too shit-faced to even tell them his name but had adamantly denied being nauseous. So, of course, the moment they had gotten into the truck, the guy had spewed. Brow wrinkling in disgust, he pulled out the longboard and the cardiac monitor. Leaving the back open to air out, he suspected the stench would deter any would-be thieves.

Shrugging the cardiac monitor onto one shoulder and the oxygen bag onto the other, he awkwardly manhandled the longboard beneath his arm. Eyeing the residence, he blew out a shaky breath. *Shit.* A rickety building leered down at him from the top of a steep hill. The faded green paint and crooked shutters caught his breath in his throat. The building was right out of his dream. Sighing tiredly, he began his ascent. He had a date with a dead guy and his reaper to get to.

The battered steps creaked disconcertingly beneath his scuffed boots, and the monitor strap bit uncomfortably into his

First On Scene: A Howling Sirens Novel

shoulder. A glacial wind nipped at him, cutting through his flimsy EMS jacket and latex gloves. From behind him, he could hear his partner's labored breathing. "Where the fuck is fire? They should have beat us here!" He growled between chattering teeth.

The town was supposed to be a three-tier system, meaning that every 9-1-1 call got an ambulance, a fire engine, and a police car dispatched to it. He was used to being the second or third team on scene and being updated on what they were walking into. Getting dispatched for the unresponsive patient might as well be an *unknown medical*. Not knowing what to expect, they had to bring in *all* of the equipment. It also guaranteed that the residence would be a pain in the ass to get to. It was Murphy's law.

After what seemed like forever, they cleared the stairs. Panting, he readied himself to bang on the front door, but it was already open. Half expecting to be met by his reaper, he froze, but neither dead man nor specter greeted him. Walking into the well-lit entryway, an image of the sallow, sobbing face flashed across his mind.

Swallowing hard he maneuvered through the narrow doorway and licked his suddenly dry lips, attempting to coax some moisture back into them. "Hello!" He bellowed, stepping deeper into the foyer. "EMS!"

"In here!" the strained female voice responded from a room just out of sight.

Kitty pushed past him, leading the way into the living room as an Arctic chill snaked down his spine. His reaper still hadn't shown himself, but he knew it was only a matter of time.

One glance around the spacious room told him everything he needed to know. Smiling faces beamed at him from the pictures hanging on the wall, a well-worn red leather couch beneath their frames, and the coffee table was covered in half-finished knitting projects. Happy people lived here. *Or at least they did*, he thought, eyeing the white, naked man lying face down in the center of the living room.

Why are they always naked? Does no one own pajamas?! Shoulders slumping, he dropped to his knees and searched for a pulse. There wasn't one.

In a single, fluid motion, he flipped the man over and onto the backboard. Vacant eyes gazed up at him from a familiar, clean-shaven face. He'd been paler in the dream, but then again, they always were. The dead guy was older, maybe in his sixties, with cropped white hair and washboard abs that screamed career military man.

Snapping an oxygen mask onto the patient's face, he cranked the oxygen up as high as it would go and began compressions. Cartilage cracked and popped under his palms. It was never not gross. Unlike many of his peers who hummed "Stayin' Alive" to find the right rhythm for compressions, he preferred to just count to himself. *One and two...*

The man's wife had positioned herself at the farthest point in the room. A frail-looking white woman, she wore only a green bathrobe, clutched against her thin frame, and long unbound gray hair hung loosely over her shoulders as her eyes glistened with unfallen tears.

Nostrils flaring and chest heaving, Angell could tell that Kitty was still winded as she dropped her gear on the floor and approached the woman. "Hi, I'm Kitty, one of the paramedics," she said, drawing in a deep breath. "Do you know what happened?"

The woman shook her head. "I woke up, and he was just gone." She paused, her lips quivering. "I called for him, and when he didn't answer, I came downstairs. That's when I found him-" She broke off, suppressing a soft sob.

"Did he have any medical problems?" Kitty placed a reassuring hand on the woman's shoulder as she waited patiently for an answer.

The woman shook her head again. "No, no problems. He takes good care of himself."

Kitty began jotting things down on her notepad. "Did he drink or take any drugs?"

Again, the woman shook her head. "No, he didn't even take medications."

Kitty gave her shoulder a comforting squeeze. "We are going to do everything we can, but I have to go help my

First On Scene: A Howling Sirens Novel

partner now."

The woman nodded, pressing a hand to her breastbone.

Angell doubted that the man truly had no medical history. It wasn't impossible, but it was unlikely. Normally, he would have sent an officer to dig around for clues, but apparently, that wasn't an option.

The constant exertion made his arms burn, his back scream, and his knees ache. Only a sense of duty kept him going. He desperately wanted to switch out with someone. To maintain good chest compressions, they were supposed to swap out compressors every two minutes, but that wasn't going to be happening either. This was the third call in a row that they'd gone to on their own. It was bullshit.

Crouching beside him, Kitty tore open the defib pads and slapped them onto the man's chest. Turning the monitor on, she stared at the screen, her lips pressing into a grim line. She knew just as well as he did that they wouldn't be bringing anyone back tonight. He felt bad for his partner. She was still a new enough medic to think that every call was a chance to save a life. The job would beat it out of her. It was only a matter of time.

"Charging!" She warned.

He waited until the last possible second to withdraw.

"Clear!" She ordered.

Angell yanked his hands back.

"Shocking." She pressed the orange lighting-shaped button, and the patient's body jerked. The patient was flatlining, and no amount of electricity was going to fix that.

Finally, Kitty took over compressions. She hummed Lady Gaga's "Bad Romance" to keep in rhythm. It wasn't wrong, but it also wasn't common. He would have found it funny under better circumstances.

"I hate this," He muttered under his breath. He'd gotten into EMS to help people and to save lives but that wasn't what they did most of the time. Sure, they provided plenty of medical care and stabilized patients, but getting to save a life was rare. Most of the time, the dead guy stayed that way.

Feeling like Billy the Kid, he palmed his trusty bone drill.

Selina Rossman

Kitty always insisted on looking for an IV, even during a code, but she was busy right now. *Why be a "vein whisperer" when you could just drill?*

Finding the right landmarks on the lower leg, he sank the drill's large gauge needle into flesh. It slid through the tissues like butter. The needle made contact with a hard surface, and he pulled the trigger. Buzzing, the needle plunged into bone. With vascular access assured, he snagged the drug box.

Angell flinched and rocked back on his heels, his heart thundering in his throat as a dark figure loomed over him. He had been wondering when it would show its cloaked face, but the sudden appearance was still startling. After all these years, he should have been used to death tagging along, but he wasn't. Averting his eyes from the specter, he ignored it, forcing himself to focus on his job.

With a hard swallow, he flipped the box open and snatched up an EPI. Popping off the cap with his teeth, he spat it onto the floor and slammed the drug home. Giving the figure from his dreams the cold shoulder, he spiked a bag of saline and tucked it under his arm to pressure fluids into the patient.

Kitty's two minutes on the chest were almost up, and he needed to switch out with her. They smoothly changed positions, and in spite of his arms objections, he took over compressions again.

Shifting the drug box closer to the patient, Kitty pulled out another EPI and shivered, goosebumps breaking out along her forearms. Glancing over her shoulder and finding nothing, she went back to pushing meds. Angell glared at his reaper over the dead man's chest. To his knowledge, she wasn't the least bit clairvoyant, but he had never seen her so aware of its presence before. Normally, she was completely oblivious to the specter.

They swapped out compressors again, and he shook out his arms as Kitty took over. When he could feel his upper extremities again, Angell glanced down at his watch and frowned. They shared a meaningful glance, and his partner nodded, ceasing her compressions.

In their district, you were only supposed to work a cardiac

First On Scene: A Howling Sirens Novel

arrest for twenty minutes. They'd passed that ten minutes ago. He had mixed feelings about the protocol. Having a hard stop point meant no false hope for the family and no dangerous transports for the crew, but it also came with difficult conversations.

Clenching his jaw, he steeled himself to talk to the man's wife. They had done all they could, and unfortunately, the corpse was here to stay. Before he could stand, though, Kitty took it upon herself to break the news. His shoulders sagged with relief as he watched her approach the older woman.

"I'm so sorry. We did all we could, but he's dead," Kitty said without leaving room for confusion. He knew she ached to lessen the blow because he always wanted to, but imprecise language only led to false hope. The patient's wife covered her mouth, suppressing a sob. Silent tears coursed down her face.

"An officer will be here soon to wait with you," Kitty drawled. He was surprised to hear it. Normally she only let her southern twang out as a joke, but he could see that the accent seemed to be having a reassuring effect on the woman.

"Wait for what?" The wife asked, voice cracking.

"With no history, the medical examiner's office is going to want to get involved. You aren't in trouble or anything. It's just policy," Kitty explained. "Besides, you shouldn't be alone right now. Is there anyone we can call for you?"

The woman nodded her head, slumping heavily against the wall. "My son."

"Okay, why don't we go into the other room and call your son then?" Kitty suggested, leading her from the room.

"Medic Two to operations. Medic Two is going to be clear shortly. Police matter." Dispatch's response was slow. *What the fuck is happening tonight?* he thought, gritting his teeth until his jaw popped. When there was no reply, he repeated the patch.

"Can we get an officer here?!" He snipped into the mic. Still waiting for dispatch to wake up and answer him as he cleaned up the mess they had made.

"We have it. Police matter. Car six is en route to your location." The radio squealed loudly. Wincing, he turned down the volume.

Selina Rossman

Kitty returned from the kitchen clutching her demographic notes. Tucking it into her breast pocket, she helped him pack up their gear. Together, they covered the body with a sheet. It felt like the right thing to do. After that, they fled the house.

With trembling hands, he shoved their gear into the still-reeking truck. Wrinkling his nose, he stripped his gloves, tossed them inside, and slammed the doors shut. Groaning, he ran a hand through his dark curls and dragged himself to the front passenger seat. Despite the frigid weather, they were soaked in sweat.

"Can I ask you a question?" Kitty dragged herself into the driver's seat.

Making a noncommittal sound in the back of his throat, he leaned back in his seat and shut his eyes. He wasn't really in the mood to play preceptor right now.

"This may sound dumb…" She hesitated. "Do you ever feel like someone is watching us when we work?"

Angell's eyes flew open, his mind racing. *Does she see the reaper? Has she been seeing it? No. Tonight was the first time she's reacted to him. Besides, we're close; she would have said something to me.* His stomach twinged guiltily. He was too scared to voice his question because saying it aloud would force him to accept that there was something more going on than just a fucked up stress reaction to the job.

Kitty looked at him expectantly, a soft flush heating up her pale cheeks.

Angell ran two fingers over his mustache as he shifted uncomfortably in his seat. "Like ghosts? I thought you didn't believe in those."

Kitty hesitated for a long moment. "I don't, but—" She trailed off, pursing her lips and turning to look out the window as her fingers played absentmindedly with the bottom of her wrinkled shirt.

A flash of blue and red drew their attention. The police were finally on the scene. "About goddamn time," he muttered and watched as the officer exited his cruiser. It wasn't someone he recognized, but he raised his hand in greeting anyway. Briefly returning the gesture, the bald man headed for the residence.

First On Scene: A Howling Sirens Novel

Returning his attention to Kitty, he braced himself for an uncomfortable conversation. "You were saying?"

She opened her mouth but snapped it shut just as quickly as she tugged on her shirt collar, and he caught a glimpse of a hickey on her neck. He'd much rather talk about her latest conquest than his hooded stalker.

Angell leaned forward, grinning broadly as he hooked a finger into her collar and took a closer look at the bruise. "And what do we have here?!"

Kitty flushed fuchsia and smacked his hand away. "You remember that neurologist from the other day?"

"Yeah," he said, waggling his eyebrows suggestively.

Smirking as she scrubbed at the back of her neck, Kitty looked out the window again. "Yeah, well- she was a biter."

The tension in his shoulders eased as Angell chuckled softly, shaking his head. "You going to see her again?"

Kitty shrugged. "Probably not."

"Why not? She was hot. And, you know, a doctor. You could do much worse than a neurologist."

Chewing on her lower lip, Kitty looked up at him. "I haven't really been doing repeats. I guess you could say I like the variety."

Angell raked a hand through his curls. "Damn girl, you make me look like a prude."

Before Kitty could defend her honor, the strained voice of dispatch interrupted them. "Medic Two, are you clear?"

"Uhg, I just want a nap," Kitty wined and picked up the radio mic. "That's affirmative. Clear and available."

"Good, please respond to Thirty-two Northboro Rd. in Marlborough for mutual aid. BLS is on scene requesting an intercept. No further information is available at this time."

"Received. You can show us responding." Groaning, Kitty hooked the mic on its holder and threw the truck in drive, flipping on the lights.

Kitty silently clutched the steering wheel as they bumped down a side street. Taking another sharp turn, the truck bounced off a curb and Angell clutched the roof handle while his stomach churned uncomfortably. In an attempt to keep the

Selina Rossman

migraine he felt brewing at bay, he he rubbed his temples. Kitty's erratic driving wasn't helping but it could be worse. She could have left the sirens on wail.

"P2, BLS is requesting you step it up!" Dispatch squealed at them. Not wanting Kitty to take her hands off the wheel, he snatched up the mic. "Received."

BLS, Basic Life Support, was where every EMT started their career. Unfortunately, not all EMTs were created equally. They had a decent scope of practice in Massachusetts, but not everyone was confident enough to use their state-sanctioned skills. The fact that they were still on scene at the long-term care facility told him everything he needed to know about the crew. An experienced EMT would have transported and tried to meet up with them on the way to the hospital.

He glanced into the patient compartment and flinched, a wave of nausea washing over him. The hooded figure sat patiently on the bench seat. *Damn it.*

"Medic Two is out!" Kitty grumped into the radio and slid out of the truck.

Following her out, Angell focused on the acrid scent of overused brake pads. Anything to not think about the angel of death still following him.

He wanted to blame the abuse of the breaks on Kitty's exhaustion, but he knew better. She was just a shitty driver that liked to speed. Not that he would tell her that.

Ignoring their silent third rider, Angell climbed into the back of the ambulance, gagging on the stench of vomit. The smell just wouldn't die.

Shoulder their gear, he abandoned the ambulance with the doors wide open. Death stalked them toward the building. Silent and useless as always. If the Grim Reaper was going to follow them around, it could at least carry something. Ever the superior partner, Kitty took the cardiac monitor and drug box from him.

They shoved their way into the building and found the closest elevator. The doors opened on the fourth floor, and the screaming began.

Angell inhaled sharply and immediately regretted

breathing. The metallic tang of blood hung heavily in the air. Choking down the rising bile at the back of his throat, he struggled not to dry heave. Even Kitty openly gagged, not helping his resolve. She normally held it together better than he did, and if her iron-clad stomach couldn't handle the smell, what chance did he have?

Kitty took a steadying breath, wrinkled her nose, and stepped off the elevator. "Are you coming?" She glanced back at him over her shoulder.

Schooling his face into neutrality, he stepped off the elevator and looked left. His reaper loitered next to the elevator, watching him with its hooded head cocked to the side. *Hope we can put on a good show for you,* he thought with a sardonic shake of his head.

Still breathing only through his mouth, he rapidly took in the scene. A woman wearing blue scrubs screeched at the two cringing EMTs, her dark skin freckled with blood. Two other staff members scrambled around the room, frantically busy but accomplishing nothing.

"Why are you still here?! Get him out!" The woman in blue screamed at two youthful-looking providers. Both of the EMTs looked more like they were playing dress-up than the uniformed men they were expected to be. Having failed to make it further out of the building, the BLS crew stood awkwardly in front of the elevator, shooting desperate looks in Angell's direction. He felt for them. He remembered what it was like to be brand new and completely out of your depth.

The elderly man inhabiting their stretcher had a grave-like pallor and gasped for air like a fish out of water while he weakly swung at anyone who dared to get too close.

Before Angell could get close enough to help, the patient erupted in foul-smelling gore as a deluge of blood burst past the man's ashen lips. He winced as the man's shirt and the two EMTs got drenched in the frothy crimson.

Nose crinkled in revulsion, Kitty approached the woman in blue scrubs, took her firmly by the arm, and dragged her away.

"Hey, guys. I'm Angell, one of the medics. Looks like you

could use a hand." He greeted and opened the first-in bag from a safe distance. Snatching out an oxygen mask, he scooted behind the stretcher and connected it to the oxygen canister. Dodging blood-soaked fingers, he snapped the mask over the patient's face.

"We are going to take care of you, Sir. This will help you breathe. Try to just breathe." He directed the patient, searching the man's face for any hint of comprehension. There was none to be found. The man gasped raggedly and continued to struggle against the gurney's seatbelts.

There was no point in trying to attach the monitor leads. They would only be torn off again, so instead, he snuck the oxygen saturation probe onto a bloody finger. Even with the mask, the patient's saturation was seventy percent. *Fuck, that's way too low*, he thought, pinching his lips into a thin line. Normal levels were at least ninety-four percent.

"What can I do to help?" one of the EMTs, a sandy-haired kid with brown eyes, asked.

"Come here," he instructed.

The kid approached him while his partner remained frozen in place with eyes the size of saucers.

Angell gave him an approving nod. "What's your name?"

"Charlie," the kid said and grinned sheepishly.

He moved to the front of the stretcher while Charlie took the back. The other EMT shook off his petrification and sidled over to them as they lowered the stretcher to a safe height. "I can help too. My name is Matt."

"Good." Angell waved across the room where Kitty had the staff members cornered. "We need to get him downstairs," he said loudly enough for her to hear as he smashed the elevator button. "Hurry up!" Kitty gave a curt nod and turned back to the woman in blue scrubs.

"We got you. Just try to breathe." Angell tugged the stretcher towards the elevator as the patient drooled blood into the mask. Struggling not to gag as he motioned for Charlie to help him push the stretcher closer to the elevator doors.

With a soft chime, the elevator doors slid open, and the three of them squeezed inside with the stretcher and all of

First On Scene: A Howling Sirens Novel

their gear. The reaper swept in with them as the doors closed and settled uncomfortably close to him.

Angell dragged his focus away from the reaper and onto the two young healthcare providers. "What can you tell me about the patient?"

Charlie shrugged, looking down at his boots. "Not much. They just kept screaming at us to hurry up and get out. I know he's been coughing up blood for the last thirty minutes. That's all they would tell us."

"It's alright. These places can be chaotic on a good day." Suppressing a sigh, Angell shook his head. Not having more to go on was frustrating, but It wasn't their fault. It took a while to get your bearings in the field. Hell, if it weren't for the mentorship of a few old, salty medics, he never would have gotten proficient at his job.

The elevator opened, and they rushed out of the building. The frigid air stung his face and lungs, but he was grateful for it. He hoped the fresh air would settle his roiling stomach.

"Do you know how to suction and bag?" He loaded the patient into the back of the ambulance, surprised to find that it had retained its warmth despite being left open.

Nodding, Charlie settled himself in the airway seat at the head of the stretcher, his partner standing awkwardly beside him.

Angell set up the suction canister, attaching the tubing, turning it on, and passing it over to Charlie. He eyed the tech station and the row of cabinets just above it and pulled a bag valve mask out. Assembling it, he tossed it at the boys. Matt caught the BVM and got ready to manually ventilate the patient. Without needing further instruction, they got to work clearing the patient's airway and assisting his erratic breathing.

After a couple of minutes, Kitty climbed into the rig and slammed the doors shut behind her, cutting off the flow of fresh air. Her icy blue eyes blazed with unspoken rage. The lingering scent of stale vomit had been replaced by the putrid smell of partially digested blood.

"The staff here are grossly incompetent, but I got them to

tell me details anyway," she growled, curling her hands into fists. "He is eighty-eight and has a history of severe mental delay, respiratory failure, and esophageal varices. His oxygen saturation tanked, and the doctor attempted to intubate him when he *suddenly* started hemorrhaging blood from his throat. That's when they decided to finally call 9-1-1." Teeth gritted, she shook her head.

He bobbed his head in acknowledgment and tossed her the IV kit. Immediately understanding his desire, she started looking for a vein while he drew up a vial of versed. The medication should relax the patient enough to stop fighting them.

"I'm going to sedate him and try to get a real airway," he informed his partner, then watched in horror as she shivered and glanced out the back window, bringing her face flush with a hooded figure, partially obscured by the large star of life on the glass. Distracted for the moment, he had forgotten about their silent third rider.

"Kitty," he snapped, suddenly unnerved.

She jerked her head in his direction. "Sorry. What?"

He repeated himself, making a point to keep his voice steady, even if his lower lip was quivering ever so slightly.

She slid onto the bench seat next to him and pulled a saline flush out of her pocket. Holding her hand out expectantly for the syringe of medication. He handed it over and grabbed the intubation kit out of a cabinet.

"Ready?" She connected her syringe to the IV port, ready to slam the Versed.

"Ready." He nodded, tube in hand.

Ready, the patient silently screamed, freeing himself from the BVM mask and projectile vomiting blood across the ambulance compartment. It splattered against the rear doors with a sickening, squelching sound. Dark clots slid soundlessly down the doors, hitting the floor with a soft little plop plop.

It was too much for Matt. The poor kid dry-heaved and stumbled out the side door. Angell could hear him vomiting on the sidewalk outside. On the other side of the doors, his

First On Scene: A Howling Sirens Novel

reaper's face, a mask of darkness, continued its vigil.

Kitty slammed the Versed, and the patient fell back against the stretcher, his limbs flaccid, blood seeping out of his gaping mouth and dribbling onto his shirt.

"Congratulations Charlie. You get to drive us to the hospital. Have your partner meet us at UMASS with your truck," he said tiredly. Charlie flipped him a thumbs up and fled the back of the ambulance, slamming the side door behind him.

The reaper quickly replaced Charlie, alighting onto the tech seat. *I guess he doesn't want to walk to the hospital*, Angell thought bitterly.

The hospital was twenty minutes away, ten if you drove fast enough. They swayed with the movement of the ambulance. Kitty took over, suctioning the patient's airway, but most of the landmarks he needed to intubate were still obscured by blood and half-chewed food. Ultimately, he just followed the air bubbles escaping the trachea into the bloody debris. He intubated the man and was met by a geyser of blood that sprayed the ceiling, the floor, and the crew. The reaper's robes remained pristine, as always.

"I'm going home sick after this," Kitty threatened and handed him some damp, bloody tape to secure the tube.

"Why didn't we wear our face shields," Angell muttered, taking in the gore-covered truck.

"Because we're too tired to think straight?" Kitty offered and yawned widely.

When they were close enough, Kitty called on the radio to warn the hospital of their impending arrival. Only half listening to her patch, Angell focused on bagging the patient, keeping his eyes on the dying man instead of the reaper.

The ambulance came to a sudden stop, flinging Kitty back into her seat. They had arrived faster than expected. The hospital was going to be pissed that they didn't call sooner.

"God damn it!" Kitty shouted.

Before she could yell at him more, Charlie threw the truck in park and scurried around to the back. Together, they unloaded the patient.

Selina Rossman

Angell glanced back into the ambulance and winced. "If you guys want to get him inside, I'll start cleaning."

"Whatever you want," Kitty said dismissively and took over ventilating their patient. Matt ran up to join them and helped push the stretcher towards the emergency room's entrance.

Rather than staying by Angell's side, the reaper crept after the patient as the team disappeared into the emergency department's vestibule.

"Fuck! We just lost pulses!" Kitty shouted at someone just out of sight. The reaper paused outside the front doors, its hooded face turned in Angell's direction.

Acting on impulse, he nodded in acknowledgment, and the reaper returned the gesture before turning to drift after the others.

Angell staggered back, sitting heavily on the back step as his head spun. He'd never been directly acknowledged before. *What is this supposed to mean?* he thought, but before he could contemplate it further, P1 screeched into the spot next to him.

"We need help," Zuri shouted as she leaped out of the ambulance and raced to the back, yanking the doors open. "Come on!" she said, shooting him an expectant look.

Angell scrambled to his feet, and they pulled the patient out. A muscular, white man with a thick, bushy beard lay motionlessly on the gurney as Vivian continued her chest compressions.

Zuri jumped onto the side of the stretcher, leaning over the man and taking over for her partner. With every compression, blood gushed out from under her hands, soaking the sheets and cascading over the gurney's sides.

"What is this," Angell asked as he eyed the jagged wounds on the man's torso.

"Not sure yet," Vivian said as they rushed into the emergency department. "Something mauled him good, though."

Pushing the stretcher out of the trauma room, he left Vivian behind to finish giving her report. Zuri followed him, stripping off her bloody buttondown as she plodded back to the truck. The sweat-soaked white tee she wore underneath

First On Scene: A Howling Sirens Novel

clung to her shapely curves. He couldn't wait for his partner's reaction and to tease her about it over breakfast.

Dragging the stretcher with her, Kitty scowled and stomped over to the ambulance while the two EMTs followed at a distance. She stopped in front of Angell, her eyes flicking from his smirking face to the destroyed patient compartment. "I thought you stayed behind to clean," she said accusingly.

Yawning widely and pulling off her soiled gloves, Zuri jumped out of the back of the ambulance. Forgotten for the moment, Angell sat down on the back bumper to watch the show.

Kitty's fair skin flushed, red creeping from her neck to the tips of her ears as her wide blue eyes locked onto her crush. "Hey," she said, walking over and grinning sheepishly.

"Hey," Zuri answered with a small smirk of her own.

Angell shooed the two EMTs back to their own vehicle and climbed into the back of P2, leaving his friends to their awkward flirting. Ever secretive about her personal life, he had no idea what Zuri's sexual orientation was. He hoped she was at least Bi, for Kitty's sake.

With the patient compartment clean and ready for their next call, he walked to the front of the truck and got in. Kitty was already sitting in the passenger seat with her eyes closed. She startled awake as he shut his door.

Scrubbing her face tiredly, Kitty slumped back into her seat. "I think I'm going to skip out post-shift breakfast today," she muttered and yawned.

"You sure?"

"Yeah," she said and closed her eyes again.

Chapter Five

Kitty skidded into the dayroom with barely a minute to spare, turning on the ancient desktop and drumming her fingers as it groaned and wheezed with a sound like death rattles. She hurriedly typed in her username when the prompt finally appeared and then waited for another full minute while she waited to be asked for her password. More seconds ticked by before the machine displayed a notification that her password was wrong.

"Fuck!" She swore, going through the whole login rigamarole again. This time, her credentials were accepted, and she shot out of the room, sprinting down the stairs to the ambulance bay, leaping over the missing step at the base of the stairs, and landing roughly on the concrete floor with a soft grunt.

Raking a hand through her still sleep-mussed hair, she did her best to flatten out the tiny hairs that stuck out in every direction. Barely waking up for her alarm after sleeping the day away, she hadn't had time to brush it. Smoothing out the creases in her uniform shirt and straightening her jacket, she strode towards the box truck. She regretted picking up overtime, but at least the transfer truck tended to be pretty low-key, and at least she was working with her crush, Zuri. If only she could figure out if she was straight or not.

She could smell the bleach before she even climbed into the

First On Scene: A Howling Sirens Novel

truck. Zuri always insisted on wiping the truck down at the beginning of every shift. Her work ethic was something that Kitty admired about her.

Hauling herself in through the side door, she caught sight of her partner and smiled wistfully. It wasn't fair how good Zuri always looked. She wore her goddess braids in a tasteful bun, her golden brown hair complimenting her dark complexion, and her hazel eyes were flecked with hints of gold that a casual observer might miss, but Kitty had spent enough time stealing glances to notice.

"I think you missed a spot," Kitty teased.

Zuri's head snapped in her direction as she thrust the wipe in her hand out like a weapon. Her eyes narrowed in on Kitty, and she blew out a soft sigh, dropping her arm to her side. "I guess that answers who I'm with tonight."

"Who did you think was coming in?" Kitty drawled lazily, starting to check out the equipment. She checked the oxygen tanks and ran diagnostics on the monitor. Venturing a glance in Zuri's direction, she caught her watching her as she nibbled on her lower lip.

"Tim. He's been picking up a lot of shifts with me lately," she said darkly.

Kitty wrinkled her nose. "Ew," she said with a shake of her head. "I'd love to tell you that the trick is to be really mean to him, but unfortunately, he completely misses the *DIE ASSHOLE* vibes," she deadpanned.

Zuri snort-laughed, covering her mouth with a hand. "You're ridiculous!"

Kitty grinned widely. She loved making people laugh, especially women. "Angell and I, call him fuck-face," she offered helpfully.

"He's looking for his next baby mama, but he's barking up the wrong tree," Zuri grumbled.

Because he's gross or-? Kitty thought, feeling a familiar fluttering in her belly.

"He had three kids with the first wife, but she slapped him with divorce papers when she found out he'd knocked up the babysitter. After that, he made an *honest woman* out of the poor girl." Zuri shook her head. "Last time we worked together, and mind you, I didn't ask, he told me all about how he is getting divorced again because he impregnated some other woman."

Kitty let out a low whistle. "I don't understand why women keep sleeping with him. They've seen him, right? And we know it's not his winning personality."

Zuri cackled, the throaty sound making Kitty's breath catch.

Kitty pulled out the orange pelican box housing their medications, set it down on the stretcher, and flopped onto the bench seat as she steeled herself for the first of the month drug check. All she had to do was jot down expirations and drug quantities. Easy, but tedious as hell.

Reaching into her breast pocket, she found it empty. "Fuck." She looked up imploringly at her partner. "I forgot my pen."

Zuri crossed her arms over her ample chest as she shook her head, a small smile playing across her lips. "I like you, but not enough to let you steal my pen."

Pouting, Kitty pressed a hand to her chest. "You wound me," she teased.

Rolling her eyes, Zuri leaned across Kitty's lap to snatch up the drug log before dropping down beside her. Taking a pen out of her breast pocket, she looked expectantly at Kitty. "You read. I'll write."

"Yes, ma'am," Kitty croaked out and cleared her throat as Zuri's close proximity made her heart stutter in her chest. This wasn't the first time that Zuri had come into her personal space, but previously, it had always been in the name of patient care.

Swallowing hard, she opened the drug box as she took a steadying breath. Her hands itched to reach out and stroke Zuri's cheek, just to see if it was as soft and inviting as it looked.

"You're from Alabama, right?" Zuri snatched up a vial of Zofran and scribbled down its expiration date.

"I thought I was reading, and you were writing?" Kitty held out her hand for the vial.

Zuri shot her a wink. "Don't worry, I can multitask."

First On Scene: A Howling Sirens Novel

Kitty blushed, glancing down at her hands. "Yeah, that's right. Not far from Birmingham."

"Has your family visited yet?"

Kitty barked out a laugh. "No," she said flatly. "And I hope they don't."

"Why not?" Zuri leaned closer, holding Kitty's gaze.

Kitty looked away uncomfortably. "I don't... It's a little complicated."

"Sorry, I didn't mean to pry," Zuri murmured, resting her hand on Kitty's thigh.

Kitty's breath hitched in her throat as she looked from Zuri's hand to her concerned expression. "It's fine," she muttered, looking around the ambulance, anywhere but at her partner. Her heart tripled its pace as Zuri squeezed her thigh encouragingly.

"My folks wanted a girly girl for a daughter, and that's not what they got. I'm confident they knew I was gay, but they never acknowledged it. Instead, they did everything in their power to dissuade it." Keeping her eyes straight ahead, Kitty blew out a shaky breath. "They made sure that I knew it was a sin and that all *faggots*," grimacing at the word, she continued, "go to hell."

Kitty absentmindedly tugged on her collar. "They stuffed me in dresses and kept me away from sports and anything else they deemed too masculine for me." Huffing out a bitter laugh, she shook her head. "The first time I wore pants, they were scrubs. And the only reason that was tolerated is because I told them I was in nursing school."

She sighed. "In reality, I was getting my EMT and working for an ambulance company a few towns over. During paramedic school, one of the guys in my class taught me how to ride and as soon as I got my medic ticket, I got my motorcycle license and bought a bike. After that, I got the hell out of there."

"Did they try to stop you from leaving?" Zuri asked.

Kitty shook her head. "I didn't even say goodbye. I just left." Frowning, she stole a glance at Zuri, half expecting to see pity in her eyes, but there was only compassion.

"I'm so sorry," Zuri said softly and scooted closer until their legs pressed together.

"Sometimes I forget most people aren't as lucky as I am when it comes to family."

"It's fine," Kitty muttered as she awkwardly patted the hand still resting on her thigh and cleared her throat. "Why don't we finish the log," she suggested, forcing all thoughts of her past from her mind.

"Is that why you sleep around so much? Zuri asked as Kitty got up and put the med box away, "because of your family?"

Cheeks burning with embarrassment, Kitty gaped at her partner. She knew she was starting to get a reputation but hadn't expected anyone to outright comment on it. It was one thing for Angell and Eric to tease her because they spent so much time together, but she had only worked with Zuri a handful of times. Usually, they kept things pretty surface, but apparently, Zuri wanted to change that tonight.

Zuri's perfect lips curled into a wicked smile. " I wasn't trying to embarrass you. I just don't see the point in beating around the bush."

"Uh-huh," Kitty muttered, at a loss for what else to say. *Is she for real right now?*

Zuri's pretty, hazel eyes trained on Kitty. "Would you ever date someone rather than just sleeping around?"

"With the right person," she ventured. After a moment, she cleared her throat, waiting

for Zuri's next uncomfortable question. Just because her body count had risen from a whopping zero since she moved to New England didn't mean she wasn't interested in having a girlfriend. She was just enjoying herself until that happened.

"Good," Zuri said, flashing Kitty an almost predatorial smirk. "Because I'm not known for playing well with others."

Wait? That's what this is? Heart hammering in her chest, Kitty sat back down on the bench seat, looking expectantly at Zuri. If she was reading this right, all her dreams were about to come true. But what if she was wrong? She was still pretty inexperienced when it came to making the first move.

Zuri closed the distance between them, curling her fingers

First On Scene: A Howling Sirens Novel

around the back of Kitty's neck as she pulled her into a deep kiss.

A shiver ran through her. The feel of Zuri's soft lips moving against her own was electrifying, and she wanted more. Kitty grasped the front of Zuri's shirt and pulled the other woman across to straddle her lap, groaning against her mouth as they kissed hungrily. Their tongues tangled together as she let her hands wander over Zuri's body, fingers tracing over soft curves and firm muscles.

They sprang apart as loud footsteps rang out in the ambulance bay. Chest heaving, Kitty licked her swollen lips as she and Zuri stared at each other for a moment. They hadn't heard the bay door opening or P2 backing in.

Straightening their uniforms, they jumped down from the ambulance, one after another, looking around for their visitor. The bay stood empty and silent. P1 was the only vehicle present, and there was no way anyone could have gone back up the stairs without making noise. Even the disgusting break room was empty.

Glancing around the bay one final time, Zuri shook her head. "This place is so fucking haunted."

Chapter Six

"Bro! Can we go get dinner?" Angell hollered and rapped his knuckles on the bedroom door without waiting for an answer.

"Yeah, I'm coming!" Eric shouted, unwedging himself from the narrow computer chair as it squeaked in protest. Shrugging on his jacket, he opened the door into the dingy hallway.

Standing in the doorway, hands tucked into his pockets with a huge smile plastered onto his face, Angell rocked on his heels. Head cocked to the side, the smile widened even further, making him look like the Cheshire cat. "Want to call off the hunger strike for one night and split a pizza?"

"You are so dramatic." Eric rolled his eyes, crossing his arms defensively over his chest.

"Watching what I eat doesn't mean I'm hunger-striking." His stomach growled in disagreement.

"You're twenty-four and in good shape. Why are you even doing this?" Shaking his head, Angell headed for the stairs to the bay.

With a beleaguered sigh, Eric followed him. "It's not bullshit. I'm trying to get ahead of my family history. It always starts with weight gain, and then the next thing you know, you're in the ground from a heart attack. It's what took my Dad."

"You're old man lived in his recliner with a scotch in his

hand and never did a day of cardio in his life. You barely even drink." Stopping abruptly on the stairs, Angell looked up at him and pressed his lips into a firm line. "You're not your father, and honestly, your mom is much happier since she remarried."

"If you say so," Eric grumbled as he raked a hand through his hair. "I still don't want to get fat."

"Is this about getting laid?" Angell asked and frowned in earnest. "Because you *save lives* for a living, and I promise, women eat that up!"

"It's not about that," Eric grumped, feeling his cheeks heating with embarrassment. "I do okay in that department."

"Okay, Crash." With a shrug, Angell trotted down the remaining stairs.

"Don't call me Crash!" He snapped.

"You'll always be Crash to me," Angell replied without looking at him.

Most people only called him by his nickname when he screwed up. Angell was the only one who insisted on calling him Crash instead of his actual name. Apparently, it was a *cool handle*, according to his partner.

A familiar series of beeps alerted them of an incoming call. "Engine Two, Paramedic Two, and Car Two, please respond to the intersection of Pine and River for the intoxicated male."

"Medic Two has it. You can show us en route," Angell grumbled into the mic and stomped the rest of the way to the truck.

Smothering a grin, Eric climbed into the passenger seat. "Bet it's our favorite outdoorsman," Eric guessed, and Angell grunted in response.

His partner would be grumpy until he got something to eat. Whoever their patient was, they were lucky that it was Eric's tech.

They were probably going for one of their regulars. Unlike Boston, Hudson didn't have a large homeless population. When they did encounter an unhoused person, they usually just wanted a blanket or a ride to the hospital for a turkey sandwich. Occasionally, someone would drink too much and an overly helpful bystander would call 9-1-1 rather than just asking if the person was okay.

Eric's favorite was a man who insisted they call him Hobo Joe. His actual name was Bradley Smith, but apparently, "Hobo Joe" got him more street cred. Or at least that's what he'd claimed when they first met.

Eric scanned the street as they parked next to a police cruiser, and Angell called them on scene. Two officers were struggling to corral a haggard-looking man while a few bystanders watched the show. He recognized Jeff, one of the officers, easily enough, mostly because Angell never shut up about his heavily tattooed arms or the way his biceps bulged under his uniform, but the other cop was a stranger. A white-blonde man leaning against one of the brick buildings seemed particularly interested in the incident, his arms crossed & lips pulled up into a grimace as he watched the officers' efforts like a hawk.

The haggard-looking man weaved and dodged around the two officers, his yellowed eyes flashing wildly as he searched for an escape.

As the man darted off the sidewalk and into the road, Eric frowned. It was Hobo Joe, all right, but he looked wrong. His clothing was torn and splattered in mud, and he moved without grace, his limbs jerking spasmodically as he avoided the officers.

His eyes shouldn't look like that. Yellow eyes meant liver failure, but Eric didn't think he drank enough to cause that.

"He looks like shit," Angell observed.

"Yeah, I think he's actually sick today."

Eric opened his door, but Angell caught the back of his shirt, keeping him in place. "Hold up, let's wait until the police get him calmed down before we go over. Jeff is really good at talking down psychs and drunks."

Eric rolled his eyes. "Just because your boyfriend is on scene doesn't mean I'm going to hide in the truck. I know how to talk people down, too." He jabbed his partner in the ribs and pulled out of his grasp.

Slamming the door behind him, he pulled on his gloves &

approached the officers. "I have a pretty good rapport with this guy. Why don't you let me try talking to him?"

At Jeff's curt nod, he pushed past them. Behind him, he heard Angell mutter something under his breath.

"Hey, bud. What's going on today?" He edged closer to the man, shuffling back and forth on the sidewalk.

Hobo Joe squinted and looked around to see who had spoken to him.

Eric had never seen him so altered before, but it happened sometimes with liver failure. Frowning, he slid closer, keeping his gloved hands out where the other man could see them. "It's Eric," he called, raising his voice. "Your favorite medic, remember?"

He could feel Angell's presence behind him and was positive that his partner already had a sedative drawn up and ready to use. Maybe they would need it, but he didn't want to use it. Sedatives were for out-of-control patients. Hobo Joe was sick, not out of control.

"I got this," Eric said firmly, not bothering to look at Angell. He was certain that his partner was scowling at his turned back, but he would have to deal with it. It was his patient and his call. *I'm not a fuck up... At least not all the time. Besides, Hobo Joe and I have a bond, and I'm going to use it.*

"Let's get you checked out," he soothed as jaundiced eyes followed his movement, glinting predatorily. Then, without warning, Hobo Joe rushed him and sank crooked, yellowed teeth into his bicep.

"Motherfucker!" Eric shouted as he flailed his arm, but it was no use. Hobo Joe wasn't about to let go. With his free hand, he frantically hammer-fisted the other man in the face. Hobo Joe held on tighter, growling as he shook his head like a pitbull with a bone.

A soft whimper escaped his throat as he watched the rivulets of his own blood run down the patient's face. "Come on, let go," he urged through gritted teeth.

Jaundiced eyes bored into him without a hint of recognition, and a throaty rumble vibrated against his entrapped flesh, making him flinch.

Selina Rossman

"Buddy, you know me. I only show up to help you. Let go of my arm!" Still struggling to break free, tears welled up in the corners of his eyes.

Hobo Joe snarled at him around the arm clamped between his teeth.

Eric could feel himself getting lightheaded as the corners of his vision darkened and narrowed. *Oh fuck, I'm totally going to pass out. That's so embarrassing.*

Karl is going to kill me, he thought, watching from across the street as the three uniformed men tackled what should have been his protégé. Hobo Joe, as the man insisted on being referred to, had been a complete and utter failure.

The blonde cop struggling to restrain the feral man was one of theirs. It was only a matter of time before Karl found out what he had done. If he was lucky, he'd be forced to clean up his mess. If he wasn't lucky, well, he didn't want to think about that.

He was starting to understand why potential members of the brotherhood had to prove themselves before being bestowed any gifts. It was a slow process, but the results spoke for themselves.

His master plan to rise up the ranks was going down in flames, and if the redheaded kid didn't die of sepsis, he'd be one more loose end he'd have to tie up.

Fuck.

Chapter Seven

Kitty's soft lips found hers. Stifling the giggle that threatened to escape, Zuri leaned into the kiss. Grasping the front of Kitty's shirt, she pulled her close, ruffling the other woman's bleach-blonde hair. Never in a million years did she see herself having the hots for a masc-presenting woman, but she couldn't help it. She loved the crew cut with its shaved sides and shaggy top. Getting a good grip on the short hair, she teasingly flicked her tongue across Kitty's lips.

Kitty moaned against her mouth as their tongues entwined, and her hands began to wander.

Zuri cracked an eye open as something buzzed beside her. The flip phone had slid just out of easy reach with its own aggressive vibration, and she groaned as she reached for it, the frivolous romance novel she had been reading before falling asleep and sliding into her lap. Flipping the phone open, she settled back into the soft cushions of the couch.

It was a text from Kitty. Her heart sped up at the memory of their one and only kiss. She hadn't been able to stop thinking about it.

Angell just messaged me. Crash got injured on a call and is in the hospital. Do you want to come with me to check on him?

Zuri frowned. This wasn't the kind of invitation she had been hoping for, but then again, she would have judged Kitty pretty harshly for asking her out over a text message. *What is wrong with me? Yeah, she's hot, but this can't be anything serious. She's human. If she wants to text me to hook up, I should let her.* Pressing her fingers to her temples, Zuri shook her head.

She had tried dating humans in the past, but it never ended well. How could it? Concealing her wolf meant keeping her partner in the dark, and ultimately, whoever she was with got fed up with the constant secrecy and dumped her. She couldn't blame them, but it still stung when they left.

Having never met anyone like herself, except her direct relatives, the local dating pool was limited. Maybe they would hook up. Hell, she might even take Kitty out to dinner first, but it would be a short-lived affair, just like it always was. If she was serious about finding a mate, she would have to venture outside of her pack's territory, and she wasn't ready to leave the only home she'd ever known.

When isn't he getting hurt? She texted back.

Kitty replied with a facepalm emoji and a devil smiley face. *Come with me anyway?*

Meet you there in half an hour.

She set the phone down. There were worse excuses to see her crush, even if Eric really was getting hurt constantly. They didn't call him Crash for nothing.

Striding up to the EMS emergency room entrance, she pressed her badge to the scanner. It beeped but didn't open the doors. With a beleaguered sigh, she slapped her badge against the reader. Again, it acknowledged her with a high-pitched beep, but the double doors stood firm. This was nothing new.

First On Scene: A Howling Sirens Novel

Something about her always screwed with electronics: badge readers failed, doors refused to open, and smartphones shorted out in her hands. It was the curse of her bloodline, but normally, she had a partner nearby to let her in:

"God damn it," she growled under her breath and hit the doorbell meant for crews coming in from out of the area. The doors buzzed and swung open. Clenching and unclenching her hands, she shoved them into the pockets of her red leather jacket and strode inside.

Standing stock still just inside the ER, Angell had his eyes glued to the trauma room, his arms crossed and fingers gripping tightly enough to make his knuckles blanch. The acidic scent of stress sweat clung to him, but beyond that the emergency room's familiar funk of disinfectant supplies and bodily fluids assaulted her senses, making it impossible to use her nose to gather more information.

With a furrowed brow, Zuri slid into the open space beside Angell and followed his gaze.

Two nurses struggled to hold Eric's jerking body down as a woman in a white lab coat drew up medication from the vial in her hands. Latching onto his arm, the blonde Doctor injected the drug into his IV port. Eric collapsed limply back onto the mattress, his cheeks flushed and speckled with his own spittle. "What the fuck happened?" Zuri murmured in a hushed voice.

Knitting his eyebrows together, Angell cocked his head in her direction. "When did you get here?"

"Just now. What happened to Crash?" She asked, placing a soothing hand on his arm.

Angell cleared his throat but didn't draw back. "We got called for Hobo Joe, and Crash insisted on trying to talk him down. It didn't go well."

"Can you be a little more specific?" She urged, her eyes darting between his pinched face and Eric's still body. They only worked together intermittently, but she had seen Eric talk down plenty of erratic psych patients and drunks in the past. It was one of his specialties. What had been about this call?

"He passed out when Hobo Joe attacked him and hit the

ground hard. Then he got super altered on the way in," Angell said, blowing out a shaky breath. "It was so bad that we had to restrain him. After that, he passed out and hasn't woken up since. Now he's having seizures, and the scans can't tell us why. No one knows what the hell is wrong with him." Shaking his head, Angell chewed on his lower lip. "And now he's spiking a fever too."

"Shit," she breathed, watching the staff in the room peel back Eric's eyelids and shine a light into his eyes. He didn't respond to their exam.

"Has Kitty seen him yet?" She wondered out loud.

"Yeah. She went to the bathroom a while ago. I don't think she's handling this well, but you've met her. She doesn't exactly talk about her feelings unless it's about her latest hook-up." Keeping a close watch on the Neurologist in the room, Angell pressed his lips into a thin line.

He was right. Kitty barely talked about her past, let alone her emotional state. Telling people about her sexual conquests was more of a brag than a conversation.

But she opened up with me the other night, Zuri thought. *Maybe she was just trying to get into my pants.* She shook her head. Keeping people at arm's length was something they shared, regardless of Kitty's reason.

"Can you go check on her? I don't want to leave him." Angell's watery eyes flitted between her and the room.

"Of course." She gave his arm a reassuring squeeze and made her way towards the back of the emergency room. She had never seen him so upset before. Normally, nothing rattled Angell. The guy could normally make a joke out of anything, and it was jarring to see him so serious.

Catching a whiff of Kitty's signature vanilla and cinnamon scent, Zuri stopped in front of the first bathroom she came across and knocked tentatively.

Kitty's strained voice answered. "Just a minute."

Finding the door unlocked as she tried the handle, Zuri pushed inside.

Bracing herself against the sink, Kitty stared at her tear-streaked reflection. Without looking away from the mirror, she

First On Scene: A Howling Sirens Novel

snapped at Zuri. "I said, I'll be out in a minute!"

Zuri swallowed hard. She hadn't expected tears. "Are you okay?" She asked, edging closer.

Kitty wiped the tears from her red, blotchy cheeks as she turned to face Zuri. "Sorry, I didn't realize it was you, and I'm just really stressed." Kitty averted her eyes and stared hard at the floor. "I know he's always getting into trouble on calls, but he has never been sick like this before and…"

"Hey, it's going to be okay," Zuri soothed, instinctively reaching out and pulling the other woman against her, the way she would, a pack member.

Kitty's shoulders shook as she stifled a sob and pressed her face into Zuri's shoulder. "It's just… Well, you know, I'm not close with that many people, and Crash is my friend, and if he dies…"

Gently grasping Kitty's chin, Zuri forced the shorter woman to look up into her eyes. *How am I supposed to comfort her? I can't promise he won't die. I don't even know what's wrong with him.* She searched Kitty's gaze for a hint of what might bring her comfort, but the pretty blue eyes staring up at her held no answers. "Eric is going to be okay. He has good people taking care of him, but we should probably go. If we stay, we'll just be underfoot."

Blowing out a shaky breath, Kitty nodded in agreement. "You're right. But Angell won't leave his side until they get him into the ICU. He's really protective when it comes to his friends."

Zuri nodded as she rubbed slow circles on Kitty's back. She understood Angell's desire to stay close. If Eric was part of her pack, she wouldn't be going anywhere either. She liked the guy, but he just wasn't her responsibility.

"Why don't we go check on the guys?" She suggested and stepped back to put a little distance between them. She could feel her wolf pacing below the surface as its discontent at the sudden lack of physical touch washed over her. *What was that?* she thought, swallowing down a whimper. *I must be more touch-starved than I thought.*

Kitty pulled her shoulders back and inhaled deeply as she

used the back of her hand to wipe away her remaining tears. "Alright, let's go talk to Angell," she said and pushed past Zuri.

Tension settled between Zuri's shoulders as she continued to silently reel at her wolf's reactions and followed Kitty out of the bathroom.

The curtains of the trauma room had been pulled closed, hiding Eric from view. Angel was talking to the blonde Doctor, his arms still cemented to his chest. Their voices were hushed, but Zuri's sensitive hearing captured their words long before they reached the pair.

"We will be keeping him sedated and monitoring him closely." The doctor explained. "Is there anyone I should call?" The doctor slipped her hands into the pockets of her white coat and gazed into Angell's grim face.

"No," he said shortly. "I'll call his folks when he wakes up."

Pursing her lips, the Doctor nodded. "Do you have to get back to work?"

"No, the supervisor knows I'm done for the day."

"Good," she replied and patted Angell on the shoulder. "Why don't you go sit with him for a while."

The neurologist eyed Kitty as she and Zuri approached. "Hey, Kitty," she said with a soft smile. "I haven't seen you around in a while."

"Uh yeah," Kitty mumbled and rubbed the back of her neck, her hand chasing a faint blush as it crept towards her face. "I've been really busy."

The doctor's smile faded from her lips. "I see," she ground out. Shaking her head, she stalked away from them and into the nurses' station.

Great, of course, she banged the doc, Zuri thought, clenching her jaw and smothering down a territorial growl. *What am I doing? I want to fuck her, not make her my mate!*

Wide-eyed, Angell looked between the nurse's station and his friends before clearing his throat and updating them on Eric's condition. Agreeing that there was no point in all three of them staying, he promised to keep them informed before disappearing behind the curtain.

First On Scene: A Howling Sirens Novel

"You ready?" Zuri cocked her head in Kitty's direction.

Shrugging, Kitty pulled out her phone. "Yeah, I just have to request an Uber," she said and stared at the blank screen.

Frowning, Zuri watched Kitty closely. "Where's the bike?"

"I had to take it to the shop because the clutch was acting up," Kitty sighed. "I should have it back in a few days."

"Are you okay? You look paler than usual."

Kitty nibbled thoughtfully on her lower lip. "Not really. I haven't eaten much today."

"In that case, why don't we go get something to eat, and I'll drop you off at home afterward," Zuri suggested, careful to keep her expression neutral.

"Actually, that sounds good."

"Great," Zuri murmured, slipping her hand into Kitty's and leading them out of the hospital.

Chapter Eight

Kitty is going to love this, Zuri thought and parked in front of the New City Microcreamery. Grinning, she got out of the jeep and hurried around to the passenger side to open the door.

"Are you taking me out for ice cream?" Kitty squeaked, her pretty blue eyes sparkling as they flicked between the ice cream sign and the woman holding the door open for her. "You opened the door for me?"

"Uh... yes?" Zuri mumbled, scuffing her shoe on the pavement.

"That's very sweet."

Zuri felt her cheeks warm as she offered Kitty her hand. "I have my moments. Now come on, I want to show you something."

Kitty let herself be pulled out of the car and followed Zuri into the ice cream shop, entangling their fingers as they walked.

Ignoring the ice cream counter, Zuri made a beeline for the back of the shop and stopped next to the bathrooms.

Cocking an eyebrow and tilting her head to the side, Kitty pulled back. "You brought me here to show me the bathrooms?"

"What?" Zuri asked, furrowing her brow and glancing between the restrooms and Kitty. "Oh, no, thats not it at all." Chuckling, she motioned for Kitty to follow her into a nook

First On Scene: A Howling Sirens Novel

adjacent to the lavatories. Leaning against the wall next to a small ornamental window that looked reminiscent of an old-timey barn's wooden double doors.

Wrinkling her nose adorably, Kitty followed Zuri into the small space.

Reaching out, Zuri flipped on a light switch, and a moment later, the window's tiny doors opened to reveal a dark-skinned man with a bright smile.

Kitty's eyes widened as she visibly flinched.

Fuck, she's cute, Zuri thought and smirked. "Two, please."

The tiny doors shut and a previously concealed entrance popped open to their right where they were ushered into the dimly lit cocktail bar.

"Welcome to the Cobbler.," their host said softly, handing them two menus as he lead them past the soapstone bar and to one of the booths in the back.

Kitty slid into the booth across from Zuri, taking in the vintage speakeasy, her wide eyes raking over the leather seating and the lit tealight candles twinkling at them from every surface but the bar. "This is amazing! I had no idea it even existed."

Zuri's eyes lingered on Kitty's slightly parted lips as she forced down the desire to lean across the table and kiss the blonde woman. Averting her gaze before she could be caught, she glanced down at the menu.

Kitty's full lips curved into a knowing smile. "So, what's good here?"

"Everything," Zuri shrugged. "But I was thinking we could get some of their boozy ice cream to start."

Kitty laughed. "You actually did take me to get ice cream huh?"

Before Zuri could reply, a thin white man with brown hair approached their table and pulled a notepad out of his apron's pocket. "Hey ladies, I'm Tyler. I'll be your waiter today. Are you ready to order?"

"Yes," Zuri said and glanced at Kitty, who nodded. "Can we please start with two Spirits and Cream?"

"Great, what else?" Tyler asked, holding his pen at the

ready.

Zuri's stomach growled loudly. "I'll have an order of wings, the baked brie, a steak tartare, two shrimp cocktails, and an order of perogies." Under normal circumstances, she wouldn't eat so much near non-pack members, but she was ravenous.

Zuri looked at Kitty as the man jotted down her enormous order. "What are you getting?"

Giggling, Kitty rolled her eyes. "I feel like that will be enough for the two of us."

Pressing her lips together, Zuri looked down at her hands.

"Oh," Kitty said, blushing. "You were being serious."

"Uh, yeah." Zuri cleared her throat. "I was planning on sharing with you, obviously," she said, rubbing the back of her neck, "but I do a lot of strength training, and it makes me eat a lot." *Or, you know, because I have the metabolism of a wild animal. What is wrong with me today?*

"Okay," Kitty murmured and looked at the waiter. "I'll have the Dandan noodles."

He jotted down her order and then, with a curt nod, walked away.

"So," Zuri said softly and looked pointedly at Kitty. "What was the deal with that doctor?"

Adorably hiding her face in her hands, Kitty groaned and peeked out at Zuri from between her fingers. "Are you always so forward?"

Barking out a laugh, Zuri grinned widely. "Almost always."

Kitty nodded slowly and dropped her hands. "I actually, really respect that."

"So..." Zuri pried.

Kitty's cheeks reddened into an impressive ruddy color. "We hooked up, but—" Huffing out a sigh, she continued. "It happened so fast that I never got her name, and I couldn't exactly ask after the fact! I tried looking at her work badge, but she doesn't wear one, and then I couldn't ask anyone else without looking like an asshole." Still blushing, she raked her fingers through the shaggy hair at the top of her head. "So, now I just avoid her."

Howling with laughter, Zuri pressed a hand to her chest.

First On Scene: A Howling Sirens Novel

"It's not funny," Kitty whined.

The waiter returned, setting down two glasses full of eggnog ice cream and presenting them with spoons. "Enjoy!"

"So, if I understand correctly," Zuri smirked evilly and took a bite of her rum and brandy-infused dessert before continuing. "You're saying that you know what the neurologist sounds like when she comes but not her name."

"Oh my god! Stop!" Kitty whimpered, her cheeks burning even redder.

"That's not a no," Zuri said pointedly and took another bite of ice cream.

"Yes, I know that! I'm a monster," Kitty groaned.

Shaking her head, Zuri laughed softly. "Relax, I'm just fucking with you."

Sighing dramatically, Kitty finally took a bite of her ice cream. "Wow."

Zuri grinned. "Just wait until you taste the food." As if summoned by her words, the waiter appeared with their meals, placing the numerous plates down in front of them.

"Thank you." Kitty took a bite of her noodles and hummed with pleasure. She eyed the feast that Zuri was already eagerly tucking into. "How's your—everything?"

"It's not everything," Zuri smirked. "I didn't get the salad."

Kitty rolled her eyes. "Sure, Zuri."

"You can call me Zee if you want," Zuri offered and popped a pierogi into her mouth.

"Zee," Kitty said softly as if testing out the name.

Smiling, Zuri looked down at her food. She liked how her nickname sounded on Kitty's lips.

"How long have you lived in Hudson?" Kitty asked, taking another bite of her food.

"I was born and raised here, but my parents and aunt moved up here from Georgia when my brother was still a toddler." She nudged the brie and crackers closer to Kitty. "Here, try some of this, you'll like it."

Kitty slathered the melted cheese onto a cracker. "So, have you done anything fun lately?"

"Besides this?" Zuri joked as she absentmindedly tugged on

a loose braid. "When I'm not working a ton, I'm usually off on a hike or curled up on the couch with a book. There are some really beautiful places to explore in the area." *Not that I can show her without pissing off the pack.*

Kitty's eyes lit up. "Oh yeah? What do you like to read?"

Sapphic romance, she thought. "A little of everything." Leaning forward, Zuri smiled suggestively. "And you? What are you into?"

Kitty cleared her throat as she blushed wildly.

Enjoying how easily she could make the other woman flush, Zuri grinned broadly. "Hmm?"

"I also read a lot. Mostly urban fantasies and science fiction." Kitty drummed her fingers on the table. "I'm also thinking about getting my first tattoo. I hear they're addictive, so maybe that will become a thing for me." Fiddling with a napkin on the table, she looked at Zuri. "Do you have any ink?"

"Nah, not my thing." Even though she would love to get something, it was pointless. Her body would heal too quickly for the ink to set. "What are you thinking of getting?"

"I haven't decided, but I know that it will be something involving wolves, though. Growing up, I must have reread *"Blood and Chocolate"* and *"The Silver Wolf"* at least a hundred times because I could only sneak in so many books." She shrugged. "I'm thinking about taking a trip out to Ipswich to check out Wolf Hollow and get some ideas."

"Have you ever seen a wolf up close before?"

"Nope," Kitty said with a wistful sigh. "We didn't have them in Alabama, and apparently, neither does Mass."

Nope, no wolves in this state, just werewolves and other beasties that go bump in the night, Zuri thought sarcastically as the waiter swung by the table to drop off the check. Grinning, she snatched the bill out of Kitty's reach and shook her head. "It's my treat."

"Are you sure? We could split it if you want," Kitty took out her wallet and placed it on the table so that a pewter wolf head stared up at Zuri from the black leather.

Oh wow, she really does have a thing for wolves, Zuri thought

First On Scene: A Howling Sirens Novel

and nudged it back into Kitty's hands. "I'm sure."

"Okay, if you're sure. Thank you."

Pulling out a wad of cash from her pocket, Zuri removed the plastic money clip and counted out enough to cover the check.

Kitty openly stared at her as she replaced the money in her jacket. "Are you a stripper on the side?".

Zuri laughed and shook her head. "No, I'm just a little bit old school." Like with most electronic devices, credit card machines tended to fizzle out near her. She'd given up on using them a long time ago.

Kitty rolled her eyes. "I literally don't know anyone else that carries cash."

"Well, you do now," Zuri said with a wide grin as she slapped enough money down to cover the bill and a tip. "Come on, let's get out of here."

Kitty directed Zuri to a large apartment complex up the street from the Danforth Falls. "I'd invite you up, but the apartment is trashed," she said, blushing fuschia, the color blooming across her face.

It's unfair how cute she looks when she blushes, Zuri thought and cocked her head to the side. "It's okay, today was stressful. You should get some rest." Keeping her voice steady to hide her disappointment.

Kitty looked down at her hands, fiddling with the hem of her shirt.

"Would you want to do this again?" Zuri asked before she could think of a reason not to. *What am I doing? I'm not supposed to be dating her. I'm supposed to be seducing her and moving on.*

"Yeah, I'd like that," Kitty said, leaning into her space and chastely brushing their lips together. The kiss was over almost as quickly as it had begun, and Zuri smothered down a disappointed whimper.

Opening the door and climbing out, Kitty glanced over her shoulder with a shy smile. "Text me, and we'll figure out the details for next time."

"I will."

Selina Rossman

With a hesitant wave, Kitty shut the door and walked away. After she had entered the building, Zuri stayed where she was. She felt out of sorts, like she and her wolf weren't on the same page. It hadn't been like that since her awkward teenage years when she had to deal with first-time shifts and puberty. It was a fate she didn't wish on anyone. The pack had gotten her through it by teaching her self-control and how to integrate the two parts of herself.

I don't get it, she thought with a shake of her head. *Sure, I like Kitty, but I've liked other women in the past and never acted like this. Shit, I need to talk to someone about this.*

Groaning, she pressed her forehead into the steering wheel. She couldn't talk to her family without telling them about Kitty. And she absolutely couldn't do that. Her father would have a fit. He never stopped harping on the importance of keeping their existence a secret. She had no intention of coming out of the fur closet but it wasn't realistic to believe that they could lead completely separate lives from the humans. Hell, her father was a lawyer, he knew that firsthand.

With a sigh, she straightened in her seat and turned the car towards home. She would have to figure this out on her own.

Chapter Nine

Eric's distorted image glared at him from beneath the fogged-over mirror. Swiping away the condensation, he continued to examine his reflection. He was flushed, his eyes bloodshot. His freshly shaved crew cut had transformed into an unkempt mass of red. *Shit, I need a haircut. Maybe Zuri will hook me up next time I see her. She usually has her supplies in her car.*

Something was different about his eyes. Frowning, he leaned closer. Flecks of pale yellow glinted back at him from the familiar aquamarine. The glimmer of yellow intensified into a stark amber, and the color crept from the corners of his irises, spreading across the white scleras and consuming his eyes in their entirety. Blown pupils gazed out at him from a sea of gold.

Heart hammering in his chest, he took a step back and slipped on the bathroom rug. With a grunt, he scrambled for the sink, steadying himself. The cool ceramic felt good beneath his burning palms. He tried to blink away the sight in front of him, but his eyes remained the same startling amber-gold.

Steam danced around his bare torso like smoke, curling over his muscular shoulders and creeping up to the hollow of his throat. It brought the scent of soggy canid with it, making his stomach flip and roil. It was repulsive.

What the hell is happening to me? Gritting his teeth, he leaned closer to the mirror, but the reflective surface provided no further information.

Without warning, agony seared the inside of his mouth. His gums felt like they were being stabbed by knives made of fire. Groaning, he sagged against the sink.

Panting shallowly, he forced his jaws apart and stared into his mouth. Puckered flesh cradling crumbling hunks of enamel had replaced the previously healthy gums and teeth. Stomach cramping in disgust, he wretched unproductively into the sink. Glancing up at his reflection, a whimper escaped his trembling lips. He hardly recognized himself.

His sinuses burned, the metallic scent of blood edging into his nares. His vision swam, and he squeezed his eyes shut, letting the sink support his weight. *This isn't happening! It can't be real! Oh my God, please don't be real!*

His jaw cracked loudly, popping out of its socket. He whined against the torrent of pain that spread across his face and down his neck. His eyes fluttered open involuntarily, staring at the dislocated mandible hanging flaccidly.

With trembling fingertips, he touched the taut skin of his face. It tightened under his touch, and tears began streaming down his face. Agony lanced up his spine and into the back of his skull. A deafening grating sounded in his ears as his jawbone elongated.

Moaning, he sank to his knees, his breath coming in ragged gasps. He tried to call out, but only blood bubbled past his lips. Convulsing, he collapsed onto his back and gave into the encroaching darkness.

"Ahhhhhhh!" He howled and thrashed, tears leaking down his face. He was blind, and something was squeezing his left arm. Heart hammering, he struggled to get away, but whatever had him only tightened its grip. Unable to pull away, he raised his right hand to bat it away, but pain flared in his right bicep, making him drop his arm to the soft surface he was lying on.

First On Scene: A Howling Sirens Novel

Even stilled, it throbbed sharply. Whatever had latched onto his other arm suddenly released him, and he blew out a shaky breath. Trembling, he attempted to raise his good arm but was met with restraint.

What the actual fuck is happening?! Running his tongue over his dried, cracking lips, he racked his brain for details of how he had ended up like this. All he could remember was a pair of bright amber eyes peering at him, but that was a dream. Wasn't it?

Curling his fingers back, he touched the soft, thick material binding his wrist. *What is this? It kinda feels like the patient restraints we use. Wait?! Do they have soft restraints on me? Does that mean I'm in the hospital?!*

Rocking his hips, he confirmed that there was a squishy mattress underneath him and that he couldn't raise either of his legs. *Okay, I'm definitely four-pointed, and the squeezing must have been the automatic blood pressure cuff going off. This has to be a hospital, but why am I here, and why did they restrain me?* He couldn't remember being violent or aggressive, but then again, he couldn't remember anything that had landed him here.

With his limited mobility, he searched the bed for clues about his predicament. His fingers brushed against a firm, elongated but soft surface. *Is this a seizure pad? I don't have a seizure disorder!*

Wanting to be sure, he strained against his bindings but froze when the movement sent a jolt of agony shooting down his injured extremity. He lay still, breathing through gritted teeth, but his arm continued to pulse painfully.

He forced himself to think. *Okay, so if I'm in the hospital and I've been having seizures, why hasn't someone come to check on me? Why am I not being monitored more closely? I was screaming my head off, for fucks sake...unless that was part of the dream?* He needed to know.

Clearing his throat, he drew in a deep breath. "HELP ME!" He bellowed as loudly as his parched throat would allow. Met by silence, he tried again. "SOMEBODY, HELP ME!"

Straining his ears, he caught the squeak of sneakers against linoleum floors growing louder.

Selina Rossman

"Hello?" He croaked.

"Eric, It's okay. I'm here, but you're all tangled up. Just hang on for a minute." A familiar feminine voice soothed.

He froze, waiting to be released. Gentle hands guided him back onto the mattress, and he blew out the breath he had been holding. He hadn't realized he was still straining to sit up.

Something slid away from his face, leaving him squinting up at fluorescent lighting. His eyes slowly adjusted to the bright room and the tight lipped face of a nurse he recognized peered down at him.

Melissa was one of the hottest nurses working at the ER. Every inch of her exposed skin, except for her face and hands, was covered in colorful flower tattoos, and studded piercings adorned her nose and ears. She tugged at his sheets, struggling to straighten out the snarled cocoon they had become.

"Mel, what happened?" His voice cracked, and he licked at his dry lips.

Frowning, Melissa picked up a muted-pink cup from the bedside table and held it up, angling the plastic straw towards his lips.

He drank greedily and eyed her tired features. Her auburn hair was pulled back into a messy bun, strands sticking out haphazardly. The dark circles under her eyes were a stark contrast against her porcelain skin. *She must be having a rough shift.*

"Crash, you've been out cold for three days, and we weren't sure you were going to wake up. You scared the hell out of everyone."

Swallowing hard, he took in his surroundings more fully while she undid his restraints. He was in the larger of the two trauma rooms and attached to the cardiac monitor hanging on the wall. His heart rate was a little fast but otherwise normal. His oxygen saturation and blood pressure looked good from what he could see. They had put an IV in his left forearm and were infusing two different types of antibiotics through it. A soft sling supported his injured arm, and a stark white bandage covered his bicep.

First On Scene: A Howling Sirens Novel

"Why am I still in the emergency room?" He hit the button to raise himself into a seated position and reached for the cup of water, careful to keep his injured arm close to his body. If he was unconscious for three days, he should have been moved to the ICU.

Melissa pulled up a chair and sat next to the bed. "We were going to bring you to the intensive care unit, but every time we tried to move you, you had another seizure. We were able to sedate you enough to get you into a CAT scan and rule out a head bleed, but after that, it was just safer to keep you here."

"Is that why I was restrained, the seizures?" He set the cup back down.

Melissa snorted, rolling her eyes. "No. Those are because you came in completely altered and swinging." Chuckling darkly, she shook her head. "You even managed to hit Angell a few times while he was trying to hold you down."

"That's awful," He murmured, dropping his gaze and staring hard at his lap.

"It is, but mostly for you."

"What do you mean?" He stared hard at her smiling face.

"You have to ask? You know I've met you guys before, right? You act like brothers, always trying to get one up on the other. The two of you are as bad as my boys." She shook her head, resting her hands on her hips. "He is going to hold this over your head for the rest of your life."

Groaning, he shut his eyes. She was right.

"Is he here?" He asked, scanning the ER for his partner's tall profile. *I'm surprised he wasn't sitting here waiting for me to wake up.* Melissa was correct in that they were known for their ridiculous antics around the ER but there was more to their relationship than that. Angell was more than his partner, he was his best friend.

Melissa shook her head, the humor vanishing from her pretty green eyes. "He's been a mess since you got brought in. He refused to leave your side for days. Doctor Ross, the neurologist who's been working on you, finally got fed up this morning with him being a fixture in the trauma room and forced him to go home for a nap and a shower. Although I think she was more concerned about Kitty showing up again rather than his well-being, that's just me."

"Wait, Kitty came to check on me?"

Melissa nodded. "Yeah, she and Zuri showed up the day you got hurt. You scared your friends pretty good this time."

I have to stop being such a fuck up, he thought, sighing heavily.

"Do you know what happened?" Melissa asked, sitting on the edge of the bed.

"Honestly, I can't remember anything. What did Angell tell you?"

"You guys were on scene for one of the frequent fliers, and when you tried to approach him, he freaked out and bit you. After that, you fell and smashed your head on the asphalt. I'm told that you woke up in the back of the ambulance, confused and combative. Angell figured it was just a bad concussion until he got you here, and you started having seizures." She pursed her lips.

Raking a hand through his hair, he silently digested the new information. *Is that what the yellow eyes and bared teeth are from? Am I remembering getting attacked by someone with jaundice?*

"Did the guy who attacked me get brought in too?" He asked, scratching at the scruff which had sprouted on his chin while he was unconscious.

Melissa nodded. "Yes, they brought Hobo Joe in too. It still blows my mind that he introduces himself like that."

"Wait, Hobo Joe attacked me? What the hell?! I thought we were cool. I bring him sandwiches and blankets all the time." Frowning, he shook his head.

"Well, in his defense, he was brought in snarling and thrashing like a wild animal. His eyes were so jaundiced that the first thing we did after we sedated him was to pull a liver panel and a tox screen. But the results were weird. The tox screen came back completely negative, his liver is healthy, and there was only a little bit of alcohol in his system."

"Is he okay now?"

"As okay as he can be. He's been comatose for the last two days." She shrugged and stood. "I'm glad you're okay. I'm going to go update the doctor. I'm sure she'll be in shortly to

First On Scene: A Howling Sirens Novel

examine you." Melissa squeezed his good arm and walked out of the room, pulling the dingy green curtain shut behind her.

Chapter Ten

Eric was discharged a couple of days later. Kitty and Angell picked up his medications and some groceries for him and made sure he was settled at home, then went out to Victoria's Diner to celebrate. Kitty had missed their weekly post-shift boozy breakfast the other day, and raising a glass to Eric's health seemed like a good excuse to spend some time with her favorite partner.

I'm definitely going to have to drive him home and come back for my bike, she thought and smirked at a slurring Angell over her mimosa. *I can't believe he just threw back three screwdrivers, and our food isn't even here. He must have really thought Eric wasn't going to wake up.*

The bell on the front door rang, and three white men with shaved heads entered the restaurant. Not waiting to be seated, they walked past Kitty's table, shooting dirty looks in Angell's direction, and claimed one of the booths in the back for themselves.

Catching a glimpse of one of the men's shoulder tattoos when he removed his jacket, she swallowed hard. He was sporting a Wolfsangel, a symbol consisting of a Z with a central horizontal bar through it. During World War Two, it had been used to signify members of the Nazi special forces. Back home, she had caught more than one church member proudly wearing the symbol around their neck. It made her sick. *So much for the liberal North.* Frowning, she forced herself to look away from the rowdy men.

"I know there has been a lot going on lately, but you haven't mentioned a sexual conquest this week, and I just wanted to check in. Are you feeling alright?" Angell teased.

"Why does it always have to be about my dating life?"

He snorted. "You call what you do dating?"

Her cheeks burned. "I'll have you know that I went on a date just the other night!" With a grimace, she bit her tongue on the rest of her words. *Shit, I don't know if Zuri thinks that was a date or not or if she would be okay with me talking about it. It's not like we've gone out again.*

"Oh?" Wide-eyed, Angell's eyebrows crept into his hairline. "Do go on."

Shit! Shit! Shit! "Okay, but you have to promise not to tell anyone."

Crossing his heart with a finger, he grinned at her. "Promise."

Rolling her eyes, she leaned forward, elbows braced on the table. "Zuri took me out to the speakeasy the other night," she admitted, looking anywhere but at him.

Glancing in the direction of the back booth, she caught the bright blue eyes of the tattooed man on her. He silently blew her a kiss, and she abruptly looked away. *Fuck. I'm going to have to be careful when we leave.*

"Really? Wait, she's gay?"

Forcing her attention back to her partner, she laughed and nodded. "Yeah, she definitely likes women."

"Kitty, that's great. Zee is awesome," he said sincerely and smiled up at their waitress when she came to set down identical stacks of pancakes in front of them.

"So what about you?" She asked and cut into her chocolate chip and strawberry pancakes.

"What about me?" He asked between bites.

"Love life? You never talk about it."

He shrugged. "There isn't much to tell. I hook up occasionally, but dating seems like more effort than it's worth."

Selina Rossman

"What makes you say that?" She pried.

Chuckling darkly, he shook his head. "We're cursed, the whole lot of us, when it comes to love. It just doesn't last in my family. My folks split up when I was a kid, my aunt and uncle ended things after a supposed affair with a witch, and the one boy I ever really caught feelings for definitely didn't return them. Why bother, you know?"

"Wait, go back to the part about the witch," she demanded and shoved a piece of bacon into her mouth.

He waved a hand dismissively. "It's a Mexican thing. The whole culture believes in Santa Muerte, communing with the dead and witches, but anyway, my Tia Nina had this close friend who was always around. She'd give readings and tell you your future, the whole thing. One day, my uncle decided they were a little too close and loses his mind about it. They got divorced pretty quickly after that." He rolled his eyes. "The bruja, it's what we call witches, used to always tell my aunt and mother about how our family was gifted with sight. Whatever that means," he scoffed.

"Wow, the only magical thing my family believed in was Jesus," she said dryly and took a sip from her mimosa.

Angell snorted. "Yeah, Jesus is big in Mexico too."

"So, who was the boy?"

Sighing wistfully, Angell shook his head. "That, my friend, is a story for another time."

She let it go. She would have to remember to ask him again when he was sober.

Kitty checked behind them as they left the restaurant, but no one appeared to pay them any mind. They could just be wannabe Nazis, but the last thing she needed was for them to mark Angell's car or stalk them back to his place.

Double-checking that they were alone, she got Angell into the passenger side of his old Ford and drove him home.

Chapter Eleven

Eric's distorted image glared at him from beneath the fogged-over mirror. Swiping away the condensation, he continued to examine his reflection. He was flushed, his eyes bloodshot. His freshly shaved crew cut had transformed into an unkempt mass of red. *Shit, I need a haircut.* Rolling his shoulders, he struggled to shake the feeling of Deja vu.

Something was different about his eyes. Frowning, he leaned closer. Flecks of pale yellow glinted back at him from the familiar aquamarine. The glimmer of yellow intensified into a stark amber, and the color crept from the corners of his irises, spreading across the white scleras and consuming his eyes in their entirety. Blown pupils gazed out at him from a sea of gold.

Heart hammering in his chest, he took a step back and nearly slipped on the bathroom rug. Reaching out, he caught hold of the sink and steadied himself. *Has this happened before?* He wondered and stared at his reflection. Everything about this moment felt eerily familiar.

Steam danced around his bare torso like smoke, curling over his muscular shoulders and creeping up to the hollow of his throat. It brought the scent of soggy canid with it, making his stomach flip and roil.

What the hell is happening to me? Gritting his teeth, he leaned closer to the mirror, glaring at his reflection. Without warning, agony seared the inside of his mouth, making his gums feel like they were being flayed open. Groaning, he sagged against the sink, the pain in his jaw chasing away any sense of familiarity.

Panting shallowly, he forced his jaws apart and stared into his mouth. Puckered flesh cradling crumbling hunks of enamel had replaced the previously healthy gums and teeth. His heart was pounding heavily against his rib cage, and his stomach cramped. Clinging to the sink, he wretched up mouthful after mouthful of green, purulent bile.

His sinuses burned, the metallic scent of blood edging into his nares. His vision swam, and he squeezed his eyes shut, letting the sink support his weight. *This isn't real! This isn't real!* He chanted to himself.

His jaw cracked loudly, popping out of its socket. He whined against the torrid of pain that spread across his face and down his neck. His eyes fluttered open involuntarily to stare at his dislocated mandible, which hung flaccidly.

With trembling fingertips, he touched the taut skin of his face. It tightened under his touch, and tears began streaming down his face. Agony lanced up his spine and into the back of his skull. A deafening grating sounded in his ears as his jawbone elongated. Blood bubbled past his lips, dribbling into the sink and intermingling with bile.

Spasms wracked his throat and chest, and he struggled to breathe. Dropping to his hands and knees, he battled with his body for control. *Look at a fixed point, goddamn it!* He ordered himself, urging his eyes to focus on his hands. He wheezed with the effort of trying to catch his breath.

His hands contracted spasmodically. The bones snapped and popped loudly, contorting and doubling in length underneath his flesh. He hissed through gritted fangs as his fingertips split. The nails grew dark and thick, lengthening into blades. Without warning, the shifting bones in his wrists gave out under his weight. He collapsed to the floor, writhing on the cool tiles beneath him.

This can't be real. I'm sick, and this is just a fucked up dream. He told himself, still squirming on the floor. *I have to wake up. Wake*

First On Scene: A Howling Sirens Novel

the fuck up! Sinking freshly formed canines into his lower lip, he bit down until blood welled up at the site of the torn tissues.

"Wake up! Wake up! Wake up!" He chanted, the words coming out as snarls. Spasms rippled up his spine, interrupting his demands. Cracking noisily and straining against the dermis at his back, his vertebrae arched posteriorly. Realigning and thickening. He was sure they would burst free of his skin any second.

"Someone help me!" He moaned into the tiles, splattering them with blood-tinged spittle. The repulsive liquid strengthened his resolve to sit up. Shoving himself into a seated position, his elongated nails clicked and scraped against the floor. Drawing his attention to them. Malformed as they were, his hands supported his weight. Flexing his spindly hand in front of his face, he stared in disbelief. The pain was gone.

Tufts of tawny, bristled, hair erupted along his hands and arms, creeping up his chest, the hair, doubling in length and darkening into a ruddy orange. Bracing against the anticipated pain that had accompanied every new change, he stiffened but no new sensations came.

A sense of calm settled over him. His rapid heart rate stabilized into a steady, slow beat that he could hear. He found the sound soothing and let it chase away his anxieties. He was oddly at peace.

Eric ran his elongated fingers through the thick red and white pelt at his chest. *Soft*, he thought simply.

The insistent beeping of his phone's alarm jarred Eric awake.

"What the fuck am I doing?" He grumbled, finding his fingertips mindlessly tracing lines along his sweaty torso. Grimacing, he wiped his sweaty hand on the sheets. *I'm so tired of this stupid dream*, he thought resentfully and shut off the alarm. It had been haunting his nights like an unwelcome specter since he was discharged from the hospital. Every night, it was a little different, always escalating in one way or another.

At first, he'd figured it was just stress. It made perfect sense. He had never been attacked on the job before, and even hearing war stories about combative patients from his coworkers hadn't prepared him. He'd known it was only a matter of time before he had to deal with a violent patient, but he hadn't expected it to be someone that he had a good rapport with. The whole thing was disheartening. He just wanted to move on, but the dream wouldn't let him.

Kicking off sweat-soaked sheets, he slid out of bed and shivered in spite of the heater blowing full blast. *Maybe I shouldn't go to work today*, he mused before shaking his head. *No, I've already been out for over a week. I need to make some money!*

"I just need a shower and to get dressed." Running a hand through his slick hair, he groaned. "Great, now I'm talking to myself," he muttered, glancing around the room for the gym shorts he'd hucked on the floor last night. That was the trouble with roommates. No nudity in shared spaces.

Light creeping in under the door illuminated the small room. Catching sight of the red and yellow shorts, he dropped into a squat and snatched them up off the floor. Shoving them on, he made his way towards the door.

Pushing into the hallway, he was immediately blinded by the light. Squinting against the brightness, he thrust his hand out in search of a light switch. Awkwardly pawing at the wall until his fingers made contact with the switch, he was able to flip off the lights. Sighing, he easily navigated in the darkness to the bathroom. Shutting the door behind him, he locked it. He decided to shower in the dark to avoid any further photophobia.

Squeezing his eyes shut, he let the scalding water cascade over him. Today was his first shift back, and he wasn't even lucky enough to be working with someone he liked. To say he disliked his partner was an understatement. Timothy Jackson, or fuckhead as he and Angell often called him, was a lazy son-of-a-bitch that cared more about getting his dick wet than doing his job. Being a generational firefighter and paramedic, the guy thought he was special. He wasn't.

Better me than any of the girls, he thought, his shoulders slumping. Letting his mind go blank, he stood in the shower until the water ran cold. It was time to get the day started.

Turning off the shower, he stepped out and toweled himself off. Since the dreams had begun, he made a point of staring at himself in mirrors. Today was no different.

Stepping up to the sink, he tensed and gazed at his reflection. His pale skin stood out against the blackness behind him. Scanning himself for any changes and finding none, he let his shoulders sag. His hair was still clean cut and his eyes their familiar shade of aquamarine blue. Raking his eyes down his torso and abdomen, he froze. *When did I get abs?*

Running his hand over his stomach, he frowned. He'd developed a six-pack overnight. Other than deadlifting patients, he really didn't work out. He knew he should do more cardio, but he hated it. He was more than strong enough to do his job but had no interest in becoming a gym rat. He'd rather control his weight through food deprivation rather than exercise.

Gaping, he flexed his arms. His injured arm had long since healed, but there was no reason for his biceps to have doubled in size. They weren't just larger. They were toned. He was cut.

"What the actual fuck is happening to me?" He asked the mirror. His pasty reflection stared back at him silently. *Nope, I'm not dealing with this right now. I'll figure this all out later.*

Shaking his head, he wrapped the cotton towel around his waist. Barely noticing the darkness, he strode into the hall and back into his bedroom. Dressing quickly in his uniform, he completed his ensemble with a pair of black sunglasses. He didn't know what was up with him, but he would be damned if he was going to squint all day.

Growling with hunger, his stomach demanded attention. He wanted to get to work early and check out the truck since his partner would be no use, but the sharp pang in his guts made his decision for him.

Selina Rossman

Breakfast it is. Groaning, he left the bedroom. Pulling the door shut behind him, it didn't catch. With a shrug, he left it ajar. Sometimes, it was just too much effort to go back. Besides, he trusted his roommates not to fuck with his stuff.

He resolutely decided against using the kitchen lights. He might as well take advantage of this newfound ability. Seeing in the dark was going to be useful on scene. He couldn't wait to try it out, even if he didn't know what had brought it on. *Maybe Hobo Joe is actually radioactive, and I'm a superhero now,* he mused, grinning at his own nerdiness. It would explain the sudden fitness.

Opening the fridge, he pulled out a pound of bacon. His usual breakfast of coffee and nothing wasn't going to cut it today. Oddly energized, he didn't feel the need to caffeinate. He did, however, feel the need to eat.

Settling a large cast iron skillet onto the stove, he tore into the package of meat. The scent of raw pork wafted toward him. Salivating, he licked his lips. Growling loudly at the enticing smell, his stomach begged for a taste. Without thinking, he pulled a strip out of the package, jamming the whole piece into his mouth. Chewing, he moaned. A smoky sweetness mingled with the bitter taste of salt on his tongue. The flavor was like nothing he'd ever experienced before. More. He wanted more. He needed it. Now.

Fisting the wad of meat, he hungrily tore chunks off. Thrusting the hunk of raw pork into the side of his mouth, shaking his head and tearing at it with his molars. Gulping down each bite. Eager for the next. Licking his fingers clean and whimpering with each swipe of his tongue. Eyeing the empty package, he considered licking it clean. Deciding against it, he rocked back on his heels contentedly. The ravenous need receded until he could think clearly again.

"What the fuck did I just do? What the actual fuck did I do?" He squealed, his voice higher pitched than normal.

Fuck it. I'm not getting trichinosis! he thought adamantly and jammed two fingers down his throat. Engaging his overly sensitive gag reflex and bypassing his stubborn stomach, he retched. Chunks of undigested pork and fatty bile splattered

First On Scene: A Howling Sirens Novel

into the sink, splashing back at him and coating his hands and arms. Torn pieces of the thick slab of bacon landed on his clenched fists. The squishy, wet feel of raw meat on his skin was enough to send him over the edge. No longer requiring any encouragement, he emptied the full contents of his stomach.

Trembling and sweating, he used paper towels to clean both the counter and himself. Blasting the sink with hot water, he watched the undigested food clump and circle the drain, then cringed at the gurgling sound of blades hitting flesh as he turned on the waste disposal. Satisfied that he'd sufficiently hidden his fucked up behavior, he shut everything off, his stomach bubbling with displeasure.

Eric no longer wanted to go to work, but he needed to. He didn't trust himself to be alone. A repeat shower and a full five minutes of brushing his teeth made him feel physically cleaner. It did nothing for the deep shame burning in his bones.

Dressed in a clean uniform and giving the kitchen a wide berth, he stalked outside. Snatching the sunglasses off his head and forcing them over his eyes to combat the blinding sunlight. The frigid air hung heavy with the threat of snow. He could smell it when the wind blew towards him. Normally, he hated the cold, but today, he relished it. The crisp of winter was something he could focus on instead of whatever was happening to him.

So far, he reasoned, it's mostly good stuff. *I can see in the dark, and I've put on some muscle. I'll just watch my diet more closely. Maybe order in more and cook less. Yeah, I'll definitely cook less*, he told himself. He had a plan. He was going to handle things like an adult and ignore the problem until it either went away or became so big that he had no choice but to deal with it.

Chapter Twelve

Still feeling uncharacteristically energized in spite of his griping stomach, he decided to walk to work. He lived close to the base, and it would save him the effort of moving his car for the plows. Focusing on the bitter cold nipping at him, he power-walked up the hill. Hands thrust into his pockets and head down, he marched down Wilkins Street towards the station. Trotting up to the faded pink door, he punched in the code and shoved his way inside.

Surprisingly, the computer was already booted up, and he quickly clocked in. It was a nice change of pace from the normal struggle. Eager to check out the ambulance and hide in his room, he headed towards the garage. Kitty intercepted him. Walking into the room, she greeted him with a smile that reached her pretty blue eyes and held out the portable radio for him to take. She wore a pair of navy blue pants and her white undershirt.

"Good night?" He asked, taking the radio and truck keys from her.

"The best I've had in a while. We got back around six last night and then didn't turn a wheel," she said, smirking earnestly.

"That's great. Hopefully, we have a good night, too," he chirped with forced optimism that he didn't feel.

"I hope so, for your sake, but I doubt it. Your partner is

already here, so Vivian took off," she replied, approaching the computer to clock out. Then, with a wink, she darted for the door. "I'm glad you are doing better, Crash," she called over her shoulder before completely disappearing from sight.

Eric ground his teeth together at the sound of his nickname. He was never going to be free of it. He knew she cared about him. If he hadn't been confident about their friendship before his latest mishap, he was now. After Angell had let her and Zuri know that he was among the living once more, they had been by his side until he was cleared to get discharged. After that, the three of them had taken turns dropping by his apartment to check on him and bring him what they deemed to be *healthy* snacks. He knew his friends loved him, but the name still stung.

Stomping down the carpeted stairs, his boots crunched. He wrinkled his nose. *This place is gross and would benefit from being burned down.* Somehow the common event of electricity arcing away from the wall outlets had yet to do any harm. It was truly too bad.

"Damn it," he swore, catching sight of the open side door of P2. He knew he couldn't avoid Tim all shift, but he wanted to do the morning check by himself, in peace.

"Hey," he said, poking his head into the patient compartment.

Tim looked up at him from the first-in bag. After staring at Eric briefly, he returned to rummaging in the bag. He wasn't an attractive man, to begin with, but his unruly brown hair and scruffy beard did him no favors, and he was looking rougher than usual. Standing at full height, he was easily six-three with broad shoulders, not that you could tell. Whether seated or standing, he was always in a hunched position. His most glaring flaw, though, was his pasty white skin, which had been repeatedly marred by pockmarks as he continued to claw at himself.

Eric had never seen him without a Red Sox baseball cap. Tim wore it low, pulling it over his eyes to hide dilated pupils and his clawed-up forehead. Constantly sniffing at an invisible nasal drip, he was always twitchy and quick to anger. The fuckhead's look was completed by a wrinkled, stained uniform shirt and unlaced Magnum boots.

The dude had all of the hallmark signs of a cocaine addict, and it was clear as day to anyone unlucky enough to get stuck working with him, but management couldn't be bothered to care. Tim had a pulse and a medic ticket.

Eric found it enraging. He had never wished for regular piss testing so hard in his life.

They checked out the rig in silence, making sure that the oxygen was full, the monitor charged, and that the narcs were signed and sealed. Eric made sure he was the one handling their controlled substances. He didn't trust his partner not to help himself. By the time the truck was ready for its first call, he was ready to escape his partner, but as usual, the EMS gods didn't give a damn about what he wanted. The speakers in the bay beeped loudly, alerting them to the incoming call.

"P2 and engine two, please respond to 495 North for the three-car, motor vehicle accident with entrapment. It is being reported just north of exit 65A." Dispatch fell silent, waiting to be acknowledged.

"Engine Two has that. You can show us responding." Fire confirmed, sirens blaring in the background.

"This shouldn't be our fucking call," Tim growled as he leaped out the side of the truck, slammed the door behind him, and stomped around to the front of the rig. "It's clearly in Marlborough, and that's their goddamn side of the highway." Shouting like a petulant child rather than the forty-something-year-old that he was, Tim threw himself into the driver's seat and continued his tantrum, repeatedly muttering that it shouldn't be their call and pounding his fists against the steering wheel in a fit of rage.

Fuck me, Eric thought loudly, clicking the mic to announce, "P2 responding." Apparently, he was teching first today. If he was being honest with himself, he would have to tech the entire shift because he didn't trust his partner to provide proper patient care. It was going to be an incredibly long twenty-four hours.

The bay door slowly eked upwards. Too slowly for Eric's

First On Scene: A Howling Sirens Novel

taste.

The sooner they made it to the scene, the sooner he could get away from the lunatic next to him. Praying his seatbelt would keep him safe, Eric clung to the door as Tim revved the engine and threw the truck in drive.

Screeching up the hill to the main street, Tim laid on the air horn even though the street was empty. Preferring to be surprised when his partner crashed them into something, Eric closed his eyes and dug his fingers into the seat.

After several sharp turns and a sudden shortstop, the sirens finally stopped wailing. Opening his eyes and prying his fingers off of his seat, Eric took in the scene. They were parked behind the two fire engines blocking off the road. Both Marlborough trucks were already on the scene, and their medics were evaluating the two drivers who had been easily extricated.

A blue Subaru hatchback was parked up the road with minimal damage to its front bumper. A red Jeep Wrangler was parked in front of it. From his vantage point, Eric couldn't see any damage, but he figured the accident could have been a simple fender bender if the third driver hadn't had such shit luck. It looked to him like the white FJ Cruiser had swerved to avoid the wreck, struck the guard rail, and flipped over it. Lying in the ditch next to the highway, wheels up, the car and its driver had seen better days.

Tim crossed his arms as he sat in the driver's seat and scowled. "It'll be a while before they need us. It'll take the jaws of life to get her out."

Eric rolled his eyes and slipped on a reflective vest as he got out of the truck and slammed the door shut. Picking his way into the ditch to take a closer look, he frowned. The hood had crunched the way it had been designed to.

Peering through the large cracks spidering across the windshield, he could make out a woman hanging upside down, held in place only by her seatbelt. Dark curly hair obscured her face so that he could only make out her left ear, an ominous trickle of blood seeping from it. Eric sucked at guessing people's ages, and today was no different. She could have been sixteen or twenty-six; all he knew for sure was that the blood smeared on the inside of the windshield meant that she had smashed her head upon impact.

Both fire crews were working together in a desperate effort to pry the driver's side door off, but it was clear they were finding the going difficult. It seemed unlikely that the driver would last long enough to be extracted.

Off to one side, a state trooper was in conference with two senior fire department officers. The Marlborough fire chief was easily identified by the distinctive 'Fire Chief' badge on the front of his gleaming white helmet. He wasn't required to be there, but he always showed up to support his people when anything big happened.

"Chief," Eric called out as soon as he was close enough to be heard, making the group of men look up from their conversation." Extrication is taking too long, and it's rush hour. We're going to need the bird. It's not snowing yet—they'll fly for this."

"Yeah. Good call." The Battalion Chief nodded, reaching for his radio as the Trooper briskly walked off to shut down the highway.

Eric marched over to the ambulance and tore open the passenger side door. "They are shutting down the highway to land the chopper. Just thought you should know," he snapped and slammed the door shut before his partner could reply. Tim glared at him through the window, his lips pulled into a thin, unhappy line as he stayed put.

It wasn't even eight A.M., and the day was an utter trash fire. He should be thrilled to be starting off his shift with a nasty trauma that let him land MedFlight in the middle of the highway, but instead, he just felt pissed off. Huffing out a sigh, he stalked away from the truck. At least he wouldn't have a chance to eat anything weird on scene. He hoped.

With the freeway closed and headlights backed up as far as the eye could see, they waited for the arrival of the helicopter. The distinct rhythmic sound of "chuff-chuff-chuff" grew louder with every passing moment. The Firefighters glanced in the direction of the sound before continuing to struggle with the car door. It just wouldn't budge for them, and Eric started to worry that they wouldn't get the patient out in time. Medflight needed clear skies to fly, and heavy cloud cover was already threatening snow. In a perfect world, they would pop the door open just as the flight team landed, but it was safe to say that wouldn't be happening.

There didn't seem much he could do to help, but at the very least, he could offer moral support. Scrambling back into the ditch, his heel caught on an exposed root and sent him tumbling into the wreck. He caught himself on the exposed frame, and the metal crumpled under his fist like a tin can.

Looking around to see if anyone else had witnessed the event, he found everyone's attention fully occupied elsewhere. Carefully withdrawing his hand, he found it none the worse for wear despite the strain it must have suffered.

A sudden wind kicked up behind him, making him turn to see the blue and white helicopter coming in to land. The rotor wash sprayed dirt and debris everywhere, and he was glad he had his shades to act as an eye shield.

With the full weight of two firefighters shoving at it, the car door finally pried away from the frame, granting access to the driver within. Eric would have cheered, but he knew it wouldn't be heard over the spinning rotors.

With the patient collared and boarded, Eric and the firefighters carried the unconscious woman up the steep incline while the Medflight team ducked to avoid the whirling rotor blades and hurried to meet them with their petite gurney.

Laying her on the stretcher, Eric made quick work of the woman's torn clothing with his trauma sheers. He had hoped that she only had a head injury, but with one look at her torso, he identified paradoxical movement. Only the right side of her chest rose when she inhaled. It meant that there were at least three ribs broken on her left side.

Eric made hard eye contact with the flight medic and pointed at the patient's injured ribs. Nodding to show that he understood, the other paramedic pressed his hand against the left chest wall to brace it. The best way to splint a flail segment like this was to intubate her, but they would have to do that on the way to the trauma center.

One of the flight medics gave Eric an affectionate pat on the back as he assisted them in loading the patient onto the chopper. The roar of engines and rotor made speech impossible, but the meaning was clear.

Head down against the wash as the aircraft lifted into the grey sky, he made his way back to the ambulance, where Tim still hadn't moved from his seated position. *What a piece of shit*, he thought and climbed into the rig to watch Medflight go.

He insisted that they stop at Burger King on the way back, where he bought a supreme breakfast sandwich, an order of french toast sticks, a breakfast burrito, and three orders of hashbrowns. Having missed breakfast altogether, he was ravenous, and he tore into the food even before he left the restaurant. By the time he was back in the truck, only the breakfast burrito remained.

Tim warily side-eyed him on the way back to the base. Ignoring him, Eric finished his meal.

"You're a mess, dude," Tim commented as he backed into the bay.

"You're one to fucking talk," Eric growled back, brushing crumbs off his chest. Balling up the paper bags, Eric glared at his partner.

Tim met his gaze but couldn't hold it, so he quickly looked away.

Pleased with himself for having established his dominance, Eric got out of the truck and stomped across the bay and up the stairs. The surge of energy he'd felt all morning was starting to fade, and he yawned widely. *I just need a few hours of sleep*, he told himself and flopped down onto the overly firm couch in his room. Stretching out, he let his eyes flutter shut.

He startled himself awake with a loud snore-turned snort. Sitting up, he wiped the drool from his face and rubbed the sleep from his eyes. Outside the window, the sun was already setting. *Did I sleep all day? What the fuck is wrong with me?*

Groaning into his hands, he stood up, cracking his neck and stretching out his arms. Figuring that he should make himself useful if they weren't running calls, he decided to go downstairs and wash the truck. Tim certainly wouldn't be doing it.

Slumping down the stairs into the ambulance bay, he felt like he was in a haze. He pushed the back of his hand against his forehead. He didn't feel hot. *I don't think I have a fever, but maybe I am getting sick.*

He filled the bucket with soapy water and dragged it over to the ambulance. After killing thirty minutes working on the truck's exterior, he decided to go the extra mile. He was bored and needed to do something with his hands. Opening the bay door, he moved the truck forward and pulled out the stretcher.

He swept and wiped down counters and scoured the floor. If it were up to him, he'd let it air dry but he never knew when the next call would be. Planning to do the next best thing, he reached into the cabinet for a towel. The truck wasn't that nice but it could at least be clean.

Without warning, a wave of nausea struck him. Gagging, he stumbled out of the ambulance. Breathing deeply through his nose, he sat heavily on the rear step. It did nothing for the queasiness.

A headache pulsed behind his eyes, and his vision swam. The room spun, intensifying the nausea. Clutching at the truck, he struggled to remain upright.

Bile burned the back of his throat. He could taste it. The flavor of salted meat and something metallic assaulted his senses. Standing, he swayed on his feet. His legs failed under his weight, sending him sprawling on the concrete floor.

"Why does this shit keep happening to me?" He grumbled, sounding more like soft snarls than words. His jaw began to throb. He felt like he was on fire. He pressed a hand to his face and winced at the heat radiating off his skin.

The throbbing in his jaw intensified. Radiating into his sinuses and down his throat. Stiffening, he braced for what came next. It was too similar to the dreams. Maybe it was a dream. Dream or not, it was painful.

He curled into the fetal position as spasms wracked his body, and it contorted into something new. Popping and snapping, his bones lengthened, and his muscles bulked. He moaned as his jaws elongated and sprouted fangs. He could taste blood. His blood.

His ears crept up his skull and sharpened into points as thick coarse hair crept over his entire body and darkened into a ruddy, red pelt. His pants split with a loud tearing sound and buttons skittered across the bay as his torn shirt fell to the ground. He yelped as, with a loud cracking, his spine extended, vertebrae budding off one another. Flesh and fur snaked around the newly formed tail, and at last, the nausea receded.

Pushing himself off the floor, he examined his paws. They were long and spindly with individual fingers. Similar to hands but covered in soft fur and tipped with razors. Rising onto his hindquarters, he scented the air. It smelled of frost and black mold. Huffing agitatedly, he dropped back to all fours.

"I need dinner," came Tim's gruff voice as the other medic rounded the corner. He froze, wide-eyed, trembling, and with his crotch dampening as he urinated on himself.

Growling at the acrid scent of urine, Eric flattened his ears against his skull. A gnawing hunger pitted in his stomach, and the seething hatred he'd felt all day spurred him forward. Slinking closer to his partner, he snarled menacingly and bared his fangs.

Quaking in front of him, Timothy openly blubbered."Ple... please don't hurt me."

Cocking his head to the side, Eric listened to the sobbing man, the sounds were familiar, but he didn't understand. He just felt hungry.

Moving closer to his prey, he waited to see if it would run. He wanted it to flee so he could give chase, but it only continued to shiver and mewl. Resigning himself to eat without hunting, he lunged for the man in front of him, jaws snapping shut around its upper leg.

Tim screamed and kept screaming. The sound echoed off the walls as he thrashed and beat against the giant wolf.

Sinking his fangs deeper, Eric was rewarded with a fresh

First On Scene: A Howling Sirens Novel

gush of hot blood. He rumbled his pleasure at the salty, metallic taste as rivulets of crimson poured out from between his clenched jaws.

Yanking, he tore off a mouthful of cloth, quadriceps, and bone. The arterial spray painted the ambulance red and spurted all over the floor and his muzzle. Crunching bone between his teeth, he gulped it down.

Latching onto Tim's belly, he shook him like a rag doll. Tim's head struck the back door; the force of the blow caved in his skull with a sickening crunch, and the man went limp.

Unwilling to be disturbed, Eric dragged Tim's motionless body into the ambulance and dropped him gracelessly onto the floor. Blood continued to dribble out of his leg stump. It mingled with suds, creating a crimson froth. Intent on marking his territory, he reared onto his hindquarters, raked his claws down the wall, and rubbed his body against it, leaving behind his scent and tufts of fur.

Returning to his meal, he dropped to all fours and buried his muzzle into the body's soft, fatty gut. Gnawing, he tore through the adipose tissue and into the abdominal wall. He knew the tastier meats were hidden inside. Instinctively, he gulped down the liver first. Tugging out the small intestine, he slurped it down like an overly long piece of spaghetti. Blood pooled in the abdominal cavity, coating the other organs. He alternated between swallowing organs whole and lapping up the sanguine liquid. Using the carcass like a bowl.

Saving the heart for last, he chewed slowly. Savoring the beefy flavor of the lean muscle. With the innards devoured, he no longer had a use for the body, so raising his leg, he pissed on the corpse and saturated it in urine. Satisfied, he leaped from the truck and padded out of the bay, his claws clicking against the concrete floor.

Ready to hunt down his next prey, he raised his blood-splattered muzzle to the moonlit sky and howled.

Chapter Thirteen

"You should be there!" A disembodied voice snapped into his ear.

Startling, his eyes raked the darkness for the speaker, but he couldn't find them in the misty fog enveloping him. Squinting, he strained his eyes and raised a hand to his face. It was completely obscured by the swirling mists.

"There are always consequences when a job is left undone." The voice hissed from somewhere nearby.

The haze of darkness parted at his feet, revealing a window into the world below. A man and a woman walked hand in hand down a moon lit path. He recognized where they were, the Assabet River trail. The asphalt road ran through a heavily wooded area, separated from the trees and brambles by a thin metal fence. *Why am I being shown this and what do they want me to do about it?* he thought anxiously, peering down at the couple and searching for clues.

Stumbling, the man fell into his date, pushing her against the fence. The railing rattled loudly. Laughing, she gripped the front of his puffy gray jacket, and drew him closer. Brushing a strand of blonde hair out of her face, he leaned in and kissed her. A chaste brushing of lips that quickly turned heated, leaving them oblivious to the amber eyes gazing out at them from the bushes.

"Your negligence is noted!" The voice screeched, its words

First On Scene: A Howling Sirens Novel

echoing around the darkness. Biting his lip, Angell kept his eyes on the scene below. *What am I supposed to do? I'll do what it wants if it stops yelling at me!*

Behind them, a mud-streaked creature with dark, matted fur crept out of the woods. Leaping over the metal railing, the enormous lupine landed soundlessly on the road. Bright amber eyes trained on its prey while it stalked forward, fangs bared and ears flattened against its skull.

Oh shit! he thought and tried shouting at the couple, but he was mute. *Why can't I speak?! If I'm not supposed to warn them, then why am I seeing this?!* He tried clearing his throat but couldn't generate a sound. Heart pounding in his chest, he reached for his throat. He couldn't find it in the mist.

"What are you doing?!" The voice demanded, making him jerk away from the sound.

I wish I fucking knew, he thought, watching in horror while the giant wolf, easily seven feet long and five feet tall, moved closer to the couple. Snarling, it reared up on its hindquarters.

Startling, the woman looked up with wide eyes and froze, her quivering lips the only noticeable movement.

"Babe, what's wrong?" The man asked, cupping her face in his hands.

Without taking her eyes off of the looming beast, she raised a single, trembling finger and pointed over his shoulder.

Brow furrowed, he turned around, coming face to face with the wolf that had just dropped to all fours. Swallowing hard, his Adam's apple bobbed up and down. Crying and shaking, the woman hid her face in her hands.

"Nice puppy," he whispered, holding out his arms, palms up.

Ears perking, the wolf took a step closer, sniffing the offered hands with a wrinkled nose.

The man stood stock still and held his ground, tears streaking down his face. "I think it's just checking us out," he whispered to the trembling woman behind him.

"We should run!" She insisted, tugging at the back of his jacket.

"No, if we run, it will attack," he mumbled, keeping his

hands raised in front of him.

Why am I being shown this?! Angell thought aggravatedly and forced down the impulse to pace. The last thing he wanted to do was to watch someone die. He did enough of that in his day to day.

The wolf lunged, snapping its jaws shut on the outstretched arm. Growling and shaking its massive head, it tore the limb free. Arterial spray drenched the animal's face and chest.

Screaming and writhing, the man crumpled to the ground.

Face blanching white, the woman ducked under the metal railing and bolted into the treeline, hurrying down the steep incline.

Crunching on the severed limb, the wolf made no attempt to follow her.

Using his remaining limbs, the man attempted to army crawl away; the lingering stump spurted blood rhythmically. The rapid pulsation of crimson quickly became a dark ooze as the man's heart slowed. Slipping, the man fell face-first into the gore and lay still.

Something moved next to the corpse. White, smoky wisps gathered, swirling and shifting into a mass the size of a humanoid. Solidifying into a translucent carbon copy of the dead man, it stood next to the body, frowning down at it.

"This is what you leave behind!" The voice growled in his ear. Trembling, he gaped at the ghost because what else could it be? Even if he could have spoken, he would have been at a loss for words. *Is this what it meant by consequences?! What was I supposed to do?* Stunned, he continued to watch on in silence.

Running a pink tongue along its bloody muzzle, the wolf slunk towards its catch.

Ripping into the jacket, the beast leaped back in an irruption of goose down. Shaking its head back and forth and pawing at its face, it tarred and feathered itself with blood.

Angell gaped at the horrendous scene. *Why am I being shown this?!* A ripple of movement from behind the hulking wolf drew his eye. It was a second wolf. *How many of these things are there? And since when do we have wolves in Massachusetts?!*

First On Scene: A Howling Sirens Novel

Dwarfed by the first hulking beast, the second wolf had sleek, jet-black fur and barely reached the other animal's shoulder. Head cocked to the side, Golden Eyes watched the blood-soaked wolf vacillate between fighting with the goose down and devouring its prey.

Ears flat to its skull and tail streaking out behind it, the smaller wolf surged forward, racing through the apparition and launching itself onto the larger beast. With a flash of ivory, the smaller wolf sank its fangs into the matted fur at the nape of the other animal's neck.

Shimmering like static, the ghost reformed and stepped aside to watch the impending battle.

The beast reared onto its hind legs with a roar. Bucking and thrashing, it snapped at its back, but the smaller wolf was out of reach. Reaching behind its head, the beast clawed at the black wolf. Its talons found purchase along the smaller animal's rib cage and raked along its sides.

Yelping, the smaller wolf squirmed out of the beast's grasp and propelled itself further up the large animal's back. Muscles bunching beneath its fur, the small wolf launched itself towards the beast's vulnerable throat. Its jaws clamped shut with a resounding snap.

Dropping to all fours, the beast shook itself like a wet dog.

The smaller wolf kept its death hold, digging its claws into the larger animal's belly and tearing at the vulnerable flesh.

Blood gushed past the black wolf's jaws, painting its muzzle and face crimson.

Yanking ineffectively at the smaller animal, the beast staggered, tripping over the savaged, goosedown-coated body of its prey. Gurgling, it dropped to its side and rolled back and forth.

Chapter Fourteen

Sitting bolt upright, Angell choked down a scream. Trembling and sweating, he clutched the thick flannel comforter against his pounding heart. Glowing neon green numbers blinked at him from across the room. It wasn't even five A.M. yet.

It's my day off. I shouldn't be up this early, he thought, flopping back against the mattress. Pushing away the sweat-soaked locs from his forehead, he stared up at the dark ceiling. Since the first appearance of his reaper, he had been plagued by strange dreams. Usually, they forewarned of his silent observer's presence and the inevitable death he was to encounter. In the past, the dreams had never involved taunting from unseen forces or being forced to watch a snuff film. He had never dreamed about ghosts before. *Maybe for once, I had an actual nightmare instead of some sort of fucked up premonition.*

Squeezing his eyes shut, he unclenched his jaw and took a deep breath. It did nothing for his tense muscles, rapid heart rate, or the unending sense of dread he felt.

"Fuck it," he muttered and climbed out of bed. If he couldn't go back to sleep, he would put his frenetic energy to use. Shaking his head, he tugged on a hoodie and a pair of sweatpants. Pulling the foldable, stationary bike out of its corner, he rolled it to the center of the room and set it up. If his heart was intent on racing, he might as well do some cardio.

First On Scene: A Howling Sirens Novel

For the next two hours, he pushed his body hard, fluctuating between peddling on a steep incline and doing deadlifts with his dumbbells. Anything to avoid thinking about Hobo Joe's vacant expression illuminated in the moonlight.

Panting, he dismounted from the bike for a final time. Raking a hand through drenched curls and wrinkling his nose. He reeked of stress sweat. He balled up his workout clothes and tossed them into the hamper as he walked into the bathroom and turned the shower on as hot as it would go. Climbing in, he let the lukewarm water cascade over his sore muscles and leaned his head back, shutting his eyes and sighing. The water never got hot enough for his liking, but it was still better than the cold sweat he had woken up in.

A monstrous wolf lunged, its saliva-flecked jaws snapping shut with a loud click. Snarling, it tore off the man's arm.

Angell's eyes flew open. Heart racing, he stumbled back, catching himself on the curtain rod before he could fall. Rushing to get out of the shower, he quickly washed himself and turned off the water.

Still dripping, he wrapped a towel around his waist and went back into the bedroom. *Well, I'm never closing my eyes again. At this rate, I may have to stop blinking*, he thought exasperatedly and shook his head. Aching for a distraction, he turned on the television and patted himself dry. 'Breaking News' flashed across the screen in bold red letters. Rolling his eyes, he waited to hear about the gunfire that had occurred overnight in Boston. The street violence wasn't as frequent during the cold months, but it never completely went away.

A white woman with brown hair and a pinched face clutched a microphone in her hands. Wearing a gray pantsuit, she stood at the Assabet River trailhead and stared straight into the camera. "Good morning! This is Barbara Stanton, reporting live from the Assabet River trail where tragedy has stuck overnight, leaving two dead."

The camera panned out to the yellow tape and milling police officers behind her before returning to her frowning face.

Selina Rossman

"It is currently believed that these deaths are the result of a bear attack. The Department of Fish and Game is urging citizens to avoid wooded areas and to stay indoors when possible. If you should encounter a bear or any other wildlife acting bizarrely, please retreat to safety and call 9-1-1." She motioned for someone off-camera to come forward. "Joining me now is the brave young woman that witnessed last night's violent affair."

The blonde woman from his dream appeared on the screen. She took the microphone from the reporter, looking into the camera with bloodshot eyes and quivering lips. "It wasn't a bear. We were attacked by a giant wolf!" She declared, her hands shaking.

No fucking way! he thought, eyes glued to the screen and mouth agape.

Pursing her lips, Barbara snatched away the microphone. "Thank you for that accounting. I'm sure it was very scary, but it couldn't be a wolf. We don't have those in Massachusetts," she said knowingly. The blonde girl reached for the microphone once more, but Barbara kept it out of reach, motioning for someone off-screen to take the witness away.

Blood thundering in his ears, he almost missed what the reporter said next.

Sighing, she turned back towards the camera and touched her earpiece. "I'm receiving an update from the studio." A glint in her eye, she drew her shoulders back. "I have just been notified that there was a second animal attack and that another body has been found at the local ambulance station. Please stay tuned for further information." The camera panned back towards the yellow police tape where two medical examiners were pushing a gurney with a body bag on it.

Turning the television off, he stared at the now blank screen. *What the fuck does this mean?!* he thought frantically, burying his fingers in his damp locs and tugging on them. Then it dawned on him. *Holly shit, yesterday was Eric's first day back at work! Fuck!*

Spinning towards the bed, he searched for his phone. Not spotting it immediately, he tore off the covers, tossing the

First On Scene: A Howling Sirens Novel

pillows and sheets over his shoulder onto the floor. Not finding it, he dragged the bedframe away from the wall.

"Where the fuck is it?!" He growled, flipping the mattress up. Shifting it aside, he caught a glimpse of his cell phone. It had somehow wedged itself between the box spring and bed frame. Snatching it up, he immediately dialed Eric's number.

Pick up! Pick up! Pick up! He silently chanted, listening to the line ring over and over. *Come on! Pick up the fucking phone!*

It went to voicemail, and he hung up. Rocking back and forth on his heels, he dialed Kitty. She picked up on the second ring.

"Hello?" Her voice was thick with sleep.

"Have you heard from Eric?!" He demanded, his voice cracking.

"No, why?"

"Haven't you seen the news?!" He spat.

"Angell, it's not even seven A.M., and it's my day off. What's going on?"

"There was an animal attack at the base, and someone is dead. Eric hasn't answered his phone, and after the nightmares..." He snapped his mouth shut. He hadn't meant to mention his dreams.

"Oh shit." She fell silent for a long moment. "I'm getting dressed right now. I'll meet you at the base."

"Okay."

"And Angell, if you're dreams are freaking you out, maybe you should talk to your family." Her tone was gentle and sincere.

"What makes you say that?" He asked, his heart leaping into his throat.

"Remember, you told me the other day that your aunt used to hang out with a Mexican witch when you were a kid?"

"Wait, when did I tell you that?"

She sighed. "The other day, when we went out to celebrate Eric getting out of the hospital, you had one too many screwdrivers. You started talking about your family and Mexico. You told me that sometimes people in your family are gifted in weird ways. I'm not really surprised that you don't remember; you were too drunk to get yourself home, so I had to give you a ride."

Well, I'm never drinking again. I can't believe I told her that, especially so early on. What is wrong with me? He shook his head and pulled on his boxers and pants. "Yeah, maybe I'll do that. I'll see you at the base, okay?"

"See you soon." She hung up.

He finished getting dressed and rushed out to the car. Kitty had a point; maybe he should call his mother. It was amazing that his partner was so open minded considering her background. He knew she had grown up sneaking books on shapeshifters, psychics, and the like but her constant curiosity about the world kept her from being dismissive. It was a good quality to have, even if it sometimes led to uncomfortable conversations for him.

Climbing into his truck, he started the engine and called his mother. She answered on the third ring.

"Mijo, do you know what time it is?" She sounded weary.

He frowned. Massachusetts was an hour ahead of Mexico. *Apparently, I'm everyone's alarm clock today.* "Yes, I'm sorry. I just..." He hesitated. *Fuck, maybe I am crazy but between the animal attacks and the dreams... I need to know for sure.* Chewing on his lower lip, he tried to figure out what to say.

"Angell, is everything okay?"

He could hear the concern in her voice. *Great, now I'm worrying her.* Rubbing his temples, he took a deep breath. "Mama, I need to talk to the bruja that used to spend time with Tia Nina," he whispered the words through gritted teeth.

His mother was silent for a long moment.

"Mama?" He implored.

"Why?"

"I can't really explain that right now, but I need to talk to her."

She sighed. "Nina hasn't spoken to her in many years. They had some sort of falling out. I know that she moved away, but I don't know where."

"I need this." His voice cracked, and he winced.

"I will see what I can find out, but are you alright?"

First On Scene: A Howling Sirens Novel

"I'm alright, but I have to go. Thank you for doing this for me." He cleared his throat. "I love you."

"Okay. Take care of yourself. We will talk soon. I love you, Mijo."

Ending the call, he peeled out of the driveway and raced towards the station. If his mother could find the bruja, then he could get some answers, but for now, all he needed to know was if Eric was still alive.

Chapter Fifteen

I killed someone.

Pacing the length of her small living room, she tangled her fingers in her braided hair and tugged. Behind her, the television babbled on inanely. In an effort to block out the sound of her upstairs neighbors having early morning sex, she had turned it on full blast. Between the woman's loud moaning and her sensitive hearing, it wasn't going well. Pressing her lips together, she ignored the throb settling between her legs. She was stressed out enough without adding arousal into the mix.

She still hadn't been able to sleep. Last night's events flashed into view every time she tried to close her eyes. In spite of her best efforts and brushing her teeth multiple times, she could still taste the metallic tang of hot blood on her tongue. She was appalled by what she had done, but her wolf was thrilled. She wasn't used to being so out of sync with her wolf, but this was the second time it happened recently. Her wolf being more surface around Kitty wasn't as bad as picking a fight with a rogue shifter but it was still becoming a problem.

She had been acting on instinct to defend her territory, and if she was being honest with herself, she had lost control of her wolf. She knew better than to take on a threat by herself. She wasn't a tactician and had never been in a real fight before. Wrestling with her brother and cousins didn't count.

First On Scene: A Howling Sirens Novel

Regardless of the reason, it didn't change the fact that someone was dead because of her.

Her chest tightened at the memory of her fangs ripping into soft flesh and the stench of the vodka-soaked musk. Shaking her head to clear it, she dropped onto the couch and groaned into her hands. *It's probably for the best that I lost control. He was so much bigger than me. It's a small miracle I survived that fight. He could have killed me.* She blew out a breath. *The pack is going to freak.*

Sinking against the soft cushions behind her, the television caught her eye.

On the screen, a serious-looking woman in a pantsuit stood in front of the Assabet Trailhead and frowned. "It is currently believed that these deaths are the result of a bear attack. The Department of Fish and Game is urging citizens to avoid wooded areas and to stay indoors when possible. If you should encounter a bear or any other wildlife acting bizarrely, please retreat to safety and call 9-1-1."

Breath catching in her throat, she propped her elbows on her knees and leaned forward.

The woman motioned toward someone off-camera. "Joining me now is the brave young woman who witnessed last night's violent affair."

Holly shit, someone saw what I did?! she thought, biting down on her lower lip to keep from screaming.

A blonde woman marched onto the screen. She took the microphone from the reporter, looking into the camera with bloodshot eyes and quivering lips. "It wasn't a bear. We were attacked by a giant wolf!" She declared, her hands shaking.

I'm so fucked. If my father is watching this right now, he is going to kill me. Oh, shit, does this mean we are going to have to worry about hunters now?! Clutching her knees tightly, she stared at the television, waiting for the next damning words to be spoken.

Pursing her lips, the reporter snatched away the microphone. "Thank you for that accounting. I'm sure it was very scary, but it couldn't be a wolf. We don't have those in Massachusetts," she said knowingly. The blonde girl reached for the microphone once more, but Barbara kept it out of reach, motioning for someone off-screen to take the witness away.

Sighing, she turned back towards the camera and touched her earpiece. "I'm receiving an update from the studio." A glint in her eye, she drew her shoulders back. "I have just been notified that there was a second animal attack and that another body has been found at the local ambulance station. Please stay tuned for further information."

Frozen in place, her mind raced. *At the base?! Another one?! Could it be a mated pair or, worse, a pack? Shit, who did it kill?*

A possessive growl rumbled out of the back of her throat. It can't be Kitty, she thought, trying to soothe her wolf. *She and Angell had the night off, and Eric is still out on injury, so my people should be fine, but then who's dead?*

She lunged for the landline as it began to ring. Only her family knew about her landline. When there was an emergency, her pack didn't have time to fight with the latest technology. It was a small miracle that they were able to use flip phones, and there was still only a fifty-fifty chance of those working.

"Zuri," her father's deep baritone rumbled into the receiver. "Are you alright?"

"I'm okay," she murmured, clutching the edge of the couch. It was only a matter of time before he asked where she was last night. She had been on her way to meet up with the pack for their monthly run when she had caught Hobo Joe's confusing scent and followed it.

"Have you seen the news?" His voice was strained.

"I have," she admitted.

"Then you know we have a problem?"

She cleared her throat. "Yes."

"Be at the falls in one hour," he said and ended the call before she could respond.

"Love you too," she grumbled and hung up the phone.

Heading into her room to get dressed, she frowned. Her father had given her an hour to get to the falls, but she knew he would want her there sooner. He was probably already planning her next twenty-four hours. She couldn't really

First On Scene: A Howling Sirens Novel

blame him, considering how little they knew about the rogue wolves, but she had been planning on taking Kitty out to dinner tonight.

Shoulders slumping, she sighed and picked up her flip phone.

I'm going to need a rain check for tonight. I have to deal with a family issue, she texted and put the phone down. It was early and the other woman was probably asleep.

Vibrating loudly, her cell phone alerted her of an incoming text message. Flipping it open, she read Kitty's reply, a smirk tugging at her lips.

I'm sorry to hear that. I hope everything works out okay. Let me know if you need anything.

I'll make it up to you, She promised.

You better, Kitty replied with a winky face emoji.

Grinning, she put down her phone and began to dress in a pair of jeans, a black T-shirt, and a pair of black and white sketchers. Shrugging on her red, faux leather jacket, she sighed. With her naturally high body temperature, she didn't need it but the well worn material looked good on her and made it easier to blend in with the humans that insisted on covering up in weather below fifty degrees.

Locking her apartment door, she tucked her keys into her jacket and hustled down the four flights of stairs between her and the street. Stepping outside, she scented the breeze. There wasn't even a hint of bear musk. *Bears!* She scoffed and headed for her jeep.

She parked next to her father's powder blue Subaru at the top of the trailhead. Bracing herself, she got out of the car and started down the trail. Under normal circumstances, the pack would never meet up during the day, but there wasn't anything normal about this morning.

She had missed their monthly run, and her family would want to know why. The moon didn't rule her, but she appreciated the illumination it offered. She could see really well in low light but not in pitch black. Hunting under the full moon always made things easier.

She was the last to arrive. Walking slowly down the path, she caught the familiar musk of wet earth, wolf, and something uniquely them. She found the smell soothing. The wolf from last night had reeked of vodka, wet dog, and burnt pine needles.

The rush of moving water grew louder, and the wind shifted to her back. Her family would smell her coming. The walk to the falls was a short one, but she drew it out. She wasn't ready to see the judgment in her father's eyes.

Pausing, she dropped into a squat in front of a graffitied boulder. A pale circular face with exed-out eyes grinned up at her from the boulder. *Do the X-eyes mean it's supposed to be dead or high?* Breathing deeply, she caught the scent of teenage boy BO, fresh paint, and a whiff of marijuana. *Guess it's supposed to be high like its creator.*

"ZURI!" Her father bellowed over the roar of the falls.

Flinching, she jumped to her feet. Lowering her head, she trotted down the remainder of the trail and to the water's edge. Her father wanted her to be submissive during pack business, and it was usually the biggest point of contention in their relationship, but today, he was going to get exactly what he wanted. She had killed someone, and all she felt was shame.

Perched on top of a large boulder, her father, Marcus, scowled down at her. He kept his salt and pepper hair cropped short, claiming that it made him look dignified. She thought it made him look old. Her brother Marcus Jr sat beside him. With broad shoulders, dark curly hair, hazel eyes, and lighter skin, he was their father's younger clone. With ebony skin and darker eyes, she took after their mother.

"Hey," she said, slinking towards her family.

Sierra, her mother, shifted to the to make room for her.

She took the offered seat and glanced around at the rest of the family. Her aunt, Raina, leaned against a tree behind the others, keeping watch while her three sons stood in a semicircle around the falls, all three with arms crossed & brows furrowed.

They were identical triplets. If she hadn't grown up with them, she probably wouldn't be able to tell them apart. Jamal and James always took themselves very seriously while Joseph was the prankster among them.

Flashing a smile in her direction, Joseph winked at her before returning to his serious demeanor. She winked back at her favorite cousin.

"You didn't come running with us last night," Marcus said, looking down at his daughter.

She recklessly held his gaze. She knew she had fucked up, but she wasn't in the habit of mindlessly submitting to him or anyone else.

Marcus bared his teeth, a low snarl escaping his curled lips.

She bared her teeth in return but didn't meet his eyes.

"Where were you last night?" He snapped through gritted teeth.

She drew in a steadying breath and kept her eyes averted. Today wasn't the time to challenge her father. "I was tracking another shifter."

"What happened?" He asked, leaning over the edge of the boulder to better see her face.

Fisting and unfisting her hands, she let the words spill past her lips in a rush. "I was leaving my apartment when I caught a whiff of an unfamiliar wolf. I was curious, so I followed the scent to the Assabet River Trail. I still hadn't met anyone like us outside of the family and wanted to see why someone new was in our territory." She swallowed hard.

"The other wolf was huge, and it was hunting humans. Before I could do anything, he killed one and tore him to pieces." Her heart raced at the memory.

Her father watched her closely, brow furrowed over hazel eyes filled with concern. "What did you do?"

She suddenly felt very young. Her wolf ached to curl into a tight ball and hide away from her alpha's prying gaze. She wasn't ready to see his empathy replaced by disappointment.

The elders of her pack had raised her to be peaceful. They

didn't hunt humans, they never did anything to expose their true identities, and they definitely didn't kill for territory.

" I killed him." She choked the words out, her voice thick with tears. "He was out of control, and I didn't have a choice," she whimpered, keeping her eyes on her lap while hot tears streamed down her face.

"Honey," Sierra breathed, pulling her into her arms and stroking her back.

Pressing her face into her mother's shoulder, she sobbed like a child. She could feel the other's eyes boring into her, and the silence was deafening.

When she felt strong enough to raise her head, she rubbed at her eyes and looked into her father's pinched face. "When he died, he shifted back, and I recognized him. It was one of the frequent fliers." Lips quivering, she hesitated. "Before last night, I could have sworn he was human."

"Who bit him?" Marcus growled.

She shook her head. "I don't know. Before this happened, I didn't think that was anything but a myth."

Marcus turned his serious yellow eyes on the rest of the pack. "I believe I already know the answer, but has anyone here bitten or scratched a human hard enough to break the skin?"

One by one, they shook their heads and averted their eyes. Her mother squeezed her tightly against her side.

Leaping down from his perch, Marcus began pacing next to the rushing water. Stopping short, he faced his family. "Not all packs are the same. There are those of us that believe humans are beneath us, nothing more than cattle. Those individuals are also the wolves that think our women should only be used for breeding." Shaking his head, he bared his teeth and went back to pacing.

Not knowing what to say, she watched him stalk back and forth like a caged animal.

After a few more long strides, he came to a stop and faced them once more. "I've met wolves like that in the past. Not only do they cling to archaic belief systems, they think only white men should have the gift of shifting, and they have

First On Scene: A Howling Sirens Novel

every intention of making more like them."

Zuri watched her father and frowned. His bared teeth seemed sharper, and his salt and pepper curls had faded to grayish-silver color.

From an early age, control and integration with your wolf were emphasized in her family. Her parents and aunt had made a point of setting the example. She had never seen her father so close to losing control of himself before.

"I thought this was a problem we had left behind in Georgia. These idiots don't understand that making more wolves comes with risk. They don't always take well to the change. The man you killed is a perfect example of that!" He growled, grayish-silver fur creeping down his neck and arms.

Wide-eyed, she shared a startled look with her brother. Holy shit!

"I need to kill something," Marcus announced, his words more akin to snarls. He turned and abruptly sprinted deeper into the surrounding woods.

Her mother gave her another supportive squeeze and slid off of the boulder. "I need to go after him and make sure he doesn't do anything he will regret later. I haven't seen him this angry since before you were born. Everyone should go home until he calms down. Then, we can figure out what our next move will be."

Sierra strode after her mate, stripping as she went. Her skin rippled, sprouting thick, dark fur. Her spine lengthened with a series of soft pops, and her inky black pelt reached her buttocks in time to cover a newly sprouted tail. Her ears crept up the side of her head, growing tufts of fur and elongating into points. Dropping to all fours, she glanced over her shoulder at her family and offered them a soft bark before trotting into the woods.

Shaking off her stunned stupor, Raina pushed herself off the tree she had been leaning on. "Sierra is right. If anyone sees something strange, I want you to back off and alert the family immediately, but for now, everyone, go home and stay there."

That was fine by Zuri. After last night, she wanted nothing more than to go home and pretend that none of this was

Selina Rossman

happening.

Chapter Sixteen

Eric's full bladder ached with urgency. Opening his eyes, he immediately regretted the decision. His head throbbed, and the world spun. Groaning, he shut them once more. His limbs felt like they were made of lead, and he could barely raise them. He hadn't been this hungover in a long time. He didn't even remember drinking. In fact, he couldn't remember anything from the previous night. *What the hell did I do?* he thought, struggling to get his bearings without moving too much.

The cold, hard surface below him felt good against his overheated bare skin. A muscular figure pressed into his side. Letting his fingers roam, he found long, silky hair and a cotton T-shirt. Not wanting to wake her, he didn't search further. *Did I get wasted and hook up with someone?* He wondered. *Good job me! It's been a minute since I got laid. Too bad I can't remember anything...*

Curiosity getting the better of him, he peered at the person next to him through half-lidded eyes. Partially blinded by the sunlight streaming into the room, he could barely make out the woman's features. Her back was turned to him, but he had been correct. She had long blonde hair and was wearing a dark green cotton T-shirt. His eyes began to adjust, and he glanced around the room. He was naked on the floor of an industrial kitchen. He recognized the space from doing a safety walk-through with the fire department. He was in one of his favorite restaurants, the Kith and Kin. Before he'd started his diet, he and Angell used to come here at the beginning of every shift to get breakfast.

Needing to know if he'd gotten lucky with one of the hot bartenders, he took a closer look at the woman beside him. Gazing down at his would-be lover, his breath caught in his throat. He'd been right. It was one of the hot bartenders, or at least what was left of her.

Torn open, her shirt exposed jagged wounds running the length of her torso. Protruding from avulsed flesh, he could make out thick wads of adipose tissue and lengths of intestine. She was mangled from the waist down. Her legs stuck out at unnatural angles, and the lower half of her right limb was missing; only a bloody stump remained. A trail of dried blood led out of the kitchen from where the bartender had been dragged. Eyeing the disfigured woman, he licked his lips. He was hungry.

"Oh fuck no!" He shouted, scrambling away from the corpse on his hands and knees. Climbing to his feet, he slowly backed away. "What the fuck is wrong with me?!" He raked a hand down his face but jerked it away. Both of his hands were painted crimson. *Is that blood? It smells like blood!*

He could feel his heart pounding against his sternum, quadruple its normal rate. *Where the hell are my clothes?* Frantically, he searched for something to hide his nudity.

Did I do this? No! I wouldn't kill anyone, he thought, shaking his head to rid himself of the horrifying idea.

Finding an apron hanging on the wall, he snatched it off the hook and slipped it around his waist. *It's not much, but at least my dick is covered.* He frowned at himself. The white apron did little to hide his blood-smeared nudity.

Creeping into the dining area, he froze just past the swinging doors. It was a disaster. Upturned tables, splintered chairs, and shattered glass littered the floor. Someone had scrabbled at the wooden floor, leaving bloody fingerprints and broken nails behind. Picking his way through the ravaged room, he was careful to avoid cutting his bare feet. I should go

First On Scene: A Howling Sirens Novel

out the back, he thought, digging his nails into his palms.

He couldn't bring himself to go back into the kitchen. He wanted nothing to do with the body. His stomach gurgled with need at the thought of the dead bartender. Gagging down his repulsion, he pushed forward through the wreckage.

The restaurant's entrance had been forced inward by something massive. Whatever it was, had split the thick wood, leaving behind deep, jagged grooves. The door hung haphazardly from one of its hinges and crumpled on the floor beside it were the remains of a security alarm. He could make out teeth marks where something had crunched on it and spat it out.

Worming his way outside, he pressed himself against the building. It was still early, and the street was uncharacteristically empty. He didn't live far away but had no idea how he would make it there without being spotted. *I don't even have my keys!* He shook his head and blew out a nervous breath. That was a problem for future him.

Keeping his back to the wall, he tensed his muscles in preparation and slunk around the corner before pushing off the wall and breaking into a run. He didn't make it far before there was a blur of movement in his periphery, and then he was down.

He gasped for air as he landed roughly on the asphalt. Rolling onto his back and curling his hands into fists, his attention was caught by the loud click-clack of claws on pavement. Still fighting to draw in a deep breath, he turned his head towards the sound.

Two enormous gray wolves paced back and forth, their yellow eyes darting between him and up the street.

Wide-eyed, he froze. Unable to hold his breath, it escaped him in rapid little gasps. Even naked and hyperventilating, he was ready to fight, but what was he supposed to do with wolves?

I gotta make a run for it. He watched the two large lupines. They weren't paying him much attention. *This could be it*, he told himself and kept his eyes on the pacing animals as he struggled to his knees. When they didn't react, he stood.

Selina Rossman

Again, he waited to see if they'd notice, but if they did, they didn't show it.

A sickening crack rang out, and he staggered forward. Another heavy blow collided with the back of his skull, and his vision blurred. A warm, slick substance drenched the nape of his neck. Swaying drunkenly, he took another step forward, and a third strike from behind brought him to his knees. A wave of nausea washed over him, and the world tilted sideways. Collapsing onto his side, he dry heaved as all coherent thought had abandoned him.

A menacing shadow fell over him, but with his eyes refusing to cooperate, he couldn't identify the figure. Darkness encroached on the edges of his vision, narrowing more with each passing breath.

"Hurry up! We shouldn't be out here like this!" A deep baritone growled.

"I know! I know!" Another man hissed.

Rough hands hefted him off the ground, and a scratchy fabric was thrust over his head. With his face covered, the darkness was absolute. Soaring weightlessly through the air, he was dumped unceremoniously onto a cold, hard surface, and two doors slammed as he heard an engine rev to life. Groaning, he used the last of his strength to roll onto his back. His arms felt like lead, and the back of his head throbbed painfully. The world around him spun nauseatingly. Unable to do much else, he lay limply and listened to the nearby conversation.

"The boss is going to fucking kill you!" Baritone snarled.

"He's not going to kill me! I've been with him since the beginning. Besides, there aren't that many of us. Which is why I was trying to help!"

Baritone scoffed. "Help?! You just wanted a higher standing."

"That's not true!" The other man whined.

"Oh, is that why you decided to throw all of our standards out the window and bite a fucking grifter?!"

"Okay, okay. I just thought that if we could successfully train a drunk hobo, then we could train anyone, and then our numbers would increase faster."

Baritone growled low in the throat. "This is why I'm the boss's second, and you aren't. We do things a certain way for a reason!"

"What reason?!"

"Are you fucking kidding right now?! Look at the mess you made. You couldn't even pick up the kid before last night! You might have jeopardized the whole plan with your stupidity!" Baritone snarled. "Now shut up! He's probably listening right now."

"No way, I hit him too hard for that." The other man argued.

Eric heard the sound of flesh on flesh and a yelp. After that, there was only silence and the rocking of the floor, soothing him to sleep.

Chapter Seventeen

"Wake up!" Someone snarled, slapping him in the face.

Groaning, Eric opened his eyes and squinted at his attacker. A stocky, shaven-headed white man stood over him. Eric could just make out a tattoo like a letter Z peeking out from under the man's shirt collar.

Eric tried to lift his arms in defense as the man moved to strike again, but he found them bound in place. *What the fuck?!* Craning his neck to look down at himself, his head throbbed painfully. He was completely naked and covered in a fresh coat of his own blood. Someone had dumped him into a metal chair and propped him up. It was bolted to the cement floor, and thick, iron manacles had been tightened down on his throat, wrists, and ankles.

Despite being barely able to turn his head, he took in his surroundings. Above him, a series of long cylindrical lights illuminated the mostly bare room. Empty wooden pallets ran the length of the space. He appeared to be in a storeroom—maybe a warehouse?

Glowering at him, the stocky man took a step back without striking him.

"Overkill, much?" He croaked, gesturing with his limited mobility towards the shackles.

Leering, the man loomed over him. He stunk of rancid fruit, dog, and grain alcohol.

First On Scene: A Howling Sirens Novel

Wrinkling his nose, Eric sank back against the chair. Anything to get away from the overwhelming stench. He swallowed hard, choking down the nauseating bile at the back of his throat. *If he hits me one more time, I'm going to puke.*

"Nah, it ain't overkill. I reckon it's just right." He spoke with a heavy southern accent, grinning menacingly to reveal uneven razors in place of teeth.

Eric blinked rapidly in an attempt to clear his vision. Did this guy have fangs? Surely not!

He strained against the restraints until pain lanced up his spine, forcing him to stop. He trembled all over as he tried to think around the pain of his throbbing head and his spasming back, but all he could focus on was how badly he wanted to put space between himself and the terrifying stranger.

"Now, is that any way to treat a guest?" A clipped voice rang out from behind him.

The brute stood ramrod straight and looked over Eric's shoulder as the color drained from his face, and he took two big steps back. "I meant no disrespect, sir. Just hazing the new guy a little."

Noticing that the man's teeth now looked remarkably normal, Eric frowned. *Am I concussed?*

An alabaster skinned man wearing a pinstripe seersucker suit with a matching tie, vest, and fedora stepped into view. The black pocket square tucked into his jacket matched black plain-toe oxfords.

Who's the fancy fuck? What do these people want from me?

"You're dismissed." The elegantly dressed man said, keeping his ice-blue eyes trained on Eric as the brute turned on his heel and left without another word. Somewhere behind him, a door slammed shut.

"I apologize for him. It was not my intention for us to meet like this." The newcomer pulled a set of keys out of one of his jacket pockets and undid the shackles.

Rubbing his burning wrists, Eric examined the divots in his skin. *Shit! Those were on tight.*

Intelligent blue eyes watched Eric closely. "The pain will subside shortly. The silver makes our skin burn."

Selina Rossman

Our skin? Why would it burn my skin? Gingerly picking up a manacle, Eric examined its inside and frowned. The fluorescent lights reflected off a white, lustrous material. Furrowing his brow, he dropped the restraint to the floor and met the other man's eyes. "Why?"

A slow smile spread across the man's lips. "You really haven't figured it out yet, have you?"

"Figured out what?" Eric stood and stretched until his back cracked. It made the pain recede slightly, but his head continued to throb, and his legs felt wobbly.

Chuckling softly, the man caught Eric's shoulder in a vice-like grip, forcing him to turn around and march toward the exit. "You're a bit slow, aren't you?"

"Get off me!" Eric huffed and dug his heels into the concrete floor. It did nothing to stop his forward momentum. The man was much stronger than he looked and easily pushed him through the open door.

Pale green walls, plump recliners, and framed pictures of smiling men created a surprisingly welcoming space. In the corner of the room sat a tall, circular high-top with two stools on either side of it. Opposite the table and chairs was a bathroom with no door.

"Go get cleaned up so we can have a civilized conversation." The man ordered and thrust him towards the small bathroom.

Eric stumbled and caught himself on the door frame and turned to glower at the other man. "And if I don't?!" He rebuked, starting to feel more like himself as the pounding behind his eyes was starting to recede.

The man shook his head with a broad smile. "I suppose if you really want to stay covered in that girl's blood, you can, but I assure you, you will not be sitting on the furniture until you shower."

Eric blanched and swallowed hard. "Fine," he ground out. "But I want answers when I'm done."

"Of course." Making a shooing gesture with one of his hands, the man took a seat in a recliner.

Hands curled into fists, Eric stepped into the bathroom,

First On Scene: A Howling Sirens Novel

searching for any means of escape. Finding only blank walls, without so much as a tiny window, he climbed into the shower, shut the curtain, and turned the water on. *Fuck, what does this guy want from me?*

Washing quickly, he tried not to look at the dark, clotted blood circling the drain. Emerging from the shower, he found a towel, a baggy T-shirt, and a pair of sweatpants folded neatly on the sink. He wasn't going to admit it to the controlling prick in the other room, but being clean made him feel much better.

Glaring at the man, he stepped out of the bathroom and folded his arms over his chest. "I did what you wanted. Now tell me what the hell is going on," he demanded.

"Of course, I'm a man of my word, after all." The dapperly dressed man gestured towards one of the recliners and removed his fedora, resting it in his lap. Undoing his ponytail, he shook out his blonde shoulder-length hair and then tied it back once more.

Eric took the offered chair, tapping his foot impatiently as he sat.

"Why don't we start with introductions? I, of course, know who you are. My name is Karl Neumann." He gave a small hand flourish.

"I'd say nice to meet you, but that would be a lie," Eric said dryly.

Karl laughed and shook his head. "We are in a bit of a predicament. You see, we have something in common, something rare. A gift, if you will, but it's not something that is given away lightly. Normally, you would have been tasked with proving your worth. Unfortunately, one of my men made a mistake."

"What the fuck are you talking about?!" Eric snapped, involuntarily baring his teeth.

Karl ignored the question. "You were recently bit by a drunk vagrant," he stated and examined his short, manicured nails. "He has since been disposed of, but I think you have potential."

Disposed of? Did this guy kill Hobo Joe?! How screwed am I right now?

"I still don't know what the hell you are talking about." Eric kept his voice even despite his clenched jaw.

Standing, Karl began removing his suit. "I know that you are a medic and that you people tend to lack imagination, so I'm going to show you rather than attempting to convince you."

Eric leaped to his feet, holding his hands out in front of him. "Whoa! I'm not interested in whatever sex cult you're trying to sell me on!"

Chuckling darkly, Karl finished stripping and draped his clothes over the back of the recliner. A toothy grin spread across his face as dense gray fur erupted out of his pale skin, and pointed ears crept up the sides of his head, coming to a stop on the top of his skull. Icy-blue eyes shifted to a deep yellow, and his face elongated into a muzzle; his nose became bulbous and darkened while his hands doubled in size, the nails growing into thick, black claws. From the waist up, he was now some kind of wolf-man, yet he was still human from the waist down.

Swallowing hard, Eric took a startled step back, collapsing into the recliner when the backs of his legs hit the edge of the chair. Heart hammering in his chest, he froze.

Karl was on him faster than his eyes could follow. Hot saliva splattered Eric's face. Pinned under the snarling beast, he trembled from head to toe, cowering openly beneath the terrifying creature.

Satisfied that he had asserted his dominance over Eric, Karl gave a soft huff and stepped back, fur receding to leave a hairless monster. His muzzle shriveled in on itself with a loud, shlooping sound.

When the change was complete, Karl slowly redressed, taking his time. "Do you understand?"

Wide-eyed, Eric offered the other man a jerky nod and swallowed hard.

"Good. Next, you are going to make sure no one comes looking for you."

"I... I don't... I don't have my phone," Eric stammered, still

First On Scene: A Howling Sirens Novel

cowering in the recliner.

"I had it retrieved."

Eric accepted his cell phone with trembling fingers. "What do I say?"

Perching on one of the stools in the room, he watched Eric closely. "The media is running with the bear attacks story." Huffing, he shook his head. "Tell your friends that you watched your partner get killed and that it terrified you out of your mind. Let them know that you are taking some time away to recover and that you will be out of town."

"Wait. Tim's dead?" His voice cracked.

Grinning toothily, Karl nodded. "Yes, he was your first kill. Now, send the message unless you don't care what happens to your friends."

Eric's shaky hands punched in the wrong code twice. Swallowing hard, he managed to unlock the phone. He quickly typed out a message telling his friends that he was okay but needed some time alone and sent it to their group chat. He knew Angell would assume he had tucked his tail between his legs and gone home to his parent's place, but he didn't care.

"Okay," he breathed.

"Good, now turn it off and hand it over." Karl stalked over and held out his hand for the phone as Eric recoiled from him but held out the phone.

"Now, I'm going to keep this short until you calm down. We are known by many names, the most common being shapeshifters and werewolves. Some are blessed with this gift from birth, and some of us are chosen. Too many squander their blessings, but I intend to use mine to its full potential."

Eric's chest constricted painfully. Grinding his teeth together to keep his mouth shut, he breathed through his nose and suppressed the urge to hyperventilate. His head was starting to throb again, and he could feel the vertigo kicking in. Digging his fingers into the plush armrests, he tried to steady himself.

"There are two more nights of the full moon left, and if you survive them, we will start your training."

Selina Rossman

"What do you mean survive?" Eric squeaked. He cleared his throat nervously and looked away.

Karl sighed. "The full moon forces you to shift. Until you learn control, you will need to be restrained. We can't have you continue to kill indiscriminately. The girl is fine, but your partner could have been useful to the cause."

What cause? Eric choked down the hot bile rising in the back of his throat.

"I'm going to go get you something to eat and will return shortly. I don't recommend attempting escape." Karl strode towards the exit, pausing in the doorway, he smirked at Eric. "Welcome to the resistance, boy." The door shut and a lock clicked into place.

Chapter Eighteen

The tones dropped, and Kitty tore her eyes from her phone, sitting up on the couch and pulling on her boots. Since being woken up by Angell's panicked phone call yesterday morning, she'd caught herself checking her phone every few minutes.

Eric had messaged their group chat, letting them know that he was alright but that he needed a few days to himself. It was the last time she had heard from him. She could respect his need for space after seeing a bear maul his partner, even if it was Tim. Zuri had gone silent since calling off their date, and Kitty was beginning to wonder if she'd fucked something up.

When she reached the bay, Angell was already stalking towards the spare truck, P8. He had been in a shitty mood since yesterday. She knew it had everything to do with Eric, but she couldn't shake the nagging feeling of guilt that had settled onto her shoulders. More often than not, being around angry people made her second guess whether or not she had done something wrong.

Meekly following in Angell's wake, she climbed into the driver's seat. She hated P8. The only good thing about it was that it was lower to the ground.

Keeping her eyes on anything but her partner, she hit the garage door opener. It rolled upward with a disconcerting clanking noise. Reaching for the aluminum lever on the side of the seat, she struggled to find it. After poking a hole in the seat's thin fabric, her fingers finally brushed against something hard. Flipping the latch up, she clutched the steering wheel tightly between her fists and waited for the old diesel to warm up.

She turned the key, and the engine grumbled to life, revving unsettlingly. *We shouldn't be in this piece of shit, but if I take it out of service, they will definitely shove us in a van. Angell can barely fit in those things.* Pursing her lips, she put the truck in drive. It shifted gears with a loud screeching noise and coughed out a cloud of black exhaust. Sighing, she coaxed the truck up the steep hill and onto the street. Setting the siren to wail, she drove towards the apartment complex to which they had been dispatched.

Parking in front of the three-story apartment building, she noticed that fire and police were already on scene. *Good. Halloween really was just a fluke!* Donning her gloves, she walked around to the back of the truck, where one of the firefighters was pulling out the stretcher, already loaded with their gear.

"Uncle Shrek," She chirped, grinning up at the taller man and grabbing the end of the stretcher.

Rolling his eyes, he returned her smile. A few months ago, it had come out that his niece called him Uncle Shrek because of his big ears and now Kitty couldn't recall his actual name.

Spying the attractive officer holding the door open for them, Kitty sped up, ignoring Angell as he shook his head in her periphery.

"Morning, Stark," She purred and winked.

Smiling shyly and playing with her wedding band, the tan officer looked away. With dirty blonde hair, piercing green eyes, and a tall, muscular frame, she always caught Kitty's attention.

She had no intent of pursuing a married woman but she couldn't help flirting, at least a little. Even if Stark was available and interested, she couldn't do much about it. Zuri had already made it crystal clear that she didn't like Kitty sleeping around.

Just inside the lobby, they found an elderly man sitting on a

First On Scene: A Howling Sirens Novel

wooden bench. He leaned heavily against a wall of silver mailboxes, his fingers curling into claws as he clutched at his chest. His complexion was ashen, and he had already sweat through his shirt. Little rivulets of water streaked down his forehead.

Shit, this guy is fixing to die! Kitty thought, rushing to lower the stretcher and pull it closer.

Dropping into a squat, Angell caught the man's wrist between his gloved fingers, checking a pulse. "Sir, we are going to get you onto our stretcher and check you out. Okay?"

The man's dilated pupils stared straight ahead, and other than his ragged breathing, he sat unmoving.

Frowning, Angell motioned for the others to help him get the patient onto the stretcher.

Settling the man on the gurney, Kitty gently removed his hand and cut off his shirt with her shears. Pulling a towel off the back of the stretcher, she patted his chest dry and put him on the monitor.

"Stay nice and still," Kitty directed.

The man continued staring straight ahead.

Biting her lower lip, she waited for the monitor to finish analyzing and print out its tracing. *Maybe I should call her. Holly shit, not right now! Focus on your patient, not your love life!* She shook her head and stared hard at the monitor while it printed out its report. *Yup, he's definitely having a heart attack.* "STEMI," she mouthed to Angell and hit the blood pressure button. The man's pressure was sky-high.

"Okay, let's go," Angell ordered, pulling the stretcher outside and towards the ambulance.

They loaded the patient into the back, and Uncle Shrek climbed into the front of the truck without having to be asked. He was good like that.

"Let me know when you guys are ready to go," he said calmly and shut the driver's door. Kitty could hear him humming along with a song on the radio.

They worked in tandem without having to speak. She sank two large bore IVs, and Angell slathered nitro paste onto the man's chest. Still not responding to them, the patient just stared straight ahead.

"We are ready to go!" Angell hollered and took another blood pressure.

"You got it!" Uncle Shrek yelled back and threw the truck in drive.

Bobbing his head, Angell grinned at her. "Nitro paste is working! His pressure looks so much better."

The rest of the call went smoothly. Very responsive to their treatments, the patient's color improved and he started to sweat less, even though he insisted on maintaining his silence.

The cardiac team met them at the back doors for a seamless transfer of care and on their way back to town they were toned out for the shortness of breath.

Strained wheezing met them at the door of the apartment, and Kitty knew they'd have to work quickly. Surprisingly, it only took a breathing treatment and a shot of adrenalin for the woman to make a turn for the better. They left Uncle Shrek with the Engine 3 team and transported the patient to the hospital.

Kitty loved working real emergencies, but as the town quieted and her phone remained silent, her mind began to race. Zuri still hadn't texted, and she was dying to know why.

Should I message her first? Kitty wondered as she huffed out a sigh and dropped down onto the uncomfortable couch in her room. *No*, she thought and kicked off her boots. She couldn't come across as clingy.

Her breast pocket vibrated, and she snatched out her phone in time to see Zuri's name flashing across the screen. *Fuck yes! Okay, be chill. I'm chill, totally chill.*

"Hey," she said softly into the phone.

"I need you…" Zuri breathed into the receiver.

Kitty swallowed hard, her heart galloping in her chest.

"…to come downstairs," Zuri purred.

"Be right there," Kitty squeaked.

"Good." Zuri hung up.

Shoving her feet into her boots, Kitty bolted out of her room and down the stairs. In her rush, she missed the broken step and tumbled the rest of the way to the hard concrete floor,

First On Scene: A Howling Sirens Novel

landing roughly on splayed knees with a startled yelp. Blushing furiously, she looked up into concerned, amber-flecked, hazel eyes.

"I didn't say you had to rush," Zuri teased and hauled Kitty to her feet. Kitty marveled at how soft Zuri's hands were and allowed her eyes to rake over the woman in front of her.

Letting her long braided hair cascade over her shoulders, Zuri was dressed in a pair of tight jeans and a low-cut, black tee that showed off her ample cleavage.

Glancing down at herself, Kitty frowned. *Shit, this uniform is so unflattering.*

"You okay?" Zuri asked.

With an audible gulp, Kitty nodded. *She is so pretty. I can't believe I've never seen her with her hair down before.*

Zuri eyed her thoughtfully for a long moment before her lips curled into a mischievous smirk. "Did you bring a spare uniform with you?"

"I always have one. Why?"

Smirking, Zuri let go of Kitty's hand. "Oh, no reason," she murmured and sauntered across the bay, her hips swaying invitingly.

Acting with a will all their own, Kitty's legs carried her forward.

Zuri casually leaned against the BLS van and waited for Kitty to catch up.

Kitty swallowed hard and cleared her throat. "So—"

"So, I have a promise to keep," Zuri said matter-of-factly.

Heart thundering so loudly in her chest that Kitty was sure Zuri could hear it, she held her breath. *What does she have planned?*

"I do feel bad that I had to cancel our date." Slipping her thumbs through her belt loops, Zuri rocked back and forth on her heels. "So... I figured it would be fun to make it up to you now." Cocking her head to the side, she grinned wolfishly and slid the ambulance's side door open.

Kitty caught a whiff of bleach. *Why did she clean the truck if she's not working? Wait... wait, am I about to get laid?!*

Stepping into the truck, Zuri grasped Kitty's hand in hers

and pulled her into the truck before sliding the door shut behind them.

Kitty leaned in for a kiss but was halted by Zuri's hand on her chest. *Fuck. Did I misread this?* She wondered as her cheeks began to burn.

Chuckling softly, Zuri gripped the front of Kitty's uniform shirt and pulled her close, brushing their lips together, gently at first, until the kiss turned heated. Zuri shoved Kitty against the door, letting her lips explore.

Shivering as Zuri's hot mouth found her earlobe and sucked, a throaty moan tore itself free, and Kitty let her eyes flutter shut. Enjoying the sensation of warm lips trailing across her jaw until they found her mouth once more, she parted her mouth invitingly, relishing the taste of mint toothpaste as their tongues stroked against one another.

Growling playfully, Zuri nipped her lower lip, and Kitty gazed up into twinkling hazel eyes that looked almost amber in the low lighting. Her stomach fluttered nervously as she allowed herself to be maneuvered against the netting separating them from the bench seat, but she quickly forgot her nerves as insistent lips found hers once more.

Using her body weight to pin the shorter woman in place, Zuri caught both of Kitty's wrists without deviating from her mission to kiss, nibble, and lick every bit of skin available to her and guided Kitty's hands above her head, binding them to the netting with a cravat. Smirking, she took a step back and admired her handiwork.

This is a way to use these better than making slings, Kitty grinned ruefully. "You know," she said, her tone teasing, "you don't have to tie me up just to kiss me."

Zuri licked her lips. "Who says all I want to do is kiss you?"

Reaching into a nearby cabinet, Zuri pulled out a pair of sheers and Kitty swallowed hard. *And now I know why she wanted to know about the spare uniform.* Straining against the restraints, she couldn't help grinning, they were well-knotted.

Zuri gripped the front of her shirt and tugged, sending buttons scattering across the floor as she quickly cut away the remaining material and sliced through Kitty's white

First On Scene: A Howling Sirens Novel

undershirt.

Cool metal grazed her bare skin, and Kitty sucked in a deep breath. "Please don't cut the bra off."

Smirking evilly, Zuri shrugged.

"Please," Kitty breathed.

Zuri winked and artfully undid the frilly red brassiere's clasps. Finding that she couldn't fully remove the bra with Kitty's hands bound, she slid it up her arms and used it as a second restraint. The feel of lace scraping up her arms and tightening around her wrists made Kitty gasp.

Gentle fingers tilted Kitty's chin upward, exposing her throat, and a thrill raced through her as Zuri sucked and nibbled on her neck. The feel of her lover's teeth scraping against the thin skin covering her bounding pulse made her shiver.

Zuri's hot mouth worked its way down to her erect nipple, lazily flicking it with her tongue before closing her teeth around it and sucking hard. In her free hand, she squeezed Kitty's other tit, rolling the nipple between her fingers.

Heat pooled between Kitty's legs as she moaned loudly. Desperate for more skin contact, she struggled against the restraints holding her in place.

Zuri yanked Kitty's belt off and tossed it onto the stretcher before cutting Kitty out of her pants. Wearing a teasing smirk, Zuri took a step back to examine her handiwork. Her eyes roamed the newly bared skin and lingered hungrily on Kitty's lacy underwear. Breathing deeply, her nostrils flared, and she licked her lips.

Squirming under Zuri's gaze, Kitty spread her legs in a silent invitation and waited to see what the hazel-eyed woman would do next.

Close enough that Kitty could feel her warm breath on her skin, Zuri ran her fingertips down Kitty's side and over her left hip until they found the panties' waistband and slipped inside.

Kitty sucked in a sharp breath as Zuri teasingly brushed a finger over her slick entrance and groaned at the sudden loss of sensation when she removed her hand.

Licking her fingertips, Zuri let out a soft moan. "You taste so good."

Trembling with need, her body screaming to be touched.

Raking her hands down Kitty's back, Zuri captured her lips once more.

"Oh fuck," Kitty hissed as the sensation of nails on flesh made her desperate for more. Her knees weakened, and she was suddenly grateful for the restraints holding her in place.

Kissing down her torso until her lips brushed against Kitty's panties, Zuri tore them off with her teeth and let the torn fabric fall to the ground before returning to her nibbling and sucking.

Groaning in frustration, Kitty arched her hips and let her head fall back against the netting as Zuri pulled away, smirking mischievously.

Eyes twinkling, Zuri licked her lips and dropped to her knees between Kitty's legs. With one last teasing swipe of her tongue, she buried her face in her lover's wetness.

Kitty moaned loudly and writhed against her restraints as Zuri lapped up her excitement while gripping her hips hard enough to leave bruises behind. Then, taking one hand from her ass, Zuri slid two fingers into her, curling them and caressing her slick walls.

"Oh my god, yes," Kitty panted, rocking her hips.

Zuri pumped into her, making Kitty moan louder with each thrust as the muscles tightened around her lover's fingers.

Kitty gasped and ground down against Zuri's hand as a third finger was added, and she slowly circled her clit with her thumb. "I'm so close," she panted.

Warm lips wrapped around her clitoris and sucked hard while fingers thrust deeply into her. Kitty screamed, an orgasm wracking her entire body. Sagging against the net, she rode out the aftershocks of pleasure with shut eyes.

Easing her lover's legs off her shoulders, Zuri stood and kissed her lightly on the lips.

Kitty forced her eyes open, her chest still heaving.

"So… am I forgiven?" Zuri asked, a cocky smile playing out on her lips.

"So forgiven," Kitty breathed.

"Would I still be forgiven if I left you like this?" Zuri asked, arching an eyebrow.

Groaning, she shook her head. "Don't. You. Dare."

Zuri pursed her lips, looking thoughtful.

"Come on... I'm still at work. Don't you know what a miracle it is that no one called 9-1-1 while we..." She paused, unsure of how to continue.

"While we fucked?" Zuri asked, nipping at her throat.

Kitty blushed. "Please?"

"Well, since you asked nicely," Zuri said, still grinning wickedly as she freed Kitty from her restraints.

With a groan, Kitty lowered her arms and collapsed onto the bench seat. Sighing contentedly, she let her eyes flutter shut.

Zuri laughed warmly and leaned down to kiss her once more.

The tones dropped, making them both jump.

"P2, please respond to Sixty-four Willow Street for the officer injured in a domestic! Police will meet you on scene," the truck radio squawked.

"Shit! I'll be right back with your uniform." Zuri darted out of the truck, slamming the door shut behind her.

So much for cuddling.

Chapter Nineteen

"Ambulance twelve!" The radio squawked.

Zuri shot her partner a questioning glance. He shrugged and reached for the mic. They hadn't even signed into service yet. The point of a BLS transfer truck was to take non-emergent patients where they needed to go, not to rush. Dispatch had some gall this morning.

"A-12 answering." Her partner, Charlie, said, using his best customer service voice. Zuri rolled her eyes. The kid normally sounded like he had gravel in his mouth.

"Ambulance twelve, please sign on with fire. You are the only truck available, and the police need an eval," dispatch directed in a pitchy tone.

"Copy that," Charlie said into the mic and switched radio channels.

Zuri sighed in annoyance and clicked her seatbelt into place. Police evals were always for the drunk, the sad person, or the uninjured human involved in a fender bender. She wasn't caffeinated enough to be starting the morning with the police's bullshit just because they didn't feel like writing a report.

"A-12 to ops. Signing on for town coverage," Charlie hailed, sitting up straight in the driver's seat.

Zuri could feel the excitement coming off him in waves. He still enjoyed responding.

"A-12, please respond to the CVS. Police are out front

First On Scene: A Howling Sirens Novel

requesting an ambulance," Fire dispatch directed them.

Charlie confirmed that they were en route and flipped on the lights. He made a point of playing DJ with the sirens as they weaved through the rush hour traffic. The wailing sirens faded into yelps and revved into power calls. Loud and insistent that cars move out of the way.

Charlie called 'on scene' and pulled in behind the fire engine.

The metallic tang hanging in the air assaulted her senses. Breathing through her mouth only made it worse as the sudden flavor of wet pennies made her grimace. There was blood on the scene, lots of it. She couldn't see the patient through the blockade of police officers, but she could smell him.

Her stomach growled expectantly. A quick glance at Charlie confirmed that he had not heard her body's betrayal. He was too busy rushing towards the police with the first-in bag slung over his shoulder to pay her any mind.

I'm here to help, not eat, she reminded her snarling guts. Shaking her head, she followed in her partner's wake.

The police parted for them, revealing a badly injured man. Surrounded by a congealing pool of blood, his muscular, nude form lay still.

Zuri stared hard at the man. His chest barely expanded as he drew in rapid, shallow breaths, but at least he was breathing.

Estimating his age, she assumed he was in his thirties. Severe facial swelling made it tough to tell. The man's eyes bulged grotesquely beneath darkened eyelids. Avulsed tissue at his chin oozed fresh ichor, and pale bones peaked out from the ragged flesh of his elbows and knees. Lacerations serpentined around the patient's torso like claw marks.

Charlie stood frozen at the man's head. His eyes begged for direction.

Always so eager to catch a serious call but never ready to handle one. Zuri furrowed her brow. She'd be taking the lead on this one.

"We are going to need a collar, O-2, and the stretcher. We're

Selina Rossman

also going to need the medics," Zuri said expectantly.

The sudden flurry of movement told her that her colleagues were snapping out of their stupor. Police ordered dispatch to send the closest medic unit, and fire rushed towards the truck to get the stretcher. Her partner raced after the firefighters.

She secured the man's neck in a collar and snapped an oxygen mask onto his face. When fire returned with the stretcher, they waited for her to give the go-ahead to move the man.

The town saw plenty of action. Public safety was well-versed in car crashes, stabbings, and even shootings. Hell, they had to shut down the highway for a fucked up car crash on a monthly basis to land the bird. The Life Flight crews were on a first-name basis with them.

But for some reason, this was different. There was something insidious to the man's injuries that gave them all pause. *Maybe I should go to medic school. I already know how to take charge of a scene.* She shook her head. *Yeah, because I totally have time for that between work and pack business. It's a small miracle I was able to sneak away long enough to see Kitty the other day. Who knows when I'll get to do that again...*

Crouching beside the patient, she pressed her fingers to his wrist. A thready pulse bounded beneath her fingertips. The man's tawny complexion was pale, his skin cool to the touch. She took a closer look at the bruising around the man's wrists. Realization struck her like a closed fist to the face, and she rocked back on her heels.

"Oh shit. Guys, he has ligature marks on both his wrists! There is no way he wasn't dragged behind a car with these injuries." Zuri frantically waved over a cop.

A balding officer with kind eyes dropped into a squat next to her and stared hard at the marks she was pointing at. His brown eyes went wide, and he jutted to his feet, standing ramrod straight, his complexion pailing.

"Shit," he swallowed hard. "I've only seen pictures of ligature marks before, but I think you're right. I'll tell the detectives to hurry up. In the meantime, try not to touch too much." He quickly strode back towards his cruiser.

First On Scene: A Howling Sirens Novel

At her nod, fire lowered the stretcher down next to her. Together, they gently transferred the patient onto the gurney.

She wanted to know who did this and why. Drawing in a deep breath, she sifted through the individual scents of stagnant blood, the stench of terror, dried piss. Catching a whiff of something acrid and smokey, she struggled to identify it.

Focusing on the vaguely familiar smell, she drew in another deep breath as they wheeled the patient towards the rig. The scent of oily sulfur clung to him; it stung her nostrils.

She frowned. *Why does he smell like fresh asphalt? The closest road work to us is two towns over. Why would someone go through the effort of dragging him all the way here just to dump him in front of a CVS? Gangbangers aren't that motivated to get caught. They would have dumped him in a ditch. Unless, of course...* She shook her head. *Not everything is rogue werewolves. Sometimes humans just do fucked up shit.*

Loading the patient into the back of the ambulance, her nares flared, registering the familiar scent of damp earth and canine musk. *Oh fuck. He wasn't dragged behind a car. A wolf did this. How the hell did they manage that without being seen?! Unless they just don't care about getting caught? Dad is going to lose his mind over this!*

Grimacing, she climbed into the back of the truck and checked on their patient. He was still barely breathing. He was going to need to be intubated as soon as the medics got there.

Charlie climbed into the patient compartment, and she ordered him to start bagging. Still wide-eyed, he did as he was told. Leaning over his shoulder under the guise of checking his work, she discreetly scented the air, but there were no other clues to capture. *They are clearly trying to send a message, but what is it?! The last thing we need is to be outed. Humans won't be able to handle that! They'll be terrified, and if this is how other wolves operate, maybe they should be.* Huffing softly, she took the man's pulse and a manual blood pressure. Both were too low. If the medics didn't show up soon, they would be working a code. *They should be here by now.*

Brakes screeching and billowing black smog from its

Selina Rossman

tailpipe, P8 came to a jerky stop next to her van. Wrinkling her nose, she stepped out of the ambulance to meet Angell.

He reached her in two long strides, oblivious to the dark aberration silently padding after him. The giant, black mastiff's jowls were flecked with saliva, and its scarlet eyes blazed even in the bright of day. It met her gaze briefly before turning its attention to her patient.

Zuri swallowed hard. *Does he know he has a Grimm tailing him? Is this new, or have I just not been paying attention?*

"Zee, you okay?"

"What?!" She asked, tearing her gaze away from the great black dog and refocusing on Angell. Eyebrows knit together and lips pursed, his eyes searched her face.

Shaking off her momentary stupor, she nodded. "Yeah, fine. Sorry." *I'll figure out what's going on with him later. Shit, I guess I can see more than ghosts.*

"What do we have?" Angell asked for the second time, drawing her back to the present moment.

"Uh, sorry." She shook her head to clear it. "A thirty-something John Doe was found down in front of CVS. His injuries are indicative of being tied up and dragged behind a car," she lied. "His vitals are shit."

Angell nodded and yanked his first-in bag and the cardiac monitor out of the side of the truck. "Can you give Crash a hand getting the rest of the gear? I'll just ride it in with you guys." Not waiting for an answer, he turned and climbed into the van.

Rounding P8, she climbed into the back to help Eric and froze. She breathed deeply and the hair on her forearms stood on end, a low snarl emanated from her throat involuntarily. Slapping a hand over her mouth she stared hard at him. *Since when is he a wolf?!* Her skin itched with the need to shift, to attack. Rubbing her arms, she forced down the impulse. *Not here!*

Peering at her with yellow-flecked eyes the size of saucers, Eric stood his ground and bared his teeth.

She took a large step back, almost falling out of the ambulance. "Eric, what happened to you?" She hissed, her

First On Scene: A Howling Sirens Novel

words barely a whisper. She knew his sensitive hearing would catch them.

"You're one of them," Eric growled through gritted teeth, his blue eyes fading to a stark yellow.

Fuck. If he loses control, we are completely screwed. I just have to get him through this call, and then we can talk.

"Eric, I need you to calm down, or you're going to shift, and that can't happen," she said, doing her best to make her voice soothing. *Did he get bit by whoever killed Tim? Why does this town suddenly have a werewolf problem?!*

Teeth still bared, Eric dropped into the tech seat and buried his face in his hands. For a long moment, he was silent. When he looked up at her again, his eyes were their normal aquamarine.

Zuri blew out a shaky breath. "Okay, I'll bring Angell the med box, and you drive P8 to UMASS. When we both get back to the base, I'll explain everything, I promise."

Eric nodded and slid the med box across the floor to her.

She grabbed the box and carefully backed out of the ambulance. Shooting him one last glance, she darted around the truck and headed for Angell.

The patient was already on the monitor, intubated, and had two bags of fluid flowing into him. *Shit, he's fast*, she thought and handed over the drug box. "Do you need anything else?" She asked, looking around for something to do.

Angell shook his head. "Nah, I'm going to have Charlie keep bagging, and I can do everything else en route. Do you mind driving?"

She nodded quickly. "Yeah, of course. Eric is going to meet us there. He said that he knew you would have everything under control." Her throat constricted painfully. She hated lying to her friends, but it was becoming more and more of a necessity.

"Okay," Angell agreed, leaning around the massive black dog, laying beside him on the bench seat, to look at the monitor.

Wait... he sees it? What does that make Angell? Swallowing hard, she shut the back doors and walked to the front of the truck.

Driving to the hospital, her mind raced. *Who bit Eric? What the hell is Angell? Since when is Hudson a hotspot for the paranormal? My dad is going to lose his ever-loving mind. Shit, I need to text the pack as soon as we stop. Someone has to know what we're dealing with by now.*

Shaking her head to clear it, she parked in the ER bay. It must have been a slow day since the only trucks in the bay were hers and P8.

Still giving her a wide berth, Eric stood near the ER vestibule. "I'll help them get him inside."

She nodded and pulled open the back doors. "Eric is holding the ER doors open for you guys. I'm going to stay here and start cleaning up," she announced and stepped aside.

Getting out of the truck, Angell glanced between the two of them and frowned. "Okay," he said skeptically and pulled the patient out. Charlie hopped out and helped push the stretcher towards the ER. The death omen trotted alongside the stretcher, its flashing red eyes never leaving the patient.

With the others out of sight, she sat heavily on the back bumper and pulled out her phone. Opening up the family group chat, she quickly typed out her message, purposely keeping it vague like her family had trained her to do. *S.O.S. Things are more out of control than we thought. I need guidance ASAP. Meet up?* She hit send and continued to stare at the tiny screen. She knew it was crazy to expect an immediate response but she was desperate for one. She just wanted someone to tell her what to do.

Sighing, she replaced the phone in her pocket and got to work cleaning and replacing gear. *Why the hell would someone bite Eric? If my dad is right, he meets the criteria for the other wolves. I mean, he's white, male, and straight, but he's not some secret racist. Right? No. Eric isn't like that. I know him.* Scoffing, she shook her head.

Charlie joined her, and she ignored his excited babbling. Chewing on her lower lip, she pulled out her phone to check her messages. No one had replied. *Relax, it's only been a couple of minutes. They're probably just busy.* Putting her flip phone away, she got out of the truck, leaving Charlie alone to finish cleaning up.

The guys returned with the stretcher. Eric immediately gathered up the ALS gear and bolted for his truck.

Pressing her lips together, she watched him go. *What the hell am I supposed to do with him? I can't even get near him without him almost shifting.* Blowing out the breath she hadn't realized she was holding, she massaged her temples with her fingers. *Hopefully, he was just startled and can hold it together for a conversation.*

The guy coded as soon as we transferred care," Angell grumbled, shoving his hands into his pockets and frowning. The black mastiff stood beside him, its tail waving lazily.

Why is the Grimm still here? I thought they only showed up when someone was about to die. She sucked on her lower lip thoughtfully. *Is Angell in danger, or is he in league with it? Can humans even do that?*

"Sorry," she offered, fingering her phone through her shirt.

"It is what it is," he huffed and shook his head. "We're going to head back to town. Eric's been in a shitty mood all day, so I'm going to feed him and see if that helps. At least he gave up that stupid diet."

Yeah, I'm sure he did. No self-respecting wolf can live on salad alone. Zuri watched him walk away, the black dog still following him.

"That was so cool!" Charlie practically shouted as they climbed into the front of the truck.

"Mmmhm," she muttered, pulling out her phone. There were still no responses. *Where the hell is everyone?* Dropping the phone into one of the cup holders, she blew out a frustrated breath and put the van in drive.

"Do you think it's busy enough for us to do more emergencies?!" Charlie chattered, not giving her time to respond. "I hope so! I want to do more *real* calls! I'm tired of doing boring transfers. Let's be real EMTs today!"

Rolling her eyes, she ignored him and navigated away from the ambulance bay and into the street, cranking the music to dissuade her partner from forcing further conversation on her.

Selina Rossman

Before she could call them back in town, the radio went off. "A-12, please take the response to 73 Park St for the hand injury."

"Hell yeah!" Her partner shouted gleefully.

Fuck! I need to get back to Eric and get ahold of the pack. I don't have time for this. Sighing, she flipped on the light bar.

"Received. Show us responding." She stomped on the gas pedal and darted up the road to their destination. Pulling up in front of the tan and white house, fire and police were nowhere to be found.

"A-12 is out," Zuri informed dispatch and killed the engine. Snatching up her phone and pocketing it, she got out.

Charlie scurried out of the truck, darting towards the back. Bounding up the front stairs, the airway bag slung on one shoulder, the first-in on the other, he beat her to the door. He knocked loudly, but no one answered.

"Hello! EMS!" He shouted, continuing to pound on the door.

Shouldering him aside, she tried the doorknob. It was unlocked. She had just pushed her way inside when she felt her phone buzz. Her heart leaped into her throat, and she quickly stepped back outside.

"You got this! It's just a hand injury," she said, giving him a gentle shove into the foyer.

Charlie swallowed so hard that his Adam's apple bobbed. "But..."

"Go get 'em, tiger," she encouraged, pulling the door shut in his face. Shaking her head, she walked back to the truck and yanked out her phone. Her brother had finally responded telling her to get to the falls immediately.

Shit.

Chapter Twenty

Eric wrapped his sweaty palms around the steering wheel and squeezed hard, only letting go when he felt the hard plastic start to give way. Blowing out a tense breath that escaped through clenched teeth in a hiss, he forced himself to keep his grip loose. *How is she one of them? I thought they were all racists fucks... no one would bite Zuri. Unless... no! She can't be part of the pack they want to kill off!*

"Dude, are you alright?" Angell asked, dropping a gentle hand onto his shoulder.

He blinked out at his surroundings. They were at the base. *I must have driven here on autopilot.*

"Yeah," he muttered, prying his tight jaws apart and repositioning the ambulance so he could back into the bay. Head still spinning with his recent discovery, he managed to scrape the side of P8 against the wall. "Fuck!"

"Do you want me to get out and back you up?" Angell examined him thoughtfully with his brow furrowed.

"No. I can do it!" He growled, throwing the truck in drive and repositioning it.

"Okay, Crash," Angell muttered, crossing his arms.

"Don't call me that!" He snapped, backing into the wall again.

Angell laughed so hard that tears welled up in his eyes. "But you make it so easy!"

Selina Rossman

"Fine! You do it!" Eric growled and threw the truck in park. Getting out, he slammed the door shut with a resounding boom and stomped his way across the bay, making it only halfway before the tones dropped.

"P2 and Engine 2, please respond to the Forestville Cemetery on the west side for the unknown medical," the ceiling speakers shouted down at him.

Angell climbed out of the car and rounded to the driver's side. "Don't worry! I'll drive!"

"Uh-huh." Shoulders slumping, Eric walked back to the truck and climbed in. *I need to talk to Zuri not to be fucking around in the cemetery! Where is she anyway?*

Angell artfully maneuvered the ambulance out of the precarious position Eric had wedged it in, flicked on the lights, and sped toward the graveyard.

Officer Stark had beat them there. He could see her waving for them from amongst the headstones, her pretty green eyes flashing in the sunlight. Eric swallowed hard. He'd had a crush on her since they'd met but not only was she way out of his league, she was married and unlike Kitty, he didn't flirt with married women.

Angell called them on scene and jutted out of the truck, making his way towards the officer and the patient. Eric rolled his eyes. He and Kitty weren't the only ones with a crush on the cop.

The fire engine rolled up behind them and Uncle Shrek met him at the back doors.

"Crash," the tall firefighter greeted with a wink and a smile.

"Hey," Eric huffed and yanked the stretcher out of the ambulance. *If I could just stop being a fuck up for longer than a few months, maybe people will stop with the damn "Crash" thing.* Shaking his head, he dragged the gurney towards his beckoning partner.

Taking up the rear, Uncle Shrek helped him navigate through the graveyard. The stretcher's wheels dug into the soft earth, leaving long, winding grooves behind.

Eric's heart fluttered nervously in his chest. He always felt strange doing calls in the cemetery. It seemed almost

First On Scene: A Howling Sirens Novel

disrespectful to rescue the living in a place of the dead. But what was he supposed to do? It was his job, after all.

A rotund white woman with curly brown hair and thick Coke bottle glasses lay on her back where she had fallen across two grave sites. She looked up at him, her cheeks flushing brightly.

"Hey, my name is Eric," pausing, he shot Uncle Shrek a hard stare, before looking once more at the patient. "Can you tell me what happened and what hurts?"

The woman blew out a breath and remained lying still. "I was cleaning off the headstones when I heard a loud pop, and my ankle just gave out. I didn't hit my head or anything but it hurts pretty bad to move."

"Do you mind if I take a look?" He asked, squatting down to examine her leg. *This is BLS all day. I should be back at the base figuring out what to tell Zuri, not doing her calls for her!*

"Go for it, just, please be careful."

"I will," he agreed and gingerly lifted up her pant leg. The right ankle had swollen to triple its normal size, and the joint was obviously displaced. The bones strained against the blue-tinged skin, threatening to break free. *Okay… so maybe she needs pain meds.*

"Alright, Ma'am. We are going to splint your ankle and then get you off the ground, okay?"

Tight-lipped, she nodded, her nares flaring when he removed her shoe to feel for a pulse.

Angell squatted down beside him and together they carefully cradled the injured joint in a pillow and taped it down. With gentle fingers, Eric confirmed that the foot still had a strong pulse.

"Ma'am, we are going to put you on a board so that we can get you onto the stretcher and take you to the hospital. It will be uncomfortable, but once we get you in the truck, I can give you some medication for the pain, alright?"

She nodded and closed her eyes.

Uncle Shrek laid the backboard on the ground next to the woman, and the three of them slowly rolled her onto the board. Whimpering, she bit down on her lower lip and kept her eyes scrunched shut.

"Okay, so this part might feel a little scary, but I promise we got you. Just don't reach out while we lift you off the ground," Eric double-checked that the straps binding her to the board were secure.

The woman gave him a curt nod without opening her eyes.

Officer Stark slid up next to him. "Do you guys want another set of hands?"

"Always," Angell answered immediately.

The four of them picked up the woman and settled her on the stretcher.

"Thanks for the help," Angell said, puffing out his chest and offering the cop an award-winning smile.

The corners of her lips quirked upwards. "No problem. You guys got it from here?"

"Yeah, absolutely," Angell replied, still beaming at her.

"Great. I'm going to clear up then. See you on the next one." Stark strode back the way they had come from and climbed into her cruiser.

Eric rolled his eyes at his partner, who was still staring at the police car. "She's married, you know that, right?"

Uncle Shrek chuckled, shaking his head.

"I know that. I'm just being friendly! You know I don't mess with people in relationships," Angell said defensively.

"Yeah, yeah, you're the King of ethics," he said, going through the motions that people expected of him. He was supposed to be joking around with his partner and treating patients. That was his norm, even though his life had been anything but since the full moon. He would just have to fake it until he could figure out what came next.

Chapter Twenty-One

Charlie had been staring daggers at her since they'd dropped off their patient in the lobby. Under normal circumstances, she wouldn't have sent him into a home alone, but she had pack business to attend to, and besides, if he couldn't handle a simple hand injury on his own, then he shouldn't be on the rig.

"I'm going home," she informed him, climbing into the driver's seat.

"Come on! We were having such a good day. You know they aren't going to find anyone to come in mid-shift," he whined and got into the passenger side.

"You should be happy. You'll get to just hang out for the day." Zuri pulled out her phone and dialed the supervisor.

"I don't want to just sit around! I want to do actual calls!"

Holding up a finger to silence him, she put the phone to her ear.

"Hello?" A familiar voice answered.

"Hey, it's Zuri on A-12. I'm sick and need to go home."

"Alright, I'll put you out for the day."

Hanging up and sliding her phone into her pocket, she looked at her partner. "Why don't you just ride with the medics for the rest of the day?"

Thrusting his lower lip out, he crossed his arms and glared out the window. "If they let me."

He's such a fucking child! she thought, rolling her eyes. "Eric

Selina Rossman

will let you. You know he hates writing up BLS reports."

"Fine. I guess you can go home then," he said, still not looking at her.

"Gee... thanks," she muttered and turned the truck towards the station. They didn't speak for the rest of the ride, and she was grateful for it. The last thing she needed was to listen to him bitch and moan because he wasn't getting his way.

Backing in beside P8, she breathed a sigh of relief. *Good, they're here.*

She rushed up the dilapidated staircase and winced at the ominous creaking beneath her boots. Yanking the door open at the top of the stairs, she stopped short. Eric was standing there waiting for her, his eyes glowing eerily in the dim light.

"Hey, Eric," she said, keeping her distance so as not to spook him.

"Hey," he murmured, stepping aside so she could enter the hallway.

"Let me clock out, and then we can go talk." She slid past with her eyes averted. Unintegrated shifters were always unpredictable, and she didn't want his wolf deciding that she was a threat and defensively shifting.

"The computer is down... again..." he huffed, shifting from foot to foot.

"Okay then. Guess it'll be a problem for later. Let's go outside so we can talk."

Eric nodded and followed her out of the base.

"Get in, she said, holding open the passenger door. "We're going to need some privacy."

Eric eyed her warily but did as he was asked.

She slammed the door and slid across the hood to enter the driver's side. "I hate to do this, but I'm going to have to keep this short. My family needs me right now."

"Uh, thanks for taking the time, I guess," Eric said softly, looking at his knees and raking a hand through his unruly red hair.

"Okay, tell me everything, but try to keep it short," she said, brushing over his awkwardness.

Eric blew out a shaky breath. "It started with Hobo Joe

First On Scene: A Howling Sirens Novel

biting me and ended with being picked up by werewolves with a white supremacy agenda."

Zuri stared hard at him for a long moment, biting down on her lower lip. "Okay, maybe not that short."

Eric flashed her a weak smile. "I got bit and woke up in the hospital. After that, I started having strange dreams and even stranger cravings. The nightmares kept getting worse, and I could barely control my appetite. I started noticing that I was putting on muscle without trying." Pausing, he flexed his bicep. It had doubled in size. "You should see my abs," he said, shaking his head.

"We're getting off track."

"Right. Anyways, the full moon came, and I shifted. I killed Tim and a bartender at the Kith and Kin..." He crossed his arms over his chest. "I don't remember any of it, but considering they're both dead and I woke up naked and covered in blood, it makes sense. After that, a couple of Karl's goons picked me up while I was trying to make it home. Karl kept me at his warehouse until all three nights of the full moon were over and let me go. For now." He shuddered.

"Who's Karl?"

"Not all werewolves know each other?" Eric frowned.

She shook her head. "Besides you and my family, I've only met one other werewolf before." *And I killed him. God, what am I supposed to tell him when he finds out it's my fault Hobo Joe is dead?*

"So who is Karl?"

"He's the leader of the sadistic fucks that picked me up. He's hell-bent on wiping out some packs in the area and adding to his numbers. I don't know what his end game is, but I'm sure it's nothing good," he sighed heavily. "And I think he had Hobo Joe killed."

Zuri's stomach twisted guiltily. "That's terrible."

Brow furrowed and shoulders slumping, he nodded slowly.

If he finds out the truth, he'll hate me, but I don't have time for that right now. She gave his shoulder a comforting squeeze.

"Zee, you know me. I'm not like these assholes. I don't want to hurt anyone, but I don't know what to do. They expect me to show up for lessons." Voice cracking and eyes glistening with unshed tears, he looked at her pleadingly.

"It's going to be okay. My Dad will know how to stop them and how to help you," she said with a confidence that she didn't feel. *At least, I hope he will.*

"So what's the plan then?"

"For now, I need you to stay here and pretend everything is normal. You haven't told anyone else about all of this, right?"

"Shit no! Who would even believe me?!"

"Good. Stay here and finish out your shift. Whatever you do, stay in control of your wolf."

"I'll try." He blew out a shaky breath.

"I just need you to hang in for a little bit longer so I can talk to my family and figure out our next move. Can you do that for me?"

He nodded slowly. "I think so."

"Good. Now go back inside and wait for my call."

Eric swallowed hard and gave her a half-hearted salute. "Talk soon?"

"Very," she promised.

Chapter Twenty-Two

Parking next to her father's car thirty minutes later, she sent up a silent prayer to anyone that might be listening that Eric continued to hold it together while she was busy. She crushed the steering wheel between her fingers as she drew in a steadying breath. *Deal with whatever is going on right now. Then, tell them about the tortured human and figure out how to help Crash.*

Exiting the car, the pungent odor of blood and the sharp, ammonia-like scent of stress pheromones struck her like a fist to the face. Reeling back, she gagged. *Oh fuck!*

Her mouth suddenly felt like the Sahara desert. Heart pounding, she snatched her medical bag out of the trunk and sprinted down the trail. The closer she got to the falls, the stronger the scent became, and the faster her heart raced. Whoever was injured should have been healing already; it was one of the perks of being a shifter, but the blood smelled too fresh to be from a closed wound.

Panting, she stopped short in front of the falls and looked around. Seeing no one, she wiggled between the large boulders at the base of the falls, shoving her medical bag ahead of her as she army-crawled down the narrow passageway until she reached the base of their den.

The naturally occurring cavern had been expanded through endless hours of digging so that she could stand up regardless of what shape she took. It was home. But now, the metallic reek of fresh wolf blood assaulted her senses, making her guts twist and chasing away any glimmer of hope that she might have clung to; someone was dying.

Two pairs of eyes locked onto her, glowing unsettlingly in the dim lighting. Back against the wall, her mother sat cross-legged, with her father's head and shoulders drawn into her lap. Junior sat next to her, pressed into his mother's side like a scared pup seeking comfort.

Breath hitching in her throat, she kneeled down next to her father's limp body, eyes raking over his wounds. "What happened?" She whispered.

Stroking her mate's sweat-drenched brow, Sierra shook her head. "We were trailing a pair of wolves from the other pack because your father thought they might lead us to their Alpha, but…" Voice cracking, Sierra looked away.

"It was a trap," Junior rasped out and swallowed hard. "Zee, their claws were tipped in silver."

Trapping her lower lip between her teeth, Zuri pulled back the blood-soaked towels with which her family had attempted to staunch her father's bleeding. Instead of the jagged claw marks she had expected, an unfamiliar symbol had been dug into his flesh. The large Z with a central horizontal bar running through it exposed torn abdominal muscles and pooling pockets of dark blood. Breathing deeply, she could smell the infection setting in. *Shit! Shit! Shit! How am I supposed to fix this?*

"I don't understand. Why isn't he healing?" She murmured more to herself than to her family and brushed her fingers over his burning skin.

Sierra swallowed hard, her throat bobbing. "There must still be silver in the wound."

Tearing into her med bag with trembling fingers, she pulled out a bottle of hydrogen peroxide. *Nothing I have is going to help with this*, she thought, dousing the open gashes in the cleaning solution until they fizzed with pink-tinted foam. Packing the wounds with all of the sterile gauze she had in her kit, she frowned. *This isn't going to be enough. I have to get the silver out so his body can heal, but that means surgery, and that's definitely*

First On Scene: A Howling Sirens Novel

not happening. Fuck, I need help!

Pursing her lips, she wracked her brain for the answer. *Okay, so I can probably cut the silver out! Yeah, that'll work! But wait, what if he bleeds out before his body can recover? If I'm going to do this, I need fluids and someone to monitor him.* Watching the shallow rise and fall of her father's chest, she frowned. *I need a medic. Shit, I need Kitty!*

Zuri cleared her throat, struggling to swallow around the lump in her throat. "I think I have an idea, but Dad wouldn't like it."

"Do it." Her mother hissed.

"Are you sure? I haven't told you my plan yet?"

Sierra shook her head. "I'd rather him be angry and alive than..." She looked away, unable to finish the sentence. "If you think it will help, just do it," she whispered.

Junior nodded, draping his arm around their mother and holding her tight. "What can I do to help?"

"I need you to keep pressure on these wounds," Zuri directed.

Junior gave his mother one last squeeze and shifted until he was kneeling next to Marcus. Hesitantly, he put his hands over the quickly darkening gauze.

"You have to push harder than that," Zuri said, demonstrating what she meant.

"Like this?" He asked, mirroring her.

"Just like that. Hold the pressure until I get back," she said, pulling back and wiping her hands on her pants.

Junior nodded, staring hard at his hands and the blood blooming beneath them.

She hurried back the way she had come, yanking out her phone the moment she made it topside.

"Hey!" Kitty answered cheerfully on the first ring.

"I need your help," she said, cutting to the chase.

"What do you need?" Kitty asked without hesitation, her tone turning serious.

Zuri bit down on her lower lip until she tasted blood. This was a big ask. "I need you to get me some medical supplies and meet me at Danforth Falls."

Selina Rossman

"I can do that, but what's going on?"

"I promise I'll explain everything when you get here, but I need you to hurry. Please, Kitty, it's important."

"Okay. Text me a list, and I'll be there as soon as I can."

"Thank you," Zuri murmured, ending the call, and quickly fired off a text with her requirements. She blew out a shaky breath. *Dad is going to kill me for bringing a human into this mess... if he lives.*

Kitty texted back. *I have a few contacts at the ER that can get me all this. If you think of anything else, just text me. See you soon.*

Zuri slumped against a large boulder, her tense shoulders sagging. She was lucky Kitty was willing to help, even if it meant telling her the truth. *I hope her contact isn't one of the women she was sleeping with.* Groaning, she raked a hand down her face. *Stop that! She's not your mate. She isn't even your girlfriend. She can fuck whoever she wants. Besides, there is no way she sticks around after this. I'll be lucky if she promises to keep her mouth shut without being threatened.*

Sliding down the smooth rock, she sat heavily on the ground, letting her head fall back and shutting her eyes. She hated everything about the situation. She was trading her relationship with Kitty for her father's life, and it might not even work.

She didn't know how much time had passed but before long she heard the loud rumble of Kitty's motorcycle. She forced herself to her feet and walked down the path to meet her. *Here's hoping she doesn't freak and that Dad is still alive by the time I get her into the den.*

Urging her stiff limbs into a trot, she made it to the small parking lot in time to see Kitty dismount her cherry apple red crotch rocket. Dressed in black riding leathers, she slung an equally dark backpack over her shoulder and removed her helmet. Her short blonde hair had been slicked back with gel so that not even the helmet could muss it.

Zuri's heart fluttered traitorously. Kitty was the only person that she knew that still rode a motorcycle during the winter,

First On Scene: A Howling Sirens Novel

and she looked damn good doing it. *Stop that! Now is not the time. Your dad is dying,* she silently chided herself.

"I got the stuff. Now tell me who's hurt," Kitty said, striding forward, her pretty blue eyes glinting in the sunlight.

"It's my dad," Zuri breathed, holding out her hand.

Kitty gripped her hand, threading their fingers together.

Shivering at her touch, she tugged the other woman down the path. "You should brace yourself because you're going to see some pretty unbelievable things today."

"Like what?" Kitty asked, pumping her legs to keep up with Zuri's steady stride.

"It's easier if I just show you and then explain afterward." Chewing her lower lip, she sped up. *If you don't run screaming first...* "You brought the lantern, right?"

"Yeah, I got it. One of the dermatologists was in the ER when I got there, so I snagged a headlamp, too."

"Okay, we're here," Zuri announced, stopping short in front of the falls.

Kitty stumbled into her and flushed. "Uh, sorry. So where is he?"

Blowing out a shaky breath, Zuri lifted her chin and met the shorter woman's eyes. "First, I need you to promise not to freak out about anything you are about to see and to wait to ask questions until it's all over."

"Don't worry, you can trust me. I know how to hold my shit together and when to keep my mouth shut. I just want to help."

"Okay. Follow me." Zuri stooped down and wiggled into the passageway that would lead them to her family. After a long moment of silence, she heard the scuff of leather rubbing against rock as Kitty followed her into the gloom. Breathing a sigh of relief, she crawled faster.

Sliding into the cavern, she stood and helped Kitty to her feet. Her stomach roiled at the stench of blood and rot that wafted up at her. She stole a glance at her mother and flinched.

Sierra stared at her wide-eyed, nares flaring and teeth pulled into a silent snarl. Her eyes narrowed in the sudden bright light as Kitty turned on the lantern and set it down next to Marcus.

Kitty glanced between Zuri and her father and dropped to her knees next to the injured man. Junior glanced up at her, his face a distortion of conflicted emotions.

"Come on, Zee, give me a hand," Kitty urged, quickly dumping the contents of her backpack on the stone floor."

They worked in a tense silence. Zuri could feel her brother and mother's eyes boring into her backside, but she did her best to ignore them. She couldn't blame them. She had done the unthinkable and brought a human into their midst.

Lips pulled into a thin, grim line, Kitty secured an IV and started dumping fluids and antibiotics into Marcus while she attended to her father's wounds.

Zuri pulled back the bloody gauze and choked down hot bile. In the short time that she had left his side, his tissues had started to turn black with necrosis. *Fuck, silver isn't a joke*, she thought with a shiver.

"Zee, this is really bad. We should get him to a hospital," Kitty murmured.

"No!" Sierra and Junior snarled in unison.

Flinching like she had been bitten, Kitty shot Zuri a questioning look. "I know this was a hate crime, but we can keep him safe," she whispered, glancing between her lover and her lover's family.

Zuri shook her head. "We can't. I'm going to try to cut out the infection." She cleared her throat. "It'll work because it has to."

"But..."

Zuri cut her off. "No. You promised no questions until afterward."

Kitty lowered her head. "Okay. Tell me what you want me to do."

"Just make sure he keeps breathing and try not to scream." Zuri drew a deep, steadying breath and focused on her fingernails until they darkened and lengthened into two-inch-long claws.

Not daring to look at either her family or Kitty, she sank her claws into her father's abdomen and began peeling back layers

First On Scene: A Howling Sirens Novel

of damaged flesh. She was fastidious in her efforts, keeping her eyes trained on the necrotic tissues before her. When she was certain that she had removed any area contaminated with silver, she drew back, letting her hand shift back. Cleansing the area a final time with sterile water, she packed his wounds with gauze and blew out the ragged breath she had been holding onto.

Fully human once more, she glanced at Kitty. The other woman openly stared at her with eyes the size of saucers.

"Now what?" Kitty asked, dropping her gaze to her feet.

"Now we wait. Our interventions will work, or they won't. Either way, we'll know shortly."

Unwilling to meet her mother's eyes, she stared at her father, willing him to wake. If he died, she had exposed their secrets for nothing.

Her father drew in a deep, shuddering breath, and his wounds began to close. His muscles knit together, and freshly formed flesh began expelling the gauze she had packed into his open abdominal cavity. He groaned, and his eyes fluttered open.

Sierra clutched her mate's face and proceeded to kiss him all over excitedly, tears streaming down her cheeks.

Grinning from ear to ear, Junior clapped Zuri on the back. "I can't believe that worked! Good Job Zee!"

"I had help," she offered, shooting Kitty a grateful look.

Mouth slightly agape, Kitty continued to stare at Marcus.

"You should probably get her out of here before he fully wakes up," Junior suggested.

He was right but she didn't want to leave. The sooner she left the den, the sooner she would have to explain things and the sooner she would lose Kitty forever—not that she had really been hers. "Come on, let's go," she said softly, gesturing for Kitty to follow her into the passageway.

Kitty gave herself a little shake and shut her mouth. "Coming," She muttered and followed Zuri out of the Den.

They made it back to the falls, and Zuri dropped onto one of the lower boulders. Holding her breath, she waited for Kitty to say something.

Selina Rossman

"I don't understand. What are you?"

Pursing her lips, Zuri tugged on one of her braids. "You can't tell anyone what you saw here today."

Kitty barked out a bitter laugh. "Zuri, I grew up gay in the south. Trust me, I can keep a secret. Now, what are you?"

Am I really going to tell her?! I mean, I already showed her, but I could deny it. No! She doesn't deserve that. She just helped me save Dad's life. Fuck it!

Swallowing hard, she ground out the words. "Kitty, I'm a werewolf."

Chapter Twenty-Three

Kitty blinked up at the other woman. *Is she fucking with me? I mean, it would make sense, but werewolves aren't real. Right?* She opened her mouth to speak, but no words came out. *Did I sleep with a werewolf? Wait, can you catch lycanthropy through sex? Is my life turning into a Sci-fi novel?! Is that something I even want? Who am I kidding? Hell, yes, I want that!*

"You can't tell anyone," Zuri said seriously and chewed on her lower lip.

"Let me guess, if I do, my life is forfeit?" Kitty asked, quoting a line from a book and failing to suppress a rueful grin.

Cocking her head to the side, Zuri eyed her like she had lost her mind. "This isn't a joke, Kitty. If you tell anyone, my family and I could be in very real danger, and they *will* retaliate with violence. You have to take this seriously."

Schooling her features into a more neutral expression, she nodded. "Zee, I understand. I won't tell a soul. I swear." *Not that anyone would believe me anyway.* Making hard eye contact, she willed Zuri to believe her, watching in fascination as the other woman's hazel eyes shifted into sparkling pools of amber. *Whoa.*

"I'm serious. Can I trust you?"

Reaching out, Kitty snagged her lover's hands in hers and pulled her close. "Don't worry. You can trust me."

Huffing softly, Zuri leaned into her, nuzzling her face into the crook of her neck. Kitty shivered at the feel of hot breath on her skin and encircled the other woman in her arms. For a long moment, they stayed like that, silent and clinging to one another.

"I want to know everything," Kitty murmured.

Zuri pulled away, averting her gaze. "I should go check on my father."

Shit! That was the wrong thing to say. "I mean, if you're willing to tell me more."

Zuri continued to look anywhere but at her, crossing her arms over her chest.

Fuck! Do something to show her you're being serious. Not knowing what else to do, she stepped forward, closing the distance between them, and kissed the woman in front of her.

Letting out a startled but adorable little yelp, Zuri threw her arms around her neck and leaned into the kiss. A soft brushing of lips quickly became heated and hungry, and she speared her fingers through Kitty's soft hair, giving it a gentle tug.

Kitty moaned, letting their bodies melt together and quivering at the rush of heat pooling between her legs as Zuri shoved her back against one of the boulders, pinning her beneath her and trailing her fingers down her chest and stomach. All of the questions she had ached to ask evaporated, leaving behind only the glorious woman kissing her.

Someone cleared their throat loudly and they sprang apart. Heart thundering in her chest and cheeks burning, Kitty struggled to catch her breath. Beside her, Zuri leaned against a large boulder, panting slightly.

Arms crossed over his chest, the young man from the cave glared at them. "Dad wants to see you. Now."

Zuri sighed. "You should go."

"Come over tonight so we can talk?" Kitty asked, hoping she wasn't coming off too desperate, but she didn't want Zuri to just disappear out of her life. Knowing her secret only made her like her more.

Arching a delicate eyebrow, Zuri grinned wolfishly. "Sure... to talk. I'll let you know when I'm on my way over."

First On Scene: A Howling Sirens Novel

For the next several hours, Kitty neurotically cleaned her tiny studio. It was three hundred and fifty square feet of jammed-in furniture. Her queen-sized bed and two bookshelves took up most of the space, leaving no room for a couch. She could barely fit her card table in the kitchen to have somewhere to eat besides the floor or the bed. But it was a fair trade for not living with other people. Zuri had dropped her off at her apartment before but had never been inside. *Is she going to judge me for how small this place is, or will she think it's cozy like a den?*

She'd covered the cheap card table in a blue linen tablecloth and set the table. She lit a pair of thin white taper candles and put out two glasses of water. She had a bottle of red wine stashed in the cabinet in case Zuri wanted it. *Do werewolves drink for show, or does booze affect them?*

The doorbell rang, and she jumped, almost spilling a glass of water. She rushed to open the door and grinned.

Zuri stood in the hallway, her hands thrust into her pockets, her pretty hazel eyes twinkling.

Kitty motioned for her to come inside and shut the door behind her.

"Are you making stew?" Zuri asked, taking a seat at the table and eyeing the candles. The corners of her mouth curved upward into a small smile.

"I figured you probably hadn't eaten much with everything going on today," Kitty shrugged, doing her best to be nonchalant despite her racing pulse. "I hope werewolves like venison as much as I do."

Cocking her head to the side, Zuri leveled an amused look in her direction. "Safe to say we do."

"Great!" Kitty chirped, setting the two brim-full bowls down on the table and sitting across from Zuri.

Zuri stared at her so intently that heat began to creep up her neck. "What?"

"Why aren't you freaked out by all of this?" Leaning forward on her elbows, Zuri stared at her expectantly. "I don't get it."

Blushing in earnest, Kitty rubbed at the back of her neck. "I guess I've read too many shapeshifter romances, and I like the idea of werewolves being real. I would have felt the same way if you told me vampires existed." She shrugged. "Wait… are vampires real too?"

Zuri laughed and shook her head. "Sorry to disappoint you, but vampires aren't real. The dead usually stay dead."

"So Zombies are real?" Kitty practically vibrated in her seat.

"Ew, no. Thankfully, shuffling corpses don't exist either." Chuckling, Zuri settled more comfortably in her seat and took a bite of the stew.

"Oh, okay." Attempting to hide her disappointment, Kitty took a bite of her food.

Zuri licked her perfect lips and grinned. " What? Werewolves aren't enough for you?"

Throat constricting, she almost choked on a hunk of venison. Blushing furiously and coughing, Kitty shook her head. "More than enough," she rasped out.

"Good." With a smirk, Zuri dug into her food in earnest.

"So… how is your Dad doing?" Kitty asked, rolling the linen tablecloth between her fingers.

Zuri sighed beleagueredly. "He's pissed, but he's alive."

"I'm glad he is alright, but why is he angry?"

Baring her teeth, Zuri shook her head. "He's livid that I brought in an outsider, but he'd be dead otherwise. He should be grateful. I know I am."

"So, does your Dad just hate all paramedics, or am I special?" Kitty snarked.

Zuri snorted adorably, and Kitty's heart fluttered.

"No one outside of other shifters is supposed to know we exist. It's a safety thing," Zuri admitted, picking up her bowl and using her lithe tongue to lap up the remaining juices.

Kitty swallowed hard and pried her eyes from Zuri's mouth. "Yeah, but you clearly have a Nazi problem. So, maybe

First On Scene: A Howling Sirens Novel

you could use some local allies."

Zuri's head shot up, the amber flecks in her eyes becoming more prominent. "How do you know they are Nazis?"

"The town I'm from had an infestation of them. That mark that was torn into your father, that's a Wolfsangel. Nazi scum thinks it's edgier than a swastika." Frowning, she raked a hand through her hair. "I've been seeing people with it tattooed on them around here for the last couple of weeks." She shook her head.

Brow furrowed, Zuri rubbed her temples. "I'm going to let that be a problem for tomorrow." Shoulders slumping, she propped herself up on the table with her elbows. "So what do you want to ask me? I'm sure you have tons of questions."

Kitty's heart galloped in her chest. She was dying to know more but didn't want to come on too strong. *Be chill*, she told herself. "I thought you weren't supposed to tell me anything?"

Zuri shrugged, tiredly propping her head up on her fist. "I mean, the wolf is out of the bag now, but if you're not interested in knowing more…"

"No!" Kitty cut her off.

Zuri yawned widely. "I'm happy to answer questions but could we stretch out on the bed while we talk? I'm beat."

"Sure. The bed works," Kitty squeaked, her pulse tripling. She had slept with plenty of women but never in *her* bed. Clearing her throat, she gestured towards the back of the apartment. "Why don't you stretch out and make yourself comfortable? I just need to put the food away."

Still yawning, Zuri nodded and made her way to the bed. She shrugged off her red leather jacket, tugged off her black combat boots, and undid her bun so that her braided hair hung loosely over her shoulders. With a soft huff, she jumped onto the mattress and stretched out on her back.

Kitty's heart stuttered. *Zuri is in my bed. Zuri is in my bed waiting for me!* Hurrying to join her, she blew out the candles, scraped the remainder of her stew into the pot, slapped a lid on top of it, and shoved the whole thing in the fridge. Sometimes, there just wasn't time for Tupperware.

Sitting beside her lover, she beamed down at her.

Selina Rossman

Smirking, Zuri rolled onto her side and propped herself up on an elbow. "Okay, fire away."

Kitty chewed on her lower lip thoughtfully. "Are there other types of shapeshifters out there?"

"I'm told there are, but I've never met one. Until this new pack moved into our territory, I'd never met any other shifters outside of my family," Zuri shrugged nonchalantly.

Does that mean another werewolf attacked her father? I'll save that question for later. I don't want to upset her. "Are you immortal?"

Zuri laughed softly. "You do read too many books."

Blushing, she looked away. Gentle fingers captured her chin, lifting her face until she was staring into sparkling hazel eyes.

"It's okay, I think it's cute." Zuri shot her a wink before dropping her hand. "We have the normal life span of a human, but as you saw today, our bodies heal remarkably quickly. Silver, severe blood loss, and decapitation will put us down faster than our bodies will heal."

"So, no tattoos once you've been bitten?"

Zuri cocked her head to the side, confusion flickering across her eyes. "Kitty, I was born like this, so no tattoos for me."

She pursed her lips thoughtfully. "But you can be bitten?"

Zuri nodded slowly. "Yes, it's part of why this other pack is a problem. They're making werewolves."

"Could there be a connection between the tattoos I've been seeing and the wolves they're making?"

"Maybe. It's certainly possible. I'll have to look into it tomorrow." Zuri yawned widely, showing off her canines.

"Okay. So what about enhanced senses? Is it like in the books where you have a crazy sense of smell and hearing?"

Zuri nodded. "Pretty much."

"And at the speakeasy, your appetite... that was just you being wolfy?"

"You could say that," Zuri said coolly.

"This is so cool!" Grinning, Kitty rolled onto her back. "I can't believe this is real!"

"Mmhmm," Zuri murmured beside her.

First On Scene: A Howling Sirens Novel

Steeling herself to ask the question that had been plaguing her since their tryst in the ambulance, she took a deep breath and blurted out what she wanted to know. "So... I gotta know. What are we doing here? Because I think this could be something real..." She tensed, waiting for Zuri's response, not daring to look at the other woman.

She held her breath for a long moment but blew it out when Zuri didn't respond. Stealing a glance at the woman in her bed, she chuckled softly, all the tension draining out of her. Curled on her side, head pillowed on her arm, Zuri lay beside her, fast asleep.

Fuck she's beautiful. I guess I'll have to wait for tomorrow for an answer. She gently replaced Zuri's arm with a pillow and pulled the blanket over her. "Sleep tight, you earned it."

Zuri gasped and startled awake. Images of the dream grew hazy the moment she opened her eyes, but the visceral memory of drowning in blood remained. Gagging, she shoved herself into a seated position and tossed off an unfamiliar gray duvet. Her skin felt like it was on fire. Choking down the lump in her throat, she willed her roiling stomach to calm down and ran a hand across her sweat-slicked brow. *Where am I?* Even without the heavy blanket, she still felt stifled and hot. *Why'd I sleep in my clothes?*

Releasing the messy bun that had shifted to the side of her head, she shook out her hair, enjoying the feel of the heavy braids cascading down her back. Rolling her shoulders, she glanced around the room, her eyes lingering on the sleeping woman beside her.

Kitty lay with her back to her, short blonde hair mussed from sleep. Tiny hairs stuck out in every direction, and Zuri ached to reach out and smooth them down.

A tiny smile tugged at her lips. *I must have fallen asleep while we were talking, and she tucked me in.* Exhausted from yesterday's events, all she had wanted was a hot meal and to curl up for the night, and that's exactly what Kitty had provided. The domesticity of it all should have made her bolt. With anyone else, it would have.

A soft whimper escaped her as her wolf demanded physical contact. Rather than fighting the impulse, she stripped off her jeans and T-shirt so that only her black lace underwear remained. Tossing her clothing to the floor, she slid beneath the blankets. Pressing herself against the woman's toned back, she draped an arm over her and nuzzled into her neck. Breathing deeply, she savored the delicious scent of vanilla and cinnamon. *Ugh, who am I right now? We didn't even have sex last night! My wolf is out of control with this girl.*

She had never spent the night at a lover's house before. In her defense, she hadn't intended to, but clearly, she'd felt secure enough to fall asleep. She could blame her lapse in vigilance on how exhausted she'd been, but if she was honest with herself, she felt safe around Kitty. And with her secret out in the open, the feeling only intensified.

I should get up and go deal with Eric and my father. At the thought of leaving, a low whine rose in the back of her throat. *Fuck it, a few more minutes won't hurt.* Huffing out a sigh, she melted against Kitty's backside. *She's not supposed to feel this good in my arms.*

Murmuring unintelligibly, Kitty flipped over so that they were facing one another.

"Hi," Zuri breathed, her lips quirking into a smirk.

"Hey," Eyes fluttering open, Kitty smiled sleepily.

A wave of guilt crashed over Zuri. *I shouldn't be lounging around when my family is still in danger... no matter how cute she is.* Furrowing her brow, she searched for the words to tell Kitty she needed to leave, even if it was the last thing she wanted.

Flushing prettily, Kitty dropped her gaze. "I know you have to go take care of your family."

How is she so cool about all of this? I've had girls dump me for less, and she hasn't wavered at all. If I'm not careful, I will end up falling for this girl, and that can't happen. Shaking her head to clear it, she pulled back, letting the covers fall away.

Kitty audibly gulped, her eyes fixing upon Zuri's bare skin.

First On Scene: A Howling Sirens Novel

"Uh… when did you…"

Grinning wickedly, Zuri kicked off the remaining blankets. "See something you like?"

Blush intensifying, Kitty licked her lips. "I mean, I'm not blind."

Snickering, she leaned in and kissed the adorable blonde in front of her. She couldn't help herself.

Kitty parted her lips invitingly, deepening the kiss.

Taking in the sweet, tangy taste of her, she groaned against her mouth. Slipping her hands beneath the soft cotton T-shirt, she raked her fingertips down Kitty's back and arms, delighting in the feel of firm muscle and soft skin. Pulling off the shirt and tossing it over the side of the bed, she squeezed the small, perky breasts before her.

Dropping her lips to her lover's throat, she nipped and sucked at the tender flesh, enjoying the way Kitty's pulse raced beneath her lips. Kissing and nibbling her way down, blowing on one erect nipple, enjoying the way it made her lover squirm.

Pulling away with a devious glint in her eyes, Kitty pinned her to the bed. Kissing her hungrily, her hands roamed, finding the waistband of her panties and slipping beneath.

Heart fluttering in her chest at the sudden loss of control, Zuri surrendered to her lover, her breath caught in her throat as gentle fingers brushed across her center, sliding through her folds and coming to rest on her clit. Kitty's mouth was everywhere at once, kissing along her jaw, down her neck, sucking on her tits, nibbling at the underside of her breast, and moving steadily lower, making her moan loudly with every touch.

Cool air brushed across her skin as Kitty tore off her underwear with her teeth. Giggling despite herself, she ran her hands over her lover's broad shoulders, urging her lower.

Kitty licked long swaths up her inner thighs, continuing to kiss and nip at the sensitive skin between her legs. Shivering, Zuri bucked her hips forward, hungry for more. Her lover's hot mouth found her core, lapping up her heat. Two fingers slid into her, alternating between thrusting and curling rhythmically.

Kitty's lips wrapped around her clit and sucked hard, almost making her come on the spot. Tangling her fingers in Kitty's short hair, she rocked her hips in sync with her lover's thrusts until a guttural moan escaped her lips, and she toppled over the edge into an earth-shattering orgasm. Trembling, she collapsed back onto the mattress. "Fuck."

Easing down beside her, Kitty kissed her. "I'm glad you decided to stay."

"Me too," she murmured, nuzzling her lover's shoulder and sighing contentedly. *Shit! Stop that! It's just sex.* Under normal circumstances, she wouldn't be so affectionate with a lover, even one that made her climax hard enough to leave her trembling, but something about Kitty made her ache to rub herself all over the woman, to mark her, to claim her.

"Sit on my face," she demanded, flashing a devious grin.

Kitty flushed furiously, crimson creeping up her neck and into her cheeks. "Yes, ma'am," she muttered and scrambled to obey.

Zuri steadied her lover while she straddled her face, placing a firm, muscular leg on either side of her head. Licking her lips, she tugged Kitty closer, showering the inside of her perfect thighs with kisses that made the woman above her squirm. *I love how reactive she is to me*, she thought, bringing Kitty's pussy flush with her mouth. A low guttural moan sounded above her, making her skin heat and her heart race.

Alternating between long, lazy swipes of her tongue and teasingly flicking at the sensitive bundle of nerves within her reach, she let Kitty's cacophony of whimpers and moans guide her. Gripping her lover's ass, she rocked her hips in sync with the long strides of her tongue. Dragging her fingers down Kitty's legs, she slid two fingers into her, pumping them in and out while circling her clit with her thumb. Grinding down on her hand, Kitty's slick walls grasped her digits possessively.

Whole body trembling, Kitty gasped and toppled over onto the bed. "How are you so good at that?" She breathed, her chest still heaving.

"Lots of practice." Zuri winked mischievously, slipping her fingers into her mouth and sucking slowly for one final taste of her lover.

Blue eyes trained on her. "Fuck, it's unreal how hot you are."

Grinning in earnest, Zuri pushed herself into a seated position and gently brushed her lips against Kitty's. Pulling back before she got lost in her lover's lips for a second time, she glanced at the clock on the wall. "Shit. I'm going to be so late."

"What are you doing today?"

"I have to go meet up with Eh..." Cheeks heating, she cleared her throat awkwardly. *I just almost told her about Eric. Shit, get it together, Zuri! Just because she knows about you and your family doesn't mean you should tell her everything! The more she knows, the more dangerous it becomes for her.*

Brow furrowed, Kitty watched her closely but didn't pry.

"Pack stuff," she said lamely, averting her eyes.

"Okay," Kitty said softly, pulling a blanket around her shoulders.

"Um, do you mind if I take a shower? I can't show up reeking of sex."

"Yeah, guess not."

Damn it, I'm screwing this up! I mean, I can't tell her everything, but I don't want to make things awkward. "You know, water conservation is something I'm pretty passionate about."

Brow furrowed, Kitty shot her a look like she had three heads. "What?"

Grinning, she slid off the bed. "Want to take a shower with me?"

"Oh... Uh, yeah! Yeah, I do!" Kitty said, immediately brightening.

A little shower sex won't hurt... I'm already late. What's a few more minutes? She held her hand out to Kitty. The moment she felt the woman's calloused grip on her palm, she intertwined their fingers and dragged her into the bathroom.

Chapter Twenty-Four

Still luxuriating in the afterglow of the morning, she rapped on Eric's front door. Knowing that the sunshine buzzing beneath her skin would abandon her the moment she stepped inside, she silently hoped that she had the wrong apartment. She would have much rather met up at the falls but her father had refused to let Eric anywhere near the den. Her word that Eric meant them no harm wasn't enough.

The door creaked open, and a wide-eyed, pale-looking Eric peered out at her. "Oh, thank fuck, you're finally here! Where have you been?"

"I got tied up with something." *I mean, not actually, but maybe next time?* Unable to help herself, she grinned toothily.

"Whatever, I'm just glad you're here now. Your dad has been making me crazy. He just sits on the couch and glares at me. He won't accept any of the food or drinks I offered him, and he's refusing to discuss anything with me until you're in the room!" he said in a rush.

Furrowing her brow, she put a finger to his lips. "Shut up, Crash! Wolf hearing, remember? He can hear you."

"Fuck!" He hissed and swallowed hard.

Winding a braid around two fingers, she sighed. "Come on, let's go in and get this over with."

Gesturing for her to follow him, he turned and strode inside. Huffing out another sigh, she followed him, shutting the door behind them.

"Hey," she greeted, taking a seat on the plush grey sofa next to her father.

"You're late," he replied, crossing his arms over his chest and glaring down at her.

"Well, I'm here now." Baring her teeth in more of a snarl than a smile, she met his gaze and held it. She wasn't in the mood for his dominance games today. Sure, he was the Alpha of her pack, but he was still her father, and she wouldn't cowtow to him.

Unable to breach their impasse, Marcus turned his amber eyes on Eric, gesturing for him to take a seat on the leather recliner across from them. Eric rushed to comply with the order.

Watching the interaction, she rolled her eyes. *Dad must be delighted to finally have someone to Alpha at.* Her pack was made up solely of her family members, and although her father was their Alpha, no one took him that seriously, and until now, there hadn't been a reason to.

"Did you seek out someone to bite you?!" Marcus barked in Eric's direction.

The younger man whipped his head back and forth in denial and shrank back into his chair.

"Dad, I already told you…"

Marcus held up a hand, cutting her off. "I want to hear it from him."

Yup, he's on a power trip. I hate when he gets like this. Shaking her head, she reclined against the couch, draping an arm over the top. *Sorry, Eric.*

Eric swallowed hard, his Adam's apple bobbing. "No, sir."

"Then how were you bitten?" Marcus leaned forward, bracing himself on his knees, amber eyes boring into the younger man.

"It was an accident," Eric squeaked. A pained expression settled on his face, and he cleared his throat. "It was an accident, Sir. I was at work dealing with one of the local drunks when he bit me. I didn't know what he was. I wouldn't have chosen this."

"What happened after?" Marcus asked, his shoulders and neck tensing.

Slouching in the chair, Eric stared hard at the carpeted floor. "I passed out and woke up in the hospital. I'm told I was running a fever and having seizures. When they finally released me, my appetite changed, and I was putting on muscle like crazy." Drawing in a shaky breath, he swallowed hard.

"And on the full moon?" Marcus pried, not letting up.

"I shifted, and I killed people," Eric spat out, raising tear-brimmed yellow eyes to meet her father's.

Baring his teeth, Marcus held his gaze until the younger man looked away.

Shit! If Dad keeps pushing him, he'll shift. Doesn't he understand that Eric doesn't have this under control? I told him this already! She nudged her father with her shoulder, but he ignored her.

"Who did you kill?" Marcus rumbled.

"My partner and a bartender." Gripping his legs tight enough to make his fingers blanch, Eric frowned, his lips quivering ever so slightly. He refused to meet her father's gaze.

"What happened after that?" Marcus demanded in a steely tone.

"Dad, lay off. I already told you all of this." She gripped her father's leg.

"I need to hear it from him," he said without looking at her.

Eric blew out a shaky breath. "A man named Karl Neumann had me picked up and tried to shove his Nazi propaganda down my throat." Clenching his fists in his lap, he shook his head. "He held me for the next two nights of the full moon and told me that I was part of his cause now. I said whatever I needed to to get him to let me go, but I won't help that sadistic fuck. I'm not like that."

"What is he planning?" Marcus growled.

Eric shrugged. "He wants to wipe out a local pack, which I'm guessing is yours. He also said that he wanted to make new members for his cause. Other than that, he wasn't particularly forthcoming."

First On Scene: A Howling Sirens Novel

"Where did they bring you?"

"Some warehouse in Chelsea. I overheard a couple of the guys talking. The place belongs to Karl's dead brother."

Frowning, Marcus slumped back against the couch. "Daniel is dead?"

"Wait, you knew his brother?" Zuri peered questioningly at her father.

He nodded slowly. "Yes, he was my friend. We moved to Massachusetts around the same time to get away from his brother."

"Wait?! There were other werewolves in Mass?!" She leaned forward, staring intently at her father.

He shook his head slowly. "No. They were human when I knew them. I don't know why anyone would bite Karl. He was a monster even when he was just a man."

Eric silently watched them, still cowering in the recliner.

Lips pulled into a grim line, Marcus dropped his head back onto the couch and shut his eyes. Zuri had never seen him look so defeated before.

"Dad?"

"Karl Neumman is the reason why we moved here. He is the reason why you, Junior, and your cousins were raised away from other packs." Marcus clenched his fists. "He was just a dirtbag lawyer turned politician back then, but from the moment he got a taste of power, he became a champion of conservative legislation. Always pushing some new bill that would chip away at the rights of people of color or the local queer population."

A tense silence fell over the room.

"Eric, why don't you go take a walk around the neighborhood for a bit," Marcus suggested tiredly without opening his eyes.

"Dad! You can't kick him out of his apartment!"

"No! I'll go stretch my legs!" Eric volunteered, leaping out of the recliner and darting for the door. Without a second glance, he bolted out of the apartment, slamming the door shut behind him.

"If only you listened that well," Marcus muttered, opening

his eyes and rubbing his furrowed brow.

Zuri rolled her eyes. "Keep dreaming, Dad. I'm not scared of the big bad Alpha wolf," she said, her tone dripping with sarcasm.

Lips pursed, Marcus shifted on the couch so that they faced each other.

"Karl is a real threat. He plays dirty and always has."

Zuri nodded, placing a gentle hand on her father's knee. "I understand. I know that I give you a hard time, but I am taking this seriously."

Marcus nodded. "And despite how stubborn you are, I do trust your judgment." He flashed her a brief grin that reached his hazel eyes. "I know you can't help your obstinate nature. You take after me."

Cracking a smile, Zuri squeezed his leg. "I know, Dad."

"So, can we trust him?" Marcus asked, serious once more.

"Eric is a good man. He's loyal and doesn't have a hateful bone in his body. He wants to help us." Zuri held her father's gaze, begging him to believe her.

He nodded slowly. "Good because I think we can use him to catch this bastard."

"Should I text him and tell him to come back?" She asked, grinning. *I can't believe he is letting me be a part of this. He never takes counsel from anyone but Mom.*

"Not yet. We need to discuss a pack contingency plan."

"Contingency plan?" She cocked her head to the side, eyeing him curiously.

"Zuri, I almost died once already, and if Karl is gunning for me, it is only a matter of time. I need to know that the pack will still be in good hands if something happens to me."

"Don't talk like that," she growled. "We're going to get him, and we're not going to let him hurt anyone else!"

"Just in case," he insisted.

"Fine. What's the plan?" She huffed.

Placing his much larger hand on top of hers, he squeezed it. "If something happens to me, I want you to take over as Alpha."

Mouth suddenly bone dry, she stared hard at her father.

"Me?"

He nodded. "You."

"But what about Mom or Junior?"

"If I die, your mother is going to be too intent on revenge to make sound decisions, and your brother..." He shook his head. "I love your brother, but I don't trust him to keep our family safe. I know I haven't always shown it, but I trust your judgment."

Swallowing hard, she nodded solemnly. "Okay, Dad. I'll keep the family safe. No matter what."

Brushing her cheek affectionately, Marcus leaned forward and kissed his daughter on the forehead. "I know."

Chapter Twenty-Five

Angell fished out his buzzing phone.

"I found her." His mother whispered into his ear.

Slamming on the brakes, he nearly dropped the phone. Cars behind him beeped impatiently, and he swerved off the main road into a gas station parking lot. Heart hammering in his chest, he threw the car in park and clutched the phone to his ear. He was taking up two parking spots, but he didn't care; this was the phone call he had been waiting for.

"Where?!" He hissed softly as if speaking too loudly would chase off the woman he was looking for.

His mother cleared her throat. "She has a shop in Xalapa."

Realizing that he was holding his breath, he released it in a soft puff. *Guess I'm going to Mexico,* he thought, pursing his lips. He hadn't been back there in ages.

In contrast with his younger self, who couldn't wait to go back after his father had moved them to America, he was hesitant to visit. He missed his mother, but she lived in the same area, and he didn't want to dredge up any old, painful memories. It was bad enough that talking about the bruja kept bringing him back to one of the last days he'd seen his unrequited love.

He had been happy to be home visiting his mother, but he had been ecstatic to be at the Dia de los Muertos festival with Miguel.

First On Scene: A Howling Sirens Novel

Crunching loudly on the amaranth seeds of his skull-shaped candy, he followed his friend's gaze. Just off to the side of the parade route sat a youthful-looking woman with long, raven locs. Her bright green eyes appraised him from behind the milling crowds. He had seen her before at family gatherings over the years. The family would sometimes consult her in times of need, but he had always given her a wide berth.

"Dare you to go ask her for a reading," Miguel challenged, grinning stupidly.

Angell shook his head. "No way, man."

"Come on, are you scared?" Miguel jeered, prodding him in the side with his thumb.

"No, I... just don't want to bother her," he said lamely.

Miguel rolled his eyes and flapped his arms, mimicking a chicken.

"I already know what a cock you are. You don't have to show me," Angell muttered, crossing his arms.

"Oh, he's scared, alright!" Miguel goaded.

Blowing out an exasperated breath, he smacked his best friend's shoulder. Immediately regretting the decision, he shook out his stinging hand. Miguel was thin, gangly, and all bones.

Grinning wildly, Miguel giggled and waggled his eyebrows at him.

"Fine. I'll go talk to her," he muttered, taking a step in the witch's direction. "Are you coming?" he asked, glancing back at Miguel who shook his head vigorously but gave him a thumbs up.

"Yeah, and I'm the chicken." Puffing out his chest, he shoved the rest of his skull candy into his mouth and marched towards the bruja's table. He didn't want a reading, but he couldn't let Miguel think he was scared.

Sitting behind a small, circular table, Isabella Garcia idly shuffled a deck of golden tarot cards. She set them down in two stacks on top of the violet-colored tablecloth and looked up at him. "Hello, Angell. Please sit."

Pulling the small wooden stool away from the table, he sat down. "I'm surprised you remember me."

Selina Rossman

The corners of her mouth flipped up into a small smile as she combined the two stacks of cards and handed them over. "Shuffle."

Angell did as he was asked and then returned the tarot to their owner, shivering when her fingers brushed his.

Setting the deck down between them, she rested a hand on top of it but did not reveal any of the cards. "Things have been difficult for your parents."

He rolled his eyes. *Yeah, because that isn't common knowledge or anything.* His mother had moved back to Mexico City after the divorce to be closer to family. *Maybe my family has been giving this lady too much credit.*

Isabella pulled three cards off the stack and laid them face up in front of him. Tapping the two of the cards, her eyes locked onto his. "The Lovers and the Three of Swords have chosen you."

Squirming under her gaze, he looked down at the spread before him. The first card held an image of two skeletons wound together in a passionate embrace. The second was a picture of a black human heart with three swords plunged into it.

"You crave a great love, but you are too afraid to ask for it," she murmured, tapping the two cards and pursing her lips knowingly.

I bet she tells everyone that, he thought, keeping his face neutral. He'd been raised on tales of magical women with powerful gifts. And while they might just be stories, he wasn't willing to risk it. He didn't need any hexes thrown his way.

Isabella pointed to a card with a hooded figure that carried a scythe in one skeletal hand and rested the other atop the head of a giant black dog with flaming red eyes. "Death."

"Am I going to die?" He asked, struggling to keep a straight face. *This is totally a scam! I'm a healthy fifteen-year-old. I won't be dropping dead any time soon!*

Her intense green eyes burned into him, and she tapped the card again. "You already have. The mark of Santa Muerte is on you. It is only a matter of time before she calls upon you."

What is that supposed to mean?! he thought, the tiny hairs on his arms standing on end.

Thin-lipped, Isabella began gathering up her belongings and packing them away.

"Uh, how much do I owe you?"

"No charge," She muttered and wandered away without so much as a goodbye.

He had watched her go and wondered if there was any truth to her words.

Trying to rid himself of the memory, Angell shook his head. Too afraid to question his mother about any near-death experiences he might have had as a child, he had pretended that the reading never happened. He didn't even tell Miguel what the cards had told him. But things had changed. A reaper haunted him, and he needed to know why and, more importantly, how to banish it.

On the other side of the line, his mother was quiet.

Shit, how long have I been lost in my head?

"Do you know the name of the shop or where in Xalapa it is?"

His mother sighed. "No. I have told you all that I know."

"If you don't have any other information, how am I supposed to find her?" He asked, his shoulders slumping.

"Miguel lives in Xalapa. He is a Policía Federal. Perhaps he can help you?"

"Fuck no," Angell grumbled under his breath. Miguel was the last person on earth that he wanted to ask for help. At one point, it had been the highlight of his year to visit his best friend in Mexico every summer, but they hadn't seen each other in years, and he was loath to change that.

"Angell?"

"That's a good idea. Can you send me his number?"

"Of course! When you come to Mexico, you will visit, yes?"

She lived in a province north of Veracruz, and he would make sure to see her before he returned to the States. "Yes,

Mama," He promised.

Chapter Twenty-Six

Wiping his sweaty palms down his jeans, Angell stepped into the airport terminal. Swallowing hard, he raked his gaze across the crowd, letting it settle on Miguel's crooked smirk and twinkling umber eyes. It had been years since they'd seen each other, and his heart fluttered at the sight of him.

Miguel's full lips and bright smile remained the same, but that was where the familiarity ended. Clean-cut with a manicured mustache and beard, a prominent jaw, and wide, brawny shoulders, the man gave new meaning to tall, dark, and handsome. His black T-shirt clung to his toned arms, partially obscuring the dragon tattoo encircling his right bicep, and his tan shorts showed off toned legs.

Oh, fuck me. When did he turn into a brown Adonis? Choking down the lump that had suddenly formed in his throat, he raised a hand in greeting and pushed his way through the crowd.

Throwing his arms around him, Miguel yanked him into a tight embrace. Patting him enthusiastically on the back before letting him go. "It's so good to see you!" He announced, grinning broadly.

"Is this really the kid I grew up with?" Angell teased, a smile tugging at his lips.

"At your service!" Miguel bowed playfully and shot him a wink.

Selina Rossman

"You look really good, man," he admitted, hooking his thumbs into his belt loops.

Miguel chuckled. "Yeah, well, the Federales don't let twigs into their ranks, so I had to put on some muscle for the job." Flexing his large biceps, he grinned. "Besides, the chicks dig it. I know my girl does."

Angel nodded, pursing his lips. *Right, he's still straight. That hasn't changed.*

Oblivious to his discomfort, Miguel spun on his heel, gesturing for him to follow. "Let's get out of here. You'll crash at my place tonight so Teresa, my girlfriend, can meet you, and then we'll get to work finding your bruja tomorrow."

"Great," Angell said dryly, stuffing his hands into his pockets and letting his childhood friend lead him toward the luggage carousel to pick up his small duffle. Snatching up the bag, he slung it over his shoulder and looked expectantly at Miguel.

"That's all you brought?"

He shrugged. "I travel light." *Because I don't want to stay a second longer than I have to.* Time and distance had let him forget the intensity of his crush but in Miguel's close proximity, the feelings came rushing back. Heart slamming in his chest and stomach churning nervously, he swallowed hard. *God, I hope he's forgotten about the last time we saw each other and doesn't think I'm still into him.*

"Great," Miguel said, turning and heading for the exit.

Following him, his eyes immediately narrowed in on the perfectly toned ass striding ahead of him. *I'm SO screwed!* he thought, forcing himself to look away and not imagine what it would feel like to run his hands over the corded muscles of his friend's legs. *Focus on your mission! You came here to find Isabella!* He silently chided himself, blowing out an exasperated breath.

The double doors slid open, and a swell of warm, fetid air rolled over him. The warmth was welcome after too many years in the frigid north, but he could live without the smell. The area around the airport had always stunk like sewage and hadn't changed in his absence.

Parked just outside in the tow zone sat an ancient-looking

First On Scene: A Howling Sirens Novel

black and white Volkswagen Beetle police car. Its red and blue lights flashed in the light of the setting sun.

Angell scoffed, grateful for the bizarre distraction. "Good to see the Mexican police are just as underfunded as ours. I feel sorry for the poor bastard stuck driving that hunk of junk."

Frowning, Miguel walked over to the car, a deep blush blooming on his cheeks. Unlocking the squad car, he looked pointedly at him. "Are you coming?"

Angell laughed so hard that he had to brace himself on his knees.

"It's not funny. I'm still not that senior on the force, so this is what they gave me," Miguel pouted, looking more like the boy he had grown up with.

"Did you piss off one of your higher-ups, or do they just hate you?!" Angell mocked, standing and pressing a hand to his stomach.

"Yeah, yeah, so funny. Now, get in the car before I lock you in the back."

"Okay, okay!" Angell said, holding up his hands and striding towards the tiny squad car. Still shaking his head gleefully, he climbed into the passenger seat. *Damn, I needed that! Good to know that just because he got hotter doesn't mean he's any less of a dork.*

Thin-lipped, Miguel squeezed into the driver's side and threw the car in drive.

Feeling remarkably lighter, Angell relaxed into his seat. "How long have you been on the force?"

"This year makes four. It's actually where I met Teresa."

"Wait? You've been in the department for four years, and they still force you to drive this clown car?" Furrowing his brow, he stared at his friend.

Miguel shrugged, keeping his eyes on the road. "It was supposed to be short term, but a couple of the squads got wrecked, and they haven't replaced them."

"I see. What about Teresa? Is she a cop, too?" He asked, clenching his teeth until pain lanced across his jaw. *Stop it! He's allowed to have a girlfriend. He doesn't belong to you and never did.*

"Nah, thankfully, she's in dispatch. I think I'd go crazy if I had to worry about her out on the streets." A soft smile settled on Miguel's lips. "We didn't get together at first, even though I wanted to. She's beautiful, smart and so funny! You'll see when you meet her tonight. But anyways, we were friends for a few years before I found the courage to ask her out."

Pressing his lips flat, Angell looked out the window. "That's good," he said blandly.

"What about you? Your mom said you're a medic? How do you like it?"

"Yeah. I've had my medic for a little over five years now. I really like the town I serve, and I have amazing partners. If I'm being honest, they're more like family than coworkers. One of my partners, Kitty, is actually one of the reasons I reached out to Mom in the first place."

"Wow, I wish I was that close with anyone in my department," Miguel admitted, shaking his head. "How's the love life? You grew into a looker. I'm sure the girls are throwing themselves at you plenty?"

Angell's cheeks burned. "I do okay." It wasn't a lie. He'd never had a problem finding a willing partner to warm his bed when the mood struck, but relationships were something else entirely.

"I knew you would." Grinning, Miguel pulled the car to a stop against the curb in front of an apartment building.

"Is this even a parking spot?"

"No, but it's fine. I park here all the time," Miguel said and got out of the cruiser.

Shaking his head, Angell slung his bag over his shoulder and followed his friend into the building's lobby. Seated behind a desk, a man with a thick, black mustache glanced up at them, offering them a nod before returning his attention to the magazine lying open in front of him.

They took the elevator to the fourth floor, enjoying a comfortable silence. The doors slid open with a soft chime.

"I'm at the very end." Tugging his keys out of his pocket, Miguel strode down the carpet-lined hallway. Stopping in front of a door, he pushed into the apartment and hollered.

First On Scene: A Howling Sirens Novel

"Honey, I'm home!"

Met by silence, Angell's shoulders sagged. He wasn't ready to face Miguel's girlfriend. Setting his bag down and closing the door behind him, he looked around. The space was segmented into a den, kitchen, and dining room. The kitchen was separated by a bar with stools tucked beneath it, and the small area allotted to the dining room was crammed with furniture. A large rectangular table sat in the middle of the room, surrounded by plastic chairs. The table's wooden top gleamed with fresh wax. The den consisted of a comfortable-looking green futon on wooden slats, a small coffee table from Ikea, and a leather rocking chair. Across from the futon was an entertainment system that harbored a PS5 and small flat-screen TV.

"Guess she's out. Probably picking up last-minute supplies for dinner," Miguel shrugged and pointed to the futon. "You'll sleep there since we only have the one bedroom."

"What, you don't want to snuggle?" Angell snarked before he could stop himself. *Uhg! I need to shut up! He probably won't find that funny.*

Miguel's eyes widened, and he hastily dashed into the kitchen. If Angell didn't know better, he would have sworn he'd caught a slight blush on the man's cheeks. But that couldn't be true. Miguel was straight. And more importantly, not interested. He never would be.

"You want a beer?" Miguel called from the kitchen.

"Sure," Angell said, dropping onto the overly firm futon and frowning. *Not sure how much sleep I'll be getting on this thing.*

Returning with a Corona for each of them, Miguel took a seat next to Angell and passed him a beer. Raising his own to his lips, he took a tentative sip. Pushing the wedge of lime deeper into the bottle, Angell raised the beer in a quiet toast and took a swig. *I got this. I just gotta keep talking to a minimum, find Isabella, and then go home. I can ignore my infatuation for a few days.*

"I know it was a joke, but you should know I had the worst crush on you when we were kids."

Selina Rossman

What?! Throat constricting, Angell coughed and spewed beer all over the coffee table. "Oh fuck! Sorry!" He gasped, his cheeks burning.

"I got it." Miguel dashed into the kitchen, quickly returning with a roll of paper towels. Tearing off a wad of paper, he soaked up the liquid. "Sorry," he murmured, refusing to look at him.

Heart hammering so hard that he could feel his pulse banging in his throat, Angell blew out an uneven breath. When he'd been younger, he would have killed for any admittance of attraction from Miguel but the timing was all wrong. The guy had a girlfriend, and he wasn't about to enable cheating. He didn't do that shit.

Stealing a glance in his direction, Miguel looked away just as quickly.

I should say something encouraging. "What the fuck, man?!" He snapped. *Or that, I guess.*

Miguel flinched like he had been struck.

Drawing in a deep breath to steady himself, Angell stared at the other man until he looked up at him. "What I mean is, where was this when we were kids? That night after the reading, I tried to tell you how I felt, and you just blew me off and then stopped talking to me." Raking a hand through his curls, he shook his head. "It's bullshit that you want to drop this in my lap now. I didn't even want to ask you for help, but I didn't have a choice, and now you just want to act like…"

Gentle lips pressed against his, effectively shutting him up. *Is this really happening right now?!* Parting his lips invitingly, he groaned at the brush of Miguel's tongue against his. The man tasted of cherry chapstick, hops, and lime. It was better than anything Angell could have imagined.

He shivered at the feel of Miguel's hot mouth searing kisses down his jaw and throat. Firm hands tangled in his curls and pushed him to the futon below them. Teeth scraped possessively over his burning skin, and he ached to lose himself in the other man's touch, but a guilty consciousness had already started gnawing at him.

"Wait," Angell hissed, shoving Miguel off of him. *Damn it,*

First On Scene: A Howling Sirens Novel

why does doing the right thing feel so bad? Erection straining uncomfortably against the rough denim of his jeans, he wanted nothing more than to feel his childhood friend's hot mouth on every inch of him, but he wouldn't help him cheat. He wouldn't be his sidepiece. He didn't mind sleeping with closeted men, but he'd be damned before he let anyone turn him into a dirty secret, even Miguel.

Confusion flashed across the handsome man's eyes, but he said nothing.

Blowing out a frustrated breath, Angell sat up. "I won't help you cheat."

Peering down at him, the tension on Miguel's face evaporated, leaving behind a wide grin. He shook his head, chuckling.

Am I being punked right now? Lips pursed, Angell stared hard at his friend.

"I'm in an open relationship, you idiot."

"What?" Angell croaked, his throat constricting.

"I'm not a cheater."

"Oh," Angell muttered, dropping back to the futon. *Are we really doing this?*

"Now, can I go back to what I was doing?" Miguel asked, his dark eyes twinkling with amusement.

Nodding, Angell swallowed hard.

Miguel straddled him, stripping him of his T-shirt and tossing it to the floor before leaning down and capturing the other man's lips with his own.

Angell melted into the kiss, his hands wandering under the man's shirt, the feel of hard, coiled muscle under his fingertips making him moan. *Fuck, he's so hot!*

Miguel's hot mouth moved lower, leaving behind a trail of heated kisses and possessive nips, and all coherent thought abandoned him.

Are we really doing this after all these years? Miguel knelt before him and started on his belt buckle. *Apparently, we are,* he thought. Sighing contentedly, he let his eyelids drift shut. *I could get used to this.*

Chapter Twenty-Seven

Oh goodie... I get to play partner roulette. Kitty frowned down at Angell's text message saying he'd be gone for the week. With a beleaguered sigh, she wandered down the stairs into the ambulance bay. She knew better than to hope a certain wolf-woman would pick up the shift with her. Even if she wasn't working the double medic truck, Zuri had her hands full.

They hadn't spoken much since the woman had left her apartment, but she couldn't stop thinking about their time together in the ambulance, in her bed, and in the shower.

Insanely hot, passionate, and not entirely human, Zuri was a fantasy come true. She'd never met anyone like her, or at least she didn't think she had. Who knew if there were werewolves in Alabama?

Shaking her head, she strode across the bay. She'd missed her chance to tell Zuri that she wanted more and probably wouldn't get another any time soon. *If she'd even date a human.* Her mouth went dry. *What if I tell her I want more, and she laughs?* She shook her head. *Nah, she's not mean like that. Would her pack even let her be with me?*

Rolling her stiff shoulders, she pried open P8's side door and climbed into the patient compartment. Rummaging through the first-in bag, an image of Zuri splayed out in her bed flashed across her mind. *Damn, I miss her,* she thought and pressed her legs together in an attempt to reign in her libido.

First On Scene: A Howling Sirens Novel

Struggling to focus, she went through the motions of checking out the truck.

The shuffle of reluctant footsteps reached her. Not sure who she was expecting to see, she peered out the side door into the bay. Boots unlaced and uniform shirt untucked, Eric slouched in her direction, a sour expression on his face. He looked paler than usual. *Wow, he looks like shit.*

Eric climbed into the truck and dropped onto the bench seat. "Hey."

"You okay?"

He shrugged. "Got forced in and just don't want to be here."

Wrinkling her nose, she examined him more closely. His sallow complexion made the dark circles under his eyes more prominent, and his pinched expression looked pained. "You sure?"

Dragging a hand through his hair, he offered her a weak smile. "I'm alright, mom. Just got a lot on my mind right now."

Rolling her eyes, she stood up and grabbed the drug box down from a shelf. "Okay, man, but I'm here if you need to talk."

He waved off her concern. "What else needs to be checked out?"

"I haven't looked at the oxygen main yet."

"Cool," he muttered, standing and hopping out of the truck.

She could hear him rummaging around in the outside compartments and grumbling to himself. *What the hell is up with him? He usually spirals after he gets hurt at work. Is that it? Is he not over getting bit?*

The tones dropped. "P2, please sign on with Berlin Fire for mutual aid."

Guess we're starting early today. Hoping out of the back, she shut the door and picked up her portable radio. She clicked the mic. "Received."

Climbing into the passenger seat, she glanced over at her partner and frowned.

White knuckled, Eric peeled out of the ambulance bay and

sped onto the main road. "Can you switch over to Berlin?"

"Yeah, can you not kill us?"

He grunted and swerved around a minivan that refused to pull to the right.

Clutching at the door handle, she scrolled through the radio channels until she found *Berlin FD* and picked up the mic. "P2 to control."

"P2, go ahead."

"Can we have the address please?"

"P2, you were canceled."

Eric smashed his hand against the steering wheel. "Fuck! I'm so tired of being jerked around!"

Kitty cringed, staring hard at her partner. "What is with you?"

"Nothing," he grunted and flipped off the lights. Cutting the wheel hard, he spun the truck around.

Switching channels, she let Hudson dispatch know they were clear and available.

"Can you please pull over and talk to me?!"

He ignored her, his nares flaring.

She smacked his shoulder. "Eric!"

Jamming on the brakes, he turned to face her, his sunken yellow eyes boring into her. "What?!"

Kitty gaped at him. "Holy shit, you're a werewolf!"

Eric blanched. "Wha… what?"

"It's okay," she soothed. "Why don't you let me drive back, and we can talk?"

He nodded and threw the truck in park.

During their return to base, the tense silence was broken only by Eric's heavy breathing. Backing into the bay, Kitty looked hard at her partner. He was still too pale, but his eyes had returned to their normal aquamarine.

"Does Zuri know?"

He barked out a laugh. "Oh, she knows."

Sucking on her lower lip, she eyed him carefully, wondering how many more werewolves were wandering around Massachusetts. "Okay."

"Okay?" Eric's voice cracked. "You're not scared?"

She shook her head. "Just surprised. I already know about Zee."

He raked a hand through his hair. "I can't believe she told you."

"It's complicated," Kitty said, holding his gaze.

"How's her dad feel about that?"

Groaning, she shook her head. "He hates it. Her entire family is pissed that I'm in her life."

He grinned at her. "Guess that makes two of us."

She evaluated him with arched eyebrows. "So this is new?"

Eric nodded. "Very. Did Zee tell you about the trouble with the other pack?"

"Yeah, you could say that," Kitty said and sighed. "Are they the ones that turned you?"

He nodded. "Yeah. The only reason Zee's family tolerates me at all is because they think they can use me against the other wolves." His shoulders sagged. "I'm getting my marching orders secondhand through Zuri."

"But you've met her family?"

Eric shook his head. "Nah, just her father, and I don't think I'll be seeing him again any time soon."

Before she could ask any further questions, the tones dropped. "P2 and engine two, please respond to the police station for the evaluation."

Huffing out a sigh, Eric snatched up the radio mic. "Received. You can show us responding."

"This conversation isn't over," she informed him and put the truck in drive.

He nodded. "Let's get this over with, and then we can talk."

Chapter Twenty-Eight

Angell rolled over, instinctively reaching out for his lover, but found only empty air. Pushing himself into a seated position, he found his nude form covered in a bright yellow blanket.

Looking around the cramped space, he found Miguel hunched over his laptop at the dining room table. As if feeling his eyes on him, Miguel glanced in his direction, offering him a lopsided grin and pointing toward a pile of neatly folded clothing on the edge of the futon. "Hey there."

"Hey," Angell murmured, his cheeks burning. Averting his gaze, he snagged his boxers from the top of the pile and slipped them on. "What are you up to?" He asked, sliding off the futon and approaching the table.

Miguel shrugged. "Figured I'd get this witch hunt started."

"Oh?" Resting his hands on the man's toned shoulders, Angell peered at the screen. "Find anything helpful?"

"The info you had was outdated, but I think I found her in Catemaco."

Worrying at his lower lip, Angell absentmindedly kneaded Miguel's shoulders. "Isn't that pretty far from here?"

Miguel nodded. "It is about a five-hour drive."

Damn, I wanted to spend more time with him! Too bad I'm going to be stuck renting a car and driving forever instead. Blowing out a frustrated breath, Angell pulled out a seat and dropped into it. "How'd you find her?"

First On Scene: A Howling Sirens Novel

Chuckling, Miguel shook his head. "Angell, I'm an officer. I can look up whoever I want."

"You aren't limited by your district?"

"I would be, but I did a stint with Interpol and managed to retain some of my privileges." Flashing Angell a lopsided grin, he glanced back down at the computer.

Impressive, Angell thought, leaning back and eyeing the handsome man next to him. His stomach growled so loudly that Miguel looked up at him.

"Why don't you take a shower?"

"What? Do I smell bad?" Grinning, Angell leaned forward, propping himself up on his elbows.

"Well, you do smell like sex... and I'd rather you not meet Teresa like that."

Cheeks burning, he stood up abruptly.

Miguel laughed at him. "Everything you need should be in the bathroom."

"Mmhm," He murmured and wandered towards the futon. Picking up the pile of clothes, he made his way into the bathroom and shut the door behind him.

After a rushed shower, Angell walked out of the bathroom and sucked down the tantalizing scent of marinated meat and something frying in oil. *Teresa must be home,* he thought, trying to ignore the way his shoulders immediately tensed. *He says he's in an open relationship, but what if he lied? He wouldn't lie, right? And if it's true, what are the rules? Do we pretend nothing happened in front of his girlfriend? Ugh, I shouldn't have let him blow me.*

Miguel was nowhere to be found. The idea of meeting Teresa without him by his side made his stomach do a somersault. Heart fluttering anxiously, he approached the bar separating the kitchen and dining room. Miguel wasn't there, but a pretty woman with sun-kissed skin, warm brown eyes, and shoulder-length black hair was humming to herself and stirring the pot in front of her.

Wow. She is beautiful. Clearing his throat, he waited for her to acknowledge him.

Teresa glanced up and flashed him a hundred-watt smile.

"You must be Angell! Welcome! It is so good to finally meet you!"

"Uh...yeah," he said, blushing under her hospitable gaze.

A warm hand clasped his shoulder, making him flinch as Miguel came up beside him, chuckling. "Glad to see you met our guest."

"Dinner is almost done," Teresa said while beaming at them. "Why don't you two go sit down."

Wetting his lips, Angell took a seat at the dining table. *She's so nice. I can't believe I fooled around with her boyfriend. I shouldn't have done that!*

Taking a seat across from him, Miguel glanced between him and the kitchen and grinned widely.

Teresa set down a plate of Gamachas and a fresh Corona in front of him before darting back into the kitchen. Licking his lips, he eyed the golden fried corn tortillas smothered in carnitas, mole sauce, diced onions, and cheese. Garnished with fresh cilantro and dried peppers, it was just like his mother used to make. He pushed the lime wedge into his beer and took a swig, enjoying the citrusy fiz of it. Picking up and biting into one of the Gamachas, he shut his eyes and groaned with pleasure. Savoring the crunch of the tortilla and the plethora of flavors dancing across his tongue, he chewed slowly, drawing the moment out.

"Miguel tells me that you two will be setting out for Catemaco tomorrow," Teresa commented.

He almost spat his food out. Not wanting to insult the cook he choked down his mouthful and stared hard at Miguel. "You don't have to do that. I can just rent a car."

Rolling his eyes, Miguel shook his head. "I'm not going to let my oldest friend go off on a witch hunt on his own."

"Thank you," he said softly, trying to ignore the way his chest constricted guiltily. *Does he want to come with me so he doesn't have to face her? Does she know what we did?*

They set out early the following morning, stopping at a gas station for road snacks and gas. Angell waited by the tiny police cruiser while his friend went inside for supplies. He had insisted on gassing up the car. It was the least he could do. The

First On Scene: A Howling Sirens Novel

pump clicked, and he removed it, replacing the fuel cap.

Striding back to the cruiser, a lopsided smirk plastered on his face, Miguel held up two bulging paper bags. "When was the last time you had a Gansito?"

"Been a minute," he admitted, eyeing the bags. "How many snacks did you get?"

"Don't worry! I just got some essentials for the trip. You know, Takis, Gansitos, Doritos, Sabritones, and of course some Vero Mango." Miguel handed over the two bags and dug into his pocket to fish out a much smaller plastic sack.

Angell licked his lips. "You didn't?"

Miguel winked and tossed a bag of roasted pumpkin seeds at him. "You know I did."

Juggling the two larger bags, he caught the seeds before they could hit the ground. *I can't believe he remembered my favorites after all this time.* Feeling his cheeks beginning to heat, he cleared his throat and looked away. "We should probably get going."

Still grinning, Miguel opened the passenger side for him.

Eyebrow arched, he glanced between the door and the man holding it open. "So chivalrous," he teased, hoping his face wasn't as red as it felt.

Rolling his eyes, Miguel scoffed. "Your arms are full. Now get in."

Wrinkling his nose, he stuck his tongue out but slid into the car, letting Miguel shut the door behind him.

Chuckling to himself, Miguel dropped into the driver's seat and started the car. Revving the engine, he peeled out of the parking lot and shot out onto the main road without bothering to look for oncoming traffic.

It's scary how much he drives like Kitty, Angell thought clutching at the door handle and scrambling to put on his seat belt. The answers he desperately sought were almost within reach, the last thing he needed was for the lunatic next to him to send them careening into another vehicle.

"She may not look like much, but this little pony has some pickup to it," Miguel bragged, making the engine roar as he cut off a Honda to get onto the highway.

"Uh huh," Angell said dryly without relinquishing his death grip on the handle.

Speeding up, Miguel cut across three lanes of traffic. Keeping his eyes straight ahead, he cleared his throat. "Are we good man? You've been pretty quiet since last night."

He stared hard at the man beside him, unspoken words dying on his lips. *How can I be? We finally hook up after all this time, and then I have to sit across the table from your girlfriend! Who, of course, is beautiful and charming and kind of perfect for you...* His shoulders sagged; he couldn't say any of that. It wasn't fair. Delaying the inevitable, he tore into the bag of Takis and popped a few into his mouth. Crunching away, he wracked his brain for something suitable to say. If he was being honest, nothing was okay. It might never be again.

"You're freaking out, aren't you?" Sucking his lower lip into his mouth in a familiar nervous tell, Miguel kept his eyes on the road.

Sucking the salty, acidic powder off his fingers, Angell blew out a nervous breath. "I'm not freaking out," he said gruffly. Clearing his throat, he glanced out the window. "But I do feel like we did something wrong. Teresa is sweet. You shouldn't be stepping out on her." Stealing a glance at Miguel, he frowned. The man was gripping the steering wheel hard enough to make his knuckles turn white. He shook his head. "I shouldn't have let that happen."

"Angell! I didn't cheat on Teresa. Fuck, have you really never met anyone in an open relationship before or heard of polyamory?!" Miguel snapped, jerking the steering wheel to the side and whipping around the slow car in front of them.

Grunting, Angell braced for an impact that didn't happen. Drawing in a deep breath, he straightened in his seat. "Oh, I've heard of them, but nine times out of ten, it's just lip service to get into my pants." Raking a hand through his curls, he shook his head. "I know better."

"God damn it, Angell! I'm not lying to you!" Miguel snapped, crushing the steering wheel between his fists. Worrying at his lower lip, he shook his head. "I promise, I had Teresa's blessing. It's why she wasn't home when we got in.

First On Scene: A Howling Sirens Novel

She wanted to give me a chance to see where things went."

Tugging at his shirt collar, Angell pursed his lips and looked out the window. *He seems sincere enough, but I still don't know.* Swallowing hard around the lump that had formed in the center of his throat, he stole a glance at his friend. "How many times have you done this with her *blessing*?" Leveling a skeptical stare in the other man's direction, he hoped for an answer that would ease his guilty conscience.

"You... uh..." Miguel coughed, a flattering blush creeping up his neck and face into his ears. "You are the only man I've been with."

Brow furrowed, Angell stared at him in earnest. *You'd never know it by the way he sucks cock.* "Really?"

"Really." Miguel squirmed in his seat, focusing hard on the open road ahead of them.

"Why?" Angell couldn't fathom why Miguel would have denied himself all of this time if he had permission to explore. Open relationships weren't common in Mexico, but he was sure Miguel could sweet talk his way into another man's bed without issue.

"I've known that I was bisexual for a long time, but I was too scared to do anything about it. Teresa encouraged me to explore that part of myself, but I mean... if I got caught..." Miguel shook his head, sucking on his lower lip. "My family would disown me and the guys on the force—God—I don't even want to think about what they would do to me. Bunch of homophobic assholes."

Shit, I'm being an ass. Reaching out, he rested his hand on Miguel's thigh, giving it a comforting squeeze. "I'm sorry I didn't believe you. This is my baggage, not yours."

"It's okay," Miguel murmured, a slight curve to the corner of his lips. "I get it. I'm sure it hasn't been easy for you either."

Angell nodded. "It's not so different in the States, depending on where you live. I'm just lucky enough to be in one of the northern states that doesn't care who you sleep with. Hell, one of my partners is an out and proud lesbian." Shaking his head, he chuckled. "Even if she weren't, anyone with eyes can tell what her preference is, but no one bothers her."

"That sounds nice."

"It is," he confirmed, a small smile tugging at his lips. "If you come to visit, I'll take you to P-town."

"What's P-town?" Miguel asked.

"It's only the gayest place on the east coast. We could hold hands in public, and no one would even blink..." Blushing hotly at what he had just said, Angell snapped his jaw shut.

"You want to hold my hand, huh?" Miguel teased, a shit-eating grin lighting up his face.

"I just meant anyone could," he said lamely and looked away.

Miguel caught his hand in his and intertwined their fingers. "It's alright. I want to hold your hand, too."

Miguel nudged him awake.

When did I fall asleep? Untangling his fingers from Miguel's, he took his hand back and rubbed the sleep out of his eyes.

"We're here," Miguel informed him, his face pinched and serious.

They were parked outside a small shop with blacked-out windows and a sign above the door that read 'El Gato negro y el Zorro naranja.' *The black cat and the orange fox, what a random name*, Angell thought and unbuckled his seat belt.

"Okay, what is the plan?"

Grinning sheepishly, Angell ran a hand through his curly hair. *To fly by the seat of my pants?*

"You don't have a plan, do you?" Miguel frowned.

"Not really. I kinda just figured I'd go in and ask her if she could help me." Tugging at the hem of his T-shirt, Angell stared hard at his lap.

"Yeah, about that. You still haven't told me *why* you need to talk to Isabella."

That was intentional. I don't need you thinking I'm crazy. Angell pursed his lips, keeping his thoughts to himself.

First On Scene: A Howling Sirens Novel

"Come on, Angell. I've taken you this far with no questions asked, but now I need to know why we are here." Miguel leveled a stubborn glare at him.

He blew out a shaky breath and closed his eyes. *Come on, you owe him this.*

"Angell?"

Clearing his throat, Angell met his best friend's eyes. "I'm being haunted by the Grim Reaper."

Miguel stared at him for a long moment. "What?"

"I know it sounds crazy, but ever since I started working as a Paramedic, I started seeing the Grim Reaper. It shows up any time a patient is going to die." He bit his lower lip until he tasted blood. "For years, I thought it was a hallucination and that if I just ignored it, I could pretend I wasn't crazy, but lately, things have escalated and..." His voice cracked. "I'm either losing my mind completely, or I'm cursed."

Miguel sucked on his lower lip, a thoughtful expression on his face. He motioned with his hand for him to continue.

Angell groaned into his hands before glancing back at Miguel, whose expression hadn't changed. "I haven't wanted to admit it, but I think I'm tapping into something real. Besides seeing the reaper, I get these insane nightmares before I lose a patient." He shook his head.

"Okay, but what does all of this have to do with Isabella? Why do you need her?"

"Do you remember how I got a reading from her when we were kids?"

Miguel nodded, still looking lost.

"Well, I never told you this... but she told me that I was touched by Santa Muerte and that it was only a matter of time before she called me to service." He swallowed hard, his Adam's apple bobbing.

Miguel paled. "Shit."

"Tell me about it," Angell murmured.

"All right then, let's get it done." Clapping his hands together, Miguel threw back his shoulders.

"Wait? You believe me?"

"The Angell I know isn't a liar. Besides, just because

something is improbable doesn't mean it is impossible." Opening his door, he glanced back at him. "You coming."

"You don't have to come in with me," Angell argued, expecting Miguel to chicken out once more.

"Shut up. I'm not letting you do this alone." Sliding out of the cruiser, Miguel waited for him to do the same.

Some things, fortunately, did change, Angell thought, shaking his head and following his friend to the front of the shop, where Miguel stepped aside, letting him take the lead.

Faced with the gravity of the situation, he hesitated. Heart hammering in his chest, Angell suddenly felt dizzy and uncertain. Struck by a wave of nausea, he licked his lips and drew in a deep breath. *You can do this,* he told himself but remained stuck to the spot. A warm hand lit upon his shoulder, sending a shiver racing down his spine. He gulped and looked back into supportive chocolate-brown eyes.

"I got you," Miguel soothed, giving him a comforting squeeze before pushing past him and opening the door. "Come on. Let's do this."

Angell had never been so grateful for anyone in his entire life. Nodding, he ducked into the shop. The thick perfume of sweet sage and earthy frankincense that permeated everything made him cough.

Light flickered ominously from numerous black candles of varying sizes. They lined the countertops, display cases, and window sills, wax dripping freely. It was a fire waiting to happen. Blinking rapidly, he urged his eyes to adjust to the dim lighting. A collection of crosses, all sizes and colors, hung from the ceiling. Some depicted the death of Jesus, while others were bare wood.

Severed monkey paws, bundles of colorful feathers, Santa Muerte statues, baby Jesus figurines, and jars containing fetuses of an unrecognizable species cluttered the shelves around them. He could make out tarot decks, voodoo dolls, crystals, and numerous jeweled knives in the display cases. Beyond the showcases, jars of herbs, dried teas, and bottled potions lingered on dusty shelves. Cages of cooing white doves cluttered the space behind the counter.

First On Scene: A Howling Sirens Novel

Dark tapestries depicting different forms of medieval torture covered the walls, which were free of wares. Examining the one closest to him, he shivered. A hooded figure grasping a short scythe in its skeletal hand loomed over him. At its side stood a massive black beast with flaming eyes and dripping jaws.

Miguel came to stand next to him. "Is that what you see?"

Swallowing hard, he nodded. "Pretty damn close. Although, it's just a reaper, no dog."

Miguel crossed his arms, squeezing himself. "Let's find Isabella and get out of here. This place gives me the creeps."

Catching movement in his periphery, Angell spun around in time to catch someone pull back a tapestry depicting a man suspended on an upside-down cross with his feet burning. The woman peering out at them looked different than he remembered, with her long dark locs shorn short into a bob and faded to a light gray. She was also thinner with sagging jowls and countless creases, she had become more crone than maiden. Yet her brilliant green eyes were the same.

"Come, I've been expecting you," she said and disappeared back behind the tapestry.

"Because that's not creepy at all," Miguel grumbled beside him.

"You don't have to come with me," Angell reminded him.

"No. I'm not letting you do this by yourself."

Angell sighed and strode forward. *Good to see some things don't change.*

They pulled back the tapestry and followed the narrow hallway into a well-lit, mostly bare room. In the center of the space stood a flimsy fold-out table and three folding chairs. Ignoring the feeling of Deja Vu, Angell clenched his jaw and marched forward.

Taking a seat at the table, she motioned for them to do the same.

He glanced back at Miguel, who met his eyes and nodded. Together, they pulled out their chairs and sat down. They sat in silence for a long moment while Isabella squinted at them, a hard smile displayed on her thin lips.

Selina Rossman

"What is it that you wish to know?" She asked finally.

Gripping the table so hard that his fingers dug into the thin plastic, Angell drew a deep breath. "I need to know what is happening to me?"

Pursing her lips, she nodded knowingly. "I warned you once that the Santa Muerte would come calling. I see she is no longer satisfied with your passivity."

"What does that even mean?" Miguel interrupted.

Angell shot him a pleading look and elbowed him in the side. "Just be quiet and let her talk, please."

"No. We came here for answers, not riddles," Miguel said firmly, crossing his arms.

Pressing her lips together, Isabella fell silent.

Angell cleared his throat. "Please continue. I'm sorry about him."

Her gaze danced between them before falling back on him. "He leaves. Then we talk."

"Absolutely not! I'm not…"

Angell clapped his friend on the shoulder. "Go. I'll be fine. Please."

"Fine," Miguel huffed. "But I'll be just outside." Standing abruptly, he stalked out of the room. "If she does anything weird yell for me!" He shouted over his shoulder and disappeared from sight.

"Now, where were we?" She asked, folding her hands in front of her.

"I need to know…" Angell paused, searching for the right words. "I died. Let's start there." He had denied the truth she had bestowed upon him all those years ago, but if he wanted to figure out what was happening to him, he couldn't do that anymore.

She nodded. "You were three years old when you drowned. It is where your fear of the water comes from."

He stared hard at her, his heart thudding in his ears. He'd never told anyone about his aquaphobia, not his parents, not Miguel, no one. "How do you know that?"

Her lips curved up into a half smile. "Your Aunt and I were once very close, and she came to me for many things," she sighed wistfully. "The day that you drowned, she brought your body to me, begging for your life."

"How did I drown?" He asked, not sure he really wanted to know but unable to let it go.

"She looked away for a moment too long, and you climbed into the fountain." She shook her head. "By the time she found you, it was too late."

"Then how am I here?"

"Is your denial truly that strong?" She countered.

Angell swallowed down the lump in his throat. "It was, but now I need to understand."

"Like you, I serve Santa Muerte. Mostly, I am meant to observe, but when the time is right, I bring her new servants."

A chill seeped into his skin, making him shiver.

"I brought you back at her behest, but I dare not speak for her," she said solemnly.

"Then how am I supposed to know what she wants with me?" Pursing his lips together, he rubbed at the back of his neck.

"You must journey to find what you seek."

"That's what I'm doing here," he growled.

She shook her head. "No, you must go on a different journey." Smiling kindly, she slid a clear plastic baggie of green disc-shaped buttons across the table towards him.

"What is it?" He asked, warily eyeing the contents of the bag.

"This is the sacrament of our Goddess."

"What?"

"I believe you might know it as peyote."

He blinked at her. "Is it safe?"

"Is anything?" She countered smugly.

"Touché, how do I use it?"

"Make a tea out of the sacrament and find somewhere natural and secluded to drink it. I suggest you bring your guard dog with you. That is all I may tell you."

Brow furrowed, he nodded. "Thank you."

Chapter Twenty-Nine

Clutching at the steering wheel like it could save him from what he had to do, Eric examined the abandoned warehouse from the security of his ancient blue Civic. The dusty beige concrete walls and steel front door were unassuming enough, even if the lack of windows was odd. Not odd enough for the general public to notice, though. The lucky bastards just went about their lives, completely oblivious to the encroaching danger.

Running his tongue along parched lips, he fiddled with his seat belt. *I can do this! He already thinks that I'm part of his pack by default, and if I tell him that I want to prove my worth, he'll believe that. Right?*

Drawing in a steadying breath, he opened the car door. Catching sight of himself in the rearview mirror, he froze. His fresh crew cut had grown shaggy with strands of red hair dangling down his neck, and his eyes were a stark yellow. *Fuck. I need to calm down! I need them to think I'm confident and ready to take up orders.* Raking his fingers through his thick locs, he wracked his brain for the advice Zuri had given him.

She said to just breathe through it. I can do that. Shutting his eyes, he tried the box breathing that he'd been taught. Inhaling deeply, he held his breath and then exhaled for four seconds. His heart still hammering in his chest and sweat trickling down his spine, he swallowed hard. *Calm down*, he ordered

First On Scene: A Howling Sirens Novel

himself and repeated the breathing technique until his pulse slowed.

He opened his eyes and glanced at his reflection. Two pools of aquamarine gazed back at him and his clean-cut hair had returned. Sighing, he let his shoulders sag. *Okay, good. Now, let's get this over with.*

Climbing out of the car, he straightened to his full height and threw back his shoulders. Projecting an air of confidence that he definitely did not feel, he strode towards the building. Ignoring the tension that had settled between his shoulder blades, he wiped his sweaty palms against his jeans and rang the doorbell.

His sensitive hearing alerted him to the offensively loud bing-bong beyond the door. Crossing his arms, he bounced his foot impatiently. *Chill out!* Forcing his leg to still, he continued to wait for someone to answer the door. The seconds ticked by, and no one came to greet him.

Frowning, he dropped his arms to his sides. *Should I have called first? No, they don't get a warning!* Curling his hand into a fist, he pounded on the door, "Open up!" He bellowed loudly enough that the scraggly-looking teenager, loitering across the street, looked up from his cell phone to stare at him. Eric shot the kid a dirty look, and he quickly glanced back down at the device in his hand.

The door creaked open, and a muscular skinhead wearing a sour expression squinted out at him. "What?" The man barked.

Swallowing hard, Eric examined the shifter before him. Like everyone else Karl had chosen to join their ranks, the man was white with blue eyes and sported a Wolfsangel tattoo on his bicep. His broad shoulders blended seamlessly into his shaved head, making Eric wonder what had happened to his neck. Held up by limbs the size of tree trunks, he was the perfect doorman to scare off intruders, but Eric couldn't let him know that.

"I'm here to see Karl." Folding his arms across his chest and pressing his lips into a thin line, Eric glared expectantly at the thuggish doorman. *Big Bad Wolf. I'm the freaking BIG BAD*

Selina Rossman

WOLF, and I got this!

The man shook his head and started to shut the door. "He's busy. Go away."

Kicking his foot forward, Eric jammed the door open. "Trust me, he wants to hear what I have to say."

Yellowing eyes flicked from Eric's face to his foot, and the man's lips curled into a silent snarl. Leaning forward, he loomed over the shorter man.

Standing his ground, Eric looked up and held the thug's gaze. *Please work! Please work! Oh god, if this doesn't work, he's going to beat me to death.* Still staring the man down, he took a step forward into his space and bared his teeth. He could feel his wolf pushing to the surface, intent on domination, even if his human side ached to sprint back to his car.

A low growl rumbled at the base of his throat, and his eyes itched with the tell-tale sign that they were beginning to shift. *It's now or never.* Gathering his courage, he moved deeper into the thug's personal space until they were only a hair's width apart. "Take. Me. To. Karl. Now," he ground out, his shoulders tensing.

Karl's thug whined deep in his throat and stepped aside, averting his eyes.

Holy shit, did that just work?! Maybe I am getting the hang of this whole werewolf thing! Head held high, Eric walked into the building like he owned it.

Ducking submissively, the larger man led him deeper into the warehouse until they reached a backroom that Eric was intimately familiar with. "Wait here," the thug murmured before striding back the way they had come.

Nodding dismissively, he took in his surroundings and swallowed hard. Mocking him from the center of the room was the chair that had restrained him throughout the last full moon. Hanging empty, the manacles glistened with fresh ichor, and a metallic scent of fresh blood clung to them.

A pang of hunger lanced between his ribs, and he licked his lips. *Shit, stop that!* Shaking his head, he backed away from the chair.

The sound of clipped footsteps caught his attention. *Okay,*

First On Scene: A Howling Sirens Novel

show time. Turning in Karl's direction, he dropped his gaze to the floor. He knew better than to attempt to dominate this man.

Coming to a stop next to him, Karl clapped him on the shoulder. "Eric, what can I do for you?"

Fighting down the urge to flinch away from his grasp, he kept his features neutral, letting his shoulders sag. "Thank you for seeing me," he murmured and swallowed hard.

Karl nodded, staring at him expectantly.

"I know that the circumstances of me joining your pack are not the norm. I was neither tested nor chosen, and that doesn't really sit well with me." Averting his gaze, he let his head droop to the floor. "You took me in when you didn't have to, and you're teaching me how to handle my wolf, but I don't want to just be here by default. I want to be a contributing member to this pack," he admitted, infusing his tone with as much sincerity as he could muster.

Strong fingers gripped his chin, and Karl raised his face to meet his ice-blue eyes. "What do you have in mind?"

Blowing out a shaky breath, he averted his eyes. "I want to help you take out the other pack."

"Oh? And how do you plan on doing that?" Karl asked, still holding his chin in his firm grip.

"I was kinda hoping that you could help me come up with a plan..." Squirming, he shifted his weight from foot to foot. "But I do have access to the other pack."

"Go on." Karl let go of him and folded his arms across his chest.

"I work with the daughter of their Alpha. She is trying to recruit me to her pack, but I know where my loyalties are." He looked up into Karl's inquisitive face, thrusting out his chin. *Is he buying this shit?*

The corners of Karl's lips curved upward. "I think we can work with that."

Yeah, he's buying this shit. Idiot.

Chapter Thirty

"Are you sure this is a good idea?" Miguel asked for the third time as he continued pacing.

Ignoring the question, Angell attached the tiny propane canister to the camping stove and started it. Clicking loudly, it lit. He poured a bottle of water into the pot and placed it on the burner, waiting for it to boil. He was preparing to take a leap of faith, and nothing he said would make that easier on his friend.

He'd been ready to go it alone in the desert but Miguel had adamantly refused, instead insisting on choosing a location that EMS could find them if everything went to hell. The sound logic had led them to the abandoned ruins of El Tajin.

By day, it was a barely frequented tourist spot; by nightfall, it was a ghost town. Built in a time before the Aztecs and destroyed by his ancestors, the pyramids had seen many gods and even more blood shed. He would have preferred a more natural location but there were worse places to invoke a death goddess.

Casting long shadows behind the Pyramid of the Niches, the sun crept lower on the horizon. Like any Mexican pyramid, it was crafted with brown flagstones and fitted together with earth mortar. Seven stories high with numerous deep niches, it had once been a pathway to the underworld. The Aztecs had sacrificed livestock and humans alike to encourage their death gods to use the tunnels for their walkways.

Most of the sculptures that once adorned the building had been stripped away by time. Only the feathered serpents remained to guard the altar space at the top of the building. He could barely make out the carved beasts gazing down at him from their seventh-story perch.

The water started to boil, and he added the peyote buttons to the pot. After a few minutes, he strained the hot liquid into a cup and eyed it warily. He'd done shrooms before and smoked plenty of weed in the past but had no experience with such a strong hallucinogen. *I hope this is similar to shrooms, but maybe without the stomach issues...*

"You don't have to do this," Miguel reminded him, his lips pulled tight.

Angell shook his head. "I promise you that I do." *How can I make him understand when I barely do? Maybe I'm crazy, or maybe Isabella is right, and I'm being called to service by Santa Muerte. Either way, this is worth the risk to find out.*

Straightening his shoulders, he took a deep breath and downed the bitter tea. The hot liquid scalded its way down his throat. *Should've stopped for some honey. At least Miguel can't tell me not to do it now.*

"Can you at least try to relax?"

Hands crammed into his pockets, Miguel continued to stride back and forth. "You don't get it. I've seen people have psychotic breaks on this stuff, and I just got..." He stopped talking abruptly.

"You just got what?" Angell pried.

"I just got you back, and I don't want to lose you again," he mumbled, clenching and unclenching his hands.

Awww, that's really sweet. Flipping the stove off, Angell pushed himself off the ground and strode over to the pacing man. Stilling his movement with a gentle hand, he pulled Miguel into a tight embrace. He nuzzled his face into Miguel's neck and huffed in the scent of cedarwood aftershave. "I'm going to be okay."

Pulling back, Miguel swiped at his eyes and looked away.

"We should take a look around before the peyote kicks in," he said thickly.

"Sure," Angell caught Miguel's hand in his, entwining their fingers and tugging him towards the steps of the pyramid. "I want to do this at the top anyway."

Night had fallen as, legs burning and chest heaving, Angell crested the top of the pyramid to reach the flat altar space of the temple. His hand had grown slick with sweat but he continued to cling to the panting man beside him.

Standing atop the square plateau, he surveyed the land and took in the stars. Thousands of sparkling diamonds and a pale sliver of moonlight illuminated the black sky. *It's beautiful here,* he thought, wondering if the stars naturally twinkled like that or if the drugs were kicking in.

"Are you feeling it yet?" Dropping his hand, Miguel took a long swig from his water bottle and offered it to him.

Shaking his head, he waved off the bottle. With a life of their own, his feet led him over to the temple's entrance. A winged serpent had been carved into the hard stone. The beast's bulky head was cocked to the side, its enormous eye staring off into space while its willowy body serpentined up the wall.

Giving in to compulsion he ran his hands over the carved flagstone, expecting it to be smooth and cool to the touch but his fingers drifted over downy feathers and rough scales. Warm and alive, it shifted beneath his fingers. "Whoa," he whispered, staggering back and nearly toppling over until firm hands steadied him.

Wide-eyed, he watched as the beast flexed razor-sharp talons and freed itself from the wall in a flurry of tangerine-colored feathers. Soaring into the air, moonlight reflected off of iridescent green scales. "Are you seeing this?" He asked in a hushed whisper.

Behind him, Miguel snickered. "Nope. Why don't you tell me about it?"

Wings flared, the dragon hovered in the air above them, its orange reptilian eye squinting down at him. Hissing, a forked blue-gray tongue flicked out of the beast's mouth. "What do you seek?"

Knees quivering, he leaned heavily against Miguel, taking advantage of the other man's strength. "I seek answers," he whispered.

"Follow," the feathered beast commanded and slithered away through the air.

Darting after it, he narrowly avoided the strong hands trying to restrain him and followed the beast into the temple's darkened passageway. An unintelligible shout rang out in his ears but quickly faded to a deafening silence.

The darkness was all-consuming. Beating erratically, his pulse raced, and his breath escaped him in ragged gasps. *Don't panic*, he told himself firmly and waited for something to happen. Forcing his breathing to slow, he drew in a slow breath. The scent of wet moss permeated the moist air but wasn't strong enough to overpower the metallic tang of blood.

Holding his breath, he strained his ears, hoping to catch any hint of his guide, but the creature had disappeared into the darkness. Indecision left him paralyzed. *Well, what am I supposed to do now?* he thought, huffing out a sigh.

Shrill laughter shattered the silence, reverberating through him and throbbing down his spine. Intensifying, the cackling settled behind his eyes, making his skull rattle.

Is this the drugs? Blindly reaching out, he searched for the person attached to the laughter, but his fingers found only open air.

The voice continued to chortle darkly, and brilliant waves of violet and cobalt crashed across his vision. *Gotta be the drugs*, he thought, shutting his eyes to avoid the blinding colors, but they continued to flare across his vision.

Intensifying in pitch, the sound evolved into a repetitive screech that pierced his skull. Pain lanced behind his eyes, driving him to his knees with a grunt. Just as suddenly as it had begun, the screech halted. Heart still thundering in his ears, he squinted out into the darkness, expecting to see a monster looming over him but he was alone in the blackness.

Panting, he forced himself to his feet and immediately staggered. The ground roiled and quaked like a living thing below him. Arms flailing wildly, he snagged his foot on an unseen obstacle and smashed face-first back to the stone floor. The metallic flavor of blood bloomed in his mouth. Groaning, he shoved himself into a kneeling position. "Fuck," he muttered and spat on the floor.

"How is this supposed to help me?" He grumbled to himself.

"It's not," a raspy voice replied. Boney fingers curled in his hair and yanked his head back.

With a startled yelp, he jerked away, nearly stumbling to the stone floor once more. Sweat beaded on his scalp, his pulse raced, and he gulped down air in short, terrified gasps. *Maybe this wasn't such a good idea. I'll have to tell Miguel that he was right if I ever see him again.*

"What do you want from me?" He asked the darkness.

"Come to me," a feminine voice demanded.

On their own accord, his feet shuffled forward, carrying him deeper into the pyramid. *Shit, this is bad. This is really bad!* he thought, struggling to halt his forward momentum and failing to do so.

With every forced step, an eerie yellow glow replaced the darkness, illuminating the long hallway that led into an enormous room. In the center of the otherwise empty space stood something straight out of his nightmares.

Made from a haphazardly stacked collection of bones stood a skeletal throne. Perched on the pile of shattered spinal columns, cracked femur bones, and fractured skulls was the embodiment of death. Fixed, dilated pupils leered out at him from beneath a husk of sallow flesh. Wisps of brittle, white hair adorned the crown of her head, and a flaccid jaw hung agape, crooked teeth exposed. With a chest that had been flayed wide open, rotted organs and chalky white ribs were on full display. Her shriveled gray heart sat between two deflated lungs. Wrongly positioned at her sides, large breasts sagged toward the ground. Nude except for a skirt of writhing black serpents, she was a horror to behold.

His feet brought him to a stop directly in front of her. Still unable to control his limbs, he swallowed hard and took in the gruesome sight before him.

"You dare to stare at me?! Don't you know who I am?!" She snarled with unmoving lips and rushed him, scattering bones in every direction.

Frozen in place, he held his ground. Sweat trickled down the nape of his neck, and his heart stuttered. *I think I'm having a bad trip. Please just let this be the drugs.*

Bony fingers raked into his flesh, stabbing into his shoulders and forcing him to his knees. Ice-cold hands tilted his head upward, and a whimper escaped him.

Dead eyes evaluated him, and the dead woman cocked her head to the side, her withered tongue lolling out of her mouth. "I am the Lady of Death, the ruler of Mictlān and its nine hells. One day, I shall swallow the stars, and all the world shall weep!" She dropped him dismissively to the stone floor.

Heart racing and hot tears streaking down his face, he pushed himself to his knees with quaking limbs.

"Why are you here?"

"I…" Mind going blank, he realized he didn't know what to say. He had come all this way and had never gotten around to making a plan.

A skeletal hand shot out, snatching up a fistful of his hair and dragging him to his feet. "Did you seek me out to waste my time? Is that what you seek? My rage?!"

Scalp screaming, feet futilely kicking, he dangled from her grasp. The stench of rot and congealed blood made him gag. "The grim reaper stalks me, and I need to know why!"

She shook her head and laughed, tossing him to the floor.

He landed roughly on his back with a soft grunt. He lay where he'd fallen, trying to catch his breath. A heavy foot pressed into his sternum, making it even harder to breathe. The death goddess' living skirt writhed above him, hissing and lunging for him. Flattening himself against the stone floor, he braced for the feel of fangs puncturing his flesh.

"I let you return to your realm. I blessed you with sight." She cocked her head to the side, her eyes burning into him. "And you have squandered my gifts!"

Breath catching in his throat, he trembled beneath her and

waited for whatever retribution she was about to bestow upon him.

"No more. As of now, you will no longer ignore your obligations," she hissed, removing her foot and dropping something heavy into his hand.

Turning his head to the side, he eyed the item he grasped. She had given him a flat board with a smooth wooden handle. The stick's sides were embedded with blades of jagged obsidian. Two centimeters in length, there were eight blades in total. *What am I supposed to do with this?*

The death Goddess had retreated back to her throne and was watching him closely.

"Uh, thanks?" He pushed himself into a seated position and glanced between the goddess and the gift she had given him.

"I require a sacrifice," she informed him.

Brow furrowing in confusion, he shook his head. "I don't understand."

"Of course you don't." Rising, she shuffled towards him, sending bones scattering in every direction. "Your hands will act as my own, and you will shepherd the dying to my lands rather than merely watching them go. You will be guided to your purpose, but first, you must bleed for me."

Vice-like hands encircled his own. Puppeteering his limbs, she forced him to strike and slash at himself with the strange weapon. The obsidian bit deeply into his forearm, and hot blood bubbled up, drenching his arms. Tears fell freely while he struggled against her.

Unphased by his efforts, she yanked his arm to her mouth and dragged her limp tongue across it.

The sensation of sandpaper grinding into his open wounds made his knees give out so that the only thing holding him up was her. The remaining blood in his body pounded in his ears, and his vision blurred. The ironclad grip on his wrist released him, and he crumpled to the floor. Trembling, he curled into a fetal position and gave in to the growing darkness behind his eyes.

Chapter Thirty-One

"Angell!" A familiar voice shouted in the distance.

Firm hands gripped his shoulders and shook him. "Wake up!" The voice hissed.

Head throbbing, he cracked open an eye, closing it just as quickly. "Go away," he ground out thickly.

"Ah, hell no," Miguel growled and shook him more insistently.

Grunting, he shoved weakly at his friend. "Five more minutes."

"Angell. You are lying in a pile of bones and covered in blood!" The high-pitched whisper informed him.

The other man's words struck him like a slap. His eyes flew open, and he sat ramrod straight, nearly colliding with Miguel's face.

Miguel scrambled back, sending bones skittering in every direction. "Get up," he ordered.

Looking down at his blood-soaked clothing, he flinched. "This is so gross." Brow furrowed, he let strong hands pull him to his feet. A wave of vertigo crashed over him, leaving him staggering. Miguel steadied him and drew him away from the throne of bones.

"Guess it wasn't just a bad trip," he muttered, leaning heavily against Miguel, who slipped an arm under his shoulder and supported his weight.

"Guess not," Miguel agreed, dragging him out of the cavernous room. "I don't know how you found this place in the dark. I had a flashlight, and it still took me hours." Shaking his head, he illuminated the path ahead of them.

Smiling weakly, he rested his head on Miguel's shoulder. "You could say I had a little help."

Pressing his lips together, Miguel arched a manicured eyebrow. "You can tell me all about it when we get out of here."

In the time it took them to escape the depths of the pyramid, his head had cleared, his gait had stabilized, and the sun had risen.

"Sit down and let me take a look at you," Miguel ordered.

Sitting down on the hard stone, he stretched out his legs gratefully. "Aren't I supposed to be the medic?"

Miguel rolled his eyes and unscrewed his water bottle, dousing him in the lukewarm liquid. "Exactly, I know what bad patients medical staff make."

Rivulets of blood ran freely down his skin, leaving behind intact flesh. Raising his arms, Angell examined them in the early morning light. *Where did all of the wounds go?*

Brow furrowed, Miguel crossed his arms. "Whose blood did you get all over yourself?"

"Mine," he muttered, looking down at his hands.

"Well, there's not a mark on you. Did you get a nosebleed or something?"

Angell shook his head. "I don't know how to explain it." The memory of the Goddess's limp, sandpaper tongue dragging across his open flesh made him shudder. Looking up, he lost himself in identical pools of concerned umber. His breath caught in his throat, and he swallowed hard.

The corners of Miguel's lips twitched upward. "Let's get out of here," he suggested, offering him a hand up.

Grasping the other man's hand tightly, he let himself be pulled to his feet. His knees wobbled. Miguel's tight hold on him was the only thing that kept him standing.

Openly grinning, the handsome man slipped an arm under him and tugged him close. "You are going to owe me big time for carrying your ass down a seven-story pyramid."

"Anything you want," Angell promised.

"Anything?" Miguel asked teasingly.

Groaning, Angell clung to the other man as they started their descent. "Anything."

Maria Sanchez-Cruz opened the door and threw her arms around her much taller son, dragging him into a tight hug. "Mi amor! ¡Estoy tan emocionado de verte! Ha pasado demasiado tiempo desde que has estado en casa. ¡He preparado todas tus comidas favoritas en honor a tu visita!" She babbled excitedly.

"Mama, my Spanish isn't what it used to be," Angell gently reminded her. Once fluent in the language, it had atrophied in his time in the States. With no one to converse with besides the occasional Spanish-speaking patient, his vocabulary had become limited.

Sighing, the petite, gray-haired woman let go of him and gazed lovingly into his face with pursed lips. "I'm sorry. I forgot in my excitement."

Cheeks burning, he tucked his thumbs into his belt loops and rocked back and forth on his heels. "Look, I brought Miguel with me."

Pretty brown eyes twinkling, she smiled brightly at the man beside him. "Is that really little Miguel all grown up?"

Grinning, he opened his muscular arms, and the older woman embraced him. "It is good to see you, too."

Chuckling, she patted his back and released him. "Come in! Come in!" Waving them forward, she hustled into the house.

Still grinning, Miguel shot him a wink and caught his hand in his, tugging him with him as he wandered after their host.

Greeted by the tantalizing scents of slowly simmered meats, fried masa, and melting cheeses, his stomach growled with anticipation. Licking his lips, he untangled their hands before his mother could notice them.

His mother shooed them towards the set table before

bustling into the kitchen and quickly returning with her arms weighed down by plates of chicken and beef empanadas, shrimp tacos, fresh ceviche, and bowls of rice and beans. She laid the food down in front of them before darting back into the kitchen and returning with a pitcher of lemonade. Filling all of their glasses, she took her seat at the head of the table and smiled.

"Angell, how has your trip been? Did you find Isabella?"

Filling his plate, he nodded. "We found her, but I think I'm going home with more questions than answers." Frowning, he tucked into his food.

"At least you got to reconnect with me and your mom," Miguel offered and dug into his food. Groaning with pleasure, he closed his eyes. "I sure have missed your cooking," he mumbled through his full mouth.

Maria laughed warmly, covering her mouth. "I'm glad that you are enjoying it."

"Mi amor, how are things in the States? Is work still going well? Have you found a special lady yet?"

Angell's cheeks burned. "Uh, no special ladies at the moment, but work is going well."

Miguel snickered into his food, nearly choking on a half-chewed empanada.

Angell pounded harder than necessary on his friend's back and scowled. "Don't choke," he muttered.

"And you, Miguel?"

Swallowing hard, he beamed at her. "I'm doing very well. I've been with the police department for long enough to have some paid time off saved up, even if the job keeps me busy. My girlfriend lives with me, so at least I have someone to come home to."

"That's wonderful!" Maria said, clasping her hands together. "Are you planning on proposing soon?"

Miguel choked down his mouthful of ceviche and held up his hands. "Easy there, there is no need to rush!"

Shaking her head, she laughed and went back to her food. "You boys…"

Angell grinned broadly as he climbed into the tiny police

First On Scene: A Howling Sirens Novel

cruiser after their meal. "I can't believe you had dinner with me and my mom."

Shrugging, Miguel slid into the driver's side. "I told you I wanted to spend more time with you. Besides, I wouldn't miss a home-cooked meal from your mother. Don't you think I earned it on our pyramid adventure?"

Barking out a laugh, Angell crossed his arms. "I mean, if that was all you were after..."

Miguel flushed handsomely and started the cruiser.

Reaching over, he intertwined their fingers and squeezed them. *I'm going to miss this. I wish we had more time together.* Eyes burning, he stared out the window. The last thing he needed was for Miguel to see him cry.

He didn't want to leave, but he didn't have an excuse to stay. Miguel had a girlfriend and would never choose him over an easy life with her. Just because they had hooked up didn't mean anything had changed.

"When do you have to go back to work?" Miguel asked, jarring him out of his bitter thoughts.

Blinking back unshed tears, he looked up in time to see Miguel swerving around a slow-moving sedan. Wrinkling his nose, he scrabbled for the door handle. *It's amazing how much he drives like Kitty.*

Blowing out a shaky breath, he shrugged. "I go back the day after I get home." Huffing out a sigh, he shook his head. "But if I'm being honest, I'm not looking forward to it."

"Why not? I thought you loved being a Paramedic?"

"I mean... I do, but after meeting the Lady of Death..." He shrugged again. "I guess I just don't know what to expect."

"Didn't she tell you that you would be guided?"

"Yeah, but what does that even mean?! I already have nightmares that warn me about impending death. For fucks sake, I have the Grim Reaper showing up on calls. Am I supposed to learn from him?" Raking his fingers through his curls, he groaned.

"There could be something more to it," Miguel suggested, pulling onto the highway.

"Like what?"

"I'm no expert, but maybe you'll be able to see ghosts. That's a thing, right?"

"You believe in ghosts?" He asked, grinning.

"Wait… You don't? Really?" Miguel's eyebrows jumped towards his hairline.

"Well, I've never seen one. The Reaper is the only dead thing I've seen. Maybe it's because of the reaper there are no ghosts?" He rubbed his chin thoughtfully.

"Maybe, but what if not everyone gets reaped?" Taking the airport exit, Miguel frowned.

Shit, we're almost there. This is almost over. Sucking his lower lip into his mouth, he chewed on it until he tasted blood.

"Didn't you tell me that your base is haunted?" Miguel asked.

"Some of my coworkers think so, but I'm not convinced." Angell continued worrying at his lower lip. "We hear a lot of strange noises there, but it's an old, dilapidated building that should have been condemned a long time ago. Besides, animals break in pretty frequently. That would explain the noises."

"What kind of animals?"

"One time, a duck fell down the chimney into the day room. Another time, it was a baby raccoon. We've had squirrels and stray cats come in through the windows, and there are always birds in the bay." Glancing at his friend's face, he grinned broadly at the horrified expression on Miguel's face.

Shaking his head, Miguel pulled into the airport garage and found a secluded parking spot. "I'd bet my life ghosts are in your station's menagerie."

"Maybe, maybe not." He tightened his hold on Miguel's hand. *I'm not ready to say goodbye yet!*

"Well… this is it," Miguel said, rubbing at the back of his neck.

"Guess it is," He agreed, but neither of them moved to get out of the car.

"I'm so glad that you reached out to me. It's been amazing catching up, and finally…" Blushing, Miguel looked away.

Capturing both of his hands in his, Angell squeezed them

affectionately. "I feel the same way, and don't worry, I'll stay in touch this time," he promised, offering his friend a small smile.

"Good. We can figure out a time for me to come visit and I'm going to hold you to your promise to take me to P-town!" Miguel offered him a smile that didn't reach his eyes.

"I'm really going to miss you," Angell murmured, blinking back unshed tears, not looking at the handsome man next to him.

"Me too." Miguel freed his hands and glanced nervously around the garage. They were alone. He gripped the front of Angell's shirt and yanked him into a passionate kiss that ended too quickly.

"You should go," Miguel said, his voice hoarse.

Angell nodded, still blinking back tears that threatened to leak down his face. "Yeah," he said roughly and climbed out of the cruiser. Shouldering his bag, he waited for Miguel to join him outside of the vehicle.

The handsome man strode around the car and pulled him into a tight embrace, patting him on the back. "You look after yourself, alright?"

"I will," he promised, taking a step back. "Do you want to walk me to the terminal?"

"I don't think that's a good idea." Miguel stared down at his feet.

"Uh, yeah, I get that. I guess this is goodbye then." Heart dropping into his toes, he forced himself to turn and walk away.

"Let me know when you land."

"I will," he called without looking back.

Chapter Thirty-Two

Angell dug through the intubation bag. *Where are all of the size eight tubes?* Huffing out an irritated sigh, he dumped the pack out onto the stretcher. The tube kit was completely empty except for a rogue laryngoscope. There wasn't even any tape.

"What idiot put this together?!" He ground out through clenched teeth and pawed through the first-in bag to make sure nothing else was missing.

"That would be me," a nasally voice answered and sat down on the bench seat with a wet squelching sound.

Ready to fire off a few scathing comments in his partner's direction, he looked up and froze. The sour taste of bile burned the back of his throat, and he could suddenly hear the rhythmic beat of his heart pounding in his head. Still staring, he swallowed hard. *Am I dreaming?*

Across from him, in the tattered remains of his uniform, sat Tim. But Tim was dead.

Slack-jawed, Tim cocked his head to the side at an unnatural angle. Sunken, glazed eyes bulged out of torn flesh. Looking like he had been ravaged by a large animal, the left side of his face had been peeled back, exposing the bone underneath. Throat torn open, his exposed trachea hung precariously by a sliver of sinew. His innards, exposed by his widely cracked ribs, had been devoured, leaving behind a gaping maw of congealed blood. Dangling bits of meat hung where his arms

First On Scene: A Howling Sirens Novel

had once been, and cracked femur bones jutted out of the shredded leg tissues.

Angell shivered as an icy chill blew down his back. "You... You're de...dead," he stuttered through chattering teeth.

"So were you," Tim gurgled, rising to his feet in a series of jerky movements. Wheezing wetly, he shambled closer until he loomed over the living man. "Not all of us are lucky enough to serve."

Angell recoiled in his seat, keeping his breathing shallow as the stench of rot and dried blood wafted over him. Barely restraining his gag reflex, he looked up into sallow eyes. "What do you want?"

Tim rose to his full height, making his exposed spine pop and snap loudly. "To teach."

Angell continued to cower in his seat as his heart galloped in his chest and a cold sweat soaked his brow. *This is just a dream. You can push back on this monster!*

Squaring his shoulders and raising his chin, he glowered up at his dead co-worker. "You were a piece of shit when you were alive and died as a bear snack," he spat venomously. "Why would she choose you to be my teacher?" *I have my reaper. I don't need a fucking zombie!*

Head lolling to the side, Tim shuffled backward until his bent legs hit the bench seat, and he gracelessly collapsed onto it. "It is not my place to question the Lady of Shadows. It is an honor to serve, even if it was not my time to die."

Cautiously, Angell leaned forward, bracing himself on his knees. "What do you mean not your time to die?"

"Everyone has a predestined death day," Tim wheezed, rivulets of dark brown blood running down his slack jaw. "I was supposed to die in the sweet embrace of a younger woman."

Angell wrinkled his nose, fighting down his impulse to gag. *God, I'm glad he's dead! Too bad he's still my problem.* His stomach roiled at the thought of Tim in a *sweet embrace* with anyone, especially in his postmortem state. "But instead, a bear got you? If these things are predestined, then how is that possible?"

Selina Rossman

"It isn't bears that have thrown the scales askew." Tim shifted in his seat, sending his head lolling in the opposite direction. "Man and beast exist with a purpose, as do the creatures in between, but just like an overgrowth of fungus can skew nature's balance, so can the other three."

He was never this well spoken when he was alive. Is this even Tim or is it just a spirit wearing what's left of his face? Brow furrowed, Angell stared hard at the corpse. "Can you stop speaking in riddles and just tell me what's happening and what I'm supposed to do about it?!"

"Werewolves walk between worlds. Their very existence creates a natural equilibrium. But their numbers grow too rapidly. Death can be the only outcome." Tim drew a rattling breath and slumped against the wall of the ambulance.

Werewolves are real? Angell thought incredulously. *What the hell am I supposed to do with that information?!* "How does this affect me?!" A surge of heat spread throughout Angell's body until sweat trickled down his neck and shoulders. Clenching his jaw, he jumped to his feet and slammed his fist against the wall. "I'm tired of being jerked around! Don't you have anything useful to tell me?" He shouted, bearing down on the corpse.

Head still cocked unnaturally, Tim stared up at him with dead eyes. "Sir, please put your seat upright and prepare for landing," he chirped cheerfully.

What the fuck?! Is this just a joke to him?!! Angell thought, dropping his hand to his side and frowning.

"Sir?" Tim said less enthusiastically.

Someone gripped his shoulder and shook him gently. Spinning on his toes to face whatever specter had joined them, Angell jarred awake.

A thin-lipped blonde woman with stern green eyes and a cabin crew uniform stared down at him. "Sir, the Captain is preparing to land. Please put your seat back in its upright position," she sniped at him.

Oh. It was just a dream. Blowing out a shaky breath, Angell ran his trembling fingers through sweat-soaked curls and nodded.

First On Scene: A Howling Sirens Novel

"Thank you," she said shortly and strode back up the aisle towards the plane's cockpit.

He raised his chair rather than risking the flight attendants' wrath and scrubbed at his face with both hands. *God, I just want to be home.* He wanted nothing more than to chalk his nightmare up to a stress dream, but he knew better. The Lady of Death was trying to communicate with him, even if he didn't understand what she was trying to tell him.

The plane started its descent and his stomach flip flopped uneasily. His ears popped painfully and he pulled out two pieces of gum, quickly shoving them in his mouth with hopes that the strong minty flavor would soothe his churning guts. He hated flying.

So, if the dream is real, then werewolves exist, and they are somehow tied to the Lady of Death? What the hell am I supposed to do with that information? And why would she use Tim as a guide? I fucking hate that guy! Huffing out a sigh, he closed his eyes and waited for the plane to touch down. *Am I going to see ghosts now?* He shook his head. He would burn that bridge when he got to it.

After a seeming eternity, he was off the plane and seated in his car. He texted Miguel to let him know that he had arrived home safely and that he missed him already.

Miguel quickly replied with a thumbs-up emoji.

He frowned down at his phone. *Damn it, it really was just a one-time thing. Guess I'll be figuring out all this Lady Death stuff on my own then.* Raking a shaky hand through his curls, he started the engine. *At least I'll be able to talk to Kitty and Crash about Miguel, even if I can't tell them about the rest of the trip.*

Squaring his shoulders, he drove out of the parking garage and pointed the car towards home. *At least I still have real friends in this country. Thank god for Kitty and Crash.*

Despite the two coffees he'd pounded, the drive to work was a blur. He was exhausted after a restless night of tossing and

Selina Rossman

turning but he hadn't wanted to have another run in with zombie Tim.

Yawning widely, he badged into the station and pushed his way inside. The moment he entered the day room, a white and blonde blur launched itself at him.

Laughing, he caught Kitty in his arms, spun her around, and squeezed her tight against his chest. Being away from his friends, even if it had only been a few days, had made him realize just how much he needed them. They were his second family, and being away from them made his heart ache.

Kitty pulled back and beamed up at him. "How was Mexico? Did you find everything you were looking for? Was your mom excited to see you? What happened with Miguel?"

"Take a breath," Angell suggested, grinning down at her. "All your questions will be answered, but not right now, okay?"

Her bright blue eyes searched his face. "Okay. But we'll get breakfast tomorrow when you get off shift and catch up?"

"Absolutely," he promised and took the truck keys and radio from her.

"Alright, I'll meet you at our spot tomorrow morning. Let me know if you get a late call."

"I will," he promised and dragged her into one last hug. When he let her go, she peered up at him with her brow furrowed. "You good?"

Angell shot her a thumbs up. "Great, just a little jet lagged." *Shit, she knows me too well*. Offering her a forced smile, he patted her on the back and headed out into the hallway. "I'll see you tomorrow."

Walking down the carpeted stairs, he cringed at the sound of them crunching beneath his boots. He hadn't missed that. Hustling down the disgusting staircase to the concrete bay floor, he peered into the kitchen. *Nope. No ghosts here. Just a grody-ass building*. Blowing out a relieved sigh, he marched across the bay to P8. The side door to the patient compartment stood open. *Good, Crash is already here.*

"What's up, buddy?!" Angell climbed into the back of the ambulance and froze.

First On Scene: A Howling Sirens Novel

Seated in the captain's chair, Crash was running diagnostics on the monitor as if everything was normal, but a weird smoky haze clung to him like some kind of aurora.

The harder he stared at his partner, the more defined the vapor became. Crash wore the sheer exoskeleton of an enormous wolf. He could still make out his human features beneath the beast, and the two bodies moved as one creature, but there was no denying what he was seeing.

Am I still tripping, or is this part of my gifts? Either way, a heads-up from Tim would have been nice. Blinking rapidly, Angell braced himself on the truck's netting, but the ghostly lupine remained.

"You okay?" The wolf's ears flattened against his skull, and Crash turned yellow eyes on him.

Ready to dismiss his partner's concerns, he opened his mouth, but no words came out.

"What? Is there something on my face?" Crash shifted uncomfortably in his seat.

Something like that. Shaking his head, Angell sidestepped the netting and dropped onto the bench seat. "I have a strange question for you."

"Okay?" Crash offered him a weak smile, and the wolf bared its fangs. Concern danced across predatory yellow eyes as he leaned forward and peered intently at Angell.

Does that mean Crash is a werewolf? Worrying at his lower lip, he stared hard at the bestial man before him. *Fuck, what even is my life right now? I was supposed to come home, vent about Miguel, and get back to normal, not suddenly have to figure out what my best friend has become. Unless he was always like this.*

"Are you good?" Wrinkling his nose, Crash cocked his head to the side as his translucent ears perked up.

"What do you know about..." Angell hesitated. *Fuck, he's going to think I'm crazy.* "What do you know about shapeshifters?"

"Why?" Crash asked, narrowing his eyes.

"Just tell him you know," a discorporated voice hissed into his ear.

The tiny hairs that ran along his arms stood on end. A

shiver raced up his spine, and he swallowed hard. *Am I losing it, or does this count as being guided?*

"Dude, are you good?"

"Tell him," the voice urged.

Tension settled between his shoulder blades, and his heart raced. Gritting his teeth, he looked hard at the transparent wolf, stretched over Crash's human form, and ground out the words that there was no coming back from. "I know what you are. I know you're a werewolf."

Crash blanched, and an unreadable expression flashed across his features. "What makes you say that?"

The voices in my head. Angell rubbed at the back of his neck. "I guess you could say I've been going through some changes lately and that I'm paying much closer attention to my surroundings."

Crash squinted at him. "Trust me, I'd know if you were like me." Eyes widening, he snapped his mouth shut.

"You've been super moody since Tim died."

Crash barked out a bitter laugh. "Uh yeah. What do you expect? I watched him get mauled to death by an animal and then ran away. You'd be in a bad mood, too. It doesn't mean I'm a mythical creature."

How am I supposed to get him to come clean? Do I tell him what I'm seeing? What if it really is just a hallucination?

The tones dropped, and dispatch's pitchy voice filled the ambulance bay. "P2, engine two, and car two, please respond to eighty-four Pond Street for the cardiac arrest."

Saved by the bell, he thought and watched Crash pick up his radio.

"P2 is en route." Dropping the mic, he frowned. "This weird ass conversation isn't over, but why don't we go deal with the dude who woke up dead before we continue it?"

Angell nodded and jumped to his feet. He glanced around the patient compartment, but his Reaper was a no-show. *Does this mean I'm going to get a save for a change?!* Heart skipping a beat, he hopped out of the truck and strode around to the front.

They responded to the residence in an awkward silence.

First On Scene: A Howling Sirens Novel

When Angell couldn't take the quiet anymore, he switched on the radio and blasted the first song that came on. Bobbing his head along to *Highway to Hell*, he turned off the main road and pulled into the patient's driveway. Turning the music off, he threw the truck in park and glanced into the rearview mirror. His reaper was still nowhere to be found. *Fuck yes!*

Crash darted out of the truck the moment it stopped moving.

Blowing out a tight breath, he climbed out of the rig and helped his partner dump their gear onto the stretcher and haul it towards the house. The pretty blonde officer that Kitty had been obsessed with before she started sleeping with Zuri held the door to the house open for them.

"Thanks, Stark," Angell murmured on his way past her.

She nodded. "I took a look already, it's a DOA."

"Then who called it in?"

She pressed her lips together. "She's got family out of state. They called for a wellness check when they couldn't get ahold of her. It's sad."

Crash stuck his nose in the air and breathed deeply. His brow furrowed while the corners of his lips dipped downward and his wolf ears flattened against his skull. "She's seen enough dead bodies to recognize one. Why don't we leave the gear out here?"

Can he smell the body? Angell wondered, pursing his lips as he helped his partner drag the stretcher to the side of the house. Pulling on his gloves, he followed Crash inside.

The tiny vestibule led to a living room straight out of the sixties. Paisley printed wallpaper lined the walls, and a thick, brown, shag carpet ran the length of the space. Directly in front of them, a frail-looking woman, easily in her eighties, lay sprawled across a leather square-armed sofa. Her skin was a waxy, sallow color. He didn't need to touch her to know she was long dead.

Crash approached the patient and gently tugged on her jaw. It was frozen shut. He shook his head and looked back at his partner. "Rigor."

"You want to put away the gear and cancel fire while I look

around for her meds?"

Crash shrugged and started for the door. "Sure."

There were no obvious pill bottles on either of the small wooden tables next to the couch. He figured they had to be in the kitchen or in her bedroom. He followed the winding hallway into the kitchen. A waif of a woman was pacing along the yellowed tiled floor and muttering to herself.

"Excuse me, ma'am, I didn't realize anyone else was in here," he announced himself. *Didn't Stark say her family was out of state?*

The woman came to an abrupt stop and wheeled around to face him. It was the woman from the couch.

His breath caught in his throat, and his heart raced. *Did she have a twin?*

"You can see me?" Her lower lip trembled.

Nope, no twins here, just ghosts. Where the hell is my Reaper?

The voice from earlier snickered in his ear, making him jump. *"Foolish boy, you don't need the Reaper. You are the Reaper."*

Angell swallowed hard. *What is that supposed to mean?!* Running his tongue over parched lips, he stared hard hard at the dead woman.

She clutched her arms to herself and rocked back and forth on her heels. "I don't understand what is happening. I woke up from a nap, and there was a woman on my couch. She looks like me…"

Frowning, he ran a hand through his curls. *What am I supposed to do with this?*

"*Reap,*" the disembodied voice whispered in his ear.

Gee, that's specific, he thought and eyed the woman.

She took a tentative step towards him. "You have to help me."

He backpedaled until his back struck the wall.

Her eyes widened, and her face grew slack, her mouth hanging open in a silent moan. She rushed him.

Oh fuck! What should I do?! Should I run? Undecided, he clenched his jaw and held out his hands to hold the specter back.

Unphased by his outstretched arms, she moved closer.

First On Scene: A Howling Sirens Novel

His breath escaped in frantic little gasps, and his heart jackhammered behind his sternum. *Tell me what to do!* he begged the voice.

"Touch her and tell her to go."

That's it?

"Do it now!"

Oh, fuck me, fine! Trembling, he reached out and brushed his fingers against the woman's arm.

Still slack-jawed, she latched onto him and pulled him close, clutching his hand to her chest.

"O… Okay. Now go," he stuttered.

She dropped his hand and took a step back. Her feral expression dissolved into a soft smile and a hazy, as a white smoke snaked up from the floor, winding around her. She let out an excited giggle and threw her arms wide. Twirling on the spot she disappeared into the growing fog and was gone.

Mouth agape, he stared at the space where she had been only moments before. *I'm never going to get used to this.*

Someone cleared their throat behind him.

Spinning to face his partner, he flinched. Crash's translucent exoskeleton was still jarring to behold.

"What the fuck are you?" Crash hissed, baring two sets of teeth.

He blew out a shaky breath. "I think I might be the new Grim Reaper."

Chapter Thirty-Three

Eric clutched the steering wheel and fought to wrap his brain around what he'd seen. *The Grim Reaper is real, and it's a human? Unless he's something else now? I can hear his heart beating a million miles a minute, so I know he's still alive.* Frowning, he backed the truck into the bay.

Angell hadn't said a word since they left the house, which only made him speculate further.

Is being a supernatural creature a prerequisite to working in Hudson now? He shook his head. *No, Kitty is still normal, even if she knows about us.*

Pursing his lips, he turned to his partner. "I think it's time we both came clean."

Angell nodded slowly and raked a hand through his dark curls. "No more secrets?"

"No more secrets," he agreed.

Shoulders sagging, his partner huffed out a sigh. "I'm so glad to hear you say that. I've been dying to talk to someone since I got back."

"Have you always been a Reaper, or did it happen when you went to Mexico?"

"Uh…Yes." Tugging at his collar, Angell stared hard at his lap.

"Yes, what?" Arching an eyebrow, Eric waited for his partner to open up.

First On Scene: A Howling Sirens Novel

Angell blew out a breath and leaned back in his seat. "I think I may have always been a Reaper, but I can't be sure. Mexico definitely intensified everything."

Eric listened attentively as the other man spilled his guts. He couldn't believe that his best friend had been suffering silently for so long or that he'd been seeing a Grim Reaper for years. If he had been seeing an entity following him around, it wouldn't have taken him years to check himself into a psych ward. Hell, he wanted to after all the crazy things he'd seen since being bitten.

"So, how'd you clock me as a shifter?"

Angell tipped back his head, blew out a breath, and shut his eyes. "It's a little difficult to explain, but I can see it. When I look at you, I can see this hazy smoke clinging to you, shaped like a giant wolf."

That sounds terrifying. "And you're not afraid of me?" Tension settled between Eric's shoulders. He didn't want to inspire fear in anyone, let alone one of his closest friends. Just because Angell had been dragged into his strange world didn't mean he would accept it. Not everyone was as strangely open-minded as Kitty.

Opening his eyes, Angell shrugged and looked at him. "You're my friend. I know you won't hurt me. Besides, I'm not exactly normal anymore, either."

Eric beamed at his friend. Being bitten had changed everything, and he'd been ready to forfeit his relationships to protect his secrets, but he wasn't going to have to. Zuri had already come clean with Kitty, and Angell had figured it out on his own. Once Karl was out of the picture, they'd be able to get back to the status quo.

"How'd you get bit?"

Eric barked out a harsh laugh. "You ought to know. You were there when it happened."

Angell stared at him, slack-jawed. "You mean...?"

"Yup, Hobo Joe." He shook his head, a tiny smirk pulling at his lips.

"Damn," Angell muttered, running a hand through his hair. "Anyone else I know a werewolf?"

"Uh... I mean, I probably shouldn't tell you this, but since you can literally see us, you'll figure it out soon enough. Zuri is a shifter, too." Tugging at his collar, he looked out the window at the empty bay. *She's going to be pissed, but he would figure it out anyway.*

A deep furrow settled between Angell's brows. "Hobo Joe bit Zee?"

Returning his gaze to his friend, he frowned. *Do I tell him the truth? It's not really mine to tell, but I don't want to lie to him.* "No," he said softly.

"Okay..." Angell cleared his throat but didn't force the subject.

"Alright, my turn. Tell me, what happened in Mexico?"

Angell blushed brightly. "It all started with reconnecting with an old friend."

"Friend, huh?" Eric asked and arched an eyebrow. *Does he finally have a man in his life or is this the one that got away?*

"Miguel is just a friend... because that is all he can be." Angell chewed on his lower lip and shook his head. "We hooked up while I was in town, and he helped me figure out what was happening to me, but..." He huffed out a long sigh. "He has a girlfriend and isn't willing to leave her."

Eric gaped at his friend. "You slept with someone in a relationship? You've never done that before."

Angell shook his head. "Miguel said he was in an open relationship, and I believe him."

Eric nodded, rubbing his chin. "Oh, okay... So, how did you figure out that you were a Reaper?"

"I did a bunch of peyote and went spelunking through an old pyramid until I found a death goddess who told me that she had work for me to do," Angell muttered dryly.

He laughed. "Come on, man, tell me what you actually did out there."

"I'm serious."

"Oh."

"P2, Engine Two, Car four, please respond to seventy-four Fig Street for the three-car motor vehicle accident." Dispatch shouted down at them through the speakers in the ceiling.

First On Scene: A Howling Sirens Novel

"I guess the EMS gods want you to know that the death goddess isn't the only one that owns you," he snarked and swapped spots with his partner.

Angell rolled his eyes and picked up the mic. "You can show P2 responding."

"Received," the radio squawked.

Angell tapped his fingers on the steering wheel and waited for the truck to warm up enough to start the engine. He turned the key, and the ambulance sputtered to life. A dark cloud of smoke billowed out of the tailpipe.

This thing is such a piece of shit. I can't wait to get P2 back, Eric thought. *Even if I'm the reason it's out of service.* He shifted uncomfortably in his seat. He wanted to get this bullshit call over with and finish hearing about Angell's Mexican adventures.

Angell pulled the truck to a stop in front of the high school. "P2 is on scene."

He hopped out of the truck to examine the multi-car accident. An unfamiliar police officer stood in the street and directed traffic while scowling.

People milled around the three pulled over cars with crossed arms and furrowed brows. There was minimal bumper damage to all three vehicles and the self extricated drivers were clearly uninjured.

Shaking his head, he looked back at the rig. "Bullshit," he mouthed to his partner and turned back towards the accident in time to see Officer Stark striding towards him.

Grinning brightly, she sauntered up to him. "You guys are going to be all set but I gotta tell you why they crashed into each other."

"Oh, God," he muttered, raking a hand through his hair.

She leaned into him and lowered her voice. "Apparently, they were caravanning to a friend's house when a giant wolf stepped onto the road on its hind legs. The first driver slammed on his brakes, and the other two got so distracted that they just plowed right into him."

Eric blanched, and his back stiffened. *That had to be one of Karl's guys. Shit, they aren't even trying to be subtle.*

Eric forced a smile while his stomach flipped uneasily. "So you're saying they're all high?"

Stark laughed and shook her head. "Surprisingly sober. It must have been a bear. We don't even have wolves in this state, and definitely not giant ones that walk on two legs."

"Seriously! You'd think people have never seen a bear before," he grumbled and swiped at the sweat beading his brow.

"Well, I'm going to clear up if you don't need me."

"Yeah, go ahead. I'll see you at the next one." Walking back to the ambulance, Eric climbed in and firmly shut the door. "They don't need us. Let's clear up."

"You okay? You look like you've seen a ghost." Angell eyed him with concern.

Ignoring the question, Eric cleared them with dispatch and leaned back in his seat.

"Come on, man, what's up?" Angell pried.

"I can't tell you until I talk to Zuri." He closed his eyes, rubbing at his temples.

They drove back to the base in a tense silence, leaving Eric alone with his fevered thoughts.

It had to be Karl's pack. But why would they be out during the day? What the hell is he planning? Are they just biting people at random now to raise their numbers? No, that doesn't make any sense. Karl's choices have all been intentional. Unless some of his wolves are going rogue again? Fuck, I hope Zuri is working today. I don't want to have this conversation over the phone.

By the time they backed into the bay, his heart was hammering in his chest. His head throbbed painfully, and his throat felt like sandpaper from the bile that insisted on creeping up it. He felt overheated and trapped in his own skin. If he didn't calm down, he was going to shift. When he had been just a human, he had struggled with panic attacks, but unlike before, he no longer had meds to combat his anxiety, and he wasn't very proficient with the breathing techniques Zuri and Karl had taught him.

He glanced into the rearview mirror, and bright yellow eyes peered back at him. *Shit! Shit! Shit!* Sudden pain lanced

First On Scene: A Howling Sirens Novel

through his gums, and he tasted blood. *Why are my fangs coming in? Fuck, I need to get Angell out of here.*

"Are you okay?" His partner rested a gentle hand on his shoulder.

He jerked away from the man. "Please just go. I need to be alone right now," he growled.

"Are you sure?" Angell hesitated.

"Please," he whined.

"Alright, but if you need me, just yell, okay?"

Eric jerked his head up and down and squeezed his eyes shut. "Go."

He waited until he heard the door slam before letting himself give in to the panic coursing through him. He groaned, thrust his face into his hands and hyperventilated. *Don't shift! Don't shift! Don't fucking shift!*

The Buffy the Vampire Slayer theme song jarred him out of his internal chanting. Even without his heightened senses, the ringtone was aggressively loud. Dropping his hands, he snatched out his phone and glared at it. Karl was calling.

Fuck, he thought and picked up. "Yeah?"

"Eric? Are you alright?" Karl's concerned voice drawled.

"Bad day," he ground out and clutched the phone between his fingers.

"You sound like you are on the verge of shifting. Where are you?!"

"I can't destroy another ambulance," he whimpered, squeezing his eyes shut.

"You aren't going to shift at work again," Karl soothed. "Do as I say, and we will get you through this."

Whimpering, he pressed his forehead into the dash. His skin burned and crawled with the need to change.

"Take a deep breath and hold it," Karl directed.

He sucked in a deep gulp of air, and his pulse rate quadrupled.

"Keep holding it."

The longest thirty seconds of his life ticked by, and he let out a shuddering breath. His erratic heart rate stuttered and calmed.

Selina Rossman

"Again," Karl ordered.

Eric repeated the exercise until the panic faded and the need to shed his flesh dissipated.

"Thank you," He breathed and opened his eyes, two pools of aquamarine sparkled at him from the rearview mirror. *Thank God he called or I'd be ripping apart the rig.*

"You need to be careful about not getting too stressed. It might be a good idea to step away from your day job."

Yeah... because it's EMS that's the problem. Wrinkling his nose, he shook his head. "I love my job. Besides, I need money."

"Just think about it. If you choose to walk away, the pack will make sure you are taken care of, but for now, I want us to take advantage of your situation."

"I'll think about it," he lied. "Now, how does being a medic help?"

"Well, as you know, we've been scouting the area for the other pack, and we've been coming up empty-handed."

"Uh, yeah?" *Does he know what set me off?*

"I've come up with a plan to flush them out." Karl cleared his throat. "Are you aware that the children will be returning to school next week?"

"Vaguely. I don't really follow their schedule." Clamping down on his lower lip, he sucked it into his mouth and chewed. *Where is he going with this?*

"A school shooting is the perfect event to draw the Alpha's daughter out."

Eric's mouth went dry. "You want to shoot up a school?" He squeaked.

Karl's beleaguered sigh filled the silence. "No, Eric. Pay attention! We are going to stage one in order to capture your partner and use her as bait."

"Oh... uh, okay. So what do you need from me?"

"Make sure that she is in the ambulance with you next Friday. I will do the rest."

"I can do that."

"Good," Karl breathed and hung up.

Well fuck, he thought and stared at his phone's dark screen.

First On Scene: A Howling Sirens Novel

Okay, I need to talk to Zuri. Raking a hand through his sweat-soaked hair, Eric opened his door and slid out.

Quickly texting Zuri to come visit the base, he plodded upstairs to wait for her. He found Angell lounging in the day room.

"Feeling better?" Angell asked, looking up.

"Something like that." Running his tongue over parched lips, Eric dropped onto one of the couches. "What are you watching?"

"The notebook," Angell muttered without looking at him.

Eric rolled his eyes. He hated rom-coms.

His phone buzzed in his pocket. It was Zuri.

Be there in twenty.

His eyes raked over her words as he blew out a nervous breath. This was their chance to set a trap for Karl, but there were hundreds of ways things could go wrong. He was glad that he wasn't the one in charge.

Time dragged by, and the cheesy love story did nothing for Eric's sour mood. He alternated between tapping his fingers on the couch's armrest and bouncing his leg. He hoped Zuri would show up before they got another call.

Angell's eyes widened when Zuri skidded into the room almost a half hour later, braided hair cascading down her shoulders. "Hey," he said after a momentary pause.

"Hey," she muttered and looked expectantly at Eric. "Downstairs?"

Eric nodded and jutted to his feet. "Be back," he called to his partner and darted out of the room after Zuri.

"So?" She demanded as soon as they reached the bay.

"I know what Karl's planning."

"Great! Fill me in," she said in a hushed tone.

He drew in a deep breath and told her everything from the werewolf that had caused the car crash to Karl's dark scheme.

"Alright, I can work with that. Is there anything else I should know?"

He scuffed the floor with his boot. "There is one more thing."

Pursing her lips, Zuri crossed her arms over her chest.

"Okay?"

"Angell knows about us," he whispered, averting his eyes.

"What?!" She demanded, her voice cracking. "You told him about us?! Eric, what the fuck?!"

Cheeks burning, Eric stared hard at the floor. "It's not like that. He's not exactly human."

"I would have smelled it if he wasn't human."

He shook his head. "Why don't you let him explain? I think he can help us."

"Fine. Go get him. We have things to discuss."

Chapter Thirty-Four

Hands thrust into his pockets, Eric paced the length of the ambulance bay. *This has to work. It'll work. Zuri knows what she's doing, right?*

"Can you relax? You're making me anxious," Zuri growled at him from her reclined stance against P1.

Huffing out a sigh, he kept moving.

She patted the hood of the ambulance and stared expectantly at him. "Eric, come here."

Averting his eyes, he shuffled over and leaned against the truck. "I'm just worried."

"It's going to be okay," Zuri said, leaning into him so that their shoulders touched. "I know all of this is scary, but after today, all you will have to focus on is learning how to be a werewolf, and you'll have my pack's full attention. Would going over the plan again make you feel better?"

Not really, he thought but nodded.

"We know that Karl and his pack are going to take over the school under the guise of an active shooter at ten. The school will go into a lockdown, keeping all the teachers and students safe and out of our way." She paused meaningfully, letting her eyes bore into him.

Briefly meeting her gaze, he looked down and tugged at his shirt collar.

She nodded. "Once we get dispatched to the scene, we'll get

out of the truck and get ready. I'll make sure I look really worried about the students and insist that we are the first team in. Then what happens?" Pressing her lips together, she prodded him in the side.

"We go in with the police and find a way to ditch them."

"And how do we do that?"

He sighed, beleaguered. "We will try to lose them, but realistically, we'll probably have to knock them out and put them somewhere safe."

"Good. What do we do next?"

"We let your family in the back door and hunt down Karl." Sweat beaded his brow and soaked his scalp. *Shit, nothing has even happened yet, and I'm already a mess. You'd think werewolves wouldn't sweat so much.*

"Perfect," she said and patted him on the back. "How are we getting Karl out with the building surrounded?"

He shrugged. "Wish I knew, but you still haven't told me our final move."

She furrowed her brow and tugged on one of her braids. "Sorry, I forgot, but you've met my father. He's a control freak and, unfortunately, wants to keep you in the dark for now."

He clenched and unclenched his hands. "It's stupid, Zee. I'm on your side. Haven't I proven that by now?"

"I know but I promise once this is all over, he's going to fully bring you into the pack."

"If you say so," he huffed.

"She squeezed his shoulder affectionately. "Tell me what Angell and Kitty will be doing?"

"They're our backup. They'll be the second team in. Hopefully, they will just be going in to keep others out, but if everything goes to hell, they can distract the cops and drag people out."

Wrinkling her nose, she nodded. "Hopefully, we don't need them to do anything, but it's good to know someone has our backs. When they get back from their coffee run, we'll go over everything one more time."

He watched her coil a braid around her fingers and tug on it. Zuri didn't have many tells, but pulling on her hair was one

First On Scene: A Howling Sirens Novel

of them. He knew she hated putting Kitty anywhere near the danger they would be facing, but they'd given her the chance to walk away, and she hadn't taken it. Angell had insisted on staying and helping, too.

The tones dropped, and he flinched. *Shit, it's too early to be go time. We're going to have to rush through whatever emergency this is and clear up quick.*

The speakers shouted down at them from the ceiling. "Car Two, Car Four, Car Five, Car Six, Car Seven, Car Eight, Ladder One, Engine One, Engine Two, Ladder Two, P2 and P1, please respond to the high school for the active shooter. Stage in the side parking lot and wait for further instructions."

A cacophony of voices signed on, and the wail of sirens echoed through the air as every responder in town raced towards the school.

Wide-eyed, Zuri and he stared at each other.

"But it's not even nine," he hissed through clenched teeth.

"I guess he decided to start early." She swallowed hard, her throat bobbing.

"Will your family be able to get into position in time?"

"I hope so," Zuri murmured, scrambling around the truck and into the driver's side.

"And if they can't do it?" He asked, dropping into the passenger seat and slamming his door shut.

"Then we go in, and *we* get that motherfucker," she growled, revving the engine.

"Zee, I don't know what I'm doing. We can't just go in without your pack," he squeaked.

She shook her head and tore out of the ambulance bay and out onto the street. "I'm not missing what might be our only chance to get Karl. All you have to do is follow my lead and listen to your instincts," she said through bared teeth and pinned her flip phone to her ear with her shoulder.

Eric could hear the other line ring multiple times until it went to Marcus's voicemail.

"Dad, it's me. They're starting early. Get everyone in place as soon as you get this. I love you." Snatching up her phone, she snapped it shut, swerved around a car, and nearly collided with a fire engine. The engine blared its horn at them but kept going.

Heart pounding in his chest, Eric clung to his seatbelt. "Can you slow down a little?"

"No!" She snapped and sped up, racing after the fire engine.

She's going to get me killed before we even get there! Clutching at the door frame for support, he swallowed down the lump in his throat.

Zuri slid sideways into the parking lot and poked her head out the window. She drew a deep breath and frowned. "This place reeks of wolf musk," she muttered and rolled up her window.

A police officer waved them in and pointed to where the other apparatuses were already parked. Just behind the trucks, a staging tent had been set up, and officers from different departments donned ballistic vests and helmets. A group of fire and police higher-ups stood around a plastic foldable table and poured over the school's blueprints while others stood milled around the area awaiting orders.

Zuri killed the lights and pulled in next to P8. With her nose thrust into the air, she slid out of the truck and joined Angell and Kitty.

Eric followed her lead. The scent of wet earth and wolf musk stung his nares. "Zee," he muttered, sliding closer to her and lowering his voice. "We are really outnumbered. Let's figure something else out."

"No," Zuri ground out through bared teeth and glared at him. "My pack will be here. We are getting this fucker. Today."

Averting his gaze, Eric held up his hands in defeat and backed away slowly until he had put a respectful distance between himself and Zuri. Feeling the side of P8 against his back, he huffed out a sigh and leaned against the truck, glancing at Angell. "You okay?" The man looked paler than he'd ever seen him.

Angell shook his head. "The cops are werewolves," he hissed in a harsh whisper.

"All of them?" Eric squeaked.

First On Scene: A Howling Sirens Novel

"Almost half," Angell muttered and raked a hand through his dark curls.

Fuck! Eric glanced pleadingly at Zuri. "Are you sure we should do this?"

Zuri sighed haughtily and leaned in closer. "Eric, we have to. If the cops are new werewolves, I can take them. Just stay out of the way, and I'll keep you safe. Besides, we're at an active *shooter* event. We can't refuse to go in."

Glancing between Zuri and their friends' worried expressions, Eric rubbed at the back of his neck. *I guess we are really doing this.*

"You have to be careful," Kitty murmured, melting against Zuri's side as the other woman wrapped her up in both arms and squeezed affectionately.

"I will," Zuri promised.

Kitty clung to her. "Is your family here yet?"

"I called them," Zuri said, shaking her head. " I know they'll be here as soon as they can."

Eric realized that he was trembling from head to toe as a comforting weight pressed into his side and a muscular arm slid around his shoulders. Angell gave him a small shake. "We are going to get through this."

"Yeah," Eric muttered.

Without warning, shots rang out from inside the building, and a fire alarm blared. Lights flashed ominously at them through the windows.

Eric swallowed hard, shooting a worried look in Zuri's direction. "I thought they weren't supposed to have guns," he hissed.

"They're not," She growled, squinting at the building with her lips pressed tightly together.

Weaving through the crowd of uniforms, a familiar face headed in their direction. Arms laden down with ballistic vests and tourniquets, Officer Stark looked beautiful and fierce, her lips pressed into a tense, thin line and her crystal blue eyes sparkling with determination.

"We are getting a strike team together," she announced, handing out the gear she'd brought them.

Eric slipped a tourniquet and hemostatic gauze into his pocket and watched the others do the same. Once his bleeding control gear was secured, he accepted a vest and helmet. "Don't we normally wait for SWAT to get here before we move in?" He asked, donning his protective gear and frowning.

The corners of Stark's lips flipped downward. "Normally, but you heard those shots just like everyone else did. The Chief wants us in there now, and it's a good thing, too, because I promise you, with or without orders, I'd be going in." She shook her head. "I won't just stand by while some psycho shoots a bunch of kids."

Zuri stepped forward. "Don't worry, we're going to get this fucker."

"I'm glad you feel that way because I need two volunteers to go in with the first team." Her hard blue eyes darted from face to face. "Who's coming?"

"We'll go first," Zuri said firmly.

Stark offered her a curt nod and strode back the way she had come to meet the gathering officers in front of the building.

We're so fucked, Eric thought, scowling as he pulled open the ambulance's back doors and yanked out the stretcher and first in bag. *It's going to be just Zuri and me in there with a bunch of Nazi werewolves*, he thought as his throat constricted tightly. *I don't know how we are supposed to get through this. But I'm stuck. I can't abandon her to do this alone. Kitty would never forgive me. Hell, I would never forgive me.*

His guts twisted painfully, and a wave of dizziness crashed over him. Staggering against the truck, he braced himself and pressed his face to the frigid metal. His heart raced, and only short little gasps passed his lips. Closing his eyes, he shivered. *I can do this. I'm a werewolf. My instincts will kick in when I need them.*

A warm hand clasped his shoulder. "Breathe," Zuri said in a hushed whisper.

Hyperventilating is breathing, his mind snarked back. He struggled to take a deep breath, but his lungs rebelled against

First On Scene: A Howling Sirens Novel

him.

"You need to slow down your breathing."

What does she think I'm trying to do?! Panting shallowly, he nodded.

Something sharp pricked his side, and he flinched away from the pain, keeping his eyes squeezed shut. His skin itched as the small puncture wound knit back together, leaving a warm splotch of blood behind.

Growling low in his throat, his eyes fluttered open and stared into flashing pools of amber. "What the hell, Zee?"

She bared her teeth and glared at him. "Did I piss you off?"

"Yeah," he huffed, feeling his lips curl into a silent snarl.

She leaned into his space. "Good. It means you aren't panicking anymore. Now use that rage and get ready," she ordered as her eyes lightened to their normal hazel.

"Thanks," he muttered and pulled the stretcher out.

"Be careful," Kitty said softly, leaning up on her tiptoes to kiss her lover's cheek. "You too," she said pointedly and winked at Eric.

"What she said." Angell clapped him on the back with a grin before turning serious. "We are here if you need us."

Ignoring the churning in his guts, he nodded to his friends. "It's time to go."

Zuri nudged his shoulder with her own and grabbed the rear of the gurney. Together, they wheeled it towards the waiting officers. Standing stiffly, the police formed a loose diamond pattern around them and waited for the signal to go in. Out of the four cops, only Stark was human.

The three newly turned officers stunk of wet earth, wolf musk and dried blood. The lieutenant, a short, clean shaven, white man with broad shoulders and a side cut scowled at Zuri from his position at the front of their group.

Stark shouldered her AR-15 and took her position at the rear. "Everybody ready?"

The lieutenant nodded and drew his Glock 22, turning and pointing it in front of him. The two officers flanking them raised their pistols and shifted closer. A fifth officer, standing at the entrance, pulled the door open, and their unit entered the building.

Choking saliva past the lump in his throat, Eric stepped inside and flinched. His ears rang with the constant shriek of the firearm, and his pulse raced in anticipation. *You're angry, not scared,* he told himself as he scanned the area for threats.

A line of blue lockers ran the length of the wide hallway, many of the metallic doors stood ajar with books and papers spilling out of them onto the dark tiled floors. All of the classroom doors had been firmly shut and locked with their blinds drawn.

Good, they are following their protocols. We don't need any kids getting caught in the crossfire of this mess. He had done multiple active shooter drills in the past but had hoped to make it to the end of his career without encountering the real thing.

A lock clicked into place behind them, and he spun towards the sound.

The officer that had let them in, now stood blocking the entrance with his muscular arms crossed over his chest, and a Wolfsangel peeking out of his collar. His lips curled into a silent snarl.

Fuck. Eric's chest constricted painfully, his eyes darting between the officer and Zuri's pinched face.

"Jake! What the hell?!" Stark snapped, marching over to the door and shoving him aside. Scowling, she reached for the lock. "This has to stay open so our backup can get in. You know that!"

Jake cocked his head to the side, his blue eyes flashing yellow.

Shit, he's going to kill her! What do we do? Eric glanced in Zuri's direction, but her hands were full with the lieutenant and the other two officers as they warily circled her. They were outnumbered, he had just barely begun his wolf training, and he wasn't sure what he could do. They were screwed.

Smirking snidely, Jake lashed out and grabbed Stark's arm before she could flip the lock.

Stark's jaw clenched as she struggled to break his vice-like grip. "What the fuck are you doing?!"

Jake grinned down at her as his plump lips elongated into a

First On Scene: A Howling Sirens Novel

fleshy muzzle.

Stark screamed as the face shifted in front of her. Scrambling for purchase, she tried to point her rifle one-handed at the creature that held her in its grip.

Fangs bared, he knocked the gun from her grasp with a throaty growl, kicking it down the hallway and out of reach. Wrapping a clawed hand around her neck, he began to squeeze as thick grey fur sprouted along his muzzle and ran down the length of his face and neck.

Stark clawed desperately at his hand, her pretty blue eyes bulging.

Tightening his grip, Jake shook Stark like a rag doll, breaking her neck with a loud snap and leaving her hanging limply in his grasp.

Jake flung her to the floor, blood seeping from her open mouth, and finished his transformation, dropping to the ground on all fours. Rumbling out a deep snarl from the back of his throat as he bared his fangs and advanced on the others.

Gulping, Eric took a quivering step back and bumped into Zuri. *I should have done something,* he thought, blinking back tears. Stark's husband and three-year-old were never going to see her again, and it was all his fault.

Zuri's warm hand settled encouragingly on his shoulder, squeezing once, then withdrawing as he glanced back at her, his heart stuttering in his throat.

The lieutenant rubbed his hands together, grinning broadly as he loomed into their space. "Now that that's taken care of. Why don't we get down to business?"

"She's mine," Eric growled, throwing back his shoulders and puffing out his chest as he stepped in front of Zuri. *Oh God, please work!*

Barking out a laugh, the lieutenant shook his head. "Your job is over. You can stand down now."

"No," Eric said and crossed his arms. "I told Karl I'd get her for him, and I'm not handing her over to anyone but him." Glancing over his shoulder at Zuri, he hoped she was catching onto his half-assed plan. "Where is he?"

"He's around here somewhere," the lieutenant said with a

shrug. "We're on the same team. You can leave here with us."

"You fucking traitor," Zuri snarled and shoved him towards the officers.

Eric staggered but quickly straightened as he shot her an exaggerated glare.

"Alright, enough. We need to get her out of here before she gets too uppity." The lieutenant nodded to the two men beside him. "Take her."

"No!" Eric snapped and stood his ground.

"Kid, orders change." The lieutenant leveled his gun and bared his teeth. "Now, get the hell out of the way!"

Eric held up his hands and stepped aside. "Fine."

"Good boy," the lieutenant condescended and waved his gun in Zuri's face.

So what now? Eric thought. *She told me we'd fight, but what does that look like?* Stealing glances at Zuri, he shifted uneasily from foot to foot. *What should I do?*

"Move," the lieutenant grunted, gesturing down the hall with his pistol.

Glaring through squinted eyes, Zuri didn't budge. Then, without warning, her foot shot out like lightning and collided solidly with the man's nuts, sending him staggering backward, clutching his crotch.

Good to know that still works on werewolves, Eric thought, barreling into the man's side and throwing him to the floor.

The lieutenant's pistol went off with a boom, and one of the officers yelped, clutching his shoulder and swearing. Blood bloomed beneath his fingers.

Zuri grabbed Eric's arm and tugged. "Run!"

Bolting down the hallway, they served left, and fled deeper into the school. The element of surprise was short lived, though, and the steady click-clack of claws on linoleum haunted their footsteps.

"In here!" Zuri skidded to a stop and pulled Eric into the cafeteria.

Tearing his belt off, Eric looped it around the bolted arm at the top of the door and tightened it down. It wouldn't be much of a delay, but it might give them enough of a head start to escape.

"Smart," Zuri complimented, weaving her way through tables strewn with empty bottles of chocolate milk, half-eaten hash browns, and partially filled breakfast trays.

Panting, Eric followed his partner towards the exit just as something heavy smashed into the jammed doors behind them with a loud thump. Jumping in fright, he wiped out in a puddle of spilled milk and crashed to the floor with a grunt, the cold liquid saturating his shirt.

Zuri backtracked and dragged him to his feet and out of the lunch room, running down another hall until they found the staircase to the second floor.

She launched herself up the stairs, skidding to a stop and drawing in a ragged breath. "We just have to make it to the gym. There will be enough equipment to barricade the doors, and we can climb up the bleachers to get outside." Gulping down another gasp of air, she took off across the walkway and down another hall.

"Sounds good to me," Eric panted and followed her into the overwhelming stench of teenage BO and Axe body spray. *Almost there,* he told himself and pumped his legs to keep up with his partner.

Sweat poured down his face, and his heart threatened to explode. It was almost over. Their plan had gone down in flames immediately, but they would figure out another way to get Karl. At least he wouldn't have to play double agent anymore.

Zuri swung down another hallway and stopped short. It was a dead end.

Unable to stop in time, he plowed right into her and sent them both crashing to the floor in a tangle of arms and legs.

"Shit," he muttered, scrambling to his feet and offering her his hand and pulling her upright. "I forgot what a maze this place is."

"Same," she agreed, speeding back the way they had just come.

Unable to remember how to get to the gym, Eric blindly followed Zuri down one hall after another. "Are we going to cut through the library?"

"We could," Zuri said without slowing. "But I don't think it's the fastest route."

They turned down yet another winding hallway but halted abruptly as an enormous gray wolf stepped into their path, blocking the way forward. Its yellow eyes glowed menacingly as it bared its fangs, and Eric's heart stuttered in his chest.

"Library," Zuri muttered and sprinted back the way they'd come.

The sounds of heavy panting and low, guttural snarls filled Eric's ears as he ran, and he couldn't tell if the feeling of hot breath on his neck was his overactive imagination or if the animal was gaining on them.

Tearing down the nearest hallway, Eric broke into a cold sweat as they were forced to stop again. It was another dead end, and the wolf had found them.

Plastering himself against the wall, Eric looked to Zuri as her fingernails lengthened into razor-sharp claws. "What do we do?"

"We fight." Zuri stepped forward to meet the wolf as it advanced menacingly down the hallway, growling low and viciously in its throat.

The beast lunged just as she rolled aside, its massive jaws snapping on empty air. Growling as it turned to find her, the wolf shook its head, sending flecks of saliva flying in every direction.

Zuri sidestepped as the beast made another lunge, dragging her claws across its throat and sending blood spraying across the walls as the wolf crashed to the floor, gurgling and pawing at its open throat.

Eric openly gaped at Zuri. *Holy shit!*

"Move it!" Zuri snapped, leaping over the writhing beast and hustling down the hallway as she waved for him to follow.

Tearing down three more hallways with the sound of claws and panting never far behind, they finally skidded to a stop in front of the gym's green double doors.

Heart hammering in his chest, Eric shoved his way into the

gymnasium and looked around. They were alone. *I can't believe we made it.*

Shoulders sagging, he took a deep breath for what felt like the first time.

"Come help me," Zuri snapped, yanking open the supply closet.

With his heart still slamming against his ribs, Eric jogged over and helped to barricade the doors with anything they could find. They overturned carts full of cones, basketballs, and tennis netting in front of the entrance and piled chairs and free weights on top of the sports gear.

"Will that be enough?" Eric asked, running a hand through his sweat-soaked hair.

"It'll have to be."

"I guess so." Heading for the bleachers, he stopped when no footsteps followed him. Frowning, he turned back to look at his partner.

She stared at him wide-eyed, mouthing a single word. "Run."

Run? Why? We're almost home free. Then he felt it. Cold steel pressed against his temple. The gun cocked, and his mouth went dry.

"Please..." He breathed. The trigger clicked.

Chapter Thirty-Five

The sudden boom of the .38 Special was deafening. A spray of blood drenched the bleachers as Eric's body twitched once and slumped to the floor. Zuri watched helplessly as blood gushed steadily from his open skull.

A high-pitched ringing echoed in her ears. Rocking back on her heels, she drew in a shuddering breath. *Get up*, she pleaded silently, unable to look away from his still form. She was sure getting shot point blank had to hurt like hell, but it wasn't enough to kill him. Time seemed to stand still, the steady flow of blood the only movement.

A bitter-tasting bile burned the back of her throat as realization dawned. Karl was using silver bullets, and Eric would never get up again.

With a guttural scream erupting past her lips, she tore her eyes from her partner's limp body and advanced on Karl, shaking and snarling, her jaw clenched until she thought her teeth might crack. *I'm going to kill this fucker!*

"Nuh-uh," He drawled, humor painting his tone. Grinning broadly, he leveled the revolver at her. "I would stay where you are unless, of course, you want to join Eric here?"

Her body tensed, ready to rip the man limb from limb. "He was one of yours," she ground out.

He rolled his eyes, scoffing and keeping the gun trained on her. "You stupid girl. Did you actually think I'd fall for his

First On Scene: A Howling Sirens Novel

pitiful excuse for acting?"

The blood drained from her face, and a tremor ran through her. *Fuck. We never had a chance.*

Her skin itched with the familiar sensation of an impending shift, and her vision began to gray out. Her eyes were always the first to go. She sucked in a slow, steadying breath. She couldn't shift; she'd be dead before she made it halfway. *I just need to keep him talking.*

"You knew?"

"Some wet behind the ears pup wasn't going to pull one over on me!" He straightened his suit collar with a laugh and a shake of his head. "Honestly, the timing couldn't have been more perfect."

Perfect for what? she thought, the hairs on the nape of her neck standing on end.

"What did you do?!" Her hands flexed involuntarily, her short, manicured nails lengthening into razor-sharp claws.

He chuckled darkly. "That's between me and your daddy."

She sucked in a deep breath, teeth bared and chest heaving with the effort it took to remain human. *Okay, think! How do I get the gun away from him?!*

"I would say that you will find out soon enough, but we both know that's not going to happen."

She swallowed hard and curled her hands into fists, letting the sharp prick of her claws keep her present. *He's right. If I run, he shoots. If I get closer, he shoots. He's got me.*

Something heavy collided with the double doors, and three massive, snarling wolves forced their way into the room, sending various sporting equipment flying in every direction. A single basketball rolled through Eric's coagulated blood and stopped at Karl's feet.

The animals advanced, their yellow eyes boring into her as they circled and snapped.

She stood her ground, heart stuttering in her chest. *Why did I think I could pull this off on my own? I have to get the hell out of here!* Unarmed and wearing only her soft human flesh, she had no way to defend herself.

I have one shot. I hope his ego is as big as I think it is. Baring her

Selina Rossman

teeth, she glared at Karl. "You're a fucking coward!"

He grinned toothily at her. "Why? Because I outsmarted you and your idiot pack?"

"Nah," she spat and shook her head. "Because you're taking the easy way out."

Karl cocked his head to the side, his amber eyes evaluating her thoughtfully. "And do tell, what is the easy way?"

She scoffed in his direction. "Wow, I guess you aren't as smart as I thought you were."

He pursed his lips and stared hard at her. His eyes darted between her scowling face and his waiting wolves.

She crossed her arms over her chest. "Eric made it seem like you were some big, bad Alpha, but I guess he just didn't know any better." Her stomach twisted guiltily, and she choked down the bile rising at the back of her throat. "Anyone can pull a trigger."

Wrinkling his nose, he sneered at her. "Don't mistake ease with cowardice," he snapped at her, cocking the gun and taking a step forward.

Here goes something. She rolled her eyes haughtily. "You're supposed to be their Alpha," she glanced at the circling wolves. "Go ahead, shoot me. Let them see that you're too scared to take me on like a real wolf."

Lips curled back into a silent snarl, he closed the distance between them and pressed the revolver's muzzle to her sternum.

Heart galloping in her chest, she met his gaze and held it. "Pussy," she growled.

He loomed over her, a vein throbbing in his tensed jaw. "Fine. I'll rip your throat out instead," he ground out and tossed the gun to the floor, kicking it aside. The revolver skidded beneath the folded-up bleachers.

Done talking, she lashed out with her claws and tackled him to the floor, pinning him beneath her as her jaw popped loudly and ground into a new shape, newly formed fangs puncturing through her gums to rain frothy blood and hot saliva down on her enemy.

The three wolves lunged forward, claws ripping into the

First On Scene: A Howling Sirens Novel

linoleum, but Karl checked them with a snarled command. "Get back!" he braced a hand against her chest, keeping her off of him. "She's mine!"

Letting her instincts take over, Zuri embraced her wolf. Her uniform shredded as ebony fur erupted from her flesh and her petite frame widened and lengthened. With a vigorous shake, she wriggled out of the ballistic vest & helmet, which had somehow remained intact, and scattered strips of fabric across the floor.

With a snarl, she snapped at Karl, straining to reach his throat with her fangs but only coming away with a mouthful of torn cloth as his fancy suit fell away in large swaths of fabric, leaving behind an enormous gray and white beast.

Before she could react, he had hooked his claws between her rib cage and reared onto his hindquarters, sending her sailing through the air with a surprised yelp to land roughly on top of Eric's corpse.

Scrambling to her feet, she shook her head violently. The stench of singed flesh and the metallic tang of blood assaulted her senses as his thick blood coated her fur.

Ears flattened against his skull, Karl dropped back to the floor on all fours, rushing her with fangs bared.

Rumbling out a low challenge, she lunged for his throat, teeth clicking shut on empty air as pain seared across her shoulder. Whimpering as fangs tore through bone and muscle to clamp onto bone, she thrashed and clawed at the larger wolf but couldn't break free.

Snarling in pain, Zuri stumbled back, blood pouring down her leg. Fighting Karl was nothing like her battle with Hobo Joe. The newly turned wolf had been all instinct and hunger, whereas Karl was pure calculation and brute strength. She needed to get out of the school, or she was going to die.

Tucking her tail between her legs, she bolted for the bleachers, launching herself at them. She struck the hard plastic with a bang and dug her claws in, propelling herself upward. Her injured shoulder burned, screaming at her to stop, but she ignored it.

Snarling viciously, Karl threw himself at the bleachers,

making them tremble beneath her as he sank his claws into the orange plastic and dragged his massive body upward to snap at her heels.

Barely avoiding a swipe of his powerful claws, she scrambled to the top and plowed head-first into a window. Glass shards slashed her face and paws, burying themselves in her flesh as she plummeted towards the ground below, blood seeping from countless wounds and the frigid air stinging her eyes.

She smashed onto the freezing asphalt, and something snapped in her lower back. Whimpering, she struggled to stand, but her hind legs had gone numb. She couldn't even lift her tail.

Shoulders spasming, she fell to her side panting. Her ribs protested at the weight of her body, but she couldn't push herself up. Her vision blurred, and the world spun. An inky blackness clouded her eyes, and her head was suddenly too heavy to keep upright.

The sound of boots on pavement echoed from somewhere nearby. Her eyelids fluttered shut, her hearing dimmed, and then there was nothing.

Chapter Thirty-Six

I should have volunteered to go in with her! Stuffing her hands into her pockets, Kitty paced between the two ambulances like a caged animal. *Not that I would have been any help.* She dropped onto the rig's rear bumper, huffing out a sigh.

Fidgeting with her belt buckle, she stared hard at the front of the building. The concrete stairs that led inside stood empty, the glass doors firmly shut. *I hope they are okay. They've been in there a long time.* Glancing down at her watch, she frowned. *It's been thirty minutes. Is it supposed to be taking this long?*

Angell sat down beside her, nudging her shoulder with his. "They've been in there a long time," he said, echoing her thoughts.

Pressing her lips into a thin line, she nodded. *Zuri wanted us to stand by as backup, but what good are we? Sure, Angell has some sort of death sight now, but how's that going to help us in a fight? Not like I bring much to the table, either. I mean, what am I going to do against a werewolf?* Her stomach flipped queasily, and her chest constricted. *I'm fucking useless.*

Angell scuffed his boot against the ground. "I don't like just sitting around."

"Same," she agreed,

His brown eyes sparkled in the sunlight. "What if we took a look around?"

Nodding, she stood and gestured for him to take the lead.

Selina Rossman

Head held high and shoulders thrown back, Angell weaved a path around the other rigs, police cruisers, and various fire apparatus. Providers from all the surrounding towns had answered the call for help. Staying close to her partner, she nodded to familiar faces as they passed by, making sure to give the command center tent a wide berth.

Even from a distance, she could hear raised voices and the wails of terrified children. *At least they were able to evacuate some of the kids,* she thought, sucking on her lower lip. The last thing they needed was for the werewolves to start snacking on students. Grimacing at the thought, she trailed Angell to the side of the building without any of the brass noticing them.

"Okay, now what?" she asked in a hushed whisper.

A loud crack of shattering glass reverberated through the air, and an animal cried out in pain. An eerie silence followed.

As one, they turned to look into each other's startled faces, then turned and sprinted in the direction of the awful noise.

Angell easily outpaced Kitty with his long legs, speeding along the side of the building and disappearing. Panting as she raced after him, she plowed into her partner's tense back as she rounded the corner.

Muttering profanities, she untangled herself and sidestepped around him to see an enormous black wolf lying crumpled on its side, surrounded by glittering shards of glass and a slowly expanding pool of blood. The animal's rib cage barely expanded as it drew a shuttering breath.

Is that her?! Kitty rushed forward, but strong hands caught her collar and yanked her back.

Sputtering and coughing, she pulled the garroting fabric off her throat. "What the fuck?!" she demanded, slapping Angell's hand away.

Eyes trained on the top of the building, he pointed.

Following his gaze, Kitty paled. Easily triple Zuri's size, a gray and white wolf bared saliva-flecked fangs and glared down at them. Snarling, it disappeared back inside.

"We need to get the fuck out of here," Angell hissed into her ear.

Kitty shivered. If they made it out of this mess alive, she

First On Scene: A Howling Sirens Novel

would be seeing those enraged amber eyes in her nightmares for years to come.

Running her tongue over parched lips, she rolled her shoulders and approached the unconscious wolf. She didn't know how long it would take for the other shifter to get outside, and she didn't want to find out. "Should we try to move her?"

Angell shook his head. "She's too big to carry."

Kitty kneeled next to the animal, careful not to impale herself on any of the scattered shards of glass. "And you're sure this is Zuri?"

"It's her," he confirmed, keeping his eyes trained on the gym's rear door.

Her chest constricted tightly as her mouth went dry. *Please don't bite me*, Kitty thought and grabbed a fistful of slick fur. Gritting her teeth, she shook the wolf as hard as she could.

Feral amber eyes shot open, and Zuri jerked back with a pained yelp. She struggled to stand, but her hindquarters refused to support her. Sinking back to the ground, her dilated pupils searching for a threat, she glowered at her friends with bared teeth.

Frozen in place, Kitty audibly gulped. "Zee, it's okay. It's just me."

Fur bristling, Zuri peered at her without recognition.

Kitty glanced back at her partner's pale, pinched face. "I don't know how to make her shift back."

Angell warily eyed the gym exit. "Keep talking to her. If that monster comes out here, we're all dead."

He was right. They had to be running out of time. Gathering up her courage, Kitty slowly extended an open palm toward the animal. "See, it's just me. You can change back," she soothed and pressed her quivering lips together.

Ears flattened against her skull, Zuri drew in a deep breath, her nares flaring. Whimpering, she looked between Kitty and Angell.

Finally, she huffed out a sigh, dropping her head to the pavement and shutting her eyes. As they watched, her body quivered and shrank, trading razor-sharp claws for fingers and toes. Blood-matted fur receded until only soft brown flesh remained. Eventually, bleary hazel eyes fluttered open and gazed up at her friends.

"Hey," she said weakly, sitting up. "Thanks."

Kitty examined the nude woman for injuries, but there wasn't a scratch on her. *I guess shifting heals her,* she mused, pushing herself off the ground and extending a hand to her lover. "Let me help you up."

When Zuri nodded, she hauled the woman to her feet and steadied her. "Let's get out of here. We'll come back for Eric."

Zuri flinched like she'd been struck. "Eric is..." She shrugged off Kitty's grasp and cleared her throat. "He's dead."

Behind them, Angell made a strangled sound. "What?!"

A thunderous boom sounded and the metal door leading into the gym dented outward. Metal screeched loudly and the door violently rattled in its frame.

Zuri looked from the door to her friends with eyes the size of saucers. "Run!" she hissed and sprinted for the treeline surrounding the school.

They bolted into the woods, racing to catch up with the nude woman.

Kitty's legs burned from the constant exertion as she struggled to keep up with the wolf-woman and her long-legged partner. Panting pitifully, she scrambled over boulders, scaled fallen trees, and picked her way through every body of water that they came across. Despite her heart threatening to explode in her chest, she followed the others through the thick conservation land.

As she scrambled down a steep slope, an upraised root snagged her foot. Her ankle popped loudly and gave out. Kitty hit the ground hard with a soft grunt as pain lanced up her leg, and she clenched her jaw to keep quiet. Sitting up, she looked around for the others, but they'd already disappeared. *Fuck!*

She strained her ears, searching for any hint of her impending doom, but nothing crashed through the woods or leaped out at her. All she could hear were bird calls. She scanned the area for movement but saw nothing suspicious. *Did we actually hide our trail?*

First On Scene: A Howling Sirens Novel

Needing to splint her injury, she tightened down her bootlaces and bit back a scream. Agony throbbed up her calf and into her hip. Gasping, she hunched over her legs and clawed at the cold, hard earth. She needed to keep going, but the pain was making her light-headed. *I'm a goner,* she despaired and shut her eyes.

"What happened?" A hushed voice asked a minute or possibly an hour later.

Tensing, she looked up into Zuri's concerned face. "Oh, thank God," she breathed, letting her shoulders slump. She pointed at her injured ankle. "I think I twisted it."

Zuri nodded once, pressing her lips into a thin line. Stooping, she scooped Kitty up into her arms and cradled her against her chest. "I'm not losing anyone else today."

Kitty's leg objected to the sudden movement but internally she swooned. Her heart fluttered behind her sternum and she swallowed down a soft whimper as the woman held her effortlessly and she snuggled against soft skin. "Where's Angell?"

Zuri grimaced. "I gave him directions to the falls."

"Isn't your family going to lose their shit?"

Zuri held her close and strode deeper into the woods. "They'll get over it."

They reached the falls without any other incidents. The wind howled at their backs, but cocooned in the arms of a furnace, Kitty barely felt the frigid air.

Head bowed, Angell paced the clearing, muttering inaudibly to himself and raking his hands through his dark, curly hair. He looked up at their approach and paled. "Zee, you shouldn't come any closer."

Frowning, Zuri stuck her nose in the air, drawing a deep breath and going rigid. "Take care of her," she ordered and set Kitty down on a large boulder before sprinting out of sight.

Angell sat down heavily next to his partner, staring vacantly at the ground.

What happened now?! Searching his face for answers, Kitty frowned. "Angell, what is she going to find?"

A guttural scream echoed, and her chest constricted

painfully.

Fuck! That has to be Zuri! Forcing herself to her feet, Kitty moaned against the pain. Determined to get to her lover, she gritted her teeth and took a shaky step forward. Her ankle rolled out from under her, and she staggered back against the boulder with a whimper.

"Stop that," Angell said thickly, scooping her up and striding in the direction Zuri had gone. Once the other woman was in sight, he stopped, averting his eyes and keeping his distance.

Kitty went rigid in his arms.

Marcus's naked body had been propped up against a tree, his wrists pinned to the bark above his head by silver spikes. His head hung limply over his flayed chest. She could see his cracked, charred ribs and didn't need a wolf's nose to know that he had been lit on fire. The putrid scent stung her nares, and her stomach churned. Gagging, she slapped a hand over her nose and mouth. Her eyes raked over the body, and she winced. Whoever had done this had torn out the man's heart and mutilated his genitals.

Arms wrapped tightly around herself, Zuri kneeled in front of her father's corpse. Tears coursing down her face, she bowed her head, sobbing brokenly. Her shoulders trembled with each ragged breath.

Kitty's chest constricted painfully. "We can't leave her like that."

Angell nodded and carried her closer. Setting her down next to Zuri, he stripped off his jacket and draped it over the grief-stricken woman's shoulders.

Kitty pulled her into a tight embrace, letting the woman collapse against her. "It's going to be okay. We'll figure this out," Kitty said helplessly.

Zuri raised her tear-streaked face to look at her lover and slowly shook her head. "Nothing is okay. Nothing will be okay ever again."

Epilogue

Two Weeks Later

They needed to leave soon but Zuri just couldn't bring herself to get up from the couch. Her father's funeral meant more than just saying goodbye. Once they had laid him to rest, she would have to officially accept her position as Alpha. Her chest constricted at the thought. She didn't deserve to lead. She was no master tactician. All her plans did was get people killed. What had her father been thinking?

Warm fingers brushed her arm. "You ready?"

She glanced at Kitty, reclining next to her, her casted foot propped up on the coffee table. She had slicked back her hair with gel and insisted on dressing in all black for the ceremony.

Zuri had told her it wasn't necessary. Werewolves had different traditions than their human counterparts. Although, once the medical examiner finally released Eric's body, they would be attending one of those, too. She didn't know how she would face his family. They'd never know what really happened to him or that it was all her fault. Her stomach twisted painfully, and she swallowed down a wave of nausea.

Kitty trailed her index finger over Zuri's clenched knuckles. "Zee?"

Relaxing a hand, she entangled their fingers. The other woman had refused to leave her side since the attack, completely ignoring her own well-being until whatever was left of Zuri's pack was found. Her family had been gathered at her aunt's house waiting on her father's call, and after delivering the devastating news, it was Kitty's arms that she had collapsed into.

"You really don't have to come," she said for the tenth time without letting go of her lover's hand.

Kitty scowled at her. "You don't have to do this alone. Hell, the only reason Angell isn't coming is because Miguel showed up unannounced on his doorstep last night."

Squeezing the soft hand in hers, she shook her head and stared vacantly at the floor. *I don't deserve them.*

Melting against her side, Kitty flipped on the television. "Why don't we see if there have been any updates before we go."

She shrugged without looking up. "If you want."

Still covering the *school shooting*, they ran the same clips ad nauseam. Distraught high schoolers swore they'd seen giant, rabid dogs, and a sorrowful-looking blonde reported on the death of the local hero paramedic, Eric Davis. There were no updates and no breaking news.

Huffing out a sigh, Zuri turned off the television. "I guess we should go."

Using the arm of the couch for support, Kitty stood awkwardly, balancing on her good leg.

Pursing her lips, Zuri dropped her lover's hand. "I'm still not comfortable with you walking down the stairs." It was her fault that Kitty had gotten hurt in the first place. She wasn't going to let it happen again.

"I can do it," Kitty whined. Furrowing her brow, she glanced around the room. "Where are my crutches?"

"In the car," Zuri smirked and scooped the short blonde up into her arms, enjoying the way it made her blush. Her heart fluttered in her chest. She was grateful that the woman had stuck by her side even if she didn't deserve it. She wasn't sure what she would do when Kitty finally went home.

She effortlessly carried her lover out of the apartment, down the stairs, and out to her car. Once Kitty was safely deposited in the passenger side, she got in and started the engine. Keeping one hand firmly planted on the steering wheel, she

First On Scene: A Howling Sirens Novel

slipped her other into Kitty's grasp and reversed out of the driveway.

The closer they got to Bolton's conservation land, the harder it was to take a full breath. Her heart galloped in her chest, and sweat broke out on her brow. She wasn't ready. She could feel Kitty's eyes on her, but the woman stayed silent, simply giving her hand a gentle squeeze. *How does she always know what I need?*

Flashing the woman beside her a weak smile, she parked the car on the side of the road and came around to get her.

"I can walk with the crutches," Kitty protested.

Zuri shook her head. "We have to cut through the woods to get there. It'll be way faster if I just carry you. I'll bring your crutches so you can get around on your own while I..." She swallowed hard, her eyes stinging.

"Okay." Kitty rested a gentle hand on her hip.

"Thank you," she said softly and pulled the crutches out of the backseat. Helping Kitty out of the car, she tucked an arm under her and lifted, grabbing the crutches with her free hand.

Kitty's cheeks burned fuchsia. "How are you so strong?"

"Werewolf," she reminded her and kicked the door closed.

By the time they reached their destination, her family had already assembled the pyre. The nearly full moon illuminated the open field and beamed down on her father's still body. He lay supine on the stacked wood, a simple white sheet draped over him.

The smell of kerosene and rot made her stomach roil. *This is really happening*, she thought, swallowing hard. Her legs trembled, threatening to give out. She quickly placed Kitty on the ground and gave back her crutches.

Her family stood at the far side of the meadow, torches lit and held at the ready. Openly scowling, Junior passed off his torch and marched across the field towards her.

Bracing for his attack, Zuri raised her head and threw back her shoulders. She couldn't fault him for his anger. She'd brought a human into their midst and not been there for their father when he needed her most. He had every right to be furious.

"You brought the fucking human?!" His eyes flashed yellow.

"She's not just a human! She's my..." Zuri hesitated. She didn't know what they were. It was obvious that they cared about each other, and they were definitely more than friends, but where did that leave them? Could a human really be her mate?

Shaking off the confusing thoughts, she glowered at her brother. "She's an ally, and she's welcome here."

Puffing out his chest and crossing his arms, Junior growled low in the back of his throat. "And what is she supposed to do while we run?"

Zuri shook her head. "There won't be a run tonight."

"But it's tradition."

"It's too dangerous."

Junior squinted at her, the moonlight reflecting off his yellow eyes. "You don't get to..."

Keeping her voice cold, she cut him off. "His obituary says he was cremated, so let's burn the body and get out of here." Shoulder checking her brother out of the way, she strode across the field.

Shaking his head and muttering obscenities, he chased after her.

Reaching her family, she realized she'd forgotten Kitty. *Shit!* Wordlessly, she turned and jogged back the way she had come.

"Sorry," she muttered, falling in step with the hobbling woman. "I got caught up in the moment."

Kitty offered her an encouraging smile. "It's okay. I know this is hard."

Zuri huffed out a sigh. "You have no idea."

"So tell me."

Winding a braid around her fingers, she looked up at the moon. "The first action of a new Alpha is to lead the pack in a run, but I can't do that." She shook her head. "Karl and his pack are still out there. I won't risk losing anyone else just because tradition demands it. I don't even know how many of them are out there."

First On Scene: A Howling Sirens Novel

They reached her family, and she nodded to them.

Her mother was no longer a wailing mess; instead, she eyed her daughter, stone-faced. "Are you ready?" Sierra held out a torch to her.

Accepting the flickering fire, she faced her pack, making a point to look her mother, cousins, aunt, and brother in the eye. She blew out a nervous breath and spoke the words that she had been practicing all week in front of her mirror. "I know that tradition dictates that we light the pyre, shift, and send our beloved Alpha to the heavens in a chorus of howls. After that, I'm tasked with leading you all in a moonlit run." She glanced at Kitty, who nodded back encouragingly. "We won't be doing that tonight. The danger Karl poses is real, and I won't risk him finding us here. Tonight, we say goodbye to the old Alpha, my father."

Swallowing hard, she turned and thrust her torch into the pyre. Flames lapped up the kerosene-soaked logs and roared to life. The fire rapidly engulfed the wood and devoured her father's body. Stiff-legged, she kept her back to her family and watched it burn.

Kitty nudged her shoulder with her own, reaching for her hand.

Without hesitating, she slipped her hand into Kitty's. Her family wouldn't like it, but they would have to get used to it. She was sure they would disagree with most of her decisions, but her father had made her Alpha, and it fell to her to make things right.

They stood in silence until the roaring fire had collapsed into coals. Turning back to her family, she gazed into their grim faces and steadied herself. "I need everyone to go home now. I'll be in touch soon."

Without waiting for their reply, she lowered her gaze and walked back the way she'd come.

Kitty hobbled along beside her. "Are you ready for what comes next?"

"What other choice is there?"

Acknowledgments

I am incredibly blessed to be surrounded by supportive colleagues, friends, and loved ones but there are two women in particular that I want to thank.

Aoibh Wood's constant patience, support, and mentorship made this book possible. Thank you for believing in me and encouraging me to turn my vision into a reality.

I also have to thank my brilliant, insightful wife, Anne Rossman, who has spent endless nights reading and rereading my work. Thank you for continuing to be my rock. I'd be lost without you, figuratively and literally.

And of course, the town that inspired this tale, Hudson Massachusetts will always hold a special place in my heart.

About the Author

Selina lives in Massachusetts with her wife and two cats. When she isn't working on the rig, she can be found leisurely wandering in nature, burying her nose in a book, or volunteering with homeless animals.

Coming Soon

New from Carson Press
Coming Fall 2024

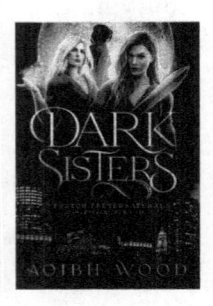

Cait is jetting off to Ireland for a crucial confrontation with the Light Fae in an effort to save her sister, Aoife. En route, an Army Medic, caught in the chaos when Cait and Nastasia escaped Boston, becomes an involuntary tagalong. It's a hostage situation for sure, but our unusual companion is as intrigued by Cait and her powerful duo as she is terrified, and there may be more to her than meets the eye.

Meanwhile, Doyle is undergoing unsettling changes. Her usual fructivorous cravings have shifted to something more carnivorous, leaving everyone baffled and worried for her. Adding to the complexity is the mysterious Rowan, likely the first vampire ever made, whose motives and intentions remain shrouded in secrecy.

Unbeknownst to Cait and her companions, something is amiss on the Emerald Isle. The typically benign Light Fae have taken on a darker, more sinister presence. Amidst this turmoil, Cait grapples with her lingering feelings for Nastasia and a strange echo of her own voice that trails her in her thoughts. Nothing is as it seems, with Fae glamour clouding reality, as they race toward a final confrontation Cait never saw coming.

Prepare for a thrilling journey where every step is fraught with danger, and trust is as elusive as the Fae themselves.

Other Titles

Other titles from Carson Press

The Cait Reagan Series
Blood Rituals
Black Mirror
Green Rath

Other Novels
The Senator's Widow